The Goddess Renewed

For Corrie

MICHELL PLESTED

CHAMPAGNE BOOK GROUP

The Goddess Renewed

Published by Champagne Book Group
2373 NE Evergreen Avenue, Albany OR 97321 U.S.A.

~ ~ ~

First Edition 2021

pISBN: 978-1-77155-513-5

Cover Art by Robyn Hart

www.champagnebooks.com

Version_1

Other books by the Author

A Jack Kane Adventure
(with J.R. Murdock)

Jack Kane and the Kaiser, 2
Jack Kane and the Statue of Liberty, 1

*To all the people who have read
and loved fantasy. Never
give up dreaming.*

Chapter One

The Great Hall practically vibrated with anticipation as a stern-faced soldier escorted the guard sergeant to stand before Duke Samuel. Gaily dressed courtiers stood in small groups watching, quietly gossiping.

"Sergeant Kheldan reporting, my lord," the guard sergeant said, his voice wavering.

Duke Samuel paced in front of his throne, his fists clenched, and he scowled. Waiting was not something he did. Not for anyone or anything and certainly not for one of his own men. He ran a hand through his dark, well-trimmed beard and looked down at his sergeant who did his best to avoid the duke's eyes. With the mood he was in, that might be a good choice.

"Well? Did you capture him?" At Duke Samuel's question, the sergeant jumped a little.

"We did not, my lord." Kheldan's reply, directed toward the floor, was barely audible.

The duke's annoyance flared to outright anger, and he briefly considered signaling the crossbowmen at the murder holes high above the floor. But no. He would deal with this fool personally.

"Why didn't you capture him?" Duke Samuel loomed over the sergeant from the raised dais. The duke straightened his emerald green tunic and wiped imagined dust from the matching hose. "I told you exactly where to go. I told you what to do when you got there. Were my instructions not clear?" His voice gained volume while he spoke, startling a pair of pigeons nesting in the rafters above. The birds circled the room once, leaving feathers in their wake.

"No, my lord." This time, Sergeant Kheldan did look up and flinched. "Captain Kerris gave us your orders, and we followed them exactly. We went to the boy's farm, and we hunkered down to hide. I kept close tabs on my men, lord. They kept quiet and still." The sergeant licked his lips nervously. "The boy showed up just about the time you said he would. Except, halfway down the lane, he stopped and went still.

He looked around then made a break for the forest. By the time we got up, he was gone into the trees."

"Are you implying the boy escaped because my orders were incorrect?" Duke Samuel let a hint of amazement flavor his words.

"No, my lord." The sergeant took an involuntary step backward. "I am merely saying the boy somehow detected us and escaped."

"And you just let him go?" Duke Samuel screamed, a vein throbbing in his right temple.

"No, my lord. We chased after him." The sergeant looked down and shuffled his booted feet. "Somehow he managed to avoid us."

"Where is the boy now? What are you doing to find him?" Duke Samuel stepped from the platform, the silver spurs on his boots ringing on the stones of the floor.

"My lord, we searched until we couldn't see anymore. Come dawn I will send riders out to sweep the roads."

"You will do nothing until dawn?" Duke Samuel's voice grew louder as he spoke with a decided note of disbelief. He addressed one of his courtiers, a fop dressed all in scarlet. "Can you believe he will do nothing until dawn?"

The fop's laugh was high-pitched and nervous. Almost a giggle. "He is a fool, Lord." The man backed into the crowd after answering.

Sergeant Kheldan ran his hands down his trousers several times. "I thought that prudent, my lord. The men do not know the forest, and I would not risk injuries to them."

The duke slapped his hand on his thigh with a crack. "Fool! By the time you send riders out, the traitor will be well gone. What makes you think he would take to the roads?"

The sergeant straightened even more. "My lord, it is what I would do. It is too easy to get lost in the forest, and travel is difficult."

"Incompetent." In two strides, the duke was beside the sergeant, grabbing him by his hair. He yanked back the man's head. "Did it not occur to you that the traitor might be familiar with the forest?"

Sergeant Kheldan gulped. "No, my lord." He held his breath.

"Did you ask anyone? Hmm?" The duke pitched his voice low when he spoke into the man's ear. Duke Samuel didn't wait for an answer. With a flip of his left hand, a blade slipped from his sleeve. In one quick move he slashed the blade across the man's throat.

Rich, red blood sprayed from the gaping wound as the man fought to free himself from the duke's grip, drumming his boot heels against the cobbles. Duke Samuel held the dying man as close as a lover as his struggles got weaker and weaker.

The duke bent close to the man's ear. "I forgive you for your errors, pig." He gave the body a shove. The corpse fell like a cut log, collapsing onto the floor with a crash and lay in a growing pool of its own blood.

Duke Samuel unbuttoned, one a time, his blood-stained doublet. Soldiers and courtiers stood in wary silence, watching him. Only the sounds of breathing and the phantom whisper of banners hung high above could be heard.

"Let this be a lesson to you all. I will *not* tolerate failure." He looked to the one man who remained at attention through the entire episode. "Marcus."

Marcus, a balding, cadaverous, little man, stiffened. "Yes, my lord?"

"Have the hunter report to me immediately."

Out of the shadows of the room a lean jackal of a man, dressed in tones of brown and grey, stepped forward. "There is no need to summon me, my lord. I am here and at your command." His hyena-like features were serene.

"Ah, Pieter, excellent." Duke Samuel wiped his hands on the bloody doublet and tossed it onto the body. "I have need of your talents."

"You wish me to track the traitor?" Pieter's expression was predatory.

"Yes. Bring him to me." He leaned down and wiped his dagger on the cooling body. "Alive, if you please."

"It will be done as you command, my lord." Pieter bowed and swept from the room.

Duke Samuel watched the hunter leave before straightening. His gaze turned to the corpse of his former sergeant. "Marcus, could you get this piece of offal removed from my court? Perhaps hang it in a crow-cage outside the gate as an example. Oh, and have wine sent to my chambers. I suddenly find myself with a terrible thirst."

He stood in the middle of the chamber, eyes focused on nothing, speaking almost as if in an afterthought. "Captain Kerris?"

"Yes, lord?" A bloated reptile of a man stepped out of the crowd.

Duke Samuel's head came down, and his gaze captured the captain's. "I seem to recall ordering you to find the traitor, not," and he waved his hands toward the corpse that was being dragged from the room, "that." He approached the captain. "Should you fail me again, it will be you, not one of your subordinates, who face my anger." He casually cleaned a fingernail with the dagger.

Captain Kerris's gaze followed the dagger in fascination.

With the speed of a striking adder, Duke Samuel slashed the captain's cheek, leaving a bloody line. "Is that clear, Captain?"

His captain didn't reach up to touch his cheek. He simply nodded.

~ * ~

Kalten stopped for a brief rest, tired at last of running.

He winced when he pulled the pack off his shoulder, scraping flesh torn raw by brambles and bushes. He rubbed his fingers over the downy brown excuse of a beard and thought for a moment.

It had seemed so simple when he left…abandoned his courier mission, actually. A turn one direction when he should have gone the other, a quick change of clothes and a little dirt on his face, then freedom. He had the presence of mind to keep the courier pouch—now hidden in a rough leather duffle—just in case he needed it.

All he had to do was travel home, collect his family then leave the kingdom. Hopefully before anyone missed him or his mother and sisters, and they would be safely away from the madness.

The plan had gone well enough. He had used his forest-craft to create a trail even a hound couldn't follow, crossing and wading through streams, doubling back and even taking to the trees for a time. He had watched for pursuit, only continuing toward home when sure there was no one behind him, still leaving a difficult path, cutting through dense brush.

Only once had he detected anyone lying in wait—maybe for him, maybe not—and they had been easily avoided. And now, he was almost there. He grinned as he imagined the welcome he would receive.

Except, something was clearly wrong. The lane to the house was thick with weeds and even had a few small trees growing in what had once been a well-travelled pathway.

Kalten's steps quickened, and it was a huge shock when he finally entered the yard.

The neat, little cottage where he'd grown up was now windowless and had holes in the thatch of the roof. The door hung off its hinges. Small trees, bushes and weeds choked the yard, and the signs of neglect were everywhere. What could have happened to his family?

The skeleton of the family cow lay in the shed, the hide shrunken around the bones like a mummy's skin. A meal, burned hard as stone, encrusted his mother's cook pot. The ghostly tatters of laundry hung on lines.

His family was gone and had been for some time. But where? Into the duke's dungeons? Or maybe they had run off after Kalten's conscription?

He knew that couldn't be true. His mother would never have left like that. She would have waited for him to come back. She was a strong woman, his mother. She would have fought anyone who tried to push her off the farm.

No, something happened to them. His stomach clenched at the thought. He could only take solace in the fact he hadn't found any bodies or bones.

Kalten scratched his head and took a last look around. Whatever the answer, he wouldn't find it here. In moments, he was back in the comforting depths of the forest, searching for a safe place to stop and plan.

He stumbled along in a daze, his thoughts heavy. He had been so certain his family would be there for him. Sure, he would finally be safe, even for a short while. He stopped to gain his bearings. Even if his head hadn't known where to go, his feet certainly had.

The greenly shaded grove surrounded a small, cool pond. Cattails swayed in the water, and the sounds of birds and frogs filled the air. The single, well-hidden pathway into the grove gave it a serene, almost spiritual feel. This was his place, a place he visited often in his youth. The place where he first met... He shook his head. No. No time for that now. He had to focus on the problems at hand.

He pulled his dusty boots off and plopped down at the bank letting the water of the pond cool his swollen feet. What to do? His family was gone, and the duke surely hunted him; he'd seen what happened to defectors. Left to rot in the crow-cages. And as a courier for the duke, Kalten might not even get that merciful a death. No, there could be no safety anywhere else in the duchy. And war was coming so there would be no safety anywhere in the kingdom soon. The duke's plans would surely devastate everything. That meant leaving Kyrglend, maybe forever.

Kalten sighed and looked around the grove. Should he search for his mother and sisters? If they were alive, he was their only hope. Leaving would eliminate any chance for them.

And if they were dead... He stopped going down that dark path. They had to be alive.

But the duke was a powerful man, and what could he, a peasant, do against someone like that?

Kalten smiled to himself. Somehow, he would find his family, and if fate was kind to him, he'd make the duke's life miserable at the same time.

Chapter Two

The three woodsmen cautiously entered the forest, their axes raised as if to ward off evil spirits. They wore muted colors and crept along as silently as they could, jumping at each snap of a twig or slap of a leafed branch.

"Remind me again why we are here," the man at the back of the group said. He led a pair of harnessed dray mules. "We have trees nearer home that aren't in this cursed forest.

"The trees near home are not large enough for the order we have received from the duke," the leader of the group said. "We had to come here; this is the only place with trees that will do. The offered commission will keep our families fed for the remainder of the year."

The middle man scanned the trees, as if expecting a monster to leap upon them. "I don't like it. And what good is that money if we aren't around to spend it?"

"You two worry too much," the leader said. "Look around us. They're just trees. I think the stories about a cursed forest are just old wives' tales. Besides, we don't have to go too far in to find the trees we need."

"Well, let's hurry. I don't want to be here any longer than I have to be," the muleteer said as he anxiously watched the trees around them.

"It's not much further," the leader said. "I came a few days ago to scout out the trees we need." He pointed at a nearby tree that had a large 'x' carved in the bark. "See there? That's one of my blazes from then." He pointed toward a towering, straight oak that could only just be seen ahead. "There is the tree I've been looking for. Come on."

All three men hurried toward the tree, stopping short when they saw the old woman standing beneath its bows.

"What are you doing here, woman?" the leader demanded.

"I would ask the same of you, boy," the old woman replied. "You are trespassing here. Begone from these woods."

"Trespassing?" The man laughed. "I have a permit from the duke himself. We are here to legally harvest trees for him."

"What duke claims this forest?" the old woman asked, her voice fierce. "These woods belong to me. No young jackanape of a duke has any authority over them. Only me."

The three men spread out, facing the woman. The leader continued to do the talking. "I don't know who you think you are, crone, but the duke considers this forest to be part of his domain."

"I know who I am," the ancient woman said. "I have been here since before this forest existed, and I will continue to be here long after it is gone."

The leader grinned. "Hear that men? This lady thinks she is some sort of immortal god or something."

"You finally have something right," the old woman said. "Now, I tell you again. Begone from here, or I will make you very sorry."

The leader's grin faded. "I don't think you are really aware of the situation you are faced with, old woman, nor do I have time to trade words with you. My companions and I are here to take that tree, and you cannot stop us."

"I can't?" The old woman sounded genuinely surprised. "I think I can."

"Barry, move her away from that tree," the leader said to the second man. "Then we can get to work."

"Sure thing," Barry said, moving to grab the old woman. As he reached for her, a flock of birds descended from the trees and pecked at his head. He covered his head with his hands and retreated. "Aiiieee! I can't get to her. These birds have gone crazy."

"Perhaps more force is necessary," the leader said. He lifted his axe and attacked the old woman. He didn't get within half-a-dozen steps of her before a large black bear lumbered out of the forest toward him.

He lowered his axe quickly, and the bear slowed but continued toward him. The lead woodsman planted his feet and took the axe in both hands, prepared for the bear's attack. He was not ready for the second bear that ran at him from behind. The bear leapt upon the unfortunate man, ripping at him with teeth and claws. More birds poured out of the trees attacking the man named Barry. The muleteer was left alone, his mouth hanging open in shock and surprise.

In moments, both the leader and the man named Barry were on the ground, dead. The old woman glared at the muleteer. "Are you going to give me any trouble? Do I need to deal with you like I did with your companions?"

'N...no, ma'am," the man said, stammering in fear. "Please. Please just let me leave this place."

"I will allow it but on the condition you tell others to stay away. This forest is my sanctuary and is under my protection. Do you understand?"

"I-I will do as you say," the man said. He had dropped the reins of the mules in the moments prior.

"Take your animals with you. They have no place here. Now get out!"

The man turned and fled, the two mules in tow.

~ * ~

Duke Samuel lounged in an overstuffed chair in front of a roaring fire in his chambers. He had kicked off his riding boots and had his legs and feet stretched toward the warmth.

There was a knock at his door.

"Enter."

Marcus, his severe-looking steward, entered the room, carrying a tray holding a carafe of wine and a cut-glass goblet. "Your wine, my lord."

"Put it beside me," Duke Samuel said, nodding toward a small table beside his chair. "Tell me, Marcus, what are your thoughts around of the goings on earlier today?"

"It is not my place to say, my lord," Marcus replied.

"That is true. But I wish to hear your thoughts regardless. Consider it a command if it makes you feel better."

"As you wish, my lord," Marcus said. He cleared his throat. "Killing the sergeant seems like a waste of material, especially over a peasant soldier."

"You might think so, although I judged a lesson for the others was needed," Duke Samuel said. "But the boy is no ordinary peasant runaway even though his desertion is enough that I want him back."

"No? I had no idea," Marcus replied.

"He is not. You might remember his father, Ewen. He was my forester until an unfortunate hunting accident."

"Ah. The accident. Yes, my lord, I remember," Marcus said.

"And you remember what led up to the accident?"

"If memory serves, young Ewen was unhappy you had exercised your lord's right with his new bride."

"Indeed," Duke Samuel said. "He was quite overwrought and was becoming something of a problem."

"That makes the boy important?"

"The boy might be my bastard," the duke said offhandedly. "That in itself is not the issue; there are others out there. But he was also privy to a great deal of important information as my courier. In fact when

14

he ran, he was carrying a very sensitive communique with Duke Ailwin. That information could be used by the bitch queen to gain support against me in the council-of-lords."

"I see. It would jeopardize your standing with the Western lords, would it not?" Marcus said. "I suspect the queen would be upset at any indication you were assembling a personal army."

"Very astute. Yes, that would be the knot in my noose, I think."

"If I may, my lord, does the boy know he is your bastard?"

"May be my bastard, Marcus. May be." The duke allowed a smile to cross his face. "The boy does not know, although I would not be surprised if others suspect it. He displays the same mismatched eyes my sire did."

"That suspicion could be a problem."

"It would not surprise me if she actually tried to replace me with the boy if his lineage got out," the duke agreed.

"I understand, my lord. I will use my own contacts to aid in the search for him," Marcus said.

"See that you do. I want him back, Marcus."

Chapter Three

The sun had almost dropped below the horizon before Kalten started looking for a place to camp. Sticking to the trees had been a very good idea. He heard several horses racing past on nearby roads over the course of the day. It was possible some of the riders were under orders to watch for and capture him. Still, the trees had a downside too. He winced a little at the scratches on his face.

He followed a game trail deeper into the trees. The trail was windy and narrow, hemmed in on either side by a thick stand of spruce that limited visibility to the next bend. A branch cracked somewhere ahead, and he froze. *What was it? Had someone tracked him and finally caught up?*

A deer thundered toward him, white tail raised like a flag. It bumped him when it raced past, almost knocking him down. He wiped his brow. Just a deer. But what could frighten a deer so badly it would risk contact with him? Then he felt the dagger pressed into the small of his back.

By unspoken command, he marched along the deer tracks, his captor walking behind, prodding him occasionally with the dagger. "Listen, I don't know who you are, but I think you've got me mistaken for someone else," Kalten said.

"Shut up and move." The voice was muffled but definitely female. Only the threat of the dagger kept Kalten from stopping and turning around.

He caught the scent of wood smoke just before he was forced off the trail through a break in the line of trees. Half a dozen steps later, he was blinded by the brightness of a fire. The light dazzled his eyes, but he was still able to get the impression of a hastily built camp with packs and gear strewn throughout the small clearing.

A figure got up at his appearance, a stout, tall man by his silhouette. "What have we here?" His voice was deep and powerful. "Caught a spy have you, Paena?"

"What's going on here... oooff." Kalten's captor knocked him to the ground. He looked up at the man. "Who are you people?"

"Quiet!" Paena ordered. "We're asking the questions here." She pulled back her hood revealing a wash of dark hair. A beautiful, fine-boned, dark-skinned face framed eyes hard as agates and full of fury. She was only slightly shorter than Kalten; tall for a woman.

He stared at the girl. Paena interrupted his reverie with a sharp slap.

"Are you listening to me, pig?" she said.

"Hmm?"

"I want to know who you are working for and why you are trailing us?"

"Who I'm working for?" Kalten couldn't believe his ears. "I'm not working for anyone. I'm just traveling out of the duchy."

The man stepped forward, suddenly interested, allowing Kalten a clear view of him. He appeared to have been powerful once, though age had long since replaced muscle with softness. "By your clothing, you are a peasant, aren't you?" Blue eyes peered at Kalten from beneath a shock of white, shoulder-length hair tied back with a black ribbon. "Do you have Duke Samuel's leave to travel?"

The thought skittered through Kalten's mind that he didn't know these people. Should he really confide in them? Did it really matter? If they were Duke Samuel's friends, he was already caught, and if they weren't? If they weren't, maybe they could help.

"If you really must know, I'm leaving because my family has disappeared." Kalten met the man's eyes. "I do not have the duke's permission to leave, nor do I care."

Paena cuffed him. "Don't be so flippant to Master Baltar. He..."

"Paena, please." Baltar raised his hands in a warding motion. "Those are pretty bold words for a peasant. Perhaps you are more than you seem." His eyes narrowed. "Who are you really working for?"

"I'm telling you, I don't work for anyone. Certainly not the duke. I came home to find my family missing and our home in shambles."

"Coming home from where, exactly?" Baltar asked, his voice quieting a little.

"That is none of your business," Kalten said. Panic jolted him. *What would these people think if they learned he was a deserter?*

Paena glared at Kalten. "Don't make me—"

"Enough, Paena," Baltar interrupted. "Listen to me closely, young man. I know of your duke—"

"He isn't my duke," Kalten insisted.

"Very well. I know of Duke Samuel. He has a dark reputation.

One that, if true, gives you ample reason to flee. Paena and I must be careful of strangers and, you must admit, you are telling us a strange tale. For all we know, you are the duke's man. Maybe even a spy for him."

"If you must be so careful, you should just let me go," Kalten demanded. The very idea he might be spying for a man he was actively trying to escape was more than ridiculous.

Paena cuffed him again, harder this time. "You will *not* talk to Master Baltar that way."

"Paena, move away, now," Baltar ordered. "I don't believe the young man means any disrespect. He has no reason to trust us and every reason to be suspicious." He studied Kalten closely. "You present an interesting puzzle. We cannot let you go, and we cannot simply trust you either." He tapped his bottom lip. "Still, if trust is to be gained, it must also be given." He thrust out his hand to Kalten. "I am, as you may have guessed, Master Baltar, a trader by profession. May I ask your name please?"

There was something going on with Paena, but somehow Master Baltar made Kalten feel at ease. If he hadn't heard the girl use the honorific, he still would have guessed Baltar was important. Jewelry glittered on the man's fingers, and the cut and style of his earth-brown garments bespoke quality and wealth. He relaxed a little. What could it hurt to introduce himself? He took Master Baltar's hand. "My name is Kalten, sir."

"Well met, Kalten. You say your family has disappeared? You have my sympathy," Baltar said kindly.

"Thank you, sir."

"Can you tell me how they disappeared? When did it happen?"

"I wish I could, sir. I was away when it happened, so I don't know."

"How long were you gone?" Paena turned to Master Baltar. "How could he not know? He must be lying."

"I'm not lying." There was definitely something wrong with her. "If you must know, I served as a soldier to Duke Samuel. I tried sending word to my family, and when I didn't get any answer, I came to find out what was wrong."

Baltar shot Paena a stern look before he spoke again. "A soldier, you say? For the duke? And you left to find out what was wrong? Go on, Kalten. Then what happened?"

"I made my way home, being careful to avoid anyone who might try to follow me. When I got there, everyone was gone. From what I could see, they had been gone for a long time." He went on to explain the state of the farm in detail.

"Why would people follow you?" Paena asked. "That doesn't make any sense."

"That's none of your business." Her attitude was definitely starting to wear on him.

Baltar put a ringed hand on Kalten's shoulder, squeezing it gently. "Kalten, if we are to help you, we need to know why Duke Samuel would come after you."

Kalten sighed. *Might as well tell them the entire story.* "I suppose it could be because I left without permission."

Paena snorted. "You're a deserter?"

"Paena, that is enough." Baltar gave Kalten a sympathetic look. "Kalten, is there any other reason he would try to capture you?"

"I have no idea."

Baltar's voice grew gentle as he said, "Kalten, secrets are my trade, and I have a feeling you are keeping one now. Tell me, why would Duke Samuel bother to chase you?"

"I suppose it's because I know things," Kalten said, taking a step away from the trader. "I was a messenger, a personal courier to the duke as well as a scout."

Paena leapt at him, wrapping an arm around his throat in a chokehold, her dagger pressing into Kalten's back near his kidney. "Did you hear that? He was the duke's personal courier. That alone should prove he's a spy."

He tried to speak, but the chokehold was too tight. Though he fought her with all his strength, his vision soon blurred. The last thing he heard was Baltar's voice.

"You may be right, Paena..."

~ * ~

Pain in his wrists and shoulders woke Kalten up. He leaned back against the coarse bark of a maple tree, his feet splayed in front and his arms stretched behind and tied around the tree. What had he done to deserve such rough treatment from these people? His head pounded.

He blearily looked around to get his bearings. It was still dark. How long had he been tied? Someone lay near the dwindling fire wrapped in blankets. While he watched, Paena marched into view. The sleeping figure had to be Baltar.

Kalten tried to speak, but his throat was dry. He coughed and spat to the side and cleared his throat. "Why have you done this to me?"

"Shut up, spy," Paena hissed. The hatred in her voice was unmistakable. "If you wake Master Baltar, I'll have your balls."

Why should she hate him so much—she didn't even know him. Kalten decided to try again, lowering his voice only slightly to say,

"Could you at least loosen these ropes, please? My arms feel like they're being pulled off."

She took two quick steps to his side. For a moment, he thought she might actually help. Instead, she gave him three sharp kicks to the ribs and belly.

"Ohh!" He tried to double over with the pain but only managed to torture his arms further.

"I said shut up," Paena said, leaning close to Kalten's face.

"Paena." Baltar got up from his blankets. "Get away from the prisoner." He strode over to Kalten. "We are not torturers. We do not behave like the enemy." With each word he seemed to get angrier.

She didn't meet the man's eyes. "My apologies, Master Baltar."

"Paena, we must be diligent." Baltar's voice had softened. "The veneer of civilization is very thin. Once we give into barbarism, all is lost. Now go finish your rounds."

She bowed and moved off into the darkness. Kalten was glad to see her go.

When Baltar spoke again, his voice was steel. "Tell me why I should believe your story. Convince me that you can be trusted."

Kalten tried to shrug. "I don't understand. I've already told you my story. Why are you doing this to me?"

"Others have come before you claiming to be victims of Duke Samuel's treachery. They have all proven to be his spies." His laugh held little mirth. "My name has often exposed their true intentions. The rest were routed by Paena's overprotective diligence."

So that was it. "But I wasn't trying to find you. I was only trying to escape."

"You would have me believe that you only happened to be near my camp." Baltar's voice grew louder. "I say you are a spy unless you can convince me otherwise."

"I am no spy." Kalten struggled against his bonds. "Who are you people?"

"We are the people who have you prisoner." Baltar squatted and looked Kalten squarely in the eyes. "So, what are you then? You say you come from Duke Samuel? He is the biggest traitor in the kingdom. You admit to being one of Samuel's soldiers and a courier on top of that. Only his most trusted men are couriers." The man stood and slapped his hand against his thigh with a crack. "What would you have me think, boy? Hmm?"

"I don't really care what you think. I just want you to let me go."

"I don't think you understand how serious I am," Baltar said. "You should know that your continued survival depends on your cooperation."

"Is that supposed to frighten me?"

"Only if you have any sense." Baltar sighed. "Listen to me very carefully. The queen has charged me to learn if the duke plans to move against her. I must gather evidence of his plots so she can expose him to the other lords. If you are working for him, you will die. If you are not, maybe we can help each other."

"What can I say to convince you I am not a spy?"

"Tell me the truth."

"I have been. I don't know what else I can tell you."

"Tell me where you were going when Paena found you."

"I don't know. I was just trying to get away from here. Find someplace safe." Kalten moved and gasped when pain shot through his shoulders. "Can you please loosen these ropes a little?"

"Very well, but if you try to escape, you will die." Baltar went behind the tree and loosened the ropes. "So, what were you going to do once you escaped?"

"Look for my family."

"That's it?"

"What else can I do? I can't go back. As you pointed out, I'm a peasant. I have nothing except my family. If they live I must save them."

Paena chose that moment to return. "Baltar, we should get moving. It's almost dawn."

"Could you begin to pack up the camp, please?"

"Yes, sir." She glanced at Kalten. "What are we going to do with him?

Baltar studied Kalten for a moment, absently tapping his chin with his index finger. "I wish I could be sure you are telling the truth. Your story rings true to my ears, but my task is too important to risk."

He turned to his companion. "Paena—" His sentence was cut short by a meaty *thunk* as an arrow buried itself into his right shoulder. Stunned, he stared down at the feathered shaft. Within moments, the air buzzed with the sound of incoming arrows masked by darkness.

Paena knocked the injured man from his feet and forced him to the ground. "Stay down, Master. I'll deal with the attackers."

"Untie me. I can help you." Kalten strained against his bonds, trying to ignore the agony of his muscles.

She laughed harshly. "Untie you? So, I have enemies both in front and behind me? You must think me a fool."

She ran off into the forest, and he listened. For several moments nothing happened. He pulled on the ropes. An arrow slammed into the tree near his chest. He watched it quiver in the bark with morbid fascination. He was a sitting target. Thank the fates Baltar had loosened the ropes. Kalten squirmed his way partially around the tree. What to do now?

A scream cut through the trees. He couldn't be sure if it was Paena or not. His arm bumped against the arrow. Maybe he could cut the rope?

He felt a tug at his wrists.

"Hold still while I untie you." Baltar had crawled up to the tree.

"Why are you helping me now? I didn't think you trusted me."

"That last arrow. I don't think your friends would try to kill you." He grunted while he worked on the rope.

"Thank you." The rope went slack, and Kalten could finally pull his arms forward. He hugged them to his chest at the rush of agony and clenched his teeth until the worst of it was past. Leaning around the tree, he helped Baltar take cover. "Let me have a look at that arrow wound."

Kalten checked the wound. The arrow was deeply buried in the shoulder. A patch of sticky, dark blood stained Baltar's brown jerkin. The man's face was a deathly pallor, almost glowing in the morning near-light. There was no telling if the arrow was iron tipped, barbed, or a simple sharpened piece of wood. The only way to tell would be to…

Kalten silently cursed his own stupidity. The attackers had narrowly missed him with an arrow. Surely it would be similar to the one embedded in Master Baltar.

Kalten reached around the trunk of the tree and fumbled around for the arrow. He located it and yanked it out, bringing bits of bark with the barbed, metal head. That would complicate things.

Another cry of pain came from somewhere out in the trees. He had to hand it to the girl. She was pretty good.

"Can you do anything with the arrow? It really hurts." Baltar's jaw clenched and unclenched at the obvious discomfort.

Kalten sighed. "It's barbed so I can't pull it out. The only way I know to remove an arrow like this one is to break off the shaft and push it through."

"I understand." Baltar looked around with glassy eyes. "Where's Paena?"

"She went into the woods to take care of our attackers. I haven't seen her since she left."

"She'll be fine," Master Baltar said, his voice hoarse. He stared at Kalten for a moment. "Why are you still here?"

That was a very good question. "I don't know. You're hurt. I can't just leave you here alone. Not with attackers in the trees."

"Thank you." Master Baltar tried to sit up only to collapse with a moan. "Do what you need to do." He lay back and closed his eyes.

"It's going to hurt," Kalten warned him.

The man only squeezed his eyes tighter in response.

"Very well, then." Kalten grabbed the shaft of the arrow and steadied it with his left hand. With his right, he snapped it off two handspans above the wound. He was careful, but Master Baltar jerked in pain and bit down on his lip to keep from crying out. "Sorry about that, sir."

He nodded, sweat beading his forehead.

"All right, then. I'm going to push it through."

"Stop talking and do it— Ahhhh!" Master Baltar slumped, unconscious. As Master Baltar had spoken, Kalten had given a hard push against the remains of the arrow, driving it down and out through the man's shoulder.

He turned Master Baltar's body to get at the arrowhead. It stuck out from the man's shoulder like some grotesque, bloodied jewelry. Kalten grabbed the arrowhead and gently pulled the remainder of the arrow from the man's shoulder. He covered the bleeding wound with some dried moss from one of the trees and used it as a pad on both sides of the injury, binding it with a scrap of cloth.

A branch cracked, and he glanced up to see a man enter the camp, a wickedly curved sword in his hand. He wore well-patched, greasy leather breeches and a filthy lambskin vest. A scar crossed one cheek, and a thick beard covered the lower half of his face. His smile was nasty as he raised his sword. Kalten tried desperately to find something to defend himself with.

Midway through a slash that would see Kalten's head split in two, the man paused, then spasmed before slowly turning around. Paena stood behind him, her sword covered in his blood. She thrust the sword into his body a second time, and he collapsed. Without a word, she wiped the sword clean on the man's vest.

Kalten had never been quite so glad to see anyone in his life.

"Back away from Master Baltar," she said, motioning with her sword. "Get away from him and lay on your stomach."

Kalten sighed. She was going to be a tough nut to crack. He lay down on his front and waited while she examined her friend.

"What did you do to him?" Her beautiful face twisted in anger.

"He'll be fine. I just removed the arrow from his shoulder. It had a barbed head and could only come out through his back." He wagged his head. "It's laying on the ground over there if you don't believe me."

She crouched and studied the arrow, careful to keep her gaze on Kalten. "Hmm. I see."

"Did you get them all?"

"Yes."

Tough nut indeed. She didn't seem willing to give him anything. Master Baltar stirred, drawing Paena to his side like a magnet.

"How are you, Master?"

He smiled at her. "Yes, Paena. I'm afraid I got a bit careless."

"Don't worry, Master. I've taken care of the attackers."

Master Baltar patted her hand. "Thank you, my dear. I knew I could count on you." He touched his injured shoulder with a slight grimace. "And thank you too, Kalten."

Kalten started pushing himself up.

"Stay down, or I'll kill you where you lie." She had somehow gone from kneeling at Baltar's side to standing in an attack posture in one smooth movement.

"Enough, Paena." Baltar tried and failed to sit up. "Kalten has proven himself to me. He stayed and helped me when he could just as easily have run off." She helped the man into a sitting position. "Kalten, please, get up. We have much to discuss."

Chapter Four

Pieter was not having a good day. How had he gotten stuck with such an ill-tempered, bad-gaited horse? The animal seemed determined to jar his bones and torture his backside. He gritted his teeth after the horse made yet another funny hop. The hostler had a lot to answer for.

Actually, when he thought about it, he decided he might have to buy the hostler a drink. The man had given him the only horse available—his own as it turned out—and Pieter was lucky to be out of there. The way Duke Samuel had been acting, any horse was better than nothing.

Pieter looked around. Nothing but trees. He didn't trust it. The leaves could hide a lot of evils, bandits being the least of them. Hidden eyes could be watching him right now and arrows could be pointing in his direction. He could only hope the combination of a sway-backed, ancient horse with a rider wearing a patched and travel-stained cloak made for a poor target. He resisted the desire to urge the horse faster. That would only make him a more compelling target. With a sigh, he rode on trying not to look around.

Despite riding for the better part of two days, he still had no idea where to go or how to find this Kalten fellow. Too bad the fool hadn't gotten himself properly captured in the first place. If that had happened, Pieter wouldn't be forced to suffer this way.

But the fool had escaped, and it was Pieter's duty as hunter to find him and bring him back. Ordinarily, it would have been an easy task for someone with Pieter's considerable tracking skills. Unfortunately, his quarry seemed to know something about tracking too. Specifically, how to avoid being followed.

The horse shied at a rabbit, almost sending Pieter crashing to the ground. *Hateful creature.* He had half a mind to dismount and send it on its way. Only the thought of walking the entire length of the kingdom stopped him. He watched the small brown blur race into the trees. A whiff of smoke caught his attention. Could it be that the young fool had stopped to camp? Pieter dismounted and tied the horse to a nearby tree. The foliage was especially thick here. Just his luck. He pulled out his dagger and followed the scent of wood smoke.

The smoldering fire ultimately led him to the camp. It was simply too well hidden. He peered through the boughs of a large spruce before entering the clearing.

Well-trampled ground surrounded the smoking ruins of a fire. A stiffening corpse lay on the ground, the camp's sole occupant. Pieter tried to judge the number of people from the tracks but simply couldn't. Too many feet made it impossible to distinguish the impressions. Maybe the corpse would offer some clues.

Pieter looked over the body with a professional eye. Sword thrust through the heart. The question was who had the victim been? He wore the colors of one of the duke's soldiers. Could this be the man he was sent to find?

Pieter bent over to get a better look at the face. No, it couldn't be Kalten. Kalten had been described as young and fair-haired. This fellow had more than a few years under his belt and had black hair flecked with silver. He certainly wouldn't be seeing any more years.

The badge on the man's chest proclaimed him a scout. Too bad it wasn't Kalten. If it were, Pieter could go home with the body and be done with it now. Feeling something wasn't quite right with the body, he searched it more thoroughly.

He checked the blood spot on the tunic. No hole. Either the man had been killed by magic or... He raised the tunic. The clean slice of a sword thrust gaped in the man's chest. If magic didn't kill him, then the clothing had been changed. But why?

Obviously, someone had meant for him or someone like him to think the body belonged to Kalten. It was all that made sense. Maybe he was on the right path after all. Pieter ripped the badge from the dead man's tunic and rushed back to his horse. Judging by what he'd seen, there was no time to lose.

~ * ~

"I know a great deal about Duke Samuel," Master Baltar said, his arm cradled in a sling made from his own cloak. "It might surprise you to know he is disobeying a royal decree just by having a soldier like you. That's probably why he has never had a single soldier leave his service and live. Especially a trusted courier."

Kalten clenched and unclenched his jaw several times while he debated how much he should confess. "There's another reason he wants me," he said, caution be damned. "I have his last communication in my pack. I kept it in case I needed it to buy my freedom."

"May I see it?" Baltar asked, his face twisting to look calm despite the excitement in his voice. "It might provide us with some important information."

"It hasn't done me any good so far." Kalten dug the courier pouch out of his pack and pulled out the communique. "Here you go. But do you really think it will help?"

Baltar unrolled the missive and scanned it quickly. "I was afraid it might be in code, but the language is plain. This message definitely incriminates him. But it isn't quite enough to turn the council completely against him. And it doesn't tell us who his co-conspirators are."

"What good is it then?" Kalten asked.

"I dare say it will confirm some of the queen's suspicions," Baltar replied. He grinned. "In the short time I've known you, you have given me more than all the investigation Paena and I have done."

"I wish that made me feel safer," Kalten said.

"That is why the less you look like one of his soldiers, the better." He held up the communication. "May I keep this? The queen will want to see it."

"As I already told you, I was keeping it as a bargaining measure in case I was captured."

"If the duke captures you, it will only prove his suspicions. It might also incriminate you if one of the queen's supporters finds it. I can offer you some protection against the latter."

"I don't know…"

"I have an idea there is a bigger role for you to play. One that will earn you the queen's favor."

"No doubt it will also earn me more of the duke's wrath too," Kalten said.

"You already did that when you deserted. All the more reason to want the queen as a friend." He considered Kalten. "I have no doubt the duke has agents scouring the countryside for you. That is the reason we had you swap clothes with that highwayman. Disguised, you are slightly safer for us all."

"I get that, but couldn't we have traded clothes with someone a little cleaner?" Kalten asked Baltar as they hiked side-by-side down the road. "This tunic feels like it's infested with fleas." He scratched at one armpit.

Paena, a few paces ahead of them, carried a bow in her hand and had a quiver of arrows at her belt. She had changed clothing too, opting to wear supple, forest green leather. An emerald green bow adorned her hair. "You sure complain a lot, Peasant Boy."

"You're pretty quick to judge. What's your story?"

"None of your business."

Whatever was wrong with her, she wasn't about to tell him. "Master Baltar, I know Duke Samuel is preparing for war. I just don't know why."

"I don't know all the reasons, but I have my suspicions." He glanced at Kalten. "How much do you know about the politics of Kyrglend?"

"Not much. Just that the queen was crowned when her father the king died." A shadow crossed the road in front of him, and he glanced up to see a hawk soaring overhead.

"Did you know that Queen Elespeth is the first woman to ever rule the kingdom?" At the shake of Kalten's head, Baltar continued, "I believe your duke sees her as a threat to his way of life. I think he wants to be the next king."

"Why? Has she done something wrong?"

"No. But some people perceive weakness where it may not exist. They see that weakness as an opportunity to gain power. That, and Duke Samuel is a power-hungry bastard."

Kalten shuddered. "I would hate to see him take power. He is a hard man and treats the peasants like cattle."

"From what I know of him, I tend to agree. That is why it is so important we stop him." Baltar pursed his lips then said, "Can you tell me where you were taken when you joined and where you trained? If we can expose his facilities, it would go a long way to garnering support to remove him."

"Not exactly. We only traveled at night. I was chained to ten other men when they first took me."

"Can you tell me how you were trained then? Did you learn to march, use a sword and shield or a bow?"

"I can tell you some of that. As to the rest, I'll do what I can to help."

"I still don't trust him," Paena said. As she spoke, she nocked an arrow and shot a hare that had been careless enough to show itself on the road. One fluid movement, and she had the makings of a meal. She never looked back at her companions.

"Trust will come. He doesn't have any reason to trust us either. Right now, we have to work together," Baltar said.

"Um… what are you talking about, Master Baltar?" Kalten asked. He silently marveled at Paena. "Work together on what?"

Baltar walked over to a large chunk of black granite and took a seat. "This might take some explaining." He patted a spot beside him on the stone. "Please sit down."

Kalten reluctantly joined him.

"While you two talk, I'm going to find us something more for dinner," Paena said. She dropped the hare—already skinned and cleaned—at Kalten's feet. *When the heck had she done that?*

"Thank you, Paena," Baltar said before turning his attention to Kalten. "You said you would be willing to work to stop Duke Samuel, right?"

"Yes, sir. But other than giving you the communication and whatever other information I have, I don't know what help I'll be."

"You are a trained soldier. Even better, you are also a scout, and you have been a courier. Those skills are very valuable." Baltar shifted into a more comfortable position and brushed a stray lock of white hair out of his eyes.

"I suppose. But remember, I must find my family before I do anything else."

"I understand your desire to find your family. Their disappearance is a tragedy." Baltar put his hand on Kalten's shoulder. "But if we don't stop the duke, there won't be anywhere safe to hide once you find them. And, I don't know if you've noticed, lad, but I'm hurt."

"What does that have to do with me?"

"Paena and I are on a mission for the queen. We are to travel Kyrglend, East, West, North, and South and determine who supports her and who supports Duke Samuel. She needs that information in her preparations to fight the duke." Baltar leaned closer to Kalten. "Now, I need to find a partner for Paena. As good as she is, she can't do the job alone. She needs someone to watch her back. With this injury I can't do that. She would never admit it, but I'm a liability to her. That's where you come in. I want to you to take my place with her."

"Partner with Paena? She hates me."

Baltar sighed. "I know she can be a bit prickly, but she has a good heart. Give her some time."

"I don't know," Kalten said, shaking his head. "I mean, I was your prisoner not so long ago, and Paena was threatening my life. Why would I want to spend more time with her?"

"Kalten, I wouldn't ask if it wasn't important. I need people I can trust. Failure could mean the end of the queen. If that happens, nothing will stop Duke Samuel from claiming the throne."

"You said something important just now," Kalten said. "You need someone you can trust. What makes you think you can trust me? Paena was pretty sure I was a spy for the duke yesterday."

"I have eyes, Kalten," the old man said with a smile. "If you were a spy for the duke you would have acted very differently during the attack."

"Maybe," he said. "But maybe I'm just a coward who deserted his post to avoid battle?"

"Are you?" Baltar asked, watching Kalten closely. "Is that what you would have me believe?"

"Well…no, I guess I'm not," Kalten said. "But all you have to go on is my word on that."

"I know people," Baltar said. "As a trader I've had to get very good at judging people quickly. I judge you to be an honorable and trustworthy man. Besides, a spy would never have handed over that communication from the duke."

"Thank you, sir," Kalten said. "I will consider your words, but I need to think about it. I believe my family is out there and in trouble, and I need to find them."

"Would you consider traveling with us for now?" he asked. "There is greater safety in numbers, and it might be that I can get word of your family through my contacts."

"I really haven't thought about where I should look first," Kalten said. "I suppose going with you is as good a place to start as any. You might as well keep that message. You're right about the trouble it could cause. I hadn't really thought it through."

Baltar smiled and clapped him on the shoulder. "Good man. You may be the edge we've been looking for."

"I haven't said I'll do anything more than travel with you," Kalten protested.

"That is enough for now," Baltar said. "I believe you will see some value in helping us. We must all unite to stop the duke."

"Can I ask you a question?"

"Of course. What is it?"

"Why Paena? Why does the queen need her to search? I can clearly see she has the skills of a fine hunter and warrior. But I've seen some of the duke's spies before. She doesn't really look the part."

"Paena has been with me a long time—ever since I rescued her after the death of her family. I have raised her since then. I've also taught her everything I know. She is very persistent and one of the few people I trust with something like this. The fact she doesn't look like a spy works in her favor."

"I guess I understand," Kalten said.

At that moment, she reappeared carrying three more hares by their hind legs. The small animals were skinned and cleaned.

"Ah, there you are, Paena. Perfect timing as usual." He grabbed Kalten's arm, and the two men stood. "Kalten has agreed to travel with us. I'm trying to convince him to be your new partner."

She laughed unpleasantly. "Good joke, Master." She glowered at Kalten. "But I wouldn't be caught dead working with this peasant. Besides, you're my partner."

"Keep an open mind, Paena," Baltar said. "I can't work with you now. Not with my wound." He moved his bad arm, and an exaggerated look of pain crossed his face. He moaned and crumpled to the ground.

She crouched at his side in an instant. "Master. Can I do anything for you?"

"No, dear Paena. This wound is causing me a great deal of pain." He winked at Kalten over her shoulder. He noticed that somehow blood stained the bandage on Baltar's shoulder.

"We have to get you back to the city, Master. You need to heal."

"There isn't time for that, Paena. Queen Elespeth's mission is critical. If you won't work with Kalten, then I must continue."

"Wait a minute. Like I told you a moment ago, I'll travel with you for now. That's all." What was the old fraud up to? Kalten could clearly see that Master Baltar faked the pain. It should be obvious even to Paena. Somehow it wasn't.

She knelt on the ground cradling Baltar's head. "I cannot let you go on, Master. Not with your wound."

"You must have a partner, Paena. The way is too dangerous to travel alone. You know as well as I do that an unescorted young woman like you in this kingdom will be challenged at every opportunity. If you will not even consider Kalten, then it must be me." Baltar tried to sit up only to collapse with a groan.

Paena sighed. "If I agree, will you promise to rest?"

"Hold on now," Kalten protested again. "I must find my family before I commit to anything else."

She glared at him. "If you agree to this ridiculous plan, I will help you find your family *after* we finish our mission."

"Will you do it, Kalten? Will you help us?" Baltar asked.

Kalten sighed. The expression on her face promised a lot more than pain if he disagreed. "I...suppose. But only if you promise to help me find my mother and sisters."

"We will help you," Baltar said. He patted her hand like a grandfather. "Are you certain of this?"

"I will do this for you, Master." Her next words, spoken to Baltar, were meant for Kalten's ears. "But if he steps out of line, I will kill him."

"Whatever you think is best, Paena," Baltar said, patting her hand again.

Chapter Five

Pieter should be happy or at the very least, content. After days scouring the countryside, he finally had the promise of a warm bed in his future and a pint of decent ale in his present. He had even managed to find a decent inn if the common room was any indication.

Clean and cozy, the room boasted a fireplace that took up half the far wall and burned with a merry blaze. The floor was well-scrubbed pine, and the dozen or so tables looked old but solid and were surrounded by benches. No, Pieter should be well pleased with his luck.

Instead, he brooded in the darkest corner of the common room, watching the other inn's patrons, farmers mostly and a couple merchants. The farmers had the dirty, lean look of men with too much work and not enough time or food. The merchants, on the other hand, had the fat, prosperous look of swine at the trough. An unlikely pairing if he had ever seen one. But it wasn't the men in the room who frustrated him.

No, it was that damnable Kalten character. How in the darkness could Pieter find the man when he only had a vague idea what he looked like? If the boy had left tracks or any trail to follow, things would be different, but he hadn't. So, what now? Travel around asking everyone he met? Pieter snorted into his beer and took another long drink then wiped the foam from his face.

Normally he would be talking to the contacts he had in every town. Unfortunately, they were inconveniently absent. He visually searched around the room for what seemed like the hundredth time, in case one of those contacts magically appeared.

But no, aside from the farmers and merchants, the room remained the same.

He was running out of ideas, and he didn't dare go back to the duke empty-handed. Duke Samuel rewarded success and failure with equal delight. Perhaps with a touch more creativity for failure. Pieter suppressed a shudder. The guard captain had been lucky. No, he couldn't fail.

The front door of the inn swept open, and a warrior marched in. Wait a minute. Not a warrior but a woman dressed like a warrior. As tall as a man, the young woman surveyed the room in a casual yet professional way. Pieter was certain she could look after herself. He snorted again. His attention was drawn back after a young peasant man staggered in supporting his grizzled grandfather. The older man appeared to be injured. Pieter sidled down the bench a little to hear better.

"Innkeeper. I need two rooms and a healer." The woman adjusted her sword belt making the innkeeper take a step back from her.

"Of course, lady. I have two rooms just up the stairs. You can have those."

She turned to the young man, speaking quietly so Pieter had to strain to hear. "Take the master up to the room. I'll get things settled with the innkeeper." The woman pulled a pouch from her belt and poured a small handful of coins onto the counter. "And make sure you get the healer here right away." She turned away. "Oh yes, and some food, hot water and towels."

"Right away, lady." The innkeeper snatched the coins and scuttled into the back of the inn.

Pieter stared at the peasant boy as he struggled to help the old man up the stairs. Could that be the man he looked for? The duke hadn't said anything about him traveling with others. Pieter quickly searched his memory: young, fair-haired peasant boy. The duke had mentioned mismatched eyes, but the distance and the darkness of the common room made it impossible to tell if he had those. The clothes he wore could belong to the corpse from the campsite. Some things seemed to match. But Pieter had to be sure.

Then he laughed. He didn't have to be sure. The duke wanted this Kalten fellow alive. If he captured the wrong man, he could easily dispose of him; it just meant one less peasant.

Pieter almost drew his sword right there, except this was too public a place, and he was only a single man. If this was the Kalten he searched for, he had to remember the man was a trained soldier. And the woman he was traveling with had the air of someone with skills of her own. Pieter had seen too much to discount her just because she was female. No, it was too risky to attack him alone.

He got up and dropped a coin onto the table. He could find men willing to earn a little extra money to take care of a problem. They'd cut into the profit but that was a necessary evil. He almost ran out of the inn to start recruiting.

It didn't take him long to find someone to help. There were always men hanging out near the local weaponsmith's shop looking for easy money. It was no different here.

"You understand what you have to do, right?" Pieter asked again. Even after repeating the instructions three times, he wasn't sure the trio of thugs quite had the idea.

"Yes, I got it," the biggest of the three rumbled. The man was huge, his face scarred and his knuckles swollen from one too many brawls. His expensive clothing and boots were totally at odds with his brutish appearance. "We'll take care of your man, won't we boys?"

The two grunts wordlessly nodded. Both were dressed in heavily patched homespun and hose with rags wrapped around their feet. Wool cowls were pulled over their heads, and a miasma of halitosis surrounded them like a cloud.

"See. Like I told you. We got it. Now hand over the money."

Pieter wagged his index finger at them. "You only get half now and half when you're done with him."

The tough cracked his knuckles and thrust out his hand. "Half now and half when we're done."

Pieter handed him a pouch of coins and nodded. "See you back here when you're done."

~ * ~

The small but comfortable room contained a single bed and table. A fireplace warmed the air, and a shuttered window opened to what smelled like the stable.

Kalten watched while Paena tucked the covers tenderly around Baltar. She straightened and beckoned for him to follow her out of the room.

She closed the door behind them. "He's finally sleeping. Let's get something to eat."

It was probably the most civil thing she said to him in days. Kalten could only nod his agreement.

The room was filled with laughing, talking people. Paena grabbed the innkeeper's arm when he rushed by with a tray of mugs. She leaned close to make herself heard. "Innkeeper, can you find us a place to sit? We need some dinner."

The innkeeper nodded and continued on, leaving them standing at the foot of the stairs. Moments later, he came back and led them to an empty table near the fireplace. "What would you like?" he shouted at them. "We have a bit of mutton and some soup. The bread was fresh this morning. You can have all three for two coppers."

Kalten and Paena's gaze met. He nodded.

"We'll both have all three," she shouted back. "And two ales."

The innkeeper bustled off, ignoring the calls of patrons. He returned moments later and thumped two tankards down on the table. "Your meal will be here shortly." He left the table to help another customer.

Kalten took a sip from his tankard. Not bad. The ale was definitely better than the swill he drank in Duke Samuel's service.

"That'll be six coppers—four for the food and two more for the ale," the innkeeper said as he delivered the two platters of food, keeping Kalten between himself and Paena.

"Pay the man," she ordered with a nod before she turned her attention to her food.

With a sigh, Kalten dug the coppers from his pouch and handed them over to the innkeeper. The man pocketed the coins without a word.

Kalten looked around as he ate. A few merchants, by their garb, were hunched around a large table in closed conversation near the fire. Scattered around the of the room were guards and farmers and a table of thugs. There was no other way to describe them, and they were all staring at him. That could mean trouble.

"There's a group of toughs sitting over there," Kalten said to Paena in a low voice. "They seem to be paying a lot of attention to me."

"Don't get excited," she replied. "Just eat your food. It's probably nothing."

The largest of the thugs, a well-dressed brute, got up from his table and sauntered over. He stopped and loomed over Paena, leering at her. "Hey, girl. My friends and I want you to have a drink with us. How about coming over to our table and keeping us company?"

She ignored the man and kept eating her meal. When he realized she wasn't going to answer him, he grabbed her by the shoulder. "I'm talking to you girl, and I expect an answer."

She knocked his hand off her shoulder. "Not interested. Now, go away and let me finish my supper."

"I don't think you heard me, girl. We want you to come over and keep us company." His mouth twisted in an ugly snarl.

"She heard you just fine. Now, go away." Kalten reached for his sword, realizing too late he left it in the room.

"Stay out of this, boy, or you'll get yourself hurt." The man tried to drag her from her chair.

She jammed her fork into the man's hand. The utensil went deep, striking bone. He howled in pain and knocked her to the floor with his good hand.

"Stab me, will you, you little bitch? I'll teach you some manners." He yanked the quivering fork from his hand before he turned back to his friends and laughed. "Shall I teach this slut some manners, boys?"

Kalten jumped up, holding his dagger, and shouted at the man's back. "Turn and face me, you worthless pig!"

The man slowly turned to face Kalten, a wicked gleam in his eyes and a smile on his puffy lips. "So, the puppy has a bark. I wasn't sure you'd be able to find your way off your mistresses' lap." He began drawing his sword.

Before it cleared its scabbard, a chunk of firewood crashed into the man's jaw, sending blood and bits of bone and teeth spraying from his mouth. "I fight my own battles, you filth," Paena said, another chunk of wood already in her hand. She stood unsteadily, her cheek swollen and a bruise starting to show.

The man swayed on his feet, blood pouring down his chin. "The next time you put one of your dirty paws on me, I won't be quite so nice." She smashed the wood into the man's nose, sending him crashing to the floor.

The thug's sidekicks got up from their table, each pulling out a long wicked-looking knife. Kalten pushed Paena away from the men and faced them, his dagger held ready in front of him. The two men stalked him, stepping over their fallen boss. He could only see the gleam of their eyes from under woolen hoods.

"We're gonna cut you good, pretty boy," the left goon said as he thrust his knife at Kalten.

Kalten sidestepped the knife. The thug was clearly used to intimidating his victims. Not much finesse. Kalten's sergeant taught him to be patient; the man would eventually leave an opening to exploit.

The man tried again, slashing across Kalten's body this time.

A quick step back avoided the strike. Kalten immediately followed up by lunging forward, leaving a shallow gash in the attacker's arm.

The man yowled in pain and jerked back. His partner sneered and lurched toward Kalten. He waited until he was within reach and lunged at the man, stabbing at him. He rotated slowly on the balls of his feet as his assailant danced out of the way. Kalten continued circling, trying to draw the men away from Paena.

He had their full attention now. The first man rejoined the fight, waving his knife as his partner worked to get behind Kalten. He backed up a little, trying to keep both men in view.

When the second man passed by Paena, she stepped behind him. She held her index finger against her lips and shook her head at Kalten. He attacked the first man as she tapped the second goon on the shoulder.

The man turned and ran into her right fist. He dropped to the floor, blood streaming from his nose. The remaining thug, distracted by his companion, gave Kalten the opening he needed.

He stabbed his dagger into the man's shoulder and wrestled him for the knife. While the man focused on Kalten, Paena stepped forward and kicked the man on the side of his knee. With a groan, he collapsed to the dirty floor and lay whimpering, clutching at his injured leg and shoulder.

The bar erupted in cheers; Kalten and Paena were suddenly being pounded on the backs and congratulated. A few of the patrons took turns kicking the downed men.

"What's all this, then?" a loud voice said. The inn went quiet.

Men in chain mail pushed their way into the inn and effectively sealed the room by blocking the only available exit.

"What is going on here?" the man in front demanded again. He wore chainmail covered in a black and silver surcoat. He gripped a mace in his right hand like a scepter and held a helmet tucked under his left arm. The glare on his face challenged everyone in the room. "Do not make me ask a third time or there will be trouble."

Kalten stepped forward. "My pardon, Captain. My friend and I were having a meal when these three," he gestured to the men on the floor, "attacked us."

"They attacked you? You two?" the captain asked. "These three bruisers attacked you two." He shook his head. "Then why are you still standing?"

"Lucky, I guess," Kalten said with a shrug.

Several people spoke up at once describing their versions of the attack. A single look from the captain cowed them to silence. One of the guards covered his mouth to hide a snicker.

The captain examined the men on the floor. "Well, well, well. I'll say you were lucky. These men are known killers." He yanked Kalten's dagger from the downed man's shoulder. "This yours?"

"Yes, sir," Kalten said.

The captain tossed the knife to Kalten. "You'll want to clean that, I expect. Corporal, put them in chains and get them out of here."

"Sir." The corporal saluted and set to work on the groaning and senseless men.

The captain watched his men for a few moments before he addressed Paena and Kalten again. "You two planning on staying in town for long?"

"No, sir," Kalten said.

"Good. See that you're gone by sun-up tomorrow. If I catch you in town after that, I'll throw you into the dungeon myself." Without another word he spun on his heel and left the inn. His remaining men formed up behind him and followed him out.

"What's going on down there?" a familiar voice demanded. Baltar stood at the top of the stairs, heavy beads of sweat plain on his forehead. "I try to get some sleep, and you all decide to throw a party."

Kalten didn't know what to say. "I'm sorry, sir. We were attacked…"

Baltar waved a hand at him then stumbled. He grabbed at the stair railing and collapsed.

Paena rushed up the stairs to him. "Master. What happened?"

Baltar smiled up at her. "I'm just tired, Paena. Help me up."

"Maybe this time you'll stay in bed where you belong," Paena said while she half led, half carried Baltar back to his room.

~ * ~

The sun was just peeking over the horizon when Kalten and Paena made their way out of the town. The captain waited for them at the gate.

"Can't say I'm sorry to see you go," he said. "That brawl may not have been your doing, but I don't need any problems in my town."

"Times are troubled," Kalten said. "We don't want to make it worse."

The captain nodded in approval. "I'm glad to hear that. Bring 'em over."

A man came out of the shadows, leading a pair of horses. The animals, one a chestnut with a single white stocking, the other a dappled grey, looked healthy to Kalten's inexperienced eye. The man handed the reins to Kalten.

"What's this?" Paena asked.

"These used to belong to those fellows you fought. They won't be needing them anymore. I thought you might take them off my hands," the captain said. "Call it a reward for capturing some dangerous criminals. You'll find rations in the saddle bags."

"Thank you, sir," Kalten said.

"Before we go, Captain, I have a request for you," Paena said. She waited until she had the captain's attention. "Our companion, an older merchant, is recovering at the inn. Robbers injured him before we came to your town. Could you look in on him from time-to-time to make sure he's all right?"

The captain was silent, likely as he considered her request for a long moment before he nodded. "I'll check in on him."

Chapter Six

Duke Samuel paced the south wall of the castle, anxiously scanning the fields and forests, when Marcus answered his summons.

Normally, he would have taken a minute to enjoy the view himself: the small, quaint village, a handful of paces below the castle walls, fields of grain and sheep that ended with the thick trees of the forest. But not today. He could see his duke was agitated, and that always required him to employ extra caution.

"Any word from the hunter, Marcus?" Duke Samuel asked as Marcus approached. His eyes were wild and his hair unkempt. Obviously, the man had not slept in some time.

"Nothing yet, lord," Marcus replied. His instincts for self-preservation screamed at him to run away. Experience told him to maintain a calm facade.

"You told him how to contact you before he left, didn't you?" The duke continued to pace and watch the horizon.

"Yes, my lord." Marcus was careful to maintain a neutral expression. He shivered and not just from the cold wind blowing over the keep's wall.

"You will inform me the moment word comes in."

"As you wish, my lord," Marcus replied. Somehow, he knew things would get worse before it got better.

The duke looked at him with reddened eyes. "If you do not hear from the hunter by this time tomorrow, dispatch a squad of my personal guard to find him and the traitor. I want him brought to me."

"And the hunter? What would you have them do with him, my lord?"

The duke waved his hand dismissively. "I don't care. He is no longer important. Kill him, I suppose."

Marcus bowed. "As you command, my lord."

~ * ~

The sky was a deep blue color and clear as the sun rose above the horizon. Kalten and Paena removed the heavy wool cloaks they had been wearing, enjoying the warming day. On either side of them were fields filled with grazing sheep and cattle. Shepherds and cattle herders moved amongst their charges, watching for signs of danger. Most were wary of the travelers, but occasionally one would raise a hand in friendly greeting.

"Do you think Master Baltar will be all right?" Kalten asked. He shifted, seeking a more comfortable position for his tailbone.

"I hope so," Paena replied. "He knows a lot of people, so probably." Somehow, despite saying it, she still sounded worried.

Kalten caught her looking at him. "What?"

"Nothing."

"Any thoughts where we should go?"

"We have reason to believe most of the Northern lords are already pledged to the duke. That's what we were trying to find out when we came across you. We were going to talk to the Eastern lords next."

"Is that where we're going, then?"

"I don't think so," Paena said, shaking her head. "Master Baltar suggested we try something else if you're willing."

"Like what?"

"Like, we try to find your duke's stronghold and army."

"I don't know exactly where we should go," Kalten said with a shrug. "Like I told you and Master Baltar, they blindfolded me before they took me in. All I know is we were trained in a massive fort surrounded by forest. When we left, we avoided towns. When I ran, we were already out in the field."

"A big forest, hmm? I don't know what's out there. Could be lots of big forests around. We'll ask when we get to the next town." She kneed her horse to a gallop.

They rode throughout the day galloping their mounts at times, walking them at others.

"I don't want to worry you, Paena, but I think we're being followed," Kalten said after catching a glimpse of someone behind them.

"Could it be another traveler going the same way we are?"

"I suppose so. But I don't want to make any assumptions. I know I had some men tracking me before I ever met you and Master Baltar, and we've been attacked twice since then."

"We should set up camp while it's still light," Paena said. "I don't want someone coming up on us in the dark until we are prepared."

"Good idea. I'll start watching for somewhere to stop," he said.

They stopped in a small clearing just off the road before the sun set. He swung off his horse and pulled the bags and saddle off the beast's back.

"Kalten, unsaddle my horse while I make a fire."

He stared at Paena for a moment, his hands still on the saddle. "Say please."

"What?"

"I said, 'Say please'. I'm not some servant you can order around. I'm your partner in this little adventure," Kalten said. Her answering frown told him he just said the wrong thing. He braced for the fight.

"No, you're not. You are just a peasant Master Baltar saddled me with. Worse, you're a deserter. You're working for me, not with me." Her face reddened as her voice grew louder.

That was more like the Paena he first met. "What is your problem?" He could feel the heat rising in his face too. "You know, I have never met anyone harder to deal with than you. I understood that you might not trust me right away, so I've done everything I could to ease your mind. Yet you still treat me like dirt."

She sneered at him. "Did I hurt your feelings? Too bad, coward! Go cry where I can't see you."

Coward? What was wrong with her? Maybe it was time to cut his losses. If that's how she felt after the last few days, there was no point staying. He could quit wasting his time with this crazy mission and get back to finding his family. Kalten turned his back on Paena and cinched up the saddle on his horse. He threw his saddlebags behind the saddle then swung back up onto his horse.

"Where are you going?"

Was that a note of fear in her voice? "I'm leaving. Master Baltar asked me to join you, not the other way around. I've more important things to do than fight with you. In case you've forgotten, my family was taken when they forced me into Duke Samuel's army. I intend to find them and take them away from all this." Kalten reined his horse around.

"And you think you have any chance of finding your family on your own? You don't even know where to begin looking. I do."

That stopped him. She had a point. But was it worth the constant battles and abuse to stay with her?

"You also seem to forget that Master Baltar is working for the queen. That means I am working for her too. If you leave now, I will have no choice but to get her guards to hunt you down."

"That's all you've got? Threats?" Kalten shook his head. "If I leave, you'll send hunters after me?"

"If I must." Her wide-eyed expression weakened the threat.

"In case you've forgotten, I've already got people hunting me. What's a few more?" He tapped the horse with his heel to get it moving.

"Wait!"

"What is it?"

"I'm sorry."

"What?" Kalten wasn't sure he heard her correctly. "Did you just apologize?"

"You're right. I have treated you badly. Unfairly too." She stared at her boots for a few moments. "You have acted honorably and deserve my trust. Please don't go."

"Just like that?"

She didn't meet his eyes. "Yes. I haven't had many times in my life where I could trust anyone. Fewer where the people I was around deserved it. Master Baltar was really the first."

Kalten studied her for a moment. She actually seemed remorseful. "You'll stop treating me like the soil beneath your boots?"

She tried to smile and failed. "I can't promise that, but I'll try."

He nudged the gelding back into the camp and dismounted. "Then I'll stay. But only if you will answer a question for me."

"That entirely depends on the question."

"Why were you always so angry when Master Baltar was around? When we first met you were ready to kill me at the drop of a hat. I've never seen anyone act so aggressive and violent before. You are so much different now."

She considered the question. "I-I owe Master Baltar everything. I cannot let him down so, I suppose, I'm always more vigilant when he's around."

"Vigilant?" Kalten asked. "That's not exactly the word I would have used. But, if I'm hearing you correctly, you have something to prove to him, right? Master Baltar mentioned something about you two being together a long time. Is that it?"

"We have been, but that story will have to wait for another time."

"Fair enough," he said.

"Since we're asking questions, can I ask you something?" she asked.

"I guess so."

"Can you tell me about your eyes?"

"What about them?"

"They're different colors, aren't they?"

"They are. So what?"

"Nothing, I suppose. Have they always been like that? Did it ever cause you trouble?"

"Some of our neighbors avoided our family, if that's what you mean. It was even worse after my father died. My family often struggled because no one was willing to help." Kalten shook his head. "I never understood it. Mother said they came from my father, but my dad, Ewen, had grey eyes. She would never say more, and I quit asking."

"Thank you for telling me. I think they are nice," Paena said.

"You're welcome, I guess," he said. Was her curiosity a breakthrough, or was she just trying to keep him off balance? He made a mental shrug. That was a question that would have to wait for another day.

~ * ~

Paena woke in darkness; only the silvery light of the waning moon lit the camp. Surely Kalten hadn't fallen asleep during his watch and forgotten to wake her. A quick, fumbling search of the campsite only increased her anxiety.

Cautious not to make too much noise by calling out to him, she checked all the likely places around the camp for him to stand watch. There was no sign of him. Their gear was missing too. She shouldn't have let her guard down. The moment she eased up on him, he turned tail and ran.

Soft laughter floated down from above her.

"Miss me?" Perched on a large branch, well above the ground, Kalten looked down at her, a big grin on his face.

"What are you doing up there? Why didn't you wake me for my watch?"

"You looked so peaceful, I decided to let you sleep."

How like him to not think things through. "We can't afford for one of us to get worn out. You should've gotten me up."

He shrugged. "I couldn't sleep anyway. I had too much on my mind." He climbed from the tree, dropping lightly to the ground.

She clenched her fists. "You bastard. I thought you left me."

"I thought you decided to trust me."

"Really? I wake up to find our gear gone, and you nowhere to be seen."

He had the grace to look embarrassed. "I guess I can see why you might think that. I'm sorry. I moved the gear out of sight in case someone wandered in. I thought I saw someone following us back on the road, remember?"

"That's fine, but if we're going to work together, we need to tell each other what we're doing. It'll be the unexpected that kills us." The panic Paena felt faded. Now, she was simply annoyed with Kalten.

"You're right. I should have told you what I was doing, but I didn't want to wake you."

"Well, let's agree to not surprise each other anymore."

"You have my word." He eyed the sky. The moon hovered low in the west. "If I'm any judge, the sun will be up soon. We should pack up the camp and get out of here."

"But you haven't had any sleep."

"Not to worry. I can probably doze a little while we ride if you keep an eye on me."

"I can do that," she said. "I was thinking we could find a village today. Maybe use it as our base of operations while we searched for the duke's camp?"

"That's as good a plan as any other," he said. "Since I'm not certain where the camp is, we can start there and work our way out."

"Exactly."

They rode for most of the day, stopping only to stretch their legs. By the time they found a place to rest the sun was just a sliver sliding down beneath the horizon.

The village was small, no more than a dry goods store, a well-kept inn, and a few houses. Still, it wasn't the road, and Paena was excited at the thought of sleeping in a bed for a night.

Leaving their horses tethered outside, Kalten and Paena entered the inn. They were caught off-guard by the brightness of the room. She gasped.

The place was beautiful. The floors and tables were meticulously clean. Oil lamps hung on every wall, lighting the entire room. The man standing behind the counter laughed warmly at their reactions.

"Never thought you'd see a place like this, now did you?" He polished the counter in front of him. "Welcome to The Queen's Own. Your comfort and relaxation are my greatest desire."

She stepped up to the counter. "You're most correct, kind innkeeper. We'd certainly never expected to find such a jewel as this here."

"A jewel, she says." He chuckled, winking at Kalten. "I thank you most kindly, lady, and offer you a warm welcome. Now, how may I and my humble establishment be of service to you?"

"We require two rooms if you have them, my good man," she said, "and I wouldn't say no to food and drink either."

Kalten extended his hand to the innkeeper. "My friend, we couldn't be happier to be here. My name is Kalten, and this lovely lady is my traveling companion, Paena. I would only add one thing to her request. You don't have somewhere to wash trail grime off do you?" His question was almost pleading.

The innkeeper laughed. "Of course, young Kalten, and well met. I am your host, Roulston, and I most certainly do have a place for you to wash. We have several tubs to bath in, in fact. Would you prefer the water hot, cold or somewhere in between?"

"Hot, most definitely, please." Kalten turned to Paena with a smile. "I haven't been this excited in weeks. I see a little comfort in my future."

She smiled back at her companion. "The hot bath sounds wonderful. Could you show us to our rooms and then the tubs? I would love a long soak before we eat supper." She gave the innkeeper a wry grin. "Before I get too far ahead of myself, I should ask how much?"

"You needn't worry too much about that my dear," Roulston said. "I think you will find my prices fair. It's six coppers per night each, plus whatever you eat and drink."

"That's more than fair," he said, surprise in his tone. "And we also have two horses outside with our gear. Could you point me toward a stall to stable them in please?"

"Certainly, young sir. But stabling two horses will be an additional five coppers each, six if you want a mash for your animals."

Kalten handed the coins over to the innkeeper. "Please have a mash prepared for each of them. We traveled a long way today, and they've earned it."

"Consider it done." Roulston went to the door and called out. "Nigel! We have guests here with two horses that need stabling. And put a mash on too, please."

A voice floated out of the darkness. "Right away, sir."

The innkeeper returned to his counter. "There you are, sir. Your horses will be set right. Now, can I show you to your rooms?"

"Absolutely. Lead the way."

~ * ~

Pieter had followed Kalten and the woman from a discreet distance since they had ridden out of the city.

His first plan had certainly gone badly. Kalten—and he was now sure the young man was his quarry based on how he had fought—had been skilled enough, but the real surprise had been the girl; she was much tougher than expected. Still, it had been a learning experience. Knowing the abilities of one's prey was critical if one was to successfully hunt and capture them, and the brawl with the thugs had clearly revealed that. Next time he would hire twice as many men.

Pieter patted the leather pouch behind his saddle. It clinked reassuringly. He had enough gold there to set him up comfortably for life. Running wasn't an option though. A man had his reputation to consider, and Pieter was one of the best. He hated failure, but a single setback didn't worry him.

Hidden by darkness, he watched Kalten disappear into the inn. The boy had taken him on a merry chase, but it was time to close in. He looked around for any people. Finally satisfied the way was clear, Pieter led his horse across the road and behind the dry goods store. He let himself into the stable and lit a lantern after closing the door.

He nodded in approval as he inspected the structure. It was a tidy little building with stalls enough for three animals. A ladder, nailed to one wall, ascended up into the ceiling and a there was a small room filled with tack and barrels of barley. A shaggy bay mare blinked at him in the light of the lantern from one of the stalls.

He had just put his horse into a stall when the door of the stable creaked open.

"Who're you, and what're you doing in my barn?" a voice demanded.

Pieter glanced over his shoulder. A fat man dressed in a gown and cap blocked the entrance of the building, a sword clutched awkwardly in his right fist.

"I'm stabling my horse," Pieter said.

"This is no inn, and my barn is for my use only." the man said with a scowl. "Now take your things and be gone before I lose my temper."

Pieter stepped out of the stall. "Is that any way to talk to one of the duke's own?" he asked. "I was told I could expect hospitality from you."

The gowned man quickly stepped into the stable, pulling the door closed behind him. "Shhh, man. Don't speak so loudly. The walls have ears in these parts." He looked around as if to roust out any hidden spies. His eyes narrowed. "If you be one of the duke's own, then prove it to me now."

Pieter smiled and plucked a marker from his pouch. He flipped it into the waiting man's hand. "By all means, have a look."

The man held the marker up in the lantern's light and examined the piece. With a sigh he handed it back. "Aye, you're genuine all right. But what do you want of me?"

"I'm following a fugitive for Duke Samuel. I need to send a message to him and a place to stay while I wait for a reply. Oh, and some food as well."

"The message I can do well enough. I've a cage of birds in the loft. You can stay up there with them if you can stay out of sight. Wait here, and I'll get something to write with." The man left the stable.

"And don't forget the food," Pieter called.

Chapter Seven

Horses stamped impatiently in the cobbled courtyard and chomped on their bits. Torches flared and sputtered in the strong evening winds, revealing the gathered men in a faint light. Soldiers paced the upper wall of the duke's castle, and riders waited at rigid attention beside their mounts while their captain received final instructions from the duke.

"We will find him, my lord," Captain Kerris said with a salute. He looked odd in armor, like a bloated spider. "We will comb the countryside until he is ours."

"Do as I command, and you will be rewarded," Duke Samuel said, shouting to be heard over the growing winds. "Fail me, and it will be the last time."

"My lord!" Marcus rushed into the courtyard. The scrawny man appeared as he always did: an emaciated but impeccably dressed scarecrow. "A bird has just arrived from one of your spies. He has word of the traitor." He stopped in front of the duke and tried to catch his breath.

"Well, out with it man. Where is he?"

Marcus gulped at the air. "The hunter reports that the traitor is in the village of Thistledown. He is traveling with a woman."

"Traveling with a woman, you say?" That changes things; he has most certainly talked. Duke Samuel smacked his hands together and rubbed them eagerly. "How soon can you be in Thistledown, Captain?" he asked.

Captain Kerris was silent for a few moments. "We can be there in two days, my lord."

"See that you are, and do not let this traitor escape," the duke said. "I don't care if you bring him back alive or dead. Just bring him to me and his woman too."

The man saluted and swept onto his mount. His men followed his example, mounting up in a single, well-choreographed motion. The captain wheeled his horse around and trotted to the head of the column. Within moments, the troop of soldiers were clattering out of the courtyard.

Duke Samuel turned toward his steward. "Marcus, send a bird back to our man. Have him tell the hunter to watch the traitor. He is not to lose him."

"As you wish, my lord."

~ * ~

Paena walked down the steps, rubbing her eyes. She had taken full advantage of the soft bed and slept late. The peace of the place invigorated her; for the first time in days, her dreams had not been filled with images of Master Baltar in trouble. The common room of the inn was deserted except for the innkeeper who scrubbed one of the tables.

"Good morning, miss," Roulston said.

"Oh, good morning, Roulston."

"Did you sleep well?"

"Better than I have in days, thank you. Have you seen my companion yet?"

"Oh, yes. He came down just before sun-up. He had breakfast and went for a stroll."

"That's Kalten. I don't think I've ever seen him get up late."

"I suspected as much." The innkeeper chuckled. "Would you like something to eat?"

"That would be lovely. What do you have?" She turned her head toward the kitchen and breathed in deeply. The rich, heady smell of fresh bread filled her with a sense of peace.

"I think we still have porridge on, or would you prefer something more substantial?"

"Porridge would be fine… with a spoonful of honey, if you have it?"

He smiled. "We do have it, lady. I'll bring it out to you shortly. Would you like some tea too?"

"Yes, please. I'll just sit down by the window and enjoy the morning sun."

"It won't be long." He turned and re-entered the kitchen.

Paena seated herself at a small table by the inn's window. The shutters had been thrown back to allow the morning sun in, and she could see that, for the villagers, the day was already well in hand. Children chased each other in play while busy men and women went about their daily business. She scrutinized the street but didn't see any sign of Kalten.

"Here you are, miss," Roulston said, setting a bowl of porridge and cup of tea in front of her. "I'll be right back with some honey for you." He returned moments later and set a large honey pot in front of her along with a small loaf of still-warm bread.

"How much do I owe you?"

"Not a thing, miss. Your young man has been helping out in the stable. Breakfast is the least I can do to repay his kindness." He paused then said, "My lady, if you don't mind me asking, do you know a trader by the name of Baltar?"

It was Paena's turn to be surprised. "Why yes, I do. He is my mentor. Why do you ask?"

"A messenger rode through yesterday and left something. He said a young woman by the name of Paena might be coming through here. The message came from Master Baltar the Trader."

A message from Baltar? "That sounds like me. What did he leave?"

Roulston removed an envelope from under his apron, an apologetic look on his face. "I should have given this to you last night, but you were obviously tired."

"Don't concern yourself, Roulston." She examined the envelope. "I'm sure a single night won't make a difference."

"Thank you, miss. I shall leave you to the message." He turned and left her alone.

What could Baltar's message be? Paena tore open the envelope and read the contents. Moments later she ran out of the inn looking for Kalten, her breakfast forgotten.

It didn't take long to find him; he was already on his way back to the inn. He flashed her a wide grin and waved.

She couldn't help but smile back at him. He did have a nice smile even if he was a commoner. She noticed a pair of young women watching him walk, talking and giggling to each other.

"Good morning, sleepy head. How was your rest?"

"Hmm? Oh, good." Paena grabbed his arm and pulled him away from the main street, glancing over her shoulder.

"What's going on?" he asked.

"We got a message from Baltar."

Kalten stiffened but kept moving. "Huh? From Baltar? How did he find us?"

"He's in charge of the queen's eyes and ears. I don't suppose he had too much trouble."

Kalten scratched his head. "That makes sense, I suppose." He stopped talking until a farmer passed, then leaned closer to Paena. "What does he have to say?"

When she spoke again, her voice was very quiet. "He warns us to be careful because it is believed that Duke Samuel has spies throughout the kingdom just like the queen. We may be in danger. "

"I expected as much. He isn't a terribly merciful man. Maybe we shouldn't have partnered up. You should probably leave."

"Where would I go? Besides, we need each other. To watch each other's backs if nothing else." Paena watched while two villagers passed, nodding pleasantly to them. When they passed, she spoke again. "Baltar seems to think the message you gave him was important. What did it say?"

"I don't actually know," Kalten admitted. "I never stopped to read it. I knew the duke was up to something, and I had the opportunity to get out. So, I did."

"You didn't think to tell anyone? You just decided to run?"

His head snapped up, and he glared at her. "Who would you have me tell? I'm a peasant, and he is my liege lord, remember? Who would listen?"

"You're right, I'm sorry."

"Look. I did what I thought I could. Maybe it wasn't brave or smart, but it's all I could think of."

She nodded. "Standing up to your duke was brave, and trying to save your family is very noble."

"Thank you, I appreciate you saying that," he said. "Did Baltar have anything else to say?"

"He requested that we first try to find Duke Samuel's hidden stronghold. Then we are to continue talking to the Eastern lords to try and learn how deep the treason runs within the kingdom."

"We did agree to use this village as our base to find the stronghold. We can start by asking around." Kalten rubbed his neck. "As to the Eastern lords? I don't know how we are supposed to do that. I'm still a peasant. Nobles won't talk to me."

"Don't worry about that. The message Roulston gave me included a warrant from the queen. If we find a noble willing to talk, that will open the doors for us. The message also says we can talk to and trust the bearer of the letter."

"Could Roulston be working for Baltar?"

Paena shrugged. "That would make the most sense."

"So, let's go talk to him. We should get started."

The innkeeper was busy polishing the counter as they entered. He waved for them to follow him into the back.

He closed the door after they entered a large storeroom. A window covered by a grill high up on the one wall provided the only light. Barrels were stacked in columns against one wall and sacks of flour against another. "You two look like you have something you want to say to me."

Paena nodded. "You know we got a message from Master Baltar. Do you know what he wrote?"

"Some of it," Roulston said, his expression unflinching. "A letter arrived for me too. It told me who you two were and asked me to help you out. It said a similar letter was sent to all the agents."

"Tell us about that please," Kalten said. "We know Master Baltar is a spy for the queen, but how are you involved?"

"Therein lies the story, Kalten," Roulston said, his mannerisms changing with every word from the friendly innkeeper to that of a battle-hardened man. "You see, in my younger days I fought for the old king and the queen after him. I was their man, you could say. When it came time for me to retire, I was asked if I would be willing to keep serving in a different way."

"As a spy?" she asked.

Roulston fidgeted. "Not exactly a spy, but I was asked if I would keep an eye on things and report back to the queen. If I did that, she would fund my inn." He mopped at his brow for a moment. "You have to understand, my pension would never have let me buy a place like this, and I still felt loyalty to Her Majesty. It was a good deal for me."

Paena put a hand on Roulston's wrist. "Make no mistake, good innkeeper, we don't think you did anything wrong. We just didn't know what Baltar was up to. This is all a surprise to us."

A smile of relief crossed Roulston's face. "I'm so glad to hear that. You two are the first people outside of Master Baltar I've told. It has been a burden all these years."

"Thank you for telling us, Roulston," Kalten said. "Your secret is safe with us."

"Have you been working for the queen ever since?" she asked.

"Yes. I've been asked to keep track of who has moved through here, and I've tried to keep track of who is loyal to the queen."

"That will prove useful to us," Kalten said. "But tell me, how much of our orders do you know?"

Roulston shrugged. "Very little. I've been instructed to help you two with whatever I can. Oh, and I've been told to give you a password in case you need to report any information through the agent network. It will work with any trader or trade house."

"Password?" Paena asked. "What is it?"

"Coltsfoot. Use that word whenever you are reporting in."

"Was there anything else?"

"No, that's it," Roulston replied, shaking his head.

"Let me tell you a bit more, then," she said. "We have been ordered to try and find Duke Samuel's hidden stronghold, and we were told to find who is loyal to the queen among the Eastern nobility."

He whistled. "That's a big order. I cannot tell you where the stronghold is or even if it is nearby. I have heard horses and men pass by here late into the night, but I have never dared look for fear of discovery. As to who is loyal, I know someone who can help. He is a local baron whose family has been loyal to the Crown for generations. I'll send him a message."

"That would be very helpful," she said.

"And you say men have passed here in the darkness of night," Kalten said. "Have there been any strange occurrences. People disappearing?"

Roulston's brow furrowed. "Yes. Several families went missing a few years ago. It was northeast of the village, I believe. We searched but never found them."

"Any thoughts on this, Paena? I think I know where we should start looking. The disappeared may have been taken like my family."

"If they are related, we may just find where your family were taken," Paena agreed. "We just need a reason to go so we don't get people asking questions."

"I can help you with that," Roulston said. "Would you be willing to deliver messages for me? That would be a perfect cover story."

"Messages?" Paena asked.

"Yes. People send messages here for their families since the inn is the center of the community. Usually someone from the various families stops by here every month or so to check. If the message is important, I'll often take it out myself."

"That would be perfect," she said with a smile.

"Very good," he said, his innkeeper persona back in place. "Now, what would you two like for dinner tonight?"

Chapter Eight

Two days later, Kalten and Paena were on foot and well away from the town just as the sun rose. At Roulston's suggestion, they had gotten up early and left before daybreak. Darkness and a quick departure had shielded them from any possible spying eyes.

They had spent the prior day delivering messages to outlying families hoping to learn about missing people. At their second-to-last stop they finally heard about an uncle who had gone quiet. The man's family wondered but had not yet visited to learn what happened.

By mutual consent, he and Paena decided to leave the horses behind and take a pony instead; the horses might be too large if they ended up traveling off the road. The pony trudged behind, loaded with fresh supplies. Kalten wasn't sure how long they'd be away, or even if they were returning to the town.

Roulston had given them a hastily drawn map of the area where they were told the uncle disappeared. They were following Roulston's map closely now.

Kalten nervously checked up and down the road. They had left open countryside shortly after leaving the village. Thick forest, perfect terrain for an ambush, bordered the road on either side. His stomach gurgled, reminding him breakfast had been much earlier. He pulled a stick of dried meat from his pack and tore a chunk off with his teeth. Paena, walking to his left, munched on a piece of trail bread.

Ahead was a break in the trees, a woodcutter's lane they'd been told about. He checked over his shoulder to see if anyone followed them. Kalten sighed gratefully that there was no one close enough to see. They scrambled off the road and up the lane.

"I'm glad to be off that road," he said. "I was afraid we might be ambushed, and I certainly don't want anybody seeing us here. The less people who know about our search, the better I'll like it."

"You worry too much. Nobody knows we're here."

"Probably not, but we don't really need anyone interested in us right now."

"I suppose. Being careful won't hurt us, either way."

Thick trees and brush overflowed into the track. "How far were we supposed to follow the path before we came onto the buildings?" Kalten asked.

"A bit farther, I think." Paena sighed. "Do you think we'll find anything this time?"

"I hope so. I don't like chasing after shadows. I'd be much happier if we could uncover proof that we were going the right way."

"We'll soon find out. There's the clearing we were told about."

They emerged from the woodcutter's track into a large clearing. Calf-high grass dotted with wildflowers grew throughout the clearing. A wagon track, worn in the grass, led directly toward the tidy little farmstead at the far end of the meadow: a small cottage, a barn, and a few small buildings.

The cottage and barn stood right next to the forest with limbs of some of the larger trees almost scratching at their thatched roofs. No animals or people were anywhere to be seen. The wagon track went past the house and right up to the door of the barn.

"Let's look around. Paena, you search the house while I investigate the buildings. Maybe we'll get lucky and find something."

Kalten tied up the pony and watched Paena go into the house before he checked around the farm.

When none of the smaller outbuildings revealed any clues, he wandered over to the barn. The inside of the building was equally unenlightening. A well-tended wagon parked inside. A harness hung on the wall, the leather well-oiled and supple. Saddles sat on racks. Covered barrels were placed off to the side against one wall.

Nothing mysterious there.

He wiped his fingers on his pants and carefully closed the barn door. It whispered shut behind him. Everything appeared like it should, but something nagged at the back of his mind.

When Paena came out of the cottage, he went over to see if she had any better luck in her search.

"Find anything?" Kalten asked.

"No. Everything is in order. In fact, I'm surprised how clean everything is. Do you remember how long ago the family stopped hearing from their uncle?"

"I thought they said it was a couple months ago. But..." Something clicked, and Kalten realized what bothered him. "Hold on... I thought something wasn't right when I went into the barn. Now I know what it is. The door on the barn. The harness. It's all clear to me now."

"Whoa. You aren't making any sense. What's clear to you?" she asked.

"Sorry about that. I just realized why something seemed wrong with the barn. Besides the missing people, I mean."

"I'm listening."

"While you were in the house, I searched the farm," he said. "None of the smaller buildings had anything, so I went over to check out the barn. The door opened smoothly without a sound. Everything looked fine, so I went in. I couldn't get over how neat and orderly everything was."

"That's exactly how the house is."

"Yes, so you said. There are saddles and a harness in the barn. I ran my fingers over the harness because it seemed so clean and well kept. The leather is still oily."

"So?"

"So, leather that's been sitting for a while, especially in a dusty place, would either be dry or feel gritty from dust settling into the oil. The harness has fresh oil on it. It can't have been hanging for months untended."

"That's it?"

"No," Kalten said. "The door works too well. It wouldn't work like that if it's been sitting unused for months. At the very least, it would have settled and been hard to open. This door has been used, and recently, I'd wager."

"You're sure?" She frowned.

"Absolutely. I feel really stupid to have missed such obvious signs."

"So, what now?"

"I don't know. I've checked most of the yard. The only place I haven't gone is behind the house and…" He stopped talking then broke into a dead run toward the barn. He continued past the barn until he stood behind it. "Paena. Come quick!"

Paena came racing around the barn, her sword drawn. "What? What's wrong?"

"I think we've just had our first break. Look at the ground and tell me what you see."

She looked down. "I see rocks, dirt, grass… What else should I be seeing?"

"What about the wagon tracks?"

"Yes. So?"

He threw his hands up in frustration. "See them coming out of the back door of the barn?"

She nodded as she scanned the ground.

"Well, where do they go?"

She carefully followed the wagon wheel-tracks. "They go into…" Understanding flared in her eyes. "They go straight into solid brush."

Kalten approached the brush, grabbed a branch, then pulled. A well-camouflaged screen fell. It had been disguised with branches and leaves to appear natural. "You can see this hasn't been here long. The leaves have barely begun to wilt."

"Very clever. They have an abandoned farm to hide their activity. Use the barn to mask any movement and store their equipment in plain sight. I'm glad you're paying attention."

"Thanks, Paena. I just wish I could be sure this is the work of the traitors."

"Who else could it be? Not too many honest folk need to hide their movement like this."

He held up his hand and ticked off points as he spoke. "It could be bandits, poachers, or slavers. It might not be the traitors at all."

"If it's any of those, don't you think we should do something about them anyway? All of them could cause the queen problems."

He rubbed at his chin. "You're right, of course. I just wish I knew for certain what we are up against." He peered down the concealed trail for a moment. "Whoever they are, we need to decide how to handle this. Do we go back to town for help, or do we go forward and see where this goes?"

"We've come this far. I think we should keep following the trail. Besides, there isn't really anyone we can bring back from town to help, is there?"

"No, there isn't." Kalten stopped to think for a moment. "But first, we need to get away from here, find a place to picket the pony, then set up camp. I don't want to be hanging around here if somebody shows up. Who knows how many men there would be?"

"Okay, but why leave? Didn't you just say we should follow the trail?"

"Yes, I did, but we can't chance getting caught on it or let anyone know we've even found it. I think we should put the screen back and get back on the road. We can always cut into the woods anywhere along it. That'll also lower our chances of being seen. There could easily be sentries all around here. I can always find the trail again, now I know where it is."

"Give me a hand then," Paena said, lifting the screen.

They wrestled the screen back into place and carefully removed all traces of their tampering. The pair collected the pony and left the farm. It had been easy going in, but with the new information, he didn't want to be caught going out.

At the end of the lane, they turned right and continued up the road, careful not to look back. Kalten thought he could feel eyes watching them leave. They hiked along several twists of the road, and then turned off onto a game trail to their right.

"Paena, this next bit isn't going to be very pleasant, I'm afraid. This trail will likely widen and narrow as it goes along. We'll have to be careful not to leave any signs that we've passed."

"Signs?"

"Yes. Like if your cloak gets snagged on a bush. You could leave bits of material behind. That sort of thing. We should probably leave our cloaks rolled up in our packs until we're done. We won't be as warm, but we can travel more quickly."

Paena frowned and shook her head. "You're the expert. Just don't ask me to strip down to my skin."

He laughed. "That won't be necessary. Not that I wouldn't enjoy following you, if you decided to." At her sharp look, he threw his hands into the air in mock surrender. "Just kidding."

They shed their cloaks then stuffed them into their packs before continuing down the path, Kalten taking the lead. He stuck to the game trail, keeping his hand near his dagger.

He stopped and pointed toward a thinning in the trees. "There's the hidden road. We should move back a ways now that we know where it is. We've been very lucky so far. In fact, I'm starting to wonder if this really is a game trail at all. It seems too good to be true that it leads right where we wanted to go."

"I don't care what kind of trail it is. Just get me somewhere a little less prickly," Paena said.

They retraced their steps back down the path before they moved off it and plunged deeper into the forest. At a good spot, they picketed the pony and unloaded it.

"We can camp here tonight and watch the trail in the morning," Kalten said.

"Fine with me. Now let's eat supper and get to bed. I'm tired."

They ate their cold meal in silence before settling in for the night.

~ * ~

Pieter had been cooped up in the merchant's stable too long. He wanted to finish the job and get back to home, even if it meant being around his crazed duke. His first thought had been to leave the building, but after watching out a crack in the wall he changed his mind. In a small town like this where everyone knew each other, he would stand out like a beacon.

The stable was warm and comfortable, but Pieter didn't like the grass to grow under his feet, and he grew bored. The twice daily visits of the merchant had even become a welcome distraction.

When the door creaked open that evening, he wanted to hug the merchant. The feeling didn't last long.

"The two you've been tracking are gone." The merchant hadn't even stepped through the door before he made his pronouncement.

"How can they be gone?" Pieter shouted. "Didn't the duke send word that a squad of his personal guard were on their way? They'll kill me if the traitor is gone."

The merchant shrugged. "It makes no difference to me." His breath stank of wine.

Pieter grabbed the man by the collar. "Listen to me, you fat swine! If the guard comes after me, I'll make sure they take you too."

The merchant paled. "You wouldn't…"

Pieter sneered. "I would in a heartbeat. You can either help me, or you will go down with me." He let go of the collar.

The man wiped his brow. "I'll see what I can find out."

"You do that." Pieter settled on a bale of hay. "Our lives probably depend on it."

Chapter Nine

Captain Kerris sat atop his horse, regarding the tiny village. Lucky for the map or he would have missed it completely. He shifted in his saddle to ease the pain in his legs and butt. No light shone from any window including that of the inn. In fact, the only light came in the form of the dim moonlight overhead. A small huddle of peasant buildings. Such an insignificant, ragged place should offer little resistance, but he couldn't afford another failure.

He licked his lips. "Sergeant!"

His second rode up beside him. "Yes, sir?" The sergeant's voice betrayed no emotion.

"Ride down into the village and make contact with our man. I'm told he is staying at the dry goods store. Find out where the traitor is." He reached out to keep the sergeant from riding off. "I know I don't need to tell you to be discrete. We cannot let the traitor escape. He is ours, dead or alive. Any failure will be dealt with harshly."

The sergeant saluted and slowly rode down the hill, dismounting in front of the store. The captain waited. His horse let out a shuddering sigh and worked its bit around in its mouth.

The company had ridden out of the duke's keep two days before and had been in the saddle ever since, sleeping and eating while they rode. Captain Kerris felt a special motivation to move quickly; his life definitely teetered in the balance. His men were professionals and followed their orders without complaint. He continued to watch and wait.

A short time later the sergeant returned to the captain.

"Report."

"The traitor is gone."

"Gone? Where?"

"They did not know. Only that the traitor and his companion left their horses behind and departed early this morning." The sergeant's face remained impassive. "They suggested the innkeeper might be involved."

"It is a start," the captain said. "Take the men down and secure the innkeeper and the inn. And Sergeant, make sure the hunter doesn't go anywhere either."

The sergeant nodded once then led his men down to the village.

~ * ~

Paena lay hidden among some shrub along the trail and tried to remain still despite the tickle of sweat trickling down her back. Small gnats swarmed around her face and head, adding to her discomfort. She squirmed a little and looked up to gauge how long she'd been there. Judging by the sun, it was just about mid-day. That would make it a quarter of a day, at least.

Did Kalten hate this as much as she did? She squinted over to where he was, barely able to make him out. If she hadn't known where to look, she wouldn't have seen him at all. He somehow managed to blend into the tall grasses and low brush like he belonged there. He was very good at this, much better than she ever imagined.

She realized he was looking at her too. She jerked her head toward their camp hoping he wanted to go. The barely perceptible shake of his head squashed her thoughts of leaving. They had that conversation too. He had quite firmly said they would wait until something turned up, end of discussion. But a girl could dream, couldn't she?

She grabbed her water bottle and took a short drink. Just after they arrived, Kalten rubbed leaf mold onto his face, but left Paena alone, explaining her darker coloring would naturally hide her. She'd been grateful at the time. But would it have kept the bugs away? She wasn't sure. He might know. She'd ask later, just to see.

A flicker of movement from the trees behind her caught her eye. She instantly went still. Someone, a man, came down the game trail toward her. And he had their pony in tow.

The trail would almost bring him close enough to touch her. Definitely close enough to see her. He couldn't possibly miss her. But he was having trouble leading the pony, and he wasn't really paying attention.

Paena got a good look at him. He wasn't anything like she expected. Dressed in grubby, patched homespun, the man appeared clean-shaven and washed. Not a common bandit then.

"Flamin' animal! I should've known something was wrong with you. Nobody leaves a good animal loose." He yanked on the rope. "Now, for the last time, come on." One last pull, and he dragged the pony out of the trees. On the trail, the animal calmed and obediently followed him. He headed off, down the road toward the farm.

She held her breath until he was out of sight.

"That was close," Kalten murmured into her ear.

She almost punched him. "Don't do that. You scared me nearly half to death."

"Sorry. When I saw him coming down the path, I thought you were done for. I was so glad you noticed him and stayed still. He never knew you were here. You did exactly the right thing."

She felt slightly better at Kalten's praise, but her heart still raced. She had to quit underestimating him. He might look like a gangly farm boy, but he kept proving to be much more than that. "What should we do now? He's got our pony."

"I'm afraid we're going to have to give the pony up for lost. You saw the direction they left in. They're on their way back toward the farm. It could be that, either he's got people coming in, or they're getting ready to leave. One way or the other, something's going to happen. And probably very soon. For now, all we can do is sit back and wait."

"You mean we've got to do more of this?"

"Yes. I definitely don't want to get caught on that road by anyone. It'd be pretty hard to explain what we're doing there." He scratched at a loose piece of leaf mold dangling from his cheek. "At least we know we're on the right track now."

"How so?"

"Didn't you see how he was dressed and armed? He came close enough to you."

"I did notice his face and clothing, but for the rest? I was a little too busy trying not to be seen. What of it?"

"Don't be mad, Paena. I just meant he was too well armed to be a common bandit. I think we've found what we're looking for."

"I sure hope so." She took a deep breath. "Just for argument's sake, couldn't he have been a slaver or something like that?"

"Nah. That sort almost always travels in packs. He didn't really look the type either."

"So, what now?"

"Just sit back. Catch a nap if you want. I'll keep watch." Kalten crept back to his hiding spot and settled into it.

She sighed, arranged her cloak against a tree and lay back against it, closing her eyes. Might as well get some sleep. Kalten wouldn't be sleeping anyway.

She awoke to find him leaning over her, hand gently pressed over her mouth. She recognized him just before she pulled the dagger she always slept with. Foolish man. She would have to speak to him about her boundaries and his continued health. That would have to wait until later though. She patted his hand. He held his finger to his lips and pointed to his ear.

Paena went still and listened. Not a bird, not a squirrel. Nothing but the occasional rattle of the wind. Then, she heard it. The soft, thumping steps of many feet.

When she turned toward the growing sound on the hidden road, she almost gasped out loud. A squad of troops came into sight, herding a crowded mass of worn peasants.

The captives were mostly women and children with a few men, toothless oldsters for the most part, among them.

Most of the captives wore threadbare clothing and some had nothing on but the barest of undergarments. Some had the worn leather tatters that served for shoes, but most were barefoot. The youngest were babies carried in the arms of the women. They shuffled along, each chained to the next by shackles on the ankles.

Clouds of dust rose when the unhappy parade went by. Kalten and Paena hid until the column passed, and then shadowed it discretely from the trees. She didn't trust the road enough to follow from there. Anyone could be behind them or watching. She could see that he struggled to stay calm.

Twice, they were forced to detour deeper into the forest. Both times he spotted someone watching the road from the trees. Clearly, these people were not taking any chances.

The setting sun finally forced them to stop. He got up, swearing quietly to himself.

"What's wrong? Are we lost?"

"No." He turned with his fists clenched. "Those people…" He waved his arms helplessly. "They could easily have been my mother and sisters. What those scum are doing is wrong, and there's nothing I… nothing we can do about it. We can't keep rattling through these trees in the dark. We'll either get lost, or caught. And they keep getting farther away."

Paena looked up at the sky. What little moon there had been was now completely obscured by gathering clouds. "What should we do?"

Kalten leaned in very close, keeping his voice low. "We really only have two choices. We either stop here and wait until morning, or we move out onto the road and trust the darkness to hide us."

"But where is here?"

"I don't know. We could be out in the open come daylight or well hidden. Without light to see, I can't really tell."

She had to squash his sense of hopelessness. "What've we got to lose, then? If there's a chance we'll be seen anyway, we might as well try using the road."

"Agreed. I hate to expose us, but the good thing right now is, if we can't see, neither can they. Stay close to me. In the dark, it's too easy to get separated."

They crept out to the road, careful not to disturb the underbrush or make noise. Once again, Paena marveled at how silent Kalten could be when he put his mind to it. She clung to a corner of his cloak just to keep track of him.

They made it onto the road without detection and began traveling along it. Once, they saw a muted glow just off the side of the trail. He had her wait while he checked it out.

When he came back, they had a quick whispered conference. "I think we should be safe to travel, now. It was another of the road sentries making himself supper when I looked."

Her first glimpse of the moving column came in the form of a bobbing light ahead on the road. The soldiers had lit torches both at the front and the back of the column. Kalten and Paena stayed back, remaining in the darkness.

The gathering clouds had long ago covered the moon, and the night was black as pitch. Cold wind blew through the trees, rattling branches and sending withered leaves flying. Unseen projectiles battered the travelers. The column ahead never slowed.

"I hope we get there soon, wherever there is," Paena said, wrapping her cloak tighter around herself. "Some of those folks won't survive if they don't get shelter and food. Most of them aren't wearing more than rags."

He frowned. "Yes, those soldiers certainly have a lot to answer for. If any of those people die…" He left his sentence unfinished, but his growing anger was clear.

She could see it was more than just cold peasants setting him off, but wisely chose not to mention it. "What should we do when they finally stop?"

"We'll go back into the forest a ways and settle in for the night. We can't do or learn anything useful until daylight, anyways."

The long march continued into the early morning. She was very glad she had a nap earlier.

She could tell they were getting close to the destination when the soldiers started pushing their prisoners to greater speed. Like a horse eager for its barn, the soldiers wanted their campfires, food, and blankets, and were in a hurry to get them. Kalten searched for a place to leave the road.

The clouds began to turn pink when he and Paena slipped off the road and into the forest. His anger had flared up with the coming dawn. He'd been ready to attack the column of soldiers by himself. She had been forced to drive him into the woods. He savagely smashed his way through the trees while she gave him some room. Stealth was forgotten. The sun was fully up before he stopped.

She had known he was upset, but never expected him to whirl around at her, eyes blazing.

"Did you see them? Did you see those women and children they've dragged from their homes? Those people could easily have been my family. I can't stand by and let this happen. We've got to do something."

"But what? There's just the two of us? What can we do that we aren't already doing? Attack them?"

"I suppose not," Kalten said. He kicked violently at an offending stone.

"Even if we attacked them and rescued those people, then what? They're quite clearly exhausted. We'd never escape." She grabbed his hands and looked into his eyes. "Now, we have a job to do. This could be the stronghold the queen is looking for. Acting foolishly now would be, well... foolish."

He sighed. "You're right, of course. What should we do?"

"We're both exhausted and not thinking straight. I think we should get something to eat, and then get some sleep. I think we should get a better idea of what we're up against, and then, I think we should come up with a plan."

"That makes sense, I guess. Tell you what. I'll take first watch, while you sleep."

She shook her head. "Not this time, Kalten. We've both traveled hard all night, and now we've come a long way into thick bush. Let's find ourselves a well-hidden spot and both get some sleep."

"I don't like taking a chance like that. What if we're discovered?"

"You've been awake for an entire day. You're swaying on your feet. How much good would you be if someone did find us?"

"I'm fine..."

"No, you're not. Now let's find a place to hide and get some sleep. You can take first watch tomorrow, if you like."

She made it very clear she wasn't going to change her mind. A wry smile on his face, he quit arguing. They started searching for the well-hidden spot to camp.

Chapter Ten

The long night had taken its toll on both Kalten and Paena. Both slept late in the small clearing they stumbled into the night before. The clearing was barely big enough for the name; the sleeping forms of the two travelers practically filled the entire space.

The rising sun brought with it a cacophony of bird song, and squirrels chattered at each other from distant trees. By mid-morning, insects made it impossible to stay asleep. Kalten heard Paena cursing softly and slapping at the biting flies long before he decided to get up. He looked over at her when she staggered to her feet. Even disheveled and dirty, she was still heart-wrenchingly beautiful. For the briefest of moments, he wondered what she thought of him.

He shook himself. No time for that sort of nonsense now. They had a job to do, and he had obligations. He pulled a small bottle out of his pack. "Here, rub some of this on your skin. A drop or two is all you'll need. It'll keep the bugs away."

She took the bottle. "Thanks. I'd thought about asking what you used to control the bugs. I'm glad you have something for them."

"Actually, I don't use the stuff. It smells too strong. Not that I need it, anyway."

"How come?" She had stopped in the middle of applying the lotion to her neck, arm still raised.

He shrugged. "In training camp, one of the first things we learned was how to ignore the bugs."

"How'd you do that?" Another biting insect had reminded her to continue applying the ointment.

"My sergeant took my squad out into the middle of a swamp and made us march around in our small-clothes. It was hot and humid, and there were clouds of insects everywhere. Anyone who broke formation to swat bugs was severely punished." He shuddered at the memory. "The punishment was much worse than the insects, so after several days of that, we learned to ignore the bites. Those who didn't stayed in the swamp."

The implication was clear. She paled, but didn't ask any further questions. For that, he was grateful. Those had been terrible days. The entire time, he hadn't been sure he'd survive. But he had, and in the struggle, learned a crucial lesson. The mind was much stronger than the body.

They ate and packed their meager belongings before leaving to scout out the enemy camp.

He took the lead. She had seemed to realize he was simply more adept in the woods than her and agreed to follow without argument.

He carefully chose a route both indirect and free of obstacles. His biggest worry was that she might accidentally reveal their position by making too much noise. The camp must have posted sentries within the woods. Their security precautions on the road testified to that.

His concern proved to be baseless. Paena followed him wherever he went and carefully shadowed his movements and steps. They arrived at the edge of the encampment without incident.

Any remaining thoughts that they were tracking a bandit group evaporated when he saw the camp. He motioned her closer and whispered into her ear, "This is the place. This is where I trained."

Except it wasn't the same any more. It had grown much bigger than he remembered. Trees had been cleared a full twenty paces from the first palisade of the fort, and a clearing extended completely around the compound. Guard stations were set within easy sight of each other, and mounted patrols road a continuous circuit around the walls.

The walls were easily thirty feet high, built of stout logs sharpened at the tops. A platform had been built around the entire inner circumference of the wall, as evidenced by the sentries patrolling at the top. How could they possibly get inside to see what was going on?

She simply stared at the camp, her face mirroring the shock and dismay he felt. Well, they'd wanted to know what they were up against. Now they knew. Time to plan.

He touched her shoulder and motioned for her to follow him. They left, going in a new direction.

They picked their way slowly around the massive camp, avoiding any sentries and soldiers. Try as he might, Kalten simply couldn't see any weakness they'd be able to take advantage of. It seemed impossible to get into the camp and rescue the prisoners.

He had seen enough and led Paena back into the forest where it would be safe to talk.

She waited until they were well into the trees before speaking. "That place is huge." Her eyes were wide.

"It wasn't that big when I trained here. The duke has really grown it into a fortress."

"But how could that be?" she asked. "It hasn't been all that long since you deserted, has it?"

"No, but I didn't desert from here. I trained here, and we were taken out into the field. I haven't been here in several seasons."

"Did you get a count of soldiers?"

Kalten considered for a moment, tallying the number in his head. "There had to be at least five-score soldiers outside the main wall. I have no idea how many might be inside the fort itself."

"That's what I thought too," she said. She settled onto the ground. "What are we going to do? We can't attack that fort by ourselves."

"I really don't know. Sneaking in is out of the question. It's simply too well guarded."

"What about going back to the village? We could bring back men from there."

"No. Those men are simple farm folk, militia at best. There aren't many of them, and they wouldn't stand a chance against that fort. I don't think they'd even clear the forest with all the hidden sentries posted along that road. Besides, we really don't have any idea how many of the enemy there are."

She frowned at him. "We can't go in, and we can't get help from the town. So what else is there?"

It was so frustrating, something Paena clearly felt too. He hated feeling so helpless, especially with all those prisoners in the fort. "Without more information, we shouldn't go anywhere. We need to be able to accurately report to Baltar what we're up against. I just wish we could get a better glimpse of what's inside those walls. Without that, any force we brought here could be destroyed. What we don't know could easily kill us."

"So, all you need is a view of the inside of the fort? You don't need to go in?"

The question startled him. "What are you suggesting?"

"I thought that instead of going into the fort, which you've already said is impossible, we should find a place to look into the fort from. Like, maybe a hill or a tall tree, for example."

Kalten jumped to his feet. "I could kiss you. Of course that would work. I don't know why I didn't think of it myself. I don't need to get past those walls at all."

"When should we do it?"

"The sooner, the better. In fact, I think I should go right now and take a look. I might be able to get some idea of their size by the number of campfires. And I'll be able to take advantage of the darkness for cover."

"What about me?" she asked, climbing to her feet.

"I want you to stay at our campsite while I scout around. I'll lead you back and wait for it to get dark. I'm more used to moving around at night, and there's less chance of discovery if there's only one of us."

"When will you be back?"

"By morning. If I'm not, don't panic. Just wait for me."

Paena stopped, her hands on her hips. "I don't panic. You should know that by now."

"Sorry. Bad choice of words," he said. "But if the worst should happen and I'm not back in a couple days, get out of here."

"Where would I go? I have no idea where we are."

"Don't worry about it. Just make sure you avoid the fort and any sentries."

"I can't leave you behind."

"Better that, than both of us captured or killed. Get back to the village and send word to Baltar. If you go west you will get to the road."

"Don't get yourself captured or killed." She smiled. "I'm starting to get used to having you around."

He grinned. "Don't worry. Everything will be fine. I just want you to be prepared in case something happens. Oh, and one other thing. If you do end up leaving here, carve your initial in a tree every fifty paces or so while you travel. Begin with a mark here in camp. I'll have an easier time finding you that way."

Kalten waved and then strode off into the darkness, leaving her alone by the fire.

Chapter Eleven

Paena paced from the fire to the edge of the camp like a caged panther. It had been three days since Kalten left and still nothing. Not a sign. Where could he be?

When he hadn't returned the first night, she convinced herself nothing was wrong. He had merely extended his scouting mission to get a better idea of the enemy's actions.

The second day was more difficult. She'd strongly considered going out to find him. Only his parting words kept her at camp: "Wait for a couple days, then get out of there and make your way back to the village."

It hadn't been easy. Anyone might think that three days with nothing to do would be restful. Anyone who thought that would be wrong. Her fingernails were chewed down to the skin. No, the waiting had not been easy.

The evening of the third day, she finally accepted he might not return. Kalten said to wait only a couple days, but somehow two had become three. She didn't want to face the trail without him.

The time had come for a tough decision. If he wasn't back by sun-up, she would leave without him. The sun would show her the way back to the village, and she would send word to Baltar. There was no choice.

That night, sleep was impossible. By first light, she had the camp packed and was ready to leave. She only took enough for herself. Everything else, she hid in a nearby thicket. A single job remained to be done, something Kalten asked her to do.

She faced the rising sun and walked to the first tree she saw. Just as he asked, she carved her initial on the trunk of the tree near the ground opposite the sunward side. He just had to be okay. Somehow, the act of carving the blaze made her feel a little better.

Nothing remained in the camp to show she'd ever been there. He would be so proud. For the thousandth time she hoped he was safe. Then, it was time to move on. She squared her shoulders and marched away.

Caution was called for to avoid the enemy fort, and the sun provided guidance for direction; always keeping it at her back, she hiked until mid-day. After a brief stop and some food, she continued her trek through the forest. The sun was now directly ahead, and shadows gradually lengthened behind her.

At the end of that day, she located a thicket to hide in and waited for morning, cat-napping through the night. By sun-up she was already well on her way.

It was the same routine for two days. A discreet trail of blazes marked her route. By mid-morning of the third, she came to the edge of the forest.

The grass meadow that marked the edge of the trees was only half a dozen paces wide. On her side, trees and brush formed a sort of loose barrier. On the other side, what could only be a new forest began. Somehow, despite Kalten's instructions, she had gotten lost.

The grass swath went in either direction to the horizons. It reminded her of a green canyon. And the longer she looked, the more certain she was that the trees opposite belonged to a very different type of forest.

The forest she just traveled through was filled with tall, well-spaced trees. Shrubs and bushes littered the empty spaces, and the ground was softly carpeted with old leaves and bracken. The journey could have been calming if not for the specter of Kalten hovering over her shoulder.

When she crossed into the trees on the other side, she knew things had changed. If the trees before were old, these ones must be ancient.

Gnarled and massive, any one of them could easily hide an entire squad of soldiers. The brooding limbs of one tree intertwined with those of its neighbors, blotting out the light of day. Rotting logs and stunted vegetation littered the ground. The result was a sort of ghastly, dank nether land. The scent of decay assaulted her nostrils from all around her. Paena's imagination ran wild, populating her surroundings with twisted, angry giants and dark creatures of every description.

The first time she stooped to carve a marker into the ancient woods, she was struck with such a sense of menace, she almost dropped the knife. Any thoughts of leaving a trail vanished. She fumbled to put her knife away for good. It was all she could do not to scream.

She started retracing her steps when, out of the corner of her eye, she spotted a spark of light. It bobbed and weaved between the mighty tree boles, seeming to beckon to her. She was afraid her eyes were playing tricks on her, but the light kept coming back.

When a second appeared, then shortly thereafter by a third, fear was replaced by curiosity. How could anything so bright and cheerful be bad? The lights danced around her, changing from white to blue to green in joyful abandon. Paena followed them through the forest, mesmerized by the colorful show.

It wasn't until the lights disappeared that she discovered what happened. Nothing was familiar. The dim light from the forest's edge was gone. Everywhere she turned, more of the menacing trees glowered over her.

She couldn't help herself. She threw herself to the ground and cowered beneath a decaying log, trying to shut out the forest. Memories of another time when she had been forced to hide rose in her mind. The night her family had been slaughtered. Huddled in her cloak, she cried herself to sleep.

She awoke befuddled, unsure of where she was. Rubbing the sleep from her eyes, she hoped against hope that the terrible, old forest had been a bad dream. But, when she could focus, the forest remained. She fought to stay calm.

A warm chuckle startled her. An old woman, as wrinkled and gnarled as the trees around her, sat waiting. She had hair like a winter's sky and her clothing, a ragged dress and shawl, blended into the forest floor. Her eyes were a pair of bright coals, glowing through the gloom.

"Well, my child, whatever are you doing in my forest?" Her voice was warm and friendly. Welcoming.

"Who are you?" Paena asked.

"Why, I am Mother Tully, my dear. This is my forest."

"I don't understand. Your forest?" Suspicion replaced fear.

"Just what I said, child. I know every plant and animal in the entire forest, and they know and obey me."

"Obey you? Were you the one who sent the lights for me?"

"Lights? Oh, you mean my wisps?" Mother Tully smiled. "Yes, I asked them to lead you here."

"Why would you do that?"

"Because you were in danger, child. This forest doesn't welcome strangers, and when you threatened it, it decided to destroy you."

"I didn't threaten anything."

"Were you not about to use your knife on one of the trees, child?"

Paena remembered the feeling she got when she tried to carve a blaze. "Yes…"

"Do you not think a knife is threatening?"

"What? But how did you know that? There wasn't anyone

around."

"I know everything that goes on in my forest. Now, tell me. Why were you going to cut into that tree?" Mother Tully's voice took on a distinct note of menace.

"I was leaving a sign for my friend to use to follow me. I had to leave him behind when he didn't come back." Paena was almost crying. "I didn't think it would hurt the tree. You must believe me."

Mother Tully went over to Paena and patted her shoulder, gently comforting her. "There, there, child. I know you did not mean it, or I would not have sent my wisps to get you. A cut like that would not hurt these old fellows, but they are awfully sensitive about blades of any kind. I am sure you noticed how angry they got when you pulled out your knife."

"I felt something." Paena shivered. "I don't know what. I almost dropped my knife."

"Everything is good now. You are with me. Nothing in this forest will harm you while you are in my care."

"Thank you. But who are you?"

"Like I told you, I'm Mother Tully, and this is my forest. That is all you need to know for now." She looked toward the sky. "It is almost dark. I think it is time we got back to my cottage for some supper. I am sure you must be very hungry."

How did Mother Tully know it was almost dark when the trees completely blocked the sky? The forest seemed to be draped in eternal twilight. But what else was there to do? Paena followed Mother Tully through the forest. Halfway to the cottage, the wisps returned to escort the two women, their colorful lights brightening the pathways for them to follow.

The cottage blended into the surrounding woods so perfectly Paena almost missed seeing it. Only the light spilling out of an unshuttered window betrayed its presence. It was the most beautiful thing she'd seen in days.

"Welcome to my home, child. Please go right in while I fetch us something for supper. Do not fear. I'll be right back."

The cottage was a single room and rustic. The remains of a fire glowed in the stone hearth, and several burning candles brightened the room with light. The scent of honey filled the air. A small table made from a piece of stump polished to a dull gleam, a pair of low stools, and a sideboard were the only furniture.

It only took a handful of dry deadfall from the wood box to rekindle the fire. Paena had a merry blaze crackling in the hearth by the time Mother Tully returned. The old woman stumped into the cottage with a smoked ham and a wheel of cheese, closing the door behind her.

She nodded approval at the fire and busied herself at the table, cutting thick slices of ham and cheese for the evening meal. She deftly tossed the slices onto an earthenware plate and then dipped out mugs of clear, cool water from a barrel in the corner of the room. A loaf of crusty bread completed the meal.

Without a word, the two women took a seat opposite each other and ate. It wasn't until the last morsel had been swallowed that either said anything.

Mother Tully leaned back in her chair and extracted a pipe and tobacco pouch from somewhere in her apron. She packed, then lit the pipe, her gaze never leaving Paena. "So, my girl, you never did say why you were wandering around in my forest."

The meal had rejuvenated her, and she began to relax. Something about Mother Tully projected comfort and trust. "People have been disappearing from their homes the past few years. My friend and I are trying to find out where they've gone. We were following a group of soldiers on a hidden forest road. They led us to a huge fort built in the middle of the woods. Kalten, that's my friend, went to scout out the fort, but he never came back. I was on my way to get help." She'd left a lot out of her story, but wasn't quite ready to tell it all to a stranger. Not yet, no matter how comforting.

"What kind of help were you hoping to find?"

"I have friends back in the village. I hoped to get them."

"Villagers? Against soldiers? They must be very great warriors."

"No, I don't think so. Still, I've got to do something to help Kalten. He's depending on me."

"You would lead untrained villagers against soldiers? This Kalten must be very important." At Paena's anguished look, Mother Tully held up her hands. "Peace, child. I will not judge you. Let me help you find your young man. I will send some of my birds out to look for him. While they search, you should rest. Right now, you are exhausted. You would never make it. You may stay here until my birds return."

"Thank you, Mother Tully, but I really should be going…"

"Nonsense. You would not last the night in my forest. You will remain here until I say you are fit. If my birds find your friend, I will take you to him. If they do not, I will guide you to the forest's edge. After that, you may continue on however you like."

Paena realized she didn't really have any choice. "I'll stay. But how will your birds know who to look for?"

"Your thoughts have told me. I have provided them with a description of your young man, including his mismatched eyes. Now, let us sit by the fire a while longer and talk. I get so little human company. The morning is soon enough to begin the search."

Chapter Twelve

Paena had ample time before the first of Mother Tully's birds returned. Paena reclined in a small meadow filled with wildflowers and sunshine when she saw the raven winging its way toward the cottage.

She ran back to the small, homey cottage and discovered Mother Tully applying salve to a burn on the creature's left wing. Up close, the big bird appeared worn and filthy.

"Just look at this," Mother Tully said, pointing to the wing. "He tells me this is the work of a dragon. A dragon in these parts. I thought I had an agreement with them. They stay away from here, and I stay out of their lands."

Dragon? Not knowing what else to say, Paena simply nodded. Was Mother Tully really crazy enough to believe in them? Dragons were myth, after all. Weren't they?

"He is lucky to have just been singed. Any closer, and he would be nothing but a bit of charcoal."

Paena couldn't restrain her curiosity any longer. "Did he see Kalten?"

"I do not think so. But he's so frazzled by his close call, he cannot seem to say anything but dragon, dragon. He needs some peace and quiet to calm before we will get anything useful out of him."

"Oh." She felt a surge of disappointment. "Is there anything I can do to help?"

"No, child. He will not hold still for anyone but me. Why don't you go back to the meadow? I will call if anything happens."

Paena nodded and trudged back to the meadow. How could she sit still when Kalten might be hurt or dying? She flopped to the ground and watched the skies for more of Mother Tully's birds.

As she lay back, the warmth of the sun and the buzzing of the bees soothed her anxieties. Kalten would make it. He had to.

By nightfall, her fear came back in full force. Nothing Mother Tully could say or do comforted her.

"Child, there is no sense in worrying about your friend. If he lives, you will see him again. If he is dead, there is nothing you can do."

"Did the raven say anything?"

Mother Tully sighed. "The raven died, my dear. The stress of the attack stopped his heart."

Paena gasped. "I'm sorry, Mother Tully." She thought for a moment before speaking again, choosing her words carefully. "Do you think Kalten is dead?"

"I do not know. If he can be found, my birds will be the ones to do it. But this forest is vast. If your young man is as good as you say, even the keenest eyed hawk will have trouble spotting him."

"I should retrace my steps and see if he's looking for me…"

"What you should do is go to bed. You are only getting yourself excited again."

"But…"

"No buts. Do you remember how long it took you to get here?"

"A couple of days, I think."

"It was more like four days. You slept one away before I fetched you. Your young man likely would not travel much faster, especially if he is tracking you. He might be well on his way to us. As I have said before, if he comes into my forest, I will know."

~ * ~

"Wake up, girl. Wake up, I say."

Paena sat up in bed, rubbing sleep from her eyes. "What is it? What's wrong?"

Mother Tully glared down at her. "Someone has entered my forest with axes and fire. They have already cut down some of my trees and are burning them. You had better hope your young man is not among them."

The malice in Mother Tully's voice frightened Paena awake. She threw back the covers of her bed and scrambled into her clothing. Mother Tully left the room when she saw Paena getting up. The old woman could be heard muttering and banging around the cottage.

"No time for food. Get your cloak and boots on now. Time is of the essence," Mother Tully said when Paena emerged from her room.

She rushed into her cloak and boots and followed Mother Tully. Without a word, the older woman strode out of the yard. Paena had to jog to keep up.

Mother Tully's wisps appeared, once again, to light the way. A rainbow-hued swarm of sparks floated just ahead of the pair. Paena was grateful; the forest floor was jumbled with roots and rocks waiting to trip her.

Mother Tully increased her speed, fairly flying through the ancient forest. Paena struggled to keep up with her.

Along the way, an army of shadowy figures gathered around them charging alongside in the trees. If the older woman was aware, she showed no sign.

One moment, they ran in the muted glow of the wisps, the next, they broke into a man-made glade. The broken branches and the stumps of trees littered the glade floor, and shredded leaves provided a thick carpet on the ground. An enormous bonfire blazed at its center. Uniformed men were sprawled around the fire laughing and drinking.

Mother Tully burst into the clearing along with rampaging animals from all sides. Wolves, bears, and large cats all sprang out of the forest and attacked the recumbent men.

Howling like a maniac, Mother Tully launched herself at a man who'd been in the process of chopping down yet another tree. She swung her walking stick like a cudgel, catching him behind the ear with a hollow thud. He went limp and collapsed.

Paena grabbed the fallen man's axe. She was ready to fight, but in the brief moments of the attack, the animals had already finished the enemy. All but one.

The man had his back to a tree, fending off a pair of wolves with nothing but his feet, kicking at them to keep them at bay. She realized that his hands were bound behind him. In the weirdly distorted light of the fire, she couldn't make out his face, but he looked familiar.

She dashed over to him, ready to help the wolves. He croaked out her name as she raised her axe to strike.

How did he know her name? She stopped, confused. His face was filthy and covered with soot. He had several days' growth of beard, and his clothing was tattered and torn. Could it be?

"Help me…"

His voice was clearer, this time. Unmistakable. She dove between him and the wolves. The animals, hackles raised and teeth bared, advanced on them.

"Stop!" The sound reverberated throughout the clearing freezing everything in its tracks.

Mother Tully stomped toward them, crackling with energy. "Why are you stopping my creatures from dealing with this destroyer," she demanded.

Paena took a step back, not meeting the old woman's gaze. She'd never seen anyone so angry. "I'm protecting him. This is my friend, Kalten."

"I do not care who he is. He has defiled my forest with these other scum," she said, arm sweeping to include the slain men. "He must pay, just like they have."

"No, wait. How could he have done this when he is so obviously a prisoner? His hands are bound. He couldn't have been involved."

"I do not care," the old woman raged. "My trees have been murdered. There must be justice."

"I see justice, Mother," Paena said. "The men who did this are all dead."

"These trees are mine. They need to be avenged." Mother Tully stopped speaking for a moment. She considered the animals spread around the clearing and cleared her throat. "My children. Feast on the bodies of these defilers and take your fill. But," she said, raising a warning finger, "carry not the carrion from this glade. Their bones must remain, in silent tribute to the fallen trees. And as a warning to any who may follow."

She turned to Paena. "Bring your... friend." She said the word like it tasted foul. "I must think on his punishment. I agree that he could not have been directly involved. Still, I think the defilers are here because of him, and for that, there must be payment."

The trip back to the cottage took forever. The wisps stayed behind in the glade as Paena, with Kalten and Mother Tully, marched through the trees in the dark. The sounds of crunching of bones and tearing of flesh followed them. Paena couldn't leave fast enough.

His hands untied, Kalten lurched along beside Paena. She tried talking to him, but he was so dazed and confused, she finally stopped. Instead, she made sure he kept up with the fuming Mother Tully, supporting him when he stumbled.

They returned to Mother Tully's home, and Paena led Kalten toward the cottage.

Mother Tully stepped in front of her. "Where are you going with him?"

"I'm taking him into the cottage to wash his wounds and feed him, Mother," Paena said.

"Only my guests may enter the cottage. He is not a guest. His status has yet to be determined. And you will not tend to him until I have decided what to do with him."

"What would you have me do with him then?" Paena said. "He's tired, hungry, and hurt. Why are you being so cruel? I have half a mind to leave with him right now."

"You may go, but he will remain until I am satisfied his debt is repaid. Even so, you would never leave this forest alive," Mother Tully proclaimed. "The creatures you saw tonight are not the worst things that dwell among these trees."

"But he needs our care."

"Do not push your luck with me, child. I have taken you in. I can just as easily cast you out."

That simple statement shook Paena. "I'm sorry, Mother Tully." Tears filled her eyes. "I don't mean to be ungrateful. I'm just worried about my friend. He's been through a lot."

"He has been through a lot? What of my beautiful trees, laid low and burned?"

"Kalten had nothing to do with that. Surely you could see he was a prisoner? He merely tried to escape those chasing him."

"Right into my forest," Mother Tully reminded her. "He could very well have taken those men on a merry chase in another direction that would have kept my forest safe."

"He had no way of knowing this forest was under your protection. Please let me help him." Paena was crying in earnest now.

Mother Tully sighed. "Oh, very well. I am not totally heartless. Take your young man to the well, bathe him, and give him a drink. Then, settle him by the front door. I will leave him a blanket and some food."

"Thank you, Mother."

"Do not get your hopes up. Blood must be paid with blood and life with life. His may still be forfeit."

Paena guided Kalten down to the well trying not to think about Mother Tully's words. She rinsed his wounds and cleaned the dirt off his face and hands before giving him a long drink.

Though she scrubbed at the dirt and wounds, he never uttered a sound. He simply stared blankly ahead, either too tired or too shocked to notice. He had lost a lot of weight and had a gauntness about him that hadn't been there before.

Done, at last, she led him to the cabin, wrapped him in a blanket then fed him. He ate carefully, but without enthusiasm and fell asleep. She tenderly covered him with a second blanket and left him to sleep, still anxious about what Mother Tully's decision might be.

~ * ~

Roulston couldn't remember things ever being this bad before. Even when he served the king and later the queen, as a soldier he had never been this afraid.

"Innkeeper!"

He looked up from the counter he had been aimlessly wiping. Captain Kerris waited impatiently before him. "Yes, sir?"

The captain glared at him. "I've called you five times. Can't you hear?"

"My apologies, Captain. I was distracted." Roulston performed a half-bow. "How may I help you?"

"My men and I will be returning shortly after dusk. Make sure you have a hot meal ready for us."

"Certainly, Captain. Do you have any special request?"

"Meat. Keep the local rabble away from here. I won't have my men distracted."

The smile never left Roulston's face. "As you wish, sir."

The captain turned away and strode out of the inn. Roulston could hear him shouting orders in the yard. He waited until the soldiers had all ridden away before leaving the inn.

He hurried to one of the houses and rapped at the door twice. The door opened, and he stepped inside. The man of the house, a stout, short man with thinning hair on his crown, ushered him in.

"Glad to see you home, Eldred," Roulston said. "I need you to take a message to Dwayne in Goose Crossing." He handed a rolled sheet of vellum to Eldred.

"Delivery to Goose Crossing, you say?" he replied. "Well, I do have some woolens that need delivering that way. I suppose I could carry a message too."

Roulston let out a sigh of relief. "Thank you, Eldred. It's important it gets there and that no one knows about it. Understand?"

The man nodded.

Roulston handed him a small pouch. "This should cover delivery. Please, go now."

~ * ~

"Innkeeper, food." Captain Kerris ordered after he strode in through the door of the inn. His squad of men trooped in behind him, laughing and joking. They trooped into the common room accompanied by the stink of old sweat and road dust and noisily sat, moving tables and chairs to better suit their whims.

Roulston hurried to bring flagons of dark beer and plates of mutton to the men. In short order, the room was quiet except for the sounds of chewing, slurping, and belching. He looked to be sure everyone was fed before he turned away.

"Innkeeper, hold a moment, if you please," the captain called out. The man waved him back into the room and pulled a chair out from his table. "Join us, please."

"Oh, no, sir," Roulston said, beginning to back away. "I make a rule to never intrude on my guests."

The captain's gaze went hard. "I insist. Sit down."

Roulston reluctantly joined the captain at the table.

The captain ate, speaking pleasantly between bites. "Tell me, innkeeper, do you know all the people in the village?"

He mopped at his brow. "Yes, sir, I guess I do."

"And, I suppose, you probably know everyone's business too, don't you?"

"I know what most people are doing, sir."

The captain stared at him. "I hoped you could tell me why a fellow named Eldred was so eager to avoid my patrol. Short, fat, bald man? We ordered him to stop just south of here, but he refused."

"I'm sure I don't know, Captain," Roulston said. "He may have thought you and your men brigands."

The captain chuckled. It was a hollow sound. "Brigands?" He looked around at his men. "Did you hear that, boys? The carter thought we were brigands."

The men answered their captain's question with roars of laughter.

He turned back to Roulston, his gaze now stone. He reached into his tunic and withdrew a roll of vellum. "Maybe you could explain this. The carter seemed most unwilling to part with it."

Roulston examined the vellum with a sinking heart, only absently noticing the blood that soaked one corner of it.

Chapter Thirteen

The glade around the cabin was still dark, and Kalten stood blearily before Mother Tully, waiting for her judgment. Impossibly large trees loomed all around, disappearing into the twilight heights. Besides the glimmer of light from the cabin windows, only the occasional growth of glowing fungus, or flight of one of the sprites, pierced the gloom. Telling the time of day was quite impossible.

All he knew of his captor was that she was short in stature, wizened like an old apple, and had somehow earned Paena's awe and fear.

The old woman scowled at him, hands on her hips. "A life for a life. That must be the punishment."

"I don't understand," he said. He tried to shake the cobwebs loose. Short of the past few hours, he only remembered being beaten by a squad of soldiers. They had run him down, surrounded him, and captured him. They hadn't been gentle.

"A life for a life," she repeated. "That is my judgment. For your part in the deaths yesterday, your life is forfeit."

My life is forfeit? What was going on? "But I was a prisoner of those men. I could no more stop them from cutting down those trees than I can fly from here."

"Perhaps not. But tell me, young man. Why were those men here?"

He looked at his feet knowing his answer would incriminate him. "They were after me. One of their sentries spotted me spying on their fortress. That group chased me for days."

"That is what I thought. If not for you, they would never have come. Therefore, you are responsible for the devastation too."

Paena watched the proceedings from a short distance off. In the dim light from the cottage, Kalten could see her eyes and nose were red from crying. "There must be something we can do to change your mind, Mother," she pleaded. "Kalten is a good man. He doesn't deserve death."

"A life for a life. The forest demands it."

"If you kill me, what will happen to Paena?" he asked.

"She will be fine. I will take her to the village."

Kalten sighed. He'd traded one death sentence for another. He knew he should care, but he was so tired, it didn't really matter anymore. "At least let me tell her what happened first. It's important that she knows why I didn't come back."

"I will grant your request. But do not try to run. This forest has a will of its own. You cannot escape."

"I won't run." It was something, at least. Paena would be able to warn Baltar and the queen of the coming danger. He took a seat on a nearby log and beckoned for her to come closer. When Mother Tully turned to leave, he said, "Stop, Mother. You'll need to hear this too. It affects you and all your forest."

The old woman nodded and squatted in front of him. Paena knelt beside the old woman, her face a picture of misery.

He waited until they were settled, before he spoke. "Paena, as you know, I left that night to scout the enemy's camp. I spent the first day scouting the area and generally learning the routine of the patrols. Then I decided to see what was in the camp. Your idea of looking into the camp was a good one, and I knew just where I could go.

"I remembered seeing a massive old tree standing on a low rise just off to one side of the fort. You may recall it. I went there. I managed to avoid the patrols and climbed up near to the top. Just as I hoped, it provided me with a perfect view inside the fort."

He collected his thoughts for a moment and cleared his throat. "It's worse than we imagined. Much worse. The prisoners were all penned up like animals in these huge, metal cages."

"How many prisoners did they have?" she asked.

"Scores. There were at least a dozen cages in total there. Those poor people had no shelter from the elements at all." He took a deep breath then spoke again, voice thick. "While I watched, they dragged away a body."

Paena's eyes grew big, but she said nothing.

He cleared his throat again before he continued, "The compound is filled with barracks and training areas. I was just about ready to leave when a group of soldiers stopped below my tree. I thought they spotted me."

"Are you still sure it's where you trained?" asked Paena.

Kalten nodded. "It's grown a lot, but it's the same place. But the most important information of all is…" He stopped for a moment, embarrassed. "Paena, what I'm about to tell you is absolutely true. I thought I imagined it at first, but there can be no mistake."

"What? What is it?"

"There were dragons. And it looks like they're working with Duke Samuel."

"Dragons?" She was dumbfounded. "Mother Tully said dragons attacked one of her birds, but I thought she was just talking crazy. Are you sure? I didn't think dragons were real."

"I'm sure. While I waited for the soldiers to leave, I heard this huge flapping sound. I looked over my shoulder to see what it was, and there they were. I almost fell out of the tree."

Mother Tully interrupted for the first time. "You thought I was crazy? Foolish girl. Just what did these dragons look like?" She leaned forward, eyes blazing. "Quickly. I must know."

He thought back to the moment he had first seen them. "They must have been at least fifteen cubits long, and one was easily twice that. They're hard to describe. They had long, flexible necks and wings. But not bird wings. More like bats. They gleamed like polished armor, and when the sun reflected off them, it blinded the eye." He shook his head. "I'll never forget it."

"Yes, yes, fine. But what colors were they?"

He frowned. "Well, they were lots of colors. There was a green one, a silver one…"

"Any gold?"

"Yes, there was a golden dragon."

Mother Tully didn't answer him, but instead got to her feet and paced around the clearing, cursing mightily under her breath.

Kalten wasn't sure what to make of her so he continued the story, "While I watched, the dragons swooped down over the cages. Each dragon grabbed two cages, one in each taloned foot, and flew off." He shook his head at the memory. "Those poor people. I could hear them screaming and crying for help. But the soldiers just stayed back and watched. They were laughing and joking like it was the most natural thing in the world. That's why I think they're working together."

"What happened, then," Paena asked.

"Once the dragons had flown out of sight, things returned to normal in the camp. I waited until dark before I climbed down the tree. There were patrols everywhere. It was a good thing I learned their routines. I was on my way back to our camp when I got careless, and a patrol spotted me. They chased me for days before they finally captured me.

"That was where you found me. They tried getting information from me. When I refused to tell them anything, they set up camp and began clearing the forest. I don't remember much. The screams during the attack woke me. Then you were there. The rest you know."

"So, you admit to bringing them here?" Mother Tully asked, her expression stern.

"I guess I did. It wasn't intentional. I had to get away from that prison camp and warn someone. There's too much at stake. And I couldn't leave Paena to wander the woods, alone."

"You have presented me with a big problem, young man," Mother Tully said. "I just do not know what to do with you."

He could only sit quietly and hope for a miracle.

"Perhaps, you can still be of use to me, after all. I will not kill you. At least, not yet. But, the forest still demands a life."

For a moment, he feared she would demand the death of Paena. "Mother, Paena is innocent of blame. Please, leave her out of this."

"Oh, be still. Paena has nothing to fear from me. No, I think I have another solution in mind." She seemed to reach a decision. "Yes, that will do nicely." She peered at him. "The life I will demand from you is one you will surrender willingly. Not today, but one day soon. When the time comes, that life will be mine. Do you agree?"

Her question caught him totally by surprise. A life he would surrender willingly? What could she possibly be talking about? Maybe she meant the life of an enemy. He'd never give up the life of a friend. But it wouldn't be right to trade an enemy's life either.

"I still don't understand. Do you mean an enemy or something?"

"At some point, you will give me a life of your own free will. It is that life I will accept in exchange for yours."

"Just agree with her, Kalten." A note of hope had crept into Paena's voice.

Kalten looked doubtful, but nodded.

"So you agree to give me a life?"

"I guess so. But only if the life is mine to grant and it's not dishonorable."

Mother Tully ignored his conditions. "And you, Paena. Do you agree to this, as well?"

Paena's eyes widened. "I don't know exactly what you're asking, but if it'll save Kalten, then yes, I agree."

"Then, the pact is made," Mother Tully intoned solemnly.

Her words were simple but struck like a hammer blow to his mind. He fell to the ground, dazed. He awoke moments later to see Paena slumped over. Mother Tully watched over them.

"Wha... What happened?"

"The force you felt was the weight of your promise. It has been registered within the very bones of the world. What has been agreed to can never be undone."

A terrible feeling filled him. What had he agreed to? At Paena's first moan, all the uncertainty disappeared. Her eyes fluttered, and she tried to lift herself up. He helped her to her feet. "What was that? What happened to me?"

"It's nothing to be concerned over," he soothed. Now was not the time to give her something more to worry about. She had enough shocks the past few days. "The only thing we need to worry about is what's next?"

She threw her arms around him. "I'm so glad Mother Tully changed her mind. I was so worried about you."

He forced a laugh and hugged her back. "Me too. After all, it was my head on the block."

Mother Tully interrupted their celebration. "Children, I released Kalten for a purpose. I have need of him. And you too, Paena. We have a journey we must undertake."

"A journey? Where?" he asked.

"The dragons you saw have broken an ancient covenant. Long ago, the dragon lords made a pact with me. If I left them and their lands alone in peace, they would not come near my realm. It is for this reason most people have never seen dragons and believe them to be stories only. We must go to their lands and learn why they have broken the accord."

He could only wonder why dragons would make any agreement with Mother Tully. True, she obviously had some power, but so did many others in the world. And, an ancient covenant? So old dragons had faded from memory to be nothing more than stories? The woman was old, that was obvious. But ancient? Cracked more likely. But he decided to humor her. It might help to clarify the situation.

"So, what do we need to do?"

"You will need to rest for the journey. Paena can help me prepare the supplies. I must also recall my birds from their search and meditate on the best route to travel. Then I will send my birds out to prepare the way for me."

"We still have our own mission to complete," he said. "To abandon it would mean the end of our land."

"We are not at cross-purposes, young man. I believe some of the knowledge you seek coincides with my needs."

"Where would you have me go, then?" Everything was moving so fast, he wasn't quite sure what was going on.

"Finish washing up here. Then Paena will show you into the house where you can have some food and sleep. I will wake you when it is time."

"Thank you. I appreciate your change of heart."

"Do not thank me yet, young man. The journey will be difficult and the trials many. And you still have a commitment to uphold." On that ominous note, she swept away into the forest, presumably to make preparation.

He didn't like the sound of that. But there wasn't anything he could do about it. Nothing, but do what she requested. He began washing up at the pump.

~ * ~

Pieter holed up in the loft of the merchant's barn and agonized. The duke's riders had taken over the entire town shortly after they arrived and him along with it. They knew he was there too, the captain having met briefly with him shortly after the inn was captured.

Pieter could feel his chances for redemption in Duke Samuel's eyes growing smaller and smaller with each moment. There was no running; he knew the captain's type too well. Had trained some of the soldiers himself, in fact. The captain would be looking for any excuse to remove Pieter from the picture.

He lay back in the straw and stared at the pigeon roosting high up in the rafter. The bird stared back at him. He fantasized for a moment that the bird would carry him up and away from that village.

But no. He was a professional. In his entire career as a hunter for the duke, not once had he failed to capture his man. Now was not the time to start. It was a matter of professional pride.

He pondered the problem. A soldier stood guard below and two outside, presumably to maintain order, but in reality, to prevent the hunter from escaping. The two outside patrolled together, which helped. They could never watch all sides of the barn at the same time. But what could he do to take advantage of the situation?

He rubbed a stalk of straw between his fingertips while he thought. Then a smile stretched his face. Of course. A fire would distract them and should allow him to escape unnoticed. He would have to time it right and wait for just the right moment.

Pieter waited and watched, and when the moment came, used his flint and steel to start a fire below him on the main floor of the barn. The dry hay, straw, and wood conspired against the barn and in moments, the fire was a raging inferno. In the ensuing chaos, no one noticed him slip out of the loft and into the forest.

Chapter Fourteen

Kalten had grown up around trees. His father had been a forester, after all. Kalten could tell you anything about a forest. What kind of trees grew there, what direction he faced, and even the time of day. At least, that was the case up until a few days ago. Now, he wasn't sure of anything.

There was something very strange about this place. It seemed to be aware of the three people moving through its depths. And worse, they were only tolerated because of Mother Tully.

He patted the sword that now swung at his hip for reassurance. She had given it to him just before they left her cabin "to seal their agreement," she'd said. That had worried him then but now he was grateful for its familiar weight.

Everywhere he looked, the unknown stared back. And it scared him. Varieties of trees and plants he'd never seen before grew everywhere. Some were ancient beyond belief. Even the vines that hung from the heights were older and thicker than most of the forests he knew. Occasional glimpses of movement teased him with even more mysteries. They were being tracked. And Kalten had no idea by what.

"Mother Tully," he whispered at one stop. "Something, or some things, are following us."

"Yes, I know," she said. "They belong to me."

"Belong to you? What are you talking about?" He had known she was slightly cracked but hadn't realized how bad.

"I thought Paena would have explained everything to you already." The old woman never turned to look at him, instead maintaining the same sedate, ground-eating pace she used since they left. "Be mindful to keep that sword of yours firmly in its sheath."

"Explained what?" He turned to Paena. "Do you know what she's talking about?"

She looked at him with frightened eyes. "Mother Tully told me she rules the forest and all its creatures, including the trees."

"That's crazy. No one can rule a forest. The next thing you'll tell me is the trees walk and the animals can dance."

"Are you questioning me?" This time Mother Tully did stop and look at him. She seemed to loom larger.

"Yes, I am. You've been making crazy claims for days now, and I'm tired of it. No one has the kind of power you say you have."

"I do not like your tone, boy!" Mother Tully snapped her fingers.

A pair of wolves appeared out of the trees and rushed toward them. Biting and snarling, they immediately attacked Kalten, backing him up against a massive tree. He drew his sword to hold them back.

He couldn't believe what happened next. While he held the wolves at bay, a branch reached down and slapped the sword from his hand. Another wrapped around his waist and lifted him high into the air. It all happened so fast he could only hang from the branch in shock.

The wolves stood under him, tongues lolling.

"Do you still doubt, Kalten?" asked Mother Tully. She snapped her fingers again, and the wolves disappeared back into the forest.

He could only shake his head, numbly. There was no denying her power.

"Good. Consider this your one and only warning." The menace was unmistakable.

The tree dropped him into a heap. Kalten climbed unsteadily to his feet, shaking with anger and shock.

"Kalten, please. We are Mother Tully's guests here. She's helping us, so don't annoy her. We all need to work together."

"I question some of her outlandish claims, and I'm annoying her?" Kalten barked a quick laugh. "That's rich."

"Are you through?" Mother Tully stared at him, arms crossed.

"I guess I'll have to be. Otherwise, you'll unleash the wrath of the gods on me."

She threw her head back and laughed. "I have changed my mind about you, boy. You are not annoying at all. You amuse me. Come." She beckoned to him and Paena. "Let us get moving again. We have a long distance to travel."

What was going on? One minute she threatened his life, the next she laughed at him. There was definitely something wrong with the old woman. And somehow, there would be a reckoning. But not now. No, this wasn't the time. They still needed her help to get out of the forest, unharmed.

"Where to next?" Kalten said. He gave his voice a note of respect.

"We continue on to the village. That is a good place to start. How we get there, you leave that to me. I know every path in this forest."

"But, Mother Tully. This forest doesn't go all the way to Thistledown, does it?" Paena looked unsure. "I mean, Kalten and I traveled a long way before we entered your trees."

"No, it does not quite go to the village. Still, I think I can gain its protection until we are almost there." She didn't elaborate further, but moved faster. Paena and Kalten had to hurry to keep up.

They traveled throughout that day and into the next, only stopping for the occasional rest or food. Then, suddenly the trees were gone. One moment, they were surrounded by dark forbidding forest, the next, they were out on a road. The hairs on his neck stood up.

"What just happened?" Paena said. "Where did the trees go?"

Mother Tully chuckled. "The forest removed its protection. We have arrived. See, just over there is Thistledown."

Sure enough. Kalten could just make out the shapes of buildings in the predawn darkness. There was no mistaking the village of Thistledown. A hint of smoke lingered in the air, but otherwise it seemed the same.

"I don't know how you did it, but I guess it doesn't really matter. The real question is, what do we do now?" He kept looking around, expecting the forest to reappear.

"I don't know about you two, but I'm exhausted," Paena said. "Can we go back to the inn before we do anything else?"

"I do not usually require much rest, child, but I do not have a better suggestion for now. Since we must wait for the town to wake up before we move on, an inn will suffice."

The three made their way through the sleeping streets of the village, back to the inn. It surprised Kalten to see light shining through the shutters. He tried the door. It was still locked, so he knocked.

In a matter of moments, the bolts were drawn back on the door. A tall, grizzled stranger opened the door. The man bowed and waved them into the inn.

He slammed the door closed behind them, and six men circled them. They had the grim look of men ready for trouble. Their weapons were drawn and ready.

"What's going on?" Kalten demanded.

The men stood in silence and waited. A creaking from the stairs announced the arrival of another person.

"Your name Kalten?" the newcomer asked. He was a fat reptilian man, slimy but with the poise of a veteran used to command.

His heart sank when he recognized the device on the breast of his tunic as Duke Samuel's. "It is."

"I have orders to take you back to my lord, Duke Samuel. You will come with us."

"And who are you?" Kalten asked.

The man drew himself up straighter. "I am the duke's captain. That is all you need to know."

"What right has your lord to do this?" Paena asked.

The older man stepped forward and backhanded her, knocking her to the floor. "That is none of your business, wench." His smile was wintery. "I think perhaps we will take you along. The duke likes to break spirited women."

"Then I will come with you as well, knave," Mother Tully said. She helped Paena up from the floor.

The captain sneered at the old woman. "We have no use for you, old crone."

"Still, I will go with you."

He nodded to one of his men. "Kill her."

As the man stepped forward Kalten drew his sword. "I suspect your duke wants you to bring me back alive. I know he always wanted to make sport of deserters in the past, anyway. If the old woman doesn't come along, I will fight you. If I win, I won't be going back, and if I lose I won't be going back alive. You lose either way."

The captain stared at Kalten for a long moment. "Very well, the old woman can come, but she will ride with the girl."

"Agreed," Kalten said. "But before we go, we must settle with the innkeeper."

"Don't you worry about that," the captain said. "I have already settled your debt with him. You will see him before you leave the village."

Curious onlookers watched from windows and doorways while they were escorted out of town and down the road. Kalten could only wonder if it wasn't the number of witnesses that kept them alive. If so, what would happen when they got to the woods? He idly noted the smoldering ruin of the merchant's stable when they left.

Just before they rode out of the village Paena let out a gasp. He followed her gaze and saw the forlorn creature swinging from a tree on the edge of town. The body had already been ravaged by birds, but the clothing proclaimed the man's identity. The captain and his men had a lot to answer for. From the look in Paena's eyes, she felt the same.

Chapter Fifteen

Kalten seethed. Why would they kill Roulston? Had the man told them anything? What would happen to Paena and Mother Tully when they reached the duke? The hard men rode almost stirrup-to-stirrup with him and blocked his horse on all sides. The horse had no bridle; only a simple halter on its head with a pair of ropes tied to it and held by the lead riders. A few lengths back, Paena and Mother Tully rode double in exactly the same formation. There was no way to break free and ride away.

They rode by the same route he and Paena had taken before. That was a cause for concern. Did the captain know something? What was going on?

His suspicions grew when they went up to the farm road and turned down the lane. He looked back at Paena, but said nothing. Her face mirrored his confusion and apprehension.

They were herded down the lane and into the meadow. At the captain's signal, the soldiers forced them from their horses and encircled them, preventing any chance of escape. One of the men led the mounts away.

Kalten looked around. The farm appeared to be unchanged. Only a fresh trail leading to the barn stood out.

The captain didn't waste any time. "Now. Why were you here a few days ago? There's no point denying it. I've had word you were spotted here. Duke Samuel would have the truth out of you now or later. I prefer now."

"I wouldn't dream of denying what your men saw. The truth is Paena and I were on an errand. We were doing a favor for a friend of ours."

"A favor for a friend?" The captain raised his eyebrows. "You expect me to believe that?"

"What you believe is up to you," Paena said. "We met some people out on the other side of town. We mentioned we were going this way, and they asked us to deliver a message to their uncle. They were very kind to us, so we happily agreed."

The captain glared at her then spoke to Kalten. "Their uncle lived here?"

He shrugged. "According to the directions they gave us."

"Was he here?"

"No. We didn't find him."

"I'm not surprised. He disappeared a few months back." The captain stared intently at Kalten for a few moments. "Who did you say sent you here, again?"

"Just some friends," he said.

"Is there something specific you want to know, Captain? Perhaps if you simply tell us we can be more helpful," Paena said.

The captain ignored her, speaking again to Kalten. "I want to know the names of your so-called friends."

"Captain, they were just some people we met in town. Why do you need to know who they are?" Paena asked.

The captain stared at her. "I'm not talking to you, girl. Keep quiet until I do."

"You do not need to be rude, Captain. She only asked you a question," Mother Tully said.

"The same rule applies to you, old crone. You'll keep quiet if you know what's good for you."

"You will mind your manners if you know what is good for you," Mother Tully said standing straighter. "You will not live to regret it if you do not."

"Sergeant," the captain said to the man closest to Mother Tully.

The man stiffened and saluted. "Yes, Captain?"

"If the old woman speaks again, gag her." He glared at Paena. "And if you say another word, girl, the same will happen to you."

Paena glared at the captain, but remained silent.

Satisfied she would stay quiet, he spoke to Kalten again. "And where did you go after you left here, boy?"

"Into the forest. We thought we'd move under cover to avoid any problems. We encountered Mother Tully in the forest and took her back to Thistledown."

"You met her and went directly back to the village?"

"That's right."

"You're lying," the captain said. "You were gone for several days. Where were you, and what were you doing?"

"I've already told you. We went through the forest. We found Mother Tully and stayed with her for a couple days before we went back to town."

The captain signaled to another one of his men. "Corporal, take the girl."

The man grabbed Paena, dragging her away from Kalten.

"What are you doing?" he shouted. He tried to get to her, only to be held back by two soldiers. He struggled against their grip, but couldn't free himself.

She fought the corporal's hold and snapped her head back into his nose. The soldier fell to the ground, blood streaming through his fingers where he lay writhing and swearing, clutching at his face.

Two other men tried to subdue Paena. She dropped one with a swift kick to the knee. The other she flipped over her shoulder. He crashed heavily to the ground and lay still.

"Stop her now! Kill her if you must," the captain shouted.

Six more soldiers piled onto her, knocking her down and pinning her arms and legs to the ground. She flailed and fought like a wildcat, kicking, biting, and scratching at the men. Her battle ended when a soldier smashed the butt of his spear against the side of her head. She slumped and lay still.

Kalten strained against his captors but remained held. He looked at the captain with hatred. "You bastard!"

The captain stepped up to Kalten and stood toe to toe with him, their noses almost touching. "Boy, I don't believe you. Tell me what I want to know or the girl dies."

"I've told you everything…"

"No, I don't think you have. Corporal, kill her."

"You will not harm the girl any further," Mother Tully commanded from where she was, alone on the grass.

"Just what are you going to do about it?" the captain said with a sneer on his face. He waved his hand carelessly. "Corporal, kill her now."

"I will do this." She gestured, and a flock of birds dove out of the sky at the corporal. There were gulls and ravens. Songbirds and raptors. A cloud of feathers, claws, and beaks pecked and tore at his face. The corporal fell shrieking to the ground. Blood and feathers were everywhere.

"What the… men, kill them! Kill them all!" the captain screamed.

Mother Tully gestured a second time, and the birds attacked the other men, leaving the corporal a bloody, lifeless mess on the ground. The birds swarmed over them, plucking eyes from sockets and tearing flesh from bodies.

The screams of the soldiers grew louder only to fall silent while they were torn apart by the relentless birds. Sickened by the carnage, Kalten had to look away. Mother Tully calmly watched the bloodbath.

"Go and look after Paena," she said. "I will settle things here."

Her voice shocked him out of his stupor. He looked dumbly at her for a moment before stumbling over to Paena's inert body, careful to avoid the corporal's corpse. She lay on the ground, head slightly turned away from him. Her hair was matted with fresh blood where she'd been struck.

"There's blood on her head. What can I do to help her?"

"You were a soldier. Do you not know how to deal with the wounded?"

"I was a scout, not a surgeon. I've never worked with the injured before."

Mother Tully strode over to them. "I need to check if she is just knocked out or if the injury is worse." The old woman ran her hands over Paena's head, gently probing the injury. "Kalten, I do not think she is going to wake up. Not without healing assistance. That blow was worse than I thought."

"Isn't there anything your magic can do?" He was beside himself with fear.

"No, I am afraid my powers do not yet extend to healing. We need more powerful magic than I possess."

"What will happen if we can't find healing for her?"

The wizened old woman seemed smaller. Her shoulders slumped, and she spoke again. "Her body will waste away until she dies."

He reeled. "Surely you know of someone with strong enough healing abilities to save her?"

Mother Tully frowned for a moment. "The only ones I know of strong enough to heal her wounds are the dragons. We were going to see them eventually anyway. Now we have no choice."

"The dragons? But aren't they the enemy? What can they do?"

"I do not think the ones you saw are the dragons I am thinking of. And if they are, they have much to answer for. Regardless, they are magical creatures with strong abilities. I believe they can heal Paena." She held up a warning finger. "But there is usually a hefty price associated with their help. Are you willing to pay whatever price they ask?"

Kalten didn't need to think about her question. Paena had proven herself ready to sacrifice everything for him. He could do no less for her. "I am willing to do whatever it takes."

"Very well. I need you to find something to carry her on. Something that will allow her to lay flat. And be quick about it. Every moment we take brings her closer to death."

He scavenged materials from around the farm, including the harness from the barn. He cut some long poles and built a sling for Paena.

He modified the harness to fit his shoulders and fastened it to the sling. A horse would have been better to pull the sling, but the horses had all fled during the battle. That meant the job fell on him. He would drag the sling until they got Paena healed.

He and Mother Tully moved Paena's body onto the sling. Mother Tully helped him to put on the modified harness. Kalten regarded Paena's motionless form and bent into his task. He pulled the sling toward the farm lane and away from the killing field.

~ * ~

Pieter had watched the soldiers and their prisoners ride out of the village, and he knew he had gotten lucky; his ruse with the fire had obviously convinced Captain Kerris he had died. Still, where could Pieter go?

After much searching, he went after the horsemen. His pride would allow nothing less. If there was any chance at redemption, he had to take it.

Now he rode as if all the powers of darkness were on his heels. He would never have believed it possible if he hadn't seen it for himself. The old woman was a witch. She had to be. How else could she have destroyed the troop of guardsmen?

When the troop turned down the lane, Pieter led his horse off the road and shadowed them on foot from inside the tree line. He had witnessed the entire massacre.

Duke Samuel needed to know what happened. That alone might save Pieter's life. Then he would have to… well he would wait for orders from him.

But maybe he should follow the traitor, the girl, and the witch instead? He reined up the horse. Duke Samuel wouldn't thank him for losing Kalten again. Pieter quailed at the thought of being discovered by the witch. Then he thought about the duke and remembered the way the failed guard captain had been killed.

That made the decision easy. The duke would surely kill him for failure. The witch only might. Pieter turned his horse and slowly rode back toward the witch and Kalten. They didn't know him yet. Perhaps that would still save him.

Chapter Sixteen

Duke Samuel stood and watched his compatriots settle around the council table. He had never liked the council chamber. It reeked of compromise and politics.

The room was bare except for the large oval oak table and chairs for ten. Two maps, one of his duchy, the other of the entire kingdom, hung on opposite walls.

He considered each of the six men seated around the table. Each one was a trusted confidant; conspirator if he were honest with himself. Each had pledged himself to the cause to remove the bitch queen.

"Samuel, what is this all about?" a portly, middle-aged man demanded. Standing up to speak, he didn't gain much additional height. "You had better have a good reason for calling us together like this."

"Patience, Count Grayal," Duke Samuel said, raising his hands in an appeasing gesture. "I will explain everything soon."

"I should hope so," said a bearded, silver-haired warrior. The man resembled nothing so much as a stern old wolf. "You put us all at dreadful risk bringing us together like this."

"Very well, gentlemen. Let me be brief." He sat and sipped at his wine before continuing. "To answer your concern, Earl Ranford, I believe we have already been compromised."

The room was in an immediate uproar.

Earl Ranford jumped to his feet. "What? How have we have been compromised, Samuel? What are you trying to pull?" He began moving toward the door.

Duke Samuel intercepted the older man, then turned him around by his shoulder. "Please, Ranford. Be seated and let me explain."

The older man searched the duke's eyes for a moment before nodding and sitting.

"My apologies for springing this upon you, my friends, but let me explain." He steepled his fingers. "One of my men made a run for it several weeks ago. Ordinarily, such an occurrence would be of no concern, however this man was one of my messengers. As such, he may know things about our plans."

"May?" the earl asked. "You dragged us here on speculation?"

"The traitor met up with the queen's eyes and ears within days of his defection. What would you think?" Duke Samuel replied.

"What have you done about this?" a count named William challenged.

"I have men searching for the traitor since he escaped, and I have alerted my commanders to search and watch for him. One of my squads reported his capture several days ago." The duke leaned forward and looked each man in the eye. "The squad in question was my best. They have not been heard from since. I can only assume the queen or someone in league with her stopped them."

"So, what now? What would you have us do?" Earl Ranford asked.

"I called you here to warn you. I believe we must begin to muster our troops and ready for war."

"So soon? We are still seasons from being fully prepared. How can we hope to get ready so quickly?" Count William said.

"We must do what we can," Duke Samuel said. "We have no choice. If I am wrong, we catch the queen unaware. If I am right, and she already knows our plans, we will not be caught ourselves." He sighed. "I know this is not ideal, but I urge you to return to your homes immediately and gather your forces. We must be ready to move in a fortnight."

"A fortnight?" The shock in the earl's voice was clear.

"Yes, my dear earl. If we fail, we might miss our chance to remove that upstart woman." Duke Samuel settled into his chair and listened to the men squabble. They could be such fools. They all wanted the queen gone, but were afraid to act. They needed someone who could make a decision.

He let them argue for some time before he slammed the flat of his hand against the table. "Gentlemen, the time for discussion is over. We must move now or we fail." He glared at each of the men. "Are you still with me?"

The looks they exchanged were far from confident, but, to a man, they replied, "We are."

~ * ~

"There is the entrance to the Dragon Lands," Mother Tully said.

Her voice shocked Kalten out of his reverie. He stumbled and almost fell. She grabbed his arm and steadied him. He looked up, not sure what to expect.

Hills stretched out in front of him to the horizon. They had the look of giant termite mounds. They were tall and almost vertical, and the sides were smooth and crumbly looking. He knew he wouldn't want to try to scale one of them.

A great arch split the line of hills and opened onto a desolate land of bubbling mud and stunted trees. The arch had a constructed look but was ancient beyond belief.

Sometime over the past number of days, she had taken over. He wasn't exactly sure when that was, but it had happened nonetheless. He'd been too focused on staying upright and moving forward to notice.

Dragging the sling out of the meadow had been easy. Kalten started out strong, confident he could persevere. That confidence lasted for about two hundred paces when fatigue set in.

Two hundred more, and he had to take a break. Mother Tully helped him out of the straps so he could sit for a few moments. He had caught his breath, and they continued on.

A couple hundred paces later, his back, shoulders, and legs ached. He kept on though. Paena's life was in the balance. He couldn't let her down.

That night, he simply collapsed, not even bothering to remove the harness or get settled in his bedroll. When he woke the next morning, he discovered Mother Tully had done all that for him while he slept.

When he tried to get up, he fell flat onto his face. Tortured muscles had stiffened up overnight. Movement was impossible.

She fixed warm poultices and applied them to his stiff and sore muscles. It took several applications to get him back on his feet.

He ate breakfast and got ready, but once on the road, the pain quickly returned. He kept chanting the same phrase over and over in his mind: "Can't stop now. Paena is dying. Can't stop now. Paena is dying." It was all that kept him going.

And she had not uttered a single sound since the meadow. She never moved but lay pale and cold on the sling, her life at the threshold of death's door. Mother Tully watched over her like a hawk, often taking her hand while they marched, entering a trancelike state.

How long their march lasted, he had no idea. How they even made it, he would never be sure. All that didn't matter now. They'd finally made it. Paena might still live.

Mother Tully shook him by the shoulder. "Kalten, did you not hear me? We are here. We have made it."

He regarded the huge rock arch in the towering cliff face. "I heard you," he croaked, shaking his head to clear the cobwebs. His mouth was dry and tasted of road dust. "I was just trying to remember how we got here."

"That is not important right now. We must get Paena some help. She is almost beyond hope. "

He looked back at her. She had lost a lot of weight during the journey. No time to think about that now. Not with help so close at hand.

He nodded to himself and squared his shoulders, ignoring the pain shooting through his body. Together they staggered through the arch. As he went through it, he realized it was more tunnel than gateway.

On the other side, he was disappointed by what he saw. A land of smooth hills, scrub trees, and bubbling mud. Not a dragon in sight. "What do we do now?"

"We go forward until they decide to recognize us. There is nothing else to do."

Kalten gritted his teeth and marched on with Mother Tully beside him. They passed massive boulders and stunted trees, well past the arch now. Still nothing happened. It was just about mid-day by the sun's position in the sky.

"We cannot stop and gawk now that we are here. Paena needs help more than ever."

He grunted and trudged on, dragging the sling along. Mother Tully dropped back to watch over her patient.

They were well into the dragon lands before he saw any sign of life. One moment they were hiking between hillocks of rock and sand, the next, they were surrounded by dragons of every color. The beasts had risen out of the sand almost magically never having uttered so much as a snuffle. Kalten could only stand and gape at his new captors.

"Why have you trespassed onto our lands?" a silver scaled dragon rumbled. "What are you doing here?" The creature was at least twenty cubits from the tip of its snout to the end of its tail. Bat-like wings were folded along its side, and a predator's head topped a long sinuous neck.

"We have come to seek help from the dragons," Mother Tully said. "This child has been gravely hurt. Only dragon magic can save her."

"What is she to us? Just one more filthy human. Dragons do *not* help humans. The whole idea is preposterous." The huge beast rumbled, as if in laughter. It sounded like stones being ground together.

"You will help this girl, or I will consider our treaty broken," Mother Tully snapped. "I know your people have left their boundaries and crossed into my lands. I know what that means to the ancient agreements. If you will not help, then you will take us to Golgoroth immediately."

"Golgoroth? Why would he deign to speak with the likes of you? And what are these lies about dragons breaking treaties? Dragons have no treaties with humans. Certainly none any human would remember." The silver dragon loomed over Mother Tully.

"There is one I remember well, and Golgoroth *will* speak with me or there will be trouble. This man has seen your people outside the dragon lands. I know the ancient treaties have been broken. Now, take me to him immediately."

The dragon inspected her. "There is something familiar about you. But the one whose likeness you bear hasn't been in these lands since I was a hatchling. No human is so long-lived."

"That is true," Mother Tully admitted. "But I am no normal human. Now do what you are told and take us to Golgoroth. I have no more time for your foolishness."

"How dare you!" The dragon roared in anger and jetted a stream of fire toward Mother Tully. The fire surged against an invisible barrier leaving the old woman unharmed.

"What madness is this," the dragon bellowed. "How is it you have not been reduced to ash?"

"Are you just about finished?" Mother Tully asked, stepping forward. She tapped the dragon lightly on the snout. "I told you. I am no ordinary human." She reached into her blouse and pulled out something on a leather thong. "Do you see this?" She held the item up for the dragon to see. "This is one of Golgoroth's teeth. He gave it to me long ago as a sign of good faith. It is this that protects me from your fire." She stared right into his eyes, and said, "I will ask you one last time. Will you take me to Golgoroth or not?"

The dragon seemed shaken by the evidence of the tooth. He took a step back from Mother Tully. "I-I..." He stopped speaking for a moment, looking confused. He finally nodded his massive head. "I... that is, we will take you to him."

"Thank you, noble dragon." She was gracious in victory. "May I ask your name?"

"My name? Why... oh very well." The dragon seemed at a loss. "My name is Lydaroth."

"Lydaroth. Your sire is the great Golgoroth himself?"

The dragon preened at the recognition and compliment to his sire. "You continue to surprise me, lady. Yes, Golgoroth is my sire. May I ask your name?"

"I will be happy to give you my name while we travel, noble Lydaroth. But we must go. The girl's lifeforce is dwindling rapidly."

"It shall be as you say, lady," the silver dragon said.

He nodded toward the other dragons. They had the same look and bearing, but all were smaller and colored differently They immediately sprang into the air. The travelers were snatched up by three of the dragons before they flew off.

Kalten almost bit through his tongue to keep from screaming when the huge green dragon grabbed him. Only when he realized there wasn't any immediate danger did he start to enjoy the ride. Below him, the rocky, barren land took on a strange beauty. The colors of the rock blended together and became a rich mosaic, visible only from the air.

They flew for some time, exactly how long Kalten couldn't be sure. By his reckoning, they were flying almost due north. The air grew warmer while they traveled.

Below, the landscape changed from one of rock to oozing, bubbling mud. A geyser surprised one of the dragons by erupting directly beneath it, catching it in boiling water. The creature gave a screech of surprise, but flew on unharmed.

Kalten and the green dragon were right beside it when it was struck. He could feel the heat from the water. He nervously watched the ground while they flew. If it had been him, he would have boiled alive. He saw no other geysers.

The party continued on into a new landscape. Kalten marveled at the massive craggy peaks and immense fields of blunt, melted rock. Occasional rivers of molten lava and mud surged below them and blasts of superheated air rose to meet them. The stench of sulfur filled the air. Kalten could hardly see through his watering eyes.

The dragons circled an enormous, raised crater and glided toward its floor. They got closer to the ground, and the dots of color became a multitude of dragons.

The dragons swooped to the bowl of the crater, depositing their passengers gently to the ground. Kalten was buffeted by wind and dust when the dragons landed around them. While the dust settled, he could see they had been joined by a host of dragons of every color.

A mighty gold dragon strode over to them, roaring. Kalten hoped Mother Tully knew what she was doing.

Chapter Seventeen

Kalten and the others were faced with a very large, very angry, gold dragon. The beast was massive, at least thirty cubits long and half again larger than the biggest of the dragons that surrounded them. Around them all were dozens of creatures from very small hatchlings barely larger than a full-grown man to some approaching Lydaroth in size. They were every color imaginable. None look pleased to see them.

"Why have you trespassed on our lands?" the golden dragon rumbled. "What reason could humans have for coming here?"

"We come for aid... and for answers," Mother Tully said. "Most importantly, this girl has been seriously hurt. Without your help, she will die."

"Then, she dies," the dragon said and turned away. "What is one fewer human to me? Lydaroth, you should not have brought them here."

The younger dragon looked ashamed, but defiant. "The lady claims we have broken an ancient treaty with the humans."

"That isn't exactly true, young Lydaroth. I said the dragon nation has broken a treaty with me."

The gold dragon spun around. "Treaty? What treaty would we have with a crone such as you?"

"She says we have left the dragon lands to trespass in the outer world," Lydaroth answered.

"You would believe a human? No dragon has left the lands, or I would have known. I thought you had more sense."

"I would not have believed her, but she carries one of your teeth, Sire. She says you made a pact with her long ago. She says dragons have been seen on the outside."

"She has one of my teeth? But I have only ever given out one..." The golden dragon carefully checked out Mother Tully. "Who are you that you carry such a thing?"

"Who I am now is of no matter. It is who I was that is important. I was one who you wished to strike a bargain with. I dealt with you in good faith and have always kept my end of the agreement."

"It is true that you resemble one who was here before. But you do not have the same power the other did."

Mother Tully smiled a rueful smile. "You are quite correct. I am no longer what I once was. It is an unfortunate truth that, over time, the world and the people in it change. I am not immune to that truth. Over the centuries, my power has dwindled to what you see now. That is unimportant here and now. What is important is that I still remember and hold our covenant. Do you?"

"Why should we honor an ancient agreement with one who no longer holds the same power she once did?"

"Because you have honor." Mother Tully glared at him. "The dragon I knew long ago would never have asked such a question."

Golgoroth chuckled. "You have not lost your fire, despite everything else, old woman." He sighed. "You are correct, though. I never would have asked that question in the past. But times have changed and not for the better. Regardless, my honor remains true."

"If that were so, then why have your people broken the agreement?"

He snarled at that. "We have not broken the agreement. Despite your ridiculous claims, we have kept the pact. None of my people have left the dragon lands."

"My lord, I don't know if that's true or not," Kalten broke in, speaking quickly, "but I have seen dragons outside of these lands. I saw them fly into an enemy camp, pick up cages full of prisoners then fly off."

"Impossible." He leaned toward Kalten. "I would have known if any of my people left our lands. What did these dragons look like?"

He tried to steady his fear and somehow managed to stand his ground. "They looked like you, my lord." Kalten couldn't help but be surprised at the question. How many kinds of dragon were there? "I'm sorry, but until I saw them, I didn't even know that dragons were real. Are there other kinds?"

"Of course there are, boy. But, I'm more interested in their casts."

"Casts? I don't understand."

"Their colors, boy. What were their colors?"

Kalten cringed. "They were many colors, Lord. There was a gold dragon, a green…"

"Were any black?"

He stopped to think for a moment. "I think there was. At least, there were a couple that appeared very dark, but I'm not sure."

"This is all very interesting," Mother Tully interrupted before they could go on. "But the girl is dying, and only your power can save her. Will you help her or not?"

"You still haven't given me any reasons why I should. It is not our way to interfere with the natural way of things."

"That she was injured was not a natural thing, but the act of violent men. Men who may be in league with those very same dragons Kalten has seen. Do it for a show of good faith and honor, if nothing else."

"You throw the word honor around very quickly, old woman," the dragon growled. "But you also come accusing my people of breaking treaties. What honor does that show coming from you?"

Kalten took a step toward the dragon. "Then save Paena so we remain to tell you everything we know. You can judge the truth of our words when she is healthy again."

"Very well. I will do what I can." He glared at the old woman. "But only so I can get to the bottom of these accusations." He strode over to Paena's still form and took a long, calculating look. "She is very near death. A healing could easily kill her. I will not be able to save her without assistance."

"Assistance?" Kalten said. "Is there anything I can do? Whatever it takes to save her, I will gladly do. Just tell me what."

"You also are very weak, boy. I don't know what the healing would do to you."

"Would it save her?"

"Possibly."

"Then what are we waiting for?" Kalten frowned. "I don't care if it kills me. Paena must be saved."

"As you wish." The dragon's voice took on a gentler tone as he said, "But you need to understand something first. The healing requires a great deal of energy. That is what you will be giving. But by putting your energies into the healing, your essences will be bonded inextricably to each other, forever.

"What does that mean?"

"I don't exactly know. I have not healed a human in over a millennium. I just know your lives will be forever intertwined."

It made no difference. The decision was easy. "Do it."

"As you wish." The dragon raised a massive, clawed talon and pointed at a table-like slab of granite nearby. "Place the girl on the rock and then lie down beside her." He called out to the silver dragon. "Lydaroth."

The silver dragon looked up at his sire's call. "Yes Sire?"

"You will add your strength to this as well."

"But Father, won't that..." Lydaroth stammered.

"Yes, it will include you in the bond. You brought them here. You believed their charges. You will be responsible for them."

"If they lie?"

"You will be responsible for them," Golgoroth repeated. "And if they speak truth, you will be my eyes and ears. These are my commands. Obey them."

"Yes, my lord." Head hanging, the silver dragon plodded over to the granite slab and crouched beside it.

Kalten hesitated. What exactly did all this mean? "Mother Tully, what should I do?"

"Put Paena onto the rock and get up there yourself and be quick about it. She is dying, and there is no time to waste. Have you changed your mind about saving her?" Despite her harsh words, Mother Tully sounded uncertain.

"Of course not, but..." Kalten shrugged. Nothing to do but go for it. He bent and gently picked up Paena. He was weaker than he thought and staggered when he lifted her.

He carried his friend over to the granite slab and gently laid her on it. He clambered up beside her and held her cold hand in his. "We're ready. Do what you need to do."

Golgoroth nodded. "Lydaroth. You also must touch the humans." His voice took on a softer note. "My son, it is necessary that you do this for me."

Lydaroth sighed and laid his mighty head onto the rock. Kalten looked into eyes like quicksilver pools. "I'm not lying. I did see dragons. I don't know what's expected of you, but that's the truth." He reached out, touched the dragon's muzzle and closed his eyes.

The dragon's lips barely moved. "It had better be, or I will have to kill you."

Kalten ignored the dragon's words. He had expected something like that.

"Do not panic," Golgoroth said. "You will feel the heat of my breath. But it will not harm you. If you open your eyes, you will see my flame. But it will not burn you."

His words were followed by pleasant warmth. Kalten couldn't resist. He opened his eyes.

Flames crackled and snapped around him. His clothing charred and burned off him, yet he felt no pain. He stared over at Paena. A nimbus of translucent blue flame surrounded her naked form. Her dark hair flowed in the crackling heat. She was the most beautiful thing he'd ever seen.

Where his fingers touched Lydaroth, the dragon shone with mirror brightness. Light swirled and writhed beneath his skin and whirlpooled toward Kalten's fingers. Strength flowed from the dragon through his fingers and body into Paena. His own body took on a glow so bright he was forced to close his eyes. How long it lasted he could not say, but gradually he sensed a lull in the flow of power. He was struck by a wave of intense fatigue.

The silver dragon's head lolled on the rock, and he had taken on a dull gray patina. Kalten's skin mirrored the dragon's grayish hue. His eyes grew heavy and extreme fatigue tugged at him. Euphoria swelled within his mind, and Kalten was dragged into the darkness of unconsciousness.

~ * ~

Pieter huddled under a rock outcropping as three dragons flew by overhead. He had seen several of the beasts since his arrival. He'd almost screamed when he saw the first dragon. There had been stories of them when he was a boy, of course. But those were fairy stories meant to frighten children into behaving. The ones he was seeing now were very real.

For the hundredth time he questioned his decision to follow Kalten into the Dragon Lands and for the hundredth time he reminded himself he had no choice.

He had seen the dragons carry Kalten and the women out of sight. As they disappeared into the distance, Pieter had known there was no going back; to return without the traitor would mean instant death. That meant going forward.

The trek thus far had been nothing short of a nightmare. Burning streams of liquid rock flowed like water. Bubbling pots of boiling mud and scalding fountains of water were everywhere, and the air held the stench of sulfur.

More than once, the seemingly solid ground turned out to be nothing more than a thin crust breaking beneath his feet. Many times, he escaped death by luck alone. He quickly learned to test each tentative step. Oh yes, this place was a nightmare indeed.

He peered out from under the rock and searched the sky. The dragons were gone. Pieter scrambled across the rocks, his gaze focused on the spot where the dragons appeared over the horizon. The path they flew only helped him to stay on target.

A scorpion skittered past him, pinchers extended and tail looped over its back. It had to be the size of a small cat. Wiping his sleeve across his brow, Pieter continued on his way, carefully watching the sky and the rocks for signs of danger. Kalten would pay for this discomfort, Pieter would see to that.

~ * ~

Kalten woke lying in a comfortable bed, naked beneath the covers. A fire burned in a hearth near the center of the room, providing the only light.

There was another person in the room. Against the opposite wall was another bed. Flames were reflected in open eyes.

The person, a woman by her silhouette, slinked past the fire to his bed. When she came closer, he realized it was Paena.

"Paena. I'm so glad to see…"

She stopped him with a fingertip against his lips. Her touch sent a shock through his body. She lifted the covers and slid into the bed next to him, her naked body hot against him.

She crushed her mouth against his, kissing him deeply, passionately. He tried to resist. This was his friend, not his lover, but her proximity and urgent need overwhelmed him. And something else compelled. He couldn't be sure what it was.

He made one last effort to stop her. "Paena, we mustn't…" But her eyes were aflame with passion. They pulled him in, and he lost himself in her desire.

Chapter Eighteen

Pieter shivered as he looked over a massive crater. How could it be so flaming hot during the day and so cold at night? Not that it mattered. He had managed the rivers of lava and the poisonous vermin, and now he was on the cusp of dealing with Kalten once and for all.

The crater appeared deserted in the darkness except for the far wall. It was a long way off, but Pieter was sure the small pinpoints of light were fires. What was around those fires he would learn soon enough. That was the most likely place to find Kalten anyway. He'd never know what hit him.

"What have we here?" a gravelly voice said out of the darkness.

If Pieter had less self-control he would have screamed. Instead, he faced the voice to see a pair of brilliant, glowing green eyes staring at him from high above the rocks.

"Don't bother trying to run or hide. I can see you very well," the voice said again. "Now, would you like to tell me who you are and why you are here?"

Pieter started standing up only to stop when a small fireball splashed against the rocks beside him. The fireball had briefly illuminated the owner of the eyes. He was in trouble.

"I said stand still!"

"I'm very sorry." Pieter's mind raced, and he tried to come up with a plausible story. "I've been wandering lost for several days. When I saw the lights down below, I thought I might be saved." It sounded possible when he said it. Maybe he'd survive the night.

"Lost? You would have me believe that you accidentally wandered into the Dragon Lands and have been lost here ever since. All without knowing where you were?"

"The Dragon Lands? I thought those were a legend only."

"You never saw any of the dragon patrols?"

Pieter kept his bluff going. "Dragons? They don't exist! They are a legend, just like the Dragon Lands."

A large taloned foot swept out of the darkness and grabbed Pieter. "Legend?" A snort of flame lit up the darkness, clearly showing the draconian face once again. "I should think dragons are not a legend."

The dragon leapt into the air, still holding him. Pieter clutched at one of the talons to steady himself. He squeezed his eyes shut to avoid looking down.

"I shall take you to Golgoroth. He will know how to deal with you."

~ * ~

Kalten stretched after he woke and hastily wrapped himself in his blankets. Light streamed into the room through its one window, but the air still held a bite of frost in it. He was alone. Clean clothing lay draped over the footboard of his bed. Two beds and a fireplace with a rug in front were the only furnishings. It had been enough.

He dressed quickly and followed the rough-hewn stone corridor from his room to a large, well-lit chamber. A huge table surrounded by high-backed chairs dominated the room.

At the far end of the hall, Mother Tully and Paena talked by a large window. Their heads were close together, and Mother Tully had her arm around Paena.

Kalten couldn't intrude on their conversation. The memories of the previous night were still too vivid. He wasn't sure he could face Paena. Not yet. Instead, he explored the room. Fine tapestries covered the walls, all depicting dragons in varying scenes.

The colors and detail were exquisite. He lost himself in his explorations wondering how such items could exist here.

A soft tap on his shoulder startled him. He turned around and came face to face with Paena.

"You've been staring at these tapestries all morning. What's so interesting?" She didn't quite meet his eyes.

"I saw you and Mother Tully talking. I didn't want to interrupt." She was so beautiful. And after last night, how could they ever stay friends? "I started looking at these tapestries. They're really something, aren't they? I wonder how they even got here?"

"Yes, they really are," she said. "Listen Kalten, about last night."

"There's nothing to talk about. I'm just glad you're well again." He tried to change the subject. "So, has Mother Tully said anything about what's next?"

"Kalten." Paena grabbed his face. "We can't ignore what's happened. I talked to Mother Tully about it. She told me the type of healing I had can cause a person to act differently. To not be themselves."

That's what I was afraid of. A surge of shame filled him. "But I wasn't healed. You were. I've betrayed your trust."

"No, you haven't. Mother Tully told me what you went through to get me here. Without you, I'd be dead."

"That's no excuse—"

"No, it's not," Paena said with a gentle smile. "But it explains a lot. You took yourself beyond exhaustion and still offered your strength to save me. It's no surprise that some of the healing went to you as well. You were affected the same way I was."

"Still, how can we be friends after this?"

"Kalten, how could we not be friends after all we've been through? Even now, I can feel your pain. You think you've betrayed our friendship. Trust me, you haven't. The bond we share now can only intensify our friendship. Mother Tully said that by giving me your strength, we were connected somehow."

"Paena, I'm so sorry. I wish I could change things, but I can't."

She gave him a hard hug. "From what I remember, I had a pretty key role last night. Don't beat yourself up. I'm a big girl."

"Are you children about finished?" Mother Tully interrupted the conversation. "Golgoroth is waiting to talk to us. After what he has done for us, we should not keep him waiting." The old woman stomped toward the exit. Kalten and Paena took a last look at each other, and then followed her out of the room.

Paena reached out and took Kalten's hand while they walked. "I've come to respect you and care about you. What happened won't change that."

The old woman led them through the windy, rock corridors until they emerged out into the brilliant sunlight. They were forced to shade their eyes from the glare.

The view was incredible. Around them, a verdant forest grew. Flowers were everywhere. Off in the distance, the crater walls rose up in jagged splendor. The sounds of a gurgling stream filled his ears. Everything was pristine and beautiful. Not at all what he expected from such a sparse and threatening land.

They entered a lush green meadow where, lounging on the grass, near the middle of the glen, lay the gold dragon, Golgoroth.

He rose when they approached him. "Welcome. It is good to see you two young ones doing so well. I was not certain you would survive, either of you."

Both Paena and Kalten nodded and bowed. "Thank you, Lord." There wasn't anything else to say.

"And thanks to you, my lady, for this splendid forest you have provided me. It reminds me of those from my youth, long ago."

Kalten stared at Mother Tully in shock. She'd caused this beautiful forest to come into being? Were there no limits to her surprises?

"It was the least I could do, my lord," she said. "After all, you did save my companions."

"Well, I consider myself well-paid for that service, Lady." He fidgeted for a moment. "But, we still have much to discuss. Specifically, your charges of dragons outside these lands."

"My lord, as I said before, I have seen dragons away from these lands," Kalten said.

"Yes, you have said so." Golgoroth scratched at a loose scale on his neck. "Young man, the charges you bring are very serious. I must be certain you tell the truth. There is too much at stake. Please excuse my caution, for if what you say is true, it will have far-reaching effects for my people. Pardon me for a moment." He leaned back on his haunches, tilted his head back and jetted a massive blast of flame into the sky.

Kalten stumbled and fell backward to the ground. What was going on?

Golgoroth was surprised to see Kalten on the ground. "Are you fatigued, young man?"

"No, I'm fine." He scrambled back to his feet, embarrassed. "You just startled me, that's all."

"My apologies. I needed to summon my son to us."

"Why do you need him?" Paena asked.

"Lydaroth has been tied to you two via the healing. His energy was used just like Kalten's was."

"What does that mean, exactly?" she said.

"I think I know," said Kalten. "It means he's going to use Lydaroth to sense if we're lying or not. That's a pretty dirty trick. You're going to use him to spy on us, whatever we do."

"I never intended that." Golgoroth's eyes showed a red tinge, and his voice grew in volume. "Your friend was near death, and you were too weak to provide all the required energy. Lydaroth needed to be taught to think before he acts, so I made him provide the necessary life force. It is that simple."

"It sounds pretty convenient."

The dragon reared up and spread his wings, clawing at the sky. "Do *not* question me. We have saved the young woman and what has been given, can be taken away."

"There, there, Golgoroth. The children are just trying to come to grips with what has happened. They do not mean any disrespect." Mother Tully glared at Kalten and Paena. "Do you?"

Kalten could not meet her eyes and looked at the ground. "No, I don't mean any disrespect, Lord. I apologize for my rudeness."

Paena stepped forward. "I'm sorry too, Lord." She put her arm around Kalten's waist. "We've been through a lot the past few days. Especially Kalten. We're very grateful for all you've done. By all means bring Lydaroth here to verify what Kalten says. I'm sure you will find we're telling the truth."

"Very well." Golgoroth appeared mollified. "I assure you, I did not intend to trick you."

"No, indeed," Mother Tully said. "In fact, it was my idea. Golgoroth and I were talking about the problem and how we could prove what is being said. Then I thought about the link you three share. Golgoroth has agreed to abide by what his son says."

As she finished speaking, Lydaroth swooped down, his wings making a thundering sound churning up the air, as he landed in the meadow.

"You summoned me, Sire?" he said.

"Yes, son. I need you to bear witness to what these humans say. The young man is about to tell us about the dragons he saw."

"Lydaroth," Mother Tully said, "can you sense any of Kalten or Paena's thoughts or feelings?"

"Why would I sense them? Do you still think I bonded with them during the healing?"

"Son, you know healing like we did with the girl can tie your essence to the injured. The same is true if another is part of the link like Kalten was. I need you to search deep within yourself and see if you're aware of any bond."

Lydaroth closed his eyes and was silent for a long time. Kalten and Paena both reclined on the grass to wait.

At long last, he let out an anguished bellow. "I can feel their minds. Oh, Sire. How can I stop this?"

"I do not know what can be done, my son, but I need you now. I need you to search out the truth of what Kalten tells us. Can you do this?"

"I-I will try, Father," Lydaroth said. "What do I need to do?"

"Just listen to what Kalten says," Mother Tully answered. "You should be able to at least see the truth of his words. Kalten, when Lydaroth is ready, please tell us about the dragons you saw."

Kalten nodded and waited for Lydaroth to ready himself. When the dragon nodded and closed his eyes, Kalten spoke.

He told of when he first saw the dragons and what they did. He spoke of how the soldiers seemed to expect the dragons. Golgoroth listened closely, interrupting with the occasional question. Kalten answered as best as he was able.

When he finished his story, Golgoroth glanced at his son. "Lydaroth, does the young human tell the truth?"

"I am sorry, Sire, but he does," Lydaroth said.

"How can this be?" Anger gripped Golgoroth. "I should know if my people are leaving the Dragon Lands, yet I do not. Is my power waning?"

"Sire, I could see the events when Kalten spoke. I did not recognize any of the dragons."

"You are absolutely sure?"

"Absolutely. There is no doubt in my mind."

Mother Tully interjected. "Have any other dragon colonies grown since the ancient days?"

"None in this part of the world, and I think I would know."

"What about the renegades, Father?"

"Renegades?" Kalten said.

"We will not speak of *them*," the old dragon said, his voice pregnant with anger.

"Golgoroth, we must investigate any possibility," Mother Tully said. "Right now, it appears your people have broken the pact and are traveling out of the Dragon Lands. I know you and your people are honorable. We must learn who is doing this thing."

"Sire, if it is them, we have a bigger problem than we thought. These humans have brought us this news, and I can tell you it is without evil intent. Kalten's words are true, without deceit. We must trust them."

The old dragon sighed. "You are right, my son. I've too long lived in distrust of outsiders. This problem will not disappear if I ignore it."

"Golgoroth, you have helped us. Please, let us return the favor," Paena said gently. She drew near the mighty beast and laid her hand on a scaled leg. "We already have a mission to help our queen. She has trusted us with her future. Clearly, you are being dragged into this conflict by unknown dragons. We will keep this knowledge safe."

"I second what Paena says," Kalten echoed.

"Marvelous," Golgoroth said. "Where did you find these two?" His question was directed toward Mother Tully.

The old lady shrugged. "They found me. And the longer I am around them, the more I wonder what forces are at work within them." She winked at him. "For me, that is saying something."

"I have decided," Golgoroth declared. "I will trust you with this secret. But I warn you, it must never go outside this forest glade."

"You have our promise," Kalten and Paena said.

Lydaroth gave a tiny nod to his sire.

"Excellent. Now, what I am about to tell you is known only to those dragons on the ruling council. Not even my own people know of it." Golgoroth paused for a moment, as if to collect his thoughts.

"The renegades my son spoke of are a group of dragons who long ago decided to ignore the pacts we have made. They decided to abandon honor. They tried to leave the Dragon Lands, violating all agreements, to take what they wanted. Such a thing could not be allowed. The council banished them to a desolate, volcanic region far from here."

"How would that stop them from simply going where they wanted?" Kalten said.

"We left guards behind to ensure they stayed put until they could fly no more."

"I don't understand," Paena said. "Why would they lose the ability to fly? You didn't damage their wings to stop them, did you?"

The dragon roared in anger. "We would never do such harm to another dragon. We are not savages." He lunged toward her, but stopped when Lydaroth dove between them.

"Sire, I don't think she understands our nature. She errs through ignorance, not insult."

"Then educate her. I must calm myself." Golgoroth shouldered through the trees, leaving them.

Chapter Nineteen

Stillness gripped the meadow after the dragon lord left. Only the burbling of the hidden stream and the occasional sound of snapping branches announcing the angry dragon's passage through the trees could be heard.

Paena and Kalten stood in stunned silence. Even Lydaroth looked shocked at his sire's sudden departure.

"Still quick to anger," Mother Tully tsked. "Even as a hatchling, Golgoroth would fly into a rage without provocation. I would have thought time might have muted his temper."

"Please forgive my sire. He is very touchy about the renegade dragons. My elder brother led them."

"I'm sorry," Paena said. "I didn't mean to upset him. I never meant to imply that you would injure your own people. That's what it sounded like to me. I mean, how else would a dragon lose its ability to fly?"

"I know the answer to that question, Paena, but the story is for Lydaroth to tell, not me."

The silver dragon spoke after several moments of silence. "It is something we never speak of to outsiders. We rarely even speak of it between ourselves." He settled back on his haunches, adjusting his wings tight against his back. He made a deep sighing sound deep in his throat. "But my sire did order me to educate you."

"If you can't tell us, we will understand," Paena said.

"No. You should know the answer to your question if we are to work together." He paused for a moment. "What do you know about the nature of dragons?"

She checked with Kalten who simply shrugged. "Not much. In fact, prior to a few days ago, I thought dragons were a child's story."

Lydaroth laughed, a deep musical rumbling. "No, the nature of which I speak is that of our physical form. You see, we are creatures of the earth. Our bodies reflect the elements in which we live."

"Reflect elements?" she asked.

"Touch my scales and tell me what you feel." He shifted slightly so she could more easily reach him.

She laid her hand on his shoulder. His scales were cold and hard to the touch. She tapped a scale and bruised her knuckles. It was like hitting a shield. "Your scales feel like metal."

"Yes, exactly like metal," he said. "My couch where I sleep is made up mainly of silver and iron. My body has gradually taken on those metal's properties, and my scales are now an iron and silver alloy. My father's couch is primarily gold along with iron. Iron is always included by the noble dragons because it adds strength to the beauty of the other metals and gems."

"How does this affect the renegade dragons and their ability to fly?" she asked.

"Paena, I am able to fly because the iron gives my wings the strength to support my body's weight in the air. The renegades have been denied iron. They do not have it to strengthen their bodies. In fact, they do not have metal at all to strengthen themselves. This lack keeps them on the ground."

"But the dragons I saw flew," Kalten said.

"Yes, most perplexing. I don't understand how the renegades could have gotten metal. The area they are in is extremely volcanic. Volcanic rock and glass are all that exists in the open. Both are brittle and weak."

"Could they dig it out themselves?" Paena asked.

"Unlikely. We dragons are not really built for digging."

"Then how do you get your gold and silver?" asked Kalten.

"Dragons have been allied with a digging folk for many millennia. They mine it for us. They are also exquisite craftsmen," Lydaroth replied. "Follow me, and I'll show you what I mean." He turned and Paena and the others trailed along behind him down a path toward the crater's rim.

As they neared the wall of the crater, she could see it was honeycombed with holes. Caves, she suspected. Around the caves, many small figures moved.

"What are they?" she asked.

"They call themselves Toupeira or Earth Children in our language," Mother Tully said. "I know this because there are a few living in my forest. They are the size of a small child and are furred with large digging claws. Their eyesight is very poor, but they are unparalleled miners and artisans."

"Yes. We formed an alliance with them long ago. They mine the metals and gems we need, and in return, we protect them from those who would hurt or exploit them. They have also created much of the artwork we possess. It is an arrangement that has worked to our mutual benefit ever since."

Paena could see them quite clearly now. They reminded her of giant moles, except these creatures were obviously organized and intelligent.

"Why couldn't they work for the renegades?" asked Kalten.

"That is part of the agreement. They have vowed to never work for our enemies. That includes those dragons banished from our lands. We also know none of our allied population have disappeared or been taken. The elders of their people would have told us."

"Can we meet them?" she asked.

"Alas, no. The Toupeira have little use for converse and are shy around strangers."

"It is true," Mother Tully affirmed. "They are a solitary people with no interest in anything save tunneling, building and digging."

"If it's not the Toupeira mining for the renegades, then who?" asked Paena.

Kalten snapped his fingers. "The stolen humans. That must be what the dragons were taking the prisoners for."

"Or for food," Lydaroth said. "We do occasionally eat meat, although we do not bother with humans. It would break our pact."

Paena and Kalten edged away from the dragon.

He noticed their movement and laughed. "I jest, of course. We have not consumed a human being in centuries and then usually only in self-defense. Wild game is more to our liking. That is not to say the renegades would not do otherwise. They are banished for good reason." He turned away from the caves and made his way down the path. "Come, let us return to the clearing. Our presence is making the Toupeira nervous."

By the time they returned, a table had been placed in the middle of the clearing. Steam rose from platters of roasted meats and vegetables, and bowls of succulent fruits covered its surface. Delightful aromas filled the entire meadow.

Mother Tully was delighted. "Lydaroth, how thoughtful. Please extend our thanks to your people for this feast."

"You are our guests and the first humans here in centuries." Lydaroth shrugged. "We had almost forgotten what it was like to have humans among us. I hope everything is to your liking."

"It's perfect," Paena said. "But how did you come by all this food? Surely not the Toupeira?"

"No," Lydaroth said. "For all their craft, they do not cook. No, we used our magic to summon this meal. I trust our distant memories of human food meets with your approval?"

"Well, it all looks and smells delicious," said Paena. "Let's eat, I'm starving."

Kalten and Mother Tully both nodded their enthusiastic agreement and started eating. Lydaroth backed away from the table a few steps and turned to leave.

Paena stopped eating. "Lydaroth, won't you join us?"

"I am sorry, but I do not have an appetite right now. I must confess to some uneasiness around you still. My awareness of your thoughts and emotions seems to be growing, and I am not yet comfortable with the alienness of them. Would you please excuse me?"

"Of course, Lydaroth," Mother Tully said around a mouthful of food. "Until we see you later."

The dragon bowed down to them and took flight. Paena could well understand. Her awareness of Kalten and his feelings grew stronger every day. It was very disturbing. But the wonderful aromas of the feast called to her empty stomach. Soon she forgot about the intruding thoughts and focused on eating.

As they ate, they discussed their plans for the future. Now that she was well again, they could continue on their assignment. It appeared the dragon assailants were now identified. The question became how they managed to fly without available metal, or more precisely, where they had gotten metal to allow them flight. Without the help of their new dragon friends, they might never learn the answer.

Almost on cue, Golgoroth pushed his way back through the trees and into the clearing. He appeared much calmer than when he left them.

"What ho, friends?" he said, as if his fit of anger had never happened. "What have you learned?"

"Your son has told us some of your history with the renegades, my lord," Paena said.

The dragon snorted, a small fireball incinerating a patch of grass. "That filth. I would not waste my time with them."

"Perhaps not, Golgoroth, but we believe them to be the ones Kalten saw taking the peasants."

"Impossible. If my son told you their history, then he has also told you why it could not be them."

"Isn't it possible someone from the outside could have helped them to escape their prison?" asked Kalten.

"Yes. Maybe they have agreed to help anyone who gives them the metal and the slaves they need?" said Paena.

"They were banished much too far from human lands," said Golgoroth.

"Are you sure about that?" said Mother Tully. "We know of some very determined men who would stop at nothing to gain allies, especially dragon allies. They would be especially committed if they had information as to the whereabouts of the renegades."

"My subjects are loyal. Most are not even aware of the banishments."

"Did any of the banished leave family behind?" Mother Tully asked.

His snout winkled for a moment. "A few, I suppose. But I still do not see how it could be done. I would know if any left my kingdom and the entrances to this land are all guarded."

"Sire, are they guarded by all your subjects or merely a select few?" asked Kalten.

"All dragons take their turns to guard. It is the duty of all to keep these lands safe."

"Is it possible that one of those doing the guarding might have had contact with a human and not told you?"

The old dragon idly scraped his claw along a rock. "It is possible. I am not admitting that any of my people have had anything to do with this though, you understand? But you've given me much to think about. Please, take relax here." Without another word, he stalked off through the trees, mumbling to himself.

~ * ~

How long were they going to keep him confined? Pieter searched the hole he had been dropped into. The walls were smooth and shear. Smooth except for a number of small scratches and graffiti, most likely courtesy of previous prisoners. He lay back on the pile of rags that made up his bed. He could easily imagine dying in such a place.

A shadow fell across him. He looked up to see a silver dragon looking down at him.

"Who are you, human? Why are you here?"

Pieter thought up a story quickly. "I got lost. I didn't know I trespassed in your lands."

The dragon snorted, bathing him in a wave of heat. "I have been told of your claim to be lost. I do not believe your story. Why are you really here?"

Pieter folded his arms across his chest. "I'm sorry you don't believe me, but it is the truth."

"As you wish." The dragon lifted his head as if listening. Moments later he dropped it again. "You still have not told me who you are."

He considered the question. "I am… a trader of exotic goods. I traveled here because I heard of people who had gems to sell."

"A trader? You would have me believe you are a trader? Where are your goods then, little trader?"

"I hid them. I always hide my valuables so I do not get robbed."

The dragon made a sound in its throat like a small avalanche. "Now I know you lie. Who would hide valuable goods when they themselves do not know where they are?" It shook its head in a very human gesture. "No, you will remain in this place until my sire has decided what to do with you. Or until you decide to tell us the truth." The dragon withdrew its head.

The conversation obviously over, Pieter tried to think of a way to escape.

Chapter Twenty

"You were right, the renegades have escaped." Three days had passed and the humans were relaxing in the meadow when Golgoroth stormed in and made his announcement. Paena had fully recovered from her ordeal and was beginning to gain back the weight she had lost while unconscious.

"I would never have thought that anyone would find or aid them." The dragon swiped at a tree with his tail, smashing it to kindling. "I sent a party to check on them. The renegades are gone, and for some time too."

"Golgoroth, you could not have known," Mother Tully soothed. "But it does present us with a bigger problem."

"What is that?"

"You may have a traitor in your midst."

"What? How dare you imply..."

"My lord, I imply nothing. You said it yourself that the renegades were in a remote area that would not be easily located except for inside information. Who else, but one of your own people would know where they were taken?"

Golgoroth considered that for a few moments. "I suppose you could be right. But, if what you say is true, I must discover who it is immediately. They threaten the peace we have enjoyed for so very long. I would not see the day when dragons and humans are once again at war with each other."

"It may be too late for that, my lord," said Mother Tully. "I do not know what alliances have been forged by these rebel dragons or with whom, but you may find yourself forced to choose sides. I do know that the ruler of the lands that surround yours is beset with enemies. She has commissioned these two to find out who they are so she can try to bring them to justice." She paced the floor. "The fact that the dragons that took the peasants were known to the soldiers makes me wonder. It is too coincidental to believe that an agent from another kingdom is at work here. It would seem more likely the soldiers are loyal to those men who are her enemies."

"Then we share a common cause. If my people, renegade or other, are breaking the ancient treaties, I must do something to stop them." Golgoroth regarded Kalten and Paena. "If you have been tasked with learning who is renegade among your own people and those same people are helping the rebel elements within my people, perhaps we can help each other."

"I agree, my lord," Kalten said. "But how? A dragon is too obvious to have as a traveling companion. How could we possibly keep in touch with you?"

The dragon chuckled to himself before he spoke. "How quickly you children forget. Sometimes fate smiles upon us all. Do you not recall that as an effect of the healing to your companion, my son now has a bond of the minds with you two?"

"I'm not sure I believe a bond still exists," Kalten said. "I haven't felt anything of your son's thoughts or emotions since the healing. Paena, have you noticed anything?"

She could only numbly nod. "Yes, I have. At first, I wasn't sure what they were. But when Lydaroth last fled, I could feel his relief at being away from us. I think the link is painful for him."

"Not painful, I should think," Mother Tully said. "More... confusing. He has never been exposed to humans before, and now to have to share his mind with two must be very stressful."

"Do not worry about my son. He will do what is necessary."

"That's rather cold-hearted, don't you think?" Paena demanded.

"Not at all, child. Quite the opposite, in fact. You see, one day he will be the lord of these lands. He must begin to bear some of the responsibility now to avoid the full impact of it when I am no more."

"Nonsense, Golgoroth," Mother Tully said. "You are not more than a few thousand years old. You have lots of life to live yet."

"Anything can happen." The dragon shrugged his massive shoulders in an almost human way. "Besides, I did not say anything would happen. Just that eventually it will. Now. Let us not get sidetracked by such morose matters. We must decide what to do next."

"I believe we should leave right away," Paena said. At the dragon's surprised expression, she quickly reassured him, "Not because of any lack on your part, my lord. But, if you have discovered that the rebels have escaped, would not others of your kind soon know that too?"

"I suppose. Why?"

"I see what you're saying, Paena," Kalten said. "If you are only now checking, after we've arrived, might we be considered a problem by those who know the rebels?"

"Exactly. One of your people might decide the disappearance of three trouble-making humans might be in order."

The dragon gawped at their suggestion. "I cannot believe I need instruction from children. I must be getting senile to have missed that. Of course, you are correct. We must get you away from here and soon or you will be in danger before long." He addressed Mother Tully. "Is it possible you have enemies among the humans?"

"Yes, I am sure of it. It was a human plot that caused Paena's injuries. Why?"

"I ask this because we discovered a human in our lands shortly after you were brought here. This man has plied us with lies whenever questioned about who he is and why he is here. Perhaps he has come because of you three."

"Another human? Here? I thought all the ones who attacked us dead." Mother Tully's brow wrinkled at the new information. "May we see this man?"

"Of course." The old dragon stared at Paena for a few moments, causing her to squirm. "Paena, will you do something for me, please?"

"Certainly, my lord. What would you have me do?"

"Call out to my son. Ask him to come here." When she drew breath to shout out Lydaroth's name, he stopped her. "No, child. Not that way. I want you to call out to Lydaroth in your mind only."

She nodded at the old dragon, feeling confused. For several moments nothing happened. But then, they heard the sound of wings, faint at first, then gradually louder.

Shortly after first hearing the wings, Lydaroth landed in the clearing. He had an odd, perplexed expression on his face and paused on the grass, mesmerized by some inner turmoil.

Golgoroth gently nudged his son. "Son, why are you here?"

"I... I do not know, Sire. I felt summoned here. A voice in my mind kept calling to me, so I came."

"I knew it," Golgoroth said. "The bond exists, at least between Paena and my son."

"What are you talking about?" Lydaroth asked.

"The voice you heard belonged to Paena. I asked her to call you with her mind only. She did, and you heard her. That is why you are here now."

"That is terrible. What can I do to stop it?" Lydaroth asked, anxiety filling his voice.

"No, my son. It is wonderful, not terrible. I have been trying to think how we can work with these humans to recapture the renegades.

Now that you have a means to communicate with them, one of our main problems is solved."

Lydaroth appeared unconvinced. "You do not know what it is like, Sire. I feel violated by her mind."

"Nevertheless, you will live with it. Recapturing the renegades is too important to allow such childishness." Golgoroth reared up to his full height, towering over his son. "You will obey me in this. For now, at least, we must ally ourselves with these humans. You will be the one to deal directly with them. I told you before you would be responsible for them and so you are."

"Yes, Father." He could not meet his sire's eyes. "Is there anything else you wish of me?"

"Yes, my son, there is. I need you to fetch the other human and bring him here. Mother Tully thinks he might be following our new allies."

Lydaroth lifted his head. "Yes, Father. I will return shortly." He leapt into the air and was gone.

"Let us take what ease we can while we wait for my son's return," Golgoroth said, settling onto the grass of the meadow.

Paena, Kalten, and Mother Tully followed his example and had only waited for a short while before Paena heard the soft clap of beating wings. Lydaroth practically plowed into the turf in his haste to land. He was trailed at a respectable distance by a smaller, bronze dragon.

"My lord. The prisoner has escaped," Lydaroth said.

"Escaped?" Golgoroth demanded. "How? When?"

"It must have happened in the night. The guards are both gone along with the prisoner."

Everyone jumped back when Golgoroth roared and gnashed his teeth. "Treason! Find those guards and bring them to me."

The bronze dragon nodded and took to the air.

Lydaroth was about to leave when Golgoroth stopped him. "Stay, my son. I have a task for you to perform."

"Yes, Sire."

"Why would your guards take a human prisoner away?" Mother Tully asked. "Unless there is some sort of agreement between them. I wonder now, more than ever, if this man was after us."

"If he was, we must move quickly to get you out of these lands and back to your own," Golgoroth said.

"Yes. And I believe it should be done secretly," Mother Tully said. "It will be safer for us all."

"But how will we go without it being known?" Paena asked. "There are dragons constantly watching the borders."

"My son will take you. He will carry you high above our borders and away from these lands."

"That will prevent us from being detected?" Kalten asked.

"I believe so. Besides, none would question or challenge my son. Lydaroth, your first task will be to take these humans back to their lands and to safety. I will tell you more upon your return."

"As you command, Sire." The younger dragon slouched over to the humans and lay down before them. "Please climb onto my back. I cannot carry you all in my claws. Not without hurting you, anyway."

"Just a moment, young one," Mother Tully said. "We must gather our belongings before we go or we will be in trouble."

Golgoroth spoke once again. "While they are doing that, assign two of your trusted lieutenants to help. You are not a beast of burden, whether these are our allies or not. You three will carry the humans and their belongings, one each, in your claws. You may be disappointed by this task, but you will humble yourself before no one."

Paena walked up to the silver dragon and laid her hand on his shoulder. "Lydaroth, if I had known what a burden my healing would be to you, I never would have allowed it."

The silver dragon turned his head to look at her. "The decision was never yours to make, human. Or mine either for that matter. We all do what we must." The dragon straightened, looking more confident. "Pull your things together as the mighty Golgoroth commands while I find others to assist me. We will meet back here shortly."

He bounded into the air and flew off. Paena and the others rushed to collect their gear. It wasn't long before three dragons and three humans were airborne and well away from the dragon lands.

~ * ~

Lydaroth refused to speak to any of them during the flight. He simply glared at whoever spoke to him. Kalten could only wonder if they'd make it out of the dragon lands alive.

Despite Kalten's misgivings, Lydaroth did honor his father's wishes and before sunrise, they were dropped off in a clearing near a town. Kalten did not know which town.

"Thank you, Lydaroth," Mother Tully said. "We appreciate everything you and your people have done for us."

The silver dragon ignored the old woman. He instead spoke to his dragon companions. "You must return now. I will follow shortly." The two dragons indicated their understanding and flew off.

He sighed heavily before turning back to Mother Tully. "My apologies, honored lady. I do not mean to insult you or your companions, but what I have been ordered to do is distasteful to me."

"What is that, exactly?" Kalten asked, backing away from the dragon. "Do you intend to do murder in these woods?" He took hold of his sword.

"No, nothing like that. My sire has made an agreement with you, and he intends to fulfill it. What I mean is, I am to be available to you should more trouble arise. My sire will not have me move directly against humans, but I will do what I can covertly."

"How will we summon you if trouble comes?" Kalten asked.

"Her," Lydaroth said, looking directly at Paena. "I can hear her in my mind. That fact should be abundantly clear after last night."

"I hear you, gentle Lydaroth. Do not fear. I will not abuse this gift."

"Gift? Pah. It is a curse I wish to have lifted. But I will do as my sire commands. Do not call me without good reason or it will be worse for you."

"Thank you again, young dragon," Mother Tully said. "Our good wishes go with you. Now perhaps you should leave before you are seen."

The dragon nodded to them then flew off. They watched him leave. Within moments of his departure, the forest erupted with the sounds of birds.

"That was unpleasant," Kalten said. "He really doesn't like us, does he?"

"He doesn't like being forced to do this," Paena said. "He would have no opinion about us one way or the other if we weren't bonded. That's what makes him so angry toward us."

"He will get over it," Mother Tully said. "Or not. Either way, it does not matter. He has his orders. And he will follow them."

"I don't trust him," Kalten said. "How do we know he'll be there if we need him?"

She shouldered her pack. "A dragon would die rather than be dishonored. He will be wherever we need him, if he can. Of that you can be certain."

"This is getting us nowhere," Paena said. "Trust me when I say this. I have seen the true Lydaroth. He will be there for us. Now, what do we do next?"

Kalten shrugged. "We go to whatever town is closest, I suppose. We can decide what to do once we get there."

"I would suggest caution," Mother Tully said. "With the renegade dragons gone and Golgoroth unsure of friend or foe within his kingdom, word of us may have spread."

He grimaced. "You're probably right." Somehow, it just didn't feel right to agree with the old woman.

"Remember, we must find a trader's post too," said Paena. "We agreed to send word to Baltar."

Kalten picked his pack off the ground and scanned the surrounding trees. "Agreed. We will go to the closest town and find the trader's post. Perhaps we can get news of what's been happening."

Chapter Twenty-One

Pieter crouched behind some bushes and watched while Kalten and his two bitches left the clearing. It was only luck he'd found them at all. That, and his two helpful dragon compatriots. His smile was grim. In all his years of service to Duke Samuel, he had never even suspected the alliances the man possessed. It was amazing.

Amazing and truly timely that two of the renegade sympathizers had let him go. Pieter had no false illusions about his chances to escape without their help. They had freed him and the three of them laid low and waited. Pieter knew Kalten would move sooner or later.

It had been easy enough to follow his little group once they left. His dragon companions had merely flown higher and stayed back farther than Kalten's. It had been damn cold, but worth the discomfort. Pieter's new allies dropped him off and promised to leave word for the duke. That was the key to all of this. Duke Samuel needed to know that he, Pieter, still tracked the traitor and had the target in sight.

~ * ~

Lydaroth's idea of close to town turned out to be much different than that of his passengers. He had dropped them in the middle of a forest, and only Mother Tully's ability to communicate with the trees and birds allowed them to gain their bearings and navigate through it.

This forest was much different from the one she lived in. The trees were younger, for one thing, and much smaller. Kalten was delighted to be able to see the sun.

Mother Tully drafted a raven to lead them to civilization. The bird flew above and through the treetops, cawing at them in the annoying way ravens do whenever the trio fell behind. It took them an extra two days of steady travel to clear the remaining distance to the town.

The town was large, surrounded by high, fortified stone walls. The south wall was undergoing construction with scaffolding erected alongside and guards patrolling on top. Rolling grassland encircled the town with scattered flocks of sheep wandering and grazing on the grass.

Shepherds followed their charges, protecting them from predators of both the two and four-legged kinds.

They decided to go into the town in the early evening, just prior to the gates being closed for the night. They reasoned that fewer people would be about to see them. Such was not the case.

A rainstorm struck, and they were soaking wet by the time they arrived at the town. Guards, both at the gate and on the walls, challenged them when they were within hailing distance. Kalten had to explain several times that they were simple travelers looking for lodging for the night.

A grizzled sergeant questioned them until well after darkness had fallen before he let them into the town proper, and only then if they were accompanied to the closest inn.

The three were reluctantly escorted to a small, bedraggled inn called, ironically enough, The King's Palace. Judging by its condition, no king had visited this particular palace for several decades, if ever.

The foul stench of rotting straw, bile, and stale beer assailed their nostrils when they went through the door. A tall, well-dressed man stood behind the counter. Kalten was surprised to see such a dapper, young man running such a disreputable looking establishment.

Paena wrung water from her hair. "Are we staying here?"

"No. But we need to get rid of our escort. The closest inn seemed a good place to start," Kalten said. "I'm probably being too careful, but I don't want to risk anything. We can slip out after they've gone and find the trader's post."

"How long should we wait?" she asked.

Mother Tully wrinkled her nose in disgust. "Not too long, I hope." She shook water off her cloak. "This place reminds me why I prefer living away from people. If it were to burn down, only the vermin would miss it."

Kalten went to the door and peered out onto the street. "I can't be sure if they are still out there or not. It's too dark to really see anything."

"Let me look." Mother Tully strode to the door and stared out into the darkness. "Yes. They are still out there watching the inn. They probably want to see what we will do next."

"How can you be sure? I can't see anything or anybody. It's too dark."

"There are more ways to see than with your eyes, young man," Mother Tully said, waving her finger at Kalten. "You must learn to use all of your senses."

"Stop it, you two. Maybe we should look for a different way out if the front is being watched." Paena walked up to the innkeeper. "Excuse me, sir."

He glanced up at her. "Yes?"

"We're wondering if there's another way out of the inn. Maybe a back door?"

He backed away a step and stared suspiciously at her. "Why would you want to know that? You running from something?"

She flashed him a disarming smile. "Not at all. We'd just like to know." She dropped a silver coin onto the counter. "Now, about that back door?"

The innkeeper examined the coin closely before slipping it into his jacket pocket. "It's back down that corridor." He waved his hand. "I don't want any trouble, so be on your way." He turned from them and began examining himself with a small mirror.

"We should get out of here now," she said. "I don't trust this fellow. I wouldn't be surprised if he runs to the guard the moment we're gone."

The three hurried down the indicated corridor and through the kitchen's back door. They stepped out of the kitchen and back into the rain and darkness of the inn's stable yard. The pungent smell of horses filled the night.

They made their way down the dark streets and found another, much cleaner inn where they got directions to the trader's outpost. Naturally, the building was located in the warehouse district of the town. The torches lining the street became fewer and fewer the further they went and more than once, Kalten felt the need to loosen his sword from its scabbard.

The building resembled a small fortress. The closest windows were two stories off the street and barred. A high wall bracketed the front of the structure with a double gate on the side. The front entry had a stout oak door that appeared capable of stopping a siege. Kalten marched up to the door and pounded on it.

The wooden panel in the door eventually opened, and a sleepy face peered out. "Who's there? We're not expecting a courier tonight. What do you want?"

"Coltsfoot," Paena said quietly.

"Eh? What's that?" the fellow demanded.

"Coltsfoot," she repeated, more loudly. "Do you recognize the word, or are we wasting our time here?"

"Oh, I recognize it, right enough."

"Then let us in," Kalten said.

The man opened the door and pulled them inside. He was a

small, pale man with the beginnings of a considerable paunch and thinning hair. Dark circles rimmed his eyes and, by his apparel, he had just come from bed. He stepped back in confusion when Mother Tully came out of the darkness.

"Who are you then? Be quick about answering or you're right back outside," the man demanded.

"We're travelers working for Master Baltar. We have news we need relayed to him," Kalten said.

"News for Master Baltar? Who are you? Come into the light so I can better see you."

Kalten and Paena both moved into the light. The man stared suspiciously at them. "Who did you say you are?"

"We are Kalten and Paena, and we have news that must be sent to the Master Trader immediately."

"If you are Kalten and Paena, who's this? No one said anything about three travelers." The man seemed ready to push them back out the door.

"No, wait," Kalten said. "This woman has been helping us. We met her near Thistledown. She's gotten us out of some pretty serious troubles."

"I'm not sure about this. The messages told me very specifically about the two of you. No one said anything about others—"

"If it'll make you feel any better, we will vouch for her," Paena said. "If there's any problem with this, it'll be on our heads."

"I don't know…"

"What will happen to you if we were here to report and you sent us away? If someone finds out you were the one responsible for blocking our report, then what?"

The man seemed to consider this before he herded them into the chamber and put his hands on his hips, scowling fiercely at them. "Where have you been? We were told to expect a report from you more than eight days ago."

"We ran into some problems," Kalten replied. The long night, the cold and wet only made the man's attitude more annoying. "Who are you to scold us? I didn't see you out there."

"My name is Randolf, and I'm not a field operative. I don't muddy my hands with such things."

"Maybe you should," Mother Tully said, speaking for the first time. "You look a little soft, boy. Maybe you need some hardening." She punctuated each word with a jab to the man's sunken chest, backing him against a wall.

For a brief moment Kalten actually liked the old woman.

"No need to get angry." Randolf held his hands up to fend her off. "We were just told you'd be coming and approximately when. The delay has everyone worried. We've had couriers riding between outposts almost without stop the past several days trying to find you."

Paena rubbed her eyes. "Well, we're here now and glad for it. A great deal has happened in the past few days, and we have vital information to get back to Lord Baltar." When the man did nothing, she pushed past him, peering through doors. "We'd dearly love to warm up and get some rest, if you don't mind."

Randolf stared at her for a few moments before shaking his head as if to clear it. "Forgive me, please. I'm clearly not awake yet." He hurried to the front door and closed it, carefully locking it. "Please follow me, and I'll take you to your rooms so you can get out of your cold, wet clothing and into something warmer."

He handed each of them a candle before he led them further into the building and up a set of stairs. Each were shown a room.

Before he left, he had a final message. "Please take your time to get settled and changed. But come to the dining room before you retire for the night. I'll have some food prepared. I can write down any messages you might have while you eat." He shrugged apologetically. "Our instructions were most clear. We were to get any information you had to give when you arrived and get it sent out to the capital."

"We'll be down shortly," Kalten said before he closed his door. He waited for a moment behind the door and listened. The trader let out a gusty sigh and mumbled something before he shambled off. Paena and Mother Tully had already gone into their rooms.

Kalten turned away from the door and held the candle up to see the room more clearly. A bed, chair, and desk were the only furnishings. A single, tiny window of real glass was set into the outside wall covered by shutters, and an unlit fireplace was inset into the wall closest to the foot of the bed. He was glad to see firewood had been set out in advance.

He lit the fire and hurried to change out of his wet clothing, shivering when the cold material touched his skin. He placed the chair near the fire and draped his travel clothes over it to dry.

The rumbling of his belly reminded him he was hungry and still expected to report their findings. He put on his spare boot liners, took the candle then left the room.

At the sound of his door closing, Paena poked her head out of her room. "Ready to go down? Wait a moment, and I'll come with you." She ducked back into her room for a few moments, and then came back out with her own candle.

"I'll let Mother Tully know we're ready," she said. She went to the old woman's door and pressed her ear against the wood. She grinned. "Kalten, come here."

He went closer to the door. The old woman's unmistakable snores could be heard rattling the window. "Maybe we should let her sleep. I don't think she needs to report anything."

Paena nodded and made her way down the stairs, Kalten right behind her. He didn't know about her, but he looked forward to finally getting the information delivered and off to Baltar. That and to sleep indoors.

Chapter Twenty-Two

Kalten woke and sat bolt upright in his bed and heard the screams again. They were unmistakably Paena's. He leapt out of the bed and rushed to her room.

She was sitting up in her bed, sobbing into her covers. He could just make her huddled form out in the glow of her fire. Mother Tully was already there, comforting the girl.

She glared at him when he ran into the room. "Took you long enough, you big lump."

"I thought I was dreaming. I didn't realize it was Paena until she screamed the second time."

"More like the third time," the old woman grumbled. "There, there dear. Calm down and tell Mother Tully what has you in such a state." The old woman held Paena like a child and slowly rocked her back and forth.

"It was horrible. Horrible!" The last word was almost a screech.

"Shhh, shhh, little one. Take a deep breath and tell me what happened." The old woman spoke to Kalten then. "Would you light the candle for us and then fetch her some tea, please? With some honey in it. She needs something to help her calm down."

He nodded and took a splinter from beside the candlestick and used it to light the candle from the fire. He then rushed down to the kitchen to make the tea.

"What's all the fuss about? What's going on?" the cook asked as Kalten entered.

"Need to make some tea. My companion has been having night terrors and needs something to settle herself." He rummaged around the kitchen, looking for tea and a pot.

"Here now, I'll do that. Don't want no strangers messing up my kitchen. You get back up to your lady, and I'll bring tea up for her shortly." The cook all but chased Kalten out of the room.

He hurried to Paena's room. Only Mother Tully was there.

"Where's the tea?"

"Cook's making it." He looked around the room. "Where's Paena?"

"Obviously, not here." The old woman frowned at him. "She went to wash up. She still has not said a word about what is bothering her."

"Do you know what's wrong?"

"Never you mind." The old woman shook her head. "You might as well come in, Paena. We are not saying anything in your absence that would not be said with you here."

Paena came into the room and glared at him.

He didn't meet her gaze. "I'm just worried about you."

"I'll be fine, Kalten."

"When start waking up in the middle of the night screaming, what am I supposed to do?"

"Yes, child. What happened to cause you to wake up like that?" Mother Tully asked.

"I had a dream. A terrible dream."

Before she could continue, Mother Tully stopped her. "Just a moment, child. Let me check on the tea with the cook and you can tell us then. Kalten, please bring the chair from my room so we can all sit comfortably." The old woman left for the kitchen, and Kalten retrieved the rocking chair that was in her room.

He stoked the fire before the old woman returned carrying a tray that included tea and small snacks.

Mother Tully set the tray down on the desk and poured out three cups of tea. She stirred a healthy spoonful of honey to one cup and forced it into Paena's trembling hands. "Drink that down, and not a word until you do."

She had no choice but to sip at her tea. Kalten and Mother Tully sat and waited, their own cups of tea cooling on the tray.

Paena finally set her cup down on the tray. The tears had dried from her cheeks. "Thank you for this. It's really helped."

"I am glad, child. Now, can you tell us what this is all about?"

"I'm not exactly sure. It was the oddest dream."

"Maybe if you talk about it, it'll make more sense to you," said Kalten.

Paena sighed and sat up in her chair. "I dreamed I was a dragon, a silver one, and I was flying high above the clouds. As I did, I noticed a speck in the distance. As I neared the speck, it kept getting bigger. For some reason, it seemed very familiar." She stopped speaking for a moment, her gaze on the fireplace.

"As I flew, I was able to see it more clearly. At first, I could only make out a gold splotch. Then I could see it was another dragon. Eventually I knew the dragon was Golgoroth." She stopped again.

"What happened then?" Kalten asked. "Your dream doesn't sound so bad. At least, not bad enough to make you wake up screaming."

"I was just getting to that." She closed her eyes and continued to talk, "As we approached one another, the clouds below got thicker and thicker. But the sun shone above me so I didn't care. I was just happy to see Golgoroth again." She paused for a second. "Isn't that odd that I would be happy to see him? I was more than a little afraid of him when I last saw him."

She shook her head. "Anyway, we had almost met when a trio of dragons burst up through the clouds and attacked Golgoroth. They were smaller than he but struck with such ferocity he was soon torn and bleeding. I tried to go and help him, but three more dragons appeared and came after me. I fled and, since I was much larger and faster than them, I evaded them easily.

"When they couldn't catch me, they joined the first three in the assault on Golgoroth." Her voice broke with a loud sob. "Before long, I saw him fall from the sky. I called out to him, but it was too late. That's when I woke up."

She buried her head in her hands crying. Mother Tully grabbed her shoulders and shook her.

"Enough of that. We need to understand the dream. Tell me, what color were the dragons in your dream?"

"I remember a green one and a blue. I'm not sure of the others. But their appearance was odd, almost dirty. The colors were not vibrant like the dragons we met in the Dragon Lands."

Mother Tully frowned. "It could very well be that the dragons in your dreams were the renegades. They would not look quite the same as those we know. They would be darker in coloring."

"But how could I know that?" Paena asked. "I've never seen any like them before."

"Unless your dream wasn't really a dream."

"How could a dream not be a dream?" Kalten asked.

"It could have been real events," Mother Tully said, "seen through the eyes of a silver dragon. A silver dragon known to us all."

"Lydaroth," Paena whispered. "Oh no. I was seeing things through his eyes." She choked back a short cry. "But that would mean that he and Golgoroth were attacked. I must get to him."

"Assuming you are correct, what could you do?" Kalten asked.

"I don't know," Paena said. "I just know I must find him and get to him."

"Why would she see this?" he asked. "Why now?"

"The bond formed by her healing is likely still growing," said Mother Tully. "How great that bond will eventually be, I do not know."

"That doesn't matter now." Paena began gathering her things. "I've got to get to him. He saved my life once and needs me. I must get to him."

Kalten grabbed her arms to stop her. "Paena, listen to me. How are you going to find him? It's the middle of the night. How are we going to get out of the city? He could be anywhere."

She twisted herself free of his grasp. "I will find him. I am sure of it. Nothing else matters."

"This is crazy," he said. "Mother Tully, tell her how foolish this is."

Mother Tully shook her head. "I am afraid I must agree with Paena. If Lydaroth and Golgoroth are in danger, we must help however we can."

"I don't understand how you think we can help them," Kalten said. "We don't have any special weapons we can use in their defense."

"Not now, we don't," Mother Tully said. "I have an idea that may work given time. But consider this: if renegade dragons are involved in the affairs of your kingdom as we believe them to be, we will need the help of the dragon nation. Without Lydaroth and Golgoroth, that aid will never come and your queen will fall."

"Can you share your idea?" Kalten asked.

"No, not yet. You will know when it is time."

"Can you help me get to him?" Paena asked. "You have magic. Perhaps you could even get us there faster?"

"I cannot," Mother Tully said. "My powers have been overtaxed as of late, and I must continue to allow them to regenerate."

"That figures. We will just fight dragons with swords and arrows, then." Kalten let out a heavy sigh. "Fine, I'll see about getting us out of the city. Maybe even with horses. Just promise you won't leave without me?" He didn't wait around to hear the answer.

Chapter Twenty-Three

"They've escaped me? Again?" Pieter couldn't believe his ears. So close to finally capturing Kalten, and the boy slips through his fingers once more. "What does the duke pay you for? Surely you have heard of the traitor Kalten?"

He and Randolf were in the stable of the trader's outpost. It was late, and all the stable hands were asleep. A few sleepy looking horses leaned out of the various stalls that ran down both sides of the barn.

He checked Pieter up and down. "Of course I've heard of him. But I couldn't have stopped him without drawing attention to myself."

Pieter grabbed the man by his collar. "You coward. You would allow a fugitive to escape to protect yourself?"

Randolf yanked his shirt from Pieter's hand. "I would allow a fugitive to escape to protect the duke." He glared at Pieter. "If they had learned who I really worked for, I would never have gotten their report. Did you ever think of that? Now I can pass their suspicions off to the duke instead of allowing them to reach the queen. Besides..." He airily waved. "I know where they are going. I've already alerted the commander of the North Eastern strike force. I'll leave it to him to capture the traitor."

"Not bad. Not bad at all." Pieter said, making a show of straightening the man's shirt. "Maybe I was wrong about you." He walked toward the door.

"Do you have any message for Duke Samuel?"

"Let him know I'll be hanging around here for a few days watching for Kalten or his women should they manage to get back."

"Where will you be? In case I need to get in contact with you?"

Pieter's grin was feral. "I'll be here and there. But don't worry, I'll check in with you if something comes in."

~ * ~

Lydaroth was out there, Paena could feel him. From the moment she realized what the dream meant, she felt his presence and his pain.

She hadn't really noticed how or when Kalten and Mother Tully bundled her out of the town. Paena had been searching for Lydaroth with her mind, probing the link to try to find exactly where he was and, more importantly, how he was.

"Can you still feel Lydaroth out there?" Mother Tully asked, startling Paena out of her reverie.

She looked around, seeing nothing but trees. "I'm sorry, Mother Tully?"

"Yes, child. Can you still feel Lydaroth's presence?"

"Yes, I can. We're getting close now."

They all heard Lydaroth long before they saw him. The forest echoed with his bellows and roars of anguish. The sound of trees being torn and shredded frightened the horses, making them difficult to control.

Kalten rode up beside her. "Paena, we should tie the horses here and go the rest of the way on foot. It won't be long before they refuse to move at all."

"He is right. These poor creatures are frightened out of their minds right now. It has been a struggle for me to keep them calm this long. We should not force them further."

Paena focused on them. "All right, let's tie them here. Lydaroth isn't far now." Stiff from the long ride, she awkwardly climbed from her horse. The animal made it more challenging, prancing and snorting with agitation.

They tied the horses to a nearby deadfall, picketing them so they could graze, before they set off toward Lydaroth. They had no trouble seeing where he had been.

Burned and ripped up trees bore mute testament to the dragon's rage and grief. They followed the swath of destruction.

They crept through the shattered forest, listening to the sounds of shattering trees. All at once, the noise stopped.

"How much farther before we find Lydaroth?" Kalten asked.

"I don't know." Paena stopped to concentrate for a moment. "Lydaroth is very close and very angry… at us." She leapt at her friends. "Get down!"

Her warning almost came too late. Kalten and Mother Tully dropped to the ground just before a massive burst of flame shot toward them.

"Lydaroth, stop. It's us," Paena said. "We came to help."

"I know who you are. But who did you come to help? Me or the renegades?" The voice of Lydaroth came from somewhere in the smoldering trees. "Have you come to gloat over the death you have caused?"

"Paena felt your pain and sensed the danger you were in," Kalten said. "We came to help you."

"We had nothing to do with the attack on Golgoroth," Paena said.

Lydaroth roared in fury and stormed over to them, smashing trees out of his way. He loomed over them and exhaled a huge ball of fire at them. Just before the fire struck, Mother Tully stepped forward, held up her hands and forced the flames around them. Grass and branches curled into ash at the fire's touch.

Kalten pulled out his sword, ready to defend against the infuriated dragon, but Mother Tully was ahead of him again. She snatched a stout branch from the ground and smacked it into the dragon's tender nose. Lydaroth leapt back from the old woman with a yelp.

"How dare you sully your sire's memory in this way!" she shrieked at him, shaking the branch in anger. "No dragon has attacked a human in centuries, and you decide to break this truce, his truce, now? What is wrong with you?"

The dragon stalked back toward Mother Tully. "Do not dare lecture me about truces and my actions, crone. I attack those responsible for his death."

"Do we look like dragons, you fool? How can even your small brain make such a mistake?"

The dragon stopped his advance. "I know you are not dragons. And you may not have been the ones who actually attacked my sire, but you are ultimately to blame. No dragon has battled another in over a thousand years. You three show up, and in less than a ten-day, not only do dragons ambush Golgoroth, but they kill him."

The old woman shook her head and sighed. "Your emotions have clouded your thinking, Lydaroth. How could the arrival of three humans prompt this action? Why would any dragon do such a reprehensible thing just because of us?"

"I-I do not know," the dragon said. "It does not make any sense."

"Lydaroth, did you recognize any of the attackers?" Paena asked. "I think I saw them through your eyes… in a dream. But they were not the ones I met earlier with you."

The confused expression returned to the dragon's face. "They seemed familiar, and not at the same time. They were not from the Dragon Lands, though. Of that I am certain."

"Could they have been from the rebel factions?" Kalten asked.

He snorted. "The rebels are not capable of flight. Do you not remember anything you were told?"

"I remember." Kalten glared at the dragon, his hands on his hips.

"So how did they escape their confinement? What you apparently don't recall is we think they might have been helped out by rebels of our own. You do recall that our queen is up against several renegade lords?"

"Do not talk down to me, boy. I could incinerate you where you stand."

"No, I do not think you could." Mother Tully tapped the branch against her boot. "You can try again, of course. But you will fail. And you have been acting very foolishly." She stared meaningfully around at the destruction surrounding them. "You should have been securing your sire's body. Instead, you chose to lay waste to everything around you in a temper tantrum. It is quite obvious to me that you have not bothered to think this entire thing through. Rather, you cling to the easiest answer you could find, regardless of how unlikely it is."

"Stop lecturing me. I am no hatchling, woman."

"Then start acting like an adult and stop acting so foolishly. You obviously do not realize the danger we are all in here."

"Danger?" asked Paena.

Mother Tully glared at her. "I hope you have not shut off your brain too. What do you suppose happened to the attacking dragons? You did not say Lydaroth defeated them. I seem to recall you saying that he fled from them. Where did they go? It seems unlikely they would abandon their attack just because he ran away."

Lydaroth ducked his head at the old woman's words. Paena understood. She felt the same. He spoke first. "What should I do, then?"

"Fly. Fly back to the Dragon Lands and gather support. With Golgoroth gone, you are more important than ever."

"I will not leave Golgoroth here. I cannot leave him here."

"Is Golgoroth alive?" Mother Tully challenged.

"No."

"Then there is nothing more you can do. If the other dragons return, you are in trouble. If humans return, we are in trouble. Would you risk everything for a corpse?"

"I would not leave him to be carved up for a prize."

"Can you carry him back with you?" Kalten asked.

Lydaroth glared at him. "No! He is much too heavy for me to lift and fly at the same time."

"Then you must either leave him or destroy his remains," Mother Tully said. "But either way, you must make haste and leave here. We cannot lose you too."

"Why do you keep saying how important I am? I am no leader."

"You will be. You must be. Both for the sake of the dragons and humans."

"There are other elders besides Golgoroth in the dragon lands. One of them will lead."

"I do not think so, Lydaroth. Your sire was well respected for his wisdom and strength. Those who admired and respected him will expect the same from you. No one but you will do. The sooner you accept this, the better."

"I will think on what you have said."

"Do that, but do not waste too much time. If you do not step up and take over where Golgoroth left off, there will be civil war in the Dragon Lands. It will be dragon against dragon on a greater scale than ever before. And while your kind battles it out, the human kingdom will also be destroyed."

Kalten frowned. "Why should our kingdom be affected by dragon affairs? It's been so long since dragons have been seen, they are considered children's stories."

Mother Tully whacked Kalten on the head with the branch. "Why have you all stopped thinking? Are you all so stupid you do not see how one thing affects the other?"

He glared at her. "Don't do that again, old woman."

Paena stepped between the two. "Kalten, please don't fight. Maybe Mother Tully will explain herself."

Mother Tully sighed. "If that is what will convince you fools to be afraid, then I will." She regarded both Kalten and Lydaroth. "Are you two paying attention, now? I do not want to explain this again."

Lydaroth nodded. Kalten just stared at her, arms folded across his chest.

"Kalten, you said dragons took cages filled with people from that fort, did you not?" At his reluctant nod, she continued, "And did you not also say they were colored but seemed to be dark, almost shadowed looking?"

"Yes."

"Does that not seem to fit the description of your attackers, Lydaroth?"

"Yes, it does," he said.

"Lydaroth, you have said that the rebels cannot fly because of their environment and the lack of strong metals available to them. Golgoroth said none of your people left the Dragon Lands. Yet Kalten has seen flying dragons taking people from a human camp, and the rebels are nowhere to be found. And the humans seem to have expected them. Does this not sound like cooperation?"

"Yes, it certainly does show cooperation. But it still does not prove who these dragons are," said Lydaroth.

"If the humans are cooperating with dragons to provide slaves, could they not also have provided the metals needed to attain flight? With those metals, could the rebels not have escaped?" Paena asked.

"Of course," he said. "But what can the humans be expecting in return?"

"Support in battle," Kalten said. "I hate to admit it, but you're probably right. I'll bet the rebel lords have convinced the renegade dragons to fight with them. They must plan to overthrow both kingdoms."

"What should I do?" Lydaroth asked.

"Go. Get back to your kingdom and prepare your people. Take control and be ready to fight," Mother Tully said.

"What will you do?"

"We will keep on our mission," Kalten said. "We'll continue to gain support for the queen and learn who her enemies are. It's the only way she can be ready for the coming war."

"I will go, and when the time comes, I will know. My connection with Paena is unwelcome, but it does provide us a means to communicate."

"What of Golgoroth?" Paena asked.

"I will hide his body as Mother Tully has suggested. I will bring back a guard of honor to return him home. I am sorry I attacked you. You have proven yourselves friends."

Mother Tully waved after he leapt into the air. "Good luck."

~ * ~

"What do we do now?" Paena asked. "Do we stay and wait for Lydaroth to come back?"

"Like we told Lydaroth…" Kalten stopped speaking as a soldier emerged out of hiding to block their path.

The man said nothing and just stood in their way, his sword drawn. Moments later they were surrounded by several grim-looking men. Every one of them had either a sword in hand or a bow drawn and ready.

"Drop your weapons," the group's leader said, taking charge. He was a beefy man dressed all in forest green leather like his men. Instead of a helmet, he wore a leather cap. A scar on his face made the right side of his face droop comically, though his expression was anything but funny.

Kalten put his hand on his sword. "By what authority do you threaten innocent travelers?"

Paena mutely shook her head, putting her hand on his wrist.

"What authority?" The man laughed. "I would say the eight men ready to kill you should be answer enough? Now, drop your weapons."

Paena unbuckled her sword belt and pulled the knife from her boot, putting them into a neat pile on the ground. Kalten followed her example.

"Move away from the weapons," the leader said with a wave of his sword. He addressed the man on his left. "Barton, take their weapons."

"Yes, sergeant." The soldier gathered their weapons into his arms and backed out of the circle.

"Now then," said the sergeant, "you are under arrest and will come with us."

"Arrest? But we have done nothing wrong. What are the charges?" Mother Tully asked.

The man laughed a hard, bitter laugh. "Don't need any charges. Same answer as before. We have orders to arrest all deserters." He scrutinized Kalten closely. "You have led the duke on a merry chase, fellow. He has been most interested in your capture."

Kalten's heart was in his throat. He'd suspected as much. Still, he could try and bluff his way out of the trouble. "You have me mistaken for someone else, Sergeant. I'm no deserter."

"You are a liar, boy. Round them up, and let's get moving," the sergeant ordered his men.

"Mother, can't you do something?" Paena asked.

"No, child. I am still too weak."

The sergeant laughed again. "There's very little you could do, old woman. Except maybe act as a pincushion for my men to practice on."

"Where are you taking us?" Paena asked.

"You'll see soon enough. Now, stop jawing." The sergeant pointed with his sword. "Move 'em out, boys." The troop formed around their prisoners and marched them away.

They traveled all that day, stopping only occasionally. By early twilight, they had reached a large open meadow where dozens of tents were pitched. Watch fires were already lit around the camp's perimeter. Campfires burned amongst the tents, and Kalten could smell the aromas of cooking food.

"Who goes there?" a sentry challenged.

"Sergeant Rossel coming back from long patrol, sentry. We bring prisoners."

"Come forward and be identified, Sergeant."

The sergeant emerged into the light of the watch fire and waited. The sentry, after handing his pike to one of his comrades, approached the sergeant. The two had a huddled conversation for a few moments before the sergeant waved his men forward. The soldiers drove Mother Tully, Paena and Kalten along with them.

"Take the prisoners to the holding pens," the sergeant ordered. "Separate 'em so they don't get any ideas."

"Sergeant, the new pen isn't ready yet, and we've only got room in the big one," one of the soldiers said.

"What's the flamin' holdup? That was to be finished days ago," the sergeant demanded.

"I'm sure I don't know, sergeant," the same soldier replied. "I've been on sentry duty for the past seven-day."

"Whatever. Throw them all in together then," the sergeant growled. "Me, I've got to report what we've found to the captain." He turned and strode off without another word.

Kalten and the others were locked inside a palisade constructed of stout logs. Two of the soldiers remained outside to stand guard.

Paena paced around the palisade.

"You doing okay?" Kalten asked, stepping in front of her.

"What? What did you say?" she said, speaking just a little too fast.

"I asked if you are all right. You seem rattled by something." He plopped himself down against the wall directly opposite the gate. "I don't need our bond to know that."

"I don't like being caged up." She crouched beside him. "And I…I don't like soldiers."

"Is that why you were so hard on me when we first met?"

"No? Maybe? I don't know."

"I don't like being caged up either. And you don't like soldiers? There's got to be more to it than that."

"I've got my reasons."

"Care to share them? I might be able to help."

"You can't help. No one can."

"Try me."

"You're not going to leave me alone until I tell you, are you?" Paena asked.

"Nope," he said.

"Fine." She sat beside him.

He straightened against the wall. "What is it?"

"Soldiers murdered my family."

"What? How?" He was dumbfounded. "Paena. I'm really sorry."

She choked back a sob. "It's not your fault. But when we were captured earlier, it reminded me so strongly of that day. It was all I could do to stay calm."

"I would never have known. You were so controlled."

"I didn't want to be," Paena said. "I wanted to attack those men, but I knew it would just get us all killed."

"Paena..."

"Please, let me finish. It reminded me of that day, and I was terrified. I still am." She leaned toward him. "I don't know if I can stand this for very long. I need you to tell me we'll get out of this."

He took her head between his hands and looked her into the eyes. "Paena, I know this is my fault, but somehow we are going to get out of here." Kalten pulled her over and held her. "Just keep it together. I need you strong so we can escape when the time comes."

She beckoned to Mother Tully. "Come sit with us, Mother, we need to stay warm."

The logs still held some of the heat of the day and brought some comfort. Kalten and the women huddled together, unsure of what was to come for him and them.

Chapter Twenty-Four

"Have any of the couriers brought word of Kalten and Paena?" Baltar paced behind his desk. Sunlight streamed through the large horizontal windows, illuminating the pile of parchment heaped his desk. Maps adorned the walls.

"No, my lord," Kenneth, his adjutant said. The man was clearly unhappy to be delivering bad news and avoided Baltar's eyes. "To make matters worse, five more riders have not reported back."

"Five?" Baltar couldn't believe his ears. "We've lost five more riders? Didn't you order them to ride the back roads only at night?"

"I did, my lord. Even with those measures, more have disappeared."

He slammed his fist down onto the desk. "Darkness take that traitorous duke!" He resumed his pacing. "The change in routes alone should have saved us couriers, and yet we have lost more than ever. The only explanation is we have a leak somewhere in our network."

"I agree, my lord. But how do we find such a leak?" Kenneth pulled off his cap and scrubbed a hand through his dark hair. "And how do we function until the leak is plugged?"

Baltar scowled. "We must continue to send the men out. But we have to track the routes they take and where they disappear. Perhaps that will lead us to the one we seek."

"Would it help if we sent the men in pairs? They might be able to protect each other that way."

Baltar sighed. "Would that I could, Kenneth. Your suggestion has merit, but we don't have the men to spare."

"My lord, if the men hear of this, we may not have any. It would be better to cover fewer routes than none at all."

"You are right. Post the orders. All men are to travel in pairs. Have them focus on the lands closer to the capital." Baltar poured himself a glass of wine and twirled the red liquid. "Let us hope that will give us enough warning. Oh, and Kenneth?"

"Yes, my lord?"

"Remind the men to keep an ear out for word of Kalten and Paena."

~ * ~

Kalten, Paena, and Mother Tully hadn't waited long in the prisoner's compound before Kalten was brought to the commanding officer's tent for interrogation.

"We were simply traveling," he said when questioned. "We were curious about the destruction and were searching the area. I don't understand why that's so hard to believe."

The captain appeared to be almost thirty and had sandy brown hair, a narrow face, and a close-cropped beard. Nothing unusual about him except for the fact he didn't wear any livery.

That was a surprise. Kalten had come in expecting to see Duke Samuel's crest everywhere, yet it was noticeably absent.

The captain was either unaware of Kalten's scrutiny or ignored it. "You must think me a fool, boy. My men reported that a dragon flew off shortly before your capture. Either you're very stupid or lying to me. No one with any sense would be near a dragon."

Kalten put on his most innocent face. "A dragon, Captain? My word. We never knew. It is a very good thing your men happened along to chase it away or we would surely have been in trouble."

"You and I both know my men had nothing to do with that monster leaving the area." The captain eyed Kalten.

"It's clear to me you were up to something." The captain shrugged. "The duke wants you whether you tell me what I want to know or not. Perhaps his jailers will be able to extract more information from you than I. If it were up to me, I'd have you flogged before you go, just to give the men a lesson on desertion, but the duke wants you intact. Mind you, he never said anything about your companions. Perhaps I could flog one of them. Maybe the old woman?"

Kalten laughed. "The last men to attack her didn't survive to tell the story."

The captain leaned forward. "Really? Tell me more."

"I think I'll let you figure it out for yourself. She's pretty harmless when not threatened, but if you cross her…" Kalten left that statement unfinished.

The captain appeared unimpressed. "Boy, it's lucky for you I don't torture women." He beckoned to a soldier. "Take him back to the pen, and then assemble a troop. They're to escort this deserter and his companions to the keep first thing in the morning."

He put special emphasis on the word, *deserter*—a mixture of contempt and outright anger.

"Yes, sir," the man said, saluting. He and a guard from outside the tent marched Kalten back to the log palisade.

Paena and Mother Tully crowded around him. "What do we do now?" Paena asked.

"Kalten, do you think the guards might be convinced to help us?" Mother Tully asked.

"Unlikely, but I could talk to them. They might relate to what we're going through, I suppose." He stepped up to the bars of the cage. "Hey, you," he called out to a guard who leaned heavily on his spear outside their jail.

The guard ignored him.

"Hey, you, guard." Kalten spoke louder this time. "I want to talk to you."

The guard regarded him with a bored expression. This man was older with the hard face of a veteran. He was dressed in the infantry standard boiled leather. "That may be, but I don't want to talk to you. Now shut up and leave me alone."

Kalten wouldn't be deterred. "They treating you well? Getting enough food and sleep?"

"Leave off. I already told you I have nothin' to say."

"You leave anyone special behind to join up? I did. Left my entire family behind. My mother, my sisters, and my sweetheart. Do you know what happened when I finally got home?"

Kalten waited. He thought the man was at least listening to him. "Do you know what happened? When I finally had enough and went home, my family was gone. And they hadn't been there for years. All the neighbors too, including my sweetheart."

He paused for a moment. "You didn't leave a sweetheart behind, did you? Or family? Are they still where you left them? Mine aren't, and no one seems to know what happened to them."

The guard turned to face him.

"Soldier," a voice commanded from the darkness. "Stand down and find your replacement. I'll watch the prisoners while you're gone." The captain appeared out of the night. "My men aren't going to listen to you, Kalten. They know the punishment for treason, as I'm sure you do. And the duke wants to make an example of you."

Kalten tried to keep his features neutral. He couldn't let the captain see how he truly felt. "I don't know what you're talking about. It's like we told you before. I'm not the man you seek. We are simple travelers, nothing more."

"That's still your story, is it? I heard you as much as tell my guard you are a deserter, just like the duke said." The captain leaned closer to Kalten. "I will be posting a double guard on you immediately. And tomorrow, you will visit my lord's keep. Perhaps he will learn something of interest from you."

As he straightened, two soldiers dressed identically to the previous one marched up and saluted him. He returned their salutes. "Ah, good. Men, guard these dangerous prisoners well. If any of them attempt to speak to you, kill the women immediately. Am I understood? I need him alive, unfortunately."

The men spoke in unison. "Yes, sir."

"Excellent." The captain took one last look at Kalten before striding back into the darkness. The two soldiers took their positions guarding the cage.

Kalten slumped back against the cage and buried his head in his hands. "Sorry, ladies. That didn't help us at all."

Paena knelt beside him. "It helped a little. We now know the duke is still looking for you."

"He knows about both of you now," Kalten said. "That's worse."

"Boy, you are a real clod," said Mother Tully. Although her words were harsh, the tone was gentle. "These men are obviously under your duke's command. He must be very powerful to operate so openly. Isn't that the information your queen seeks?"

"Hush. The guards will hear you," Kalten said at the mention of the queen. "We can't go mentioning her where anyone can overhear. Besides, I don't think this would qualify as new information. Certainly not proof."

"They will not hear us, nor will the spies standing just outside the light trying to listen in. I have made it so they cannot hear our words. I may be old, but I am not feeble-minded."

"You can do that?" Paena said, in wonder.

"That and much more."

"What else?" he demanded. "Why haven't you summoned your birds and animals to attack our guards? Maybe break us out of here?"

Mother Tully glared at him. "If you take a more civil tone with me, I might tell you, boy."

"Apologize to Mother Tully, Kalten," Paena said, her tone worried. "She hasn't done anything wrong."

For a moment, he thought about refusing. First, Mother Tully threatened to kill him. Now, every time he started relaxing around the old woman, another secret came out. Could she ever be trusted? But being hard-headed wouldn't get them out of this situation. He sighed. "I'm sorry."

"What was that? I could not hear you, boy."

"Please, Mother Tully. Can't we just forget about this? We need everyone working together, or we won't survive."

"Very well, child. But I do not appreciate his lack of respect."

Paena ignored the old woman's complaint. "I'm glad that's settled." Her tone left no room for argument. "Mother, is there anything you can do to help us get out of here?"

For the briefest moment, Kalten thought he could see an expression of glee on the old woman's face. But as soon as it appeared it was gone again. Must have been the light playing tricks on his eyes.

"Well, there was a time I could have done more, but those days are long gone. I'm afraid my powers are all but faded now." She shook her head sadly.

"Faded? I've seen you command a flock of birds to destroy a squad of soldiers. That doesn't sound faded to me," he said.

"You are content to make me repeat how weak I've become, boy. But yes, there was a time I could have raised every creature within the kingdom to do my bidding. Compared to that, my powers are considerably weakened. I have also been using my powers to some degree for the past few days. That has weakened me even more."

"Is there nothing you can do?" Paena asked.

The old woman considered for a moment. "I should still be able to call upon some of my old abilities, but I must regain some of strength first." She woman moved away and laid down. Within moments her snores echoed within the space.

~ * ~

"I can get us out of here, but it would require sacrifice on your part." The old woman hadn't slept long before she made the pronouncement.

"What would we have to do?" Paena asked.

"Wait a minute. Sacrifice? What kind of sacrifice?" Kalten said. He had a sick feeling he wasn't going to like what she had to say. Hadn't he already promised a life back in the witch's glade?

The old woman chuckled. "Nothing a strapping lad like yourself cannot afford to give, I assure you."

"Then, what?" he said.

"A bit of blood and an oath from each of you would probably be enough."

He was skeptical. "What would that do?"

"It would give me enough power to get us all out of here and on to safety. Surely the price is worth the reward?"

He swore to himself. "How will some blood and an oath give

you that power? You're not making any sense."

"Mother Tully, I must confess, I don't understand this either," Paena said.

"Do either of you follow any gods?" The question was unexpected.

"What's that got to do with anything?" It figured. Try to get an answer from her, and she responded with another question. Kalten had almost had enough.

"It is a simple question. Your answer will help me to explain things better."

"My family believed in several gods," Paena said. "Mostly the gods of our ancestors. I stopped worshiping them when my family died."

"Kalten?"

He sighed. "Very well. Yes, we had our gods too. My mother and sisters made sacrifices to them. I didn't hold much faith in them myself."

"Then you both know certain rituals can help with the harvest and trade."

"That's what my family believed," he said. "I never saw much proof of it."

"Take my word for it, those rituals and sacrifices are very important. Much of my power comes from the observance of such things."

"So, you're trying to tell us an oath with some blood will give you the power to get us out of here?" He laughed. "I don't believe you."

Mother Tully shot him a dirty look. "You know nothing of the deep magic. Whether you believe me or not, that is the sacrifice the gods demand for my power."

"What gods? What oath?" He turned to Paena. "Paena, I know she can do amazing things, but surely this is too much. You cannot believe her, do you? It's too wild."

"Kalten, I don't know what to believe. I only know we are trapped here, and she says a small sacrifice will help us escape."

He couldn't believe his ears. "She's said a lot of things."

"Even after everything you've seen?" Paena asked.

Something just didn't sit right. "Come on. A little blood, and she can save us? If that's all it takes, she shouldn't need us at all."

"Oh no, you two are very important. The sacrifice must be made by another on my behalf." The old woman practically quivered with anger. "After everything I have done for you children, you still question me?"

"I'm sorry, Mother—" Paena began.

Kalten interrupted. "You make it very hard to trust you, old woman. You threatened to kill me when we first met. Since then, you have continued to threaten me. How can I possibly believe you or trust you?"

Mother Tully turned her back to him. "As you wish, boy. You get us out of here. I will do nothing."

He spoke to her back. "You know I can't get us out of here. What would you do differently?"

"Without your sacrifice, you will never know." The old woman looked over her shoulder at Paena. "Maybe you can convince this fool to listen to me."

"Mother, can't you tell us more? You want our help, but you don't tell us anything."

Mother Tully shook her head. "What more would you have me say? The gods demand a sacrifice to fill me with the power I need to free us. It is that simple. Without your cooperation, I can do nothing."

"I don't understand."

"Then let me speak plainly. The only sacrifice I need from each of you is an oath of bonding and a small amount of blood. In ordinary times, blood alone might have been enough, but I have grown too weak for that to change anything."

"An oath? What kind of oath?" Paena asked.

"You must swear to obey me and my gods. You must become my warriors, my protectors, and my Keepers of the Faith."

"But I don't even like you. Why would I ever bind myself to you?" Kalten demanded.

Mother Tully looked him in the eye. "Because if you do not do this, I will not be able to free any of us. You, Paena, and the baby she carries will all be imprisoned and probably killed."

Paena gasped and collapsed. "Baby? What are you talking about?"

"You have felt ill since shortly after we left the Dragon Lands, child. You told me you and Kalten lay together after the healing."

"What? No!" he said, anguish filling his voice.

Mother Tully continued to speak, ignoring him. "Child, you became pregnant that night. I only kept my peace because I knew it would cause you distress. We were in enough danger without you worrying about something you cannot change."

"I don't want to have a baby," Paena moaned.

"I am afraid the choice has been taken from you."

A baby changed everything. But what if Mother Tully was lying about Paena's pregnancy? Could he afford to put her at risk? It was that question that decided him. "What do I have to do?" He felt dazed and defeated when he spoke. "Whatever it is, I will do it. I can't risk Paena or the baby."

Mother Tully nodded. "Paena, will you do this thing as well?"

She mutely agreed, her eyes brimming with tears.

"Then let us be done with it and escape our jailers. Quickly, you two. Come over to me."

Kalten and Paena lurched over to Mother Tully and huddled around her. Both knelt quietly while the old woman took them, each by the left hand, and slashed once at their palms with a jagged rock.

She gravely made a cut to her own left hand and took their bleeding hands into her own bloodied one and held them tight.

Raising her right hand above their heads, she and made two passes, drawing symbols in the air before she finally spoke. "Do you, Paena and Kalten, freely bind your lives and your spirits to me from now and for always?"

"I do," they each whispered, not meeting each other's eyes.

"Do you promise to obey my word as law and live as my warriors and protectors?"

"I do," they repeated again.

For a few moments, Mother Tully chanted in an unknown language, making passes above their heads with her right hand. Then, her grip on their hands eased, and she slumped into them.

They caught her and held her until she regained consciousness. "We are bound," the old woman said. She chuckled for a moment. "I had not known how weak I truly was until just now."

"What now?" he asked.

"I need a bit of time to gain strength, but we will be gone before the first rays of morning light."

"How will we escape?" he asked.

Paena hugged her knees to her chest, weeping silently.

"I should be able to change our forms to those of lesser creatures." Mother Tully nodded. "Once that happens, we can slip through the bars of this cage and escape into the darkness."

"When?"

"I will tell you. Now take Paena and talk to her. She must accept what has happened or all might still be lost. I must have time to regain my strength."

"Me? Don't you think you would be better at handling this with her?"

"You and she ultimately caused the problem and her distress. You must deal with it." With that said, the old woman moved to the far side of the cage. Soon, she was snoring once again.

Pretty darned convenient. But she was right. He needed to deal with the problem sooner or later. And that wasn't even considering the other problem he had.

What about his promise to the old woman?

Chapter Twenty-Five

Kalten wrapped an arm around Paena's shoulders, half expecting her to shrug him off. Instead, she buried her head into his chest and cried in earnest.

Stroking her hair, he silently let her cry. They sat like that for most of the night before she lifted her head.

The darkness masked all but the most severe results of her tears. He could see puffiness around her eyes, but nothing more. "Are you all right?"

"No! I'm pregnant. How should I be?"

"I don't know. Some women are happy to learn they're pregnant."

"Well, not me. I never wanted children." She emphasized the point with a sharp poke to his chest.

"Paena, I'm so sorry. I never expected any of this."

Her voice softened as she said, "I don't blame you, Kalten. What happened was because of the healing. Neither of us had any control of it." She went quiet for a few moments. "It's just that I grew up in a family of such love…"

"Wouldn't that make you want to have children of your own?"

"No." Her voice was cold, hard. Her entire body stiffened and turned unwelcoming. "My family was murdered because they were loving and trusting." She glared at Kalten. "By soldiers."

"Do you hate me for being a soldier?"

"I did. Not anymore. That's all behind us."

"Okay, your parents were murdered. I can understand why you'd hate soldiers. But why would that turn you against children?"

"I'm not against children. I love children. But you must understand, it is my duty as a faithful daughter to find the men who murdered my family and kill them. What kind of life would any child have with a parent like that?"

"Then why were you trying to join the queen's guard? They

wouldn't allow a quest like that."

"I tried to join them, because I thought it might bring me closer to the guilty men. I thought it might help my search."

"I still don't understand." Kalten shook his head. "Why would joining a guard unit bring you closer to those men?"

"Because the men who killed my family wore the queen's livery. They were her soldiers."

"You don't think she had anything to do with it, do you?" A horrifying thought hit him. "You weren't simply trying to get closer to her, were you? To kill the queen?"

Paena shrugged. "When I first learned that the soldiers were hers, I might have thought that way. But Baltar convinced me she is a good person and couldn't possibly have been involved. He thinks they were either renegades or were being commanded by someone trying to discredit her."

"That makes sense, I suppose," Kalten said. "So why are you here? I can't believe you weren't good enough to join the queen's guard."

Paena turned away. "My skills are good enough, but I got into too many fights with the other trainees."

He nodded. "I can see that."

She slapped his chest and twisted to get a better look at him. "But what about you? Was that story you told the commander true?"

"You mean about me searching for my family?"

"Yes, that one."

"Of course, it's true. I told you that the first time we met." He paused for a moment. "You know, my world fell completely apart that day. I'd been dreaming for more than two years of seeing my family again, but when I got home, everyone was gone. My mother, my sisters, even my neighbors. I ran away from the duke's army because of the things I saw him do to people like my family. I thought I could save them. Except, I've let myself be distracted by the queen's mission. Heck, I couldn't even save myself—stuck in a cage waiting for punishment."

"The queen's mission was to save the entire kingdom. I wouldn't call that distracted. And, if it's any consolation, I'm glad you're here with me now," she said. "You're a good friend."

He gave her a quick hug. "I'd better wake Mother Tully. It's almost light. If we're going to escape, we should do it now."

"I'm awake," the old woman said from where she lay. "I wanted to give you two time to stop feeling sorry for yourselves." She stretched. "I feel much stronger, thanks to you, so the escape should not be a problem. What will be a problem is Paena's pregnancy."

She gasped. "What do you mean?"

158

"To escape, I will be changing our forms to those of lesser animals. Those forms will allow us to slip out of this cage to freedom. But I do not know what the change would do to your unborn child. The child could be fine, or it could be changed to reflect the nature of your temporary animal form. I do not want to risk that."

"So, what can you do?" he asked.

"I can take the unborn baby from Paena's body and personally protect it. The child would not be affected by the form change, that way."

"Is it dangerous?" Paena asked. She clutched at his arm while she spoke.

"No, child," Mother Tully replied. "It will take most of my remaining strength, and I will have to withdraw for a time, but I will take very good care of the baby."

"You promise?" Paena's voice caught. She cleared her throat and wiped her eyes on her sleeve. "Do you promise to look after the baby while we escape? Nothing will happen to it?"

Mother Tully nodded solemnly. "You have my word. No harm shall come to it."

"Very well." Paena squared her shoulders and took Kalten's hand. "What do you want us to do?"

"Make three long piles of straw in that corner," Mother Tully said, pointing to the northeast corner of their prison. "Make them the approximate size of us sleeping on the ground. I can make it appear to be us to the casual observer. That might gain us some time."

Kalten and Paena quietly gathered straw and grass from the floor of their prison and did what the old woman asked. When they were done, she came over and inspected their work. The final product looked exactly like what it was. Straw under blankets.

Mother Tully was satisfied with the results, however. "That is what I wanted. Thank you." She knelt on the ground beside the straw piles. "Now come and kneel beside me." She raised an admonishing finger. "Be careful not to disturb the piles."

The three huddled together on the ground of the cage. "What I am going to do first is take the baby from Paena." She touched the girl's shoulder. "Do not be frightened, child. This will feel a bit strange, but will not hurt you or the baby in any way."

Mother Tully waited until Paena had taken a deep breath and nodded. She put her hands onto Paena's belly and closed her eyes. Kalten watched her very carefully.

For a few moments, nothing happened. Then she took a deep, surprised breath, and Mother Tully drew her hands away from Paena's belly. A softly glowing orb of blue light floated between them.

The old woman deposited the orb into a pouch at her belt and smiled at Paena. "Do not worry. The baby is safe. The glowing ball is there to protect it from harm."

"How do you feel?" Kalten asked.

"I don't know. That felt so strange." Paena touched her midriff. "I feel hollow, empty. But fine otherwise."

"You're sure?"

"I'm fine but thank you for worrying about me."

"Children, we do not have much time."

"We're ready," Paena said.

"I need you both to sit very still. This will not take long, but it will be unpleasant. What I am going to do is change your forms to something smaller that can slip through the bars of this cage. You will feel like you are being squeezed. That is because your physical forms must fit into much smaller ones." She caught their gazes and stared intently at them for a few moments.

"Try very hard not to make any noise, despite the pain. You will suffer this for the entire time your forms are changed, so we cannot maintain it for long. When I nudge you, follow me, whatever form I take and do not look back. Do you understand?"

"But..." Kalten began.

"There is no time for questions now. You must trust me. This will not be pleasant, but it is our only chance. Now, we will begin. Remember to come with me, no matter what."

The old woman placed her hands on him and Paena's heads. There was a wrench and then tremendous pressure, as if a mighty fist gripped his entire body.

He gasped and tried to pull away, but the old woman's hand held him fast. While the terrible pressure continued, he could feel his body twisting and changing. Beside him he could sense Paena struggling hard to escape the torture.

Abruptly, the horrible sensation of the world turning inside out was gone, but the intense pressure remained. There was a nudge, almost imperceptible beside the pain, and he opened tear-filled eyes.

Banging insistently against him was what looked like a large rat. It was a mottled grey color with a short, stubbly pelt and extremely long tail. He knew immediately it was Mother Tully. Beside him crouched another large rat. This one was a dark, satiny black color with sleek, silky fur. If a rat could be attractive, this one was. It had to be Paena. The Mother Tully animal moved off toward the darker side of the prison and slipped through a small hole in the bars.

So, they were rats now. But where were their clothes? Where

was Mother Tully holding the baby? Would she be able to change them back?

Kalten took a step and tripped over his feet, sprawling onto the ground. He picked himself up and slowly tried coordinating the extra set of legs to drunkenly go after the old woman.

Every moment was torture, but he still spared a moment to look over his shoulder to check on Paena. Her converted form staggered after him. The change in body obviously caused her the same problems he faced.

They crept through the bars to escape their prison and lurched into the woods that surrounded the enemy camp. Every step was a battle. With each movement, the pressure seemed to increase while his body fought to regain its natural form.

They continued the painful journey long after they entered the forest. When he could stand it no longer Kalten collapsed onto the ground and waited to die. The pain was too much. Death was welcome to come and claim him.

And then, the pressure disappeared. He almost cried with relief. He opened his eyes. No extra legs, no fur, just his own body fully clothed. He climbed to his feet, swaying for a moment while he gained his balance.

Paena lay on the ground very near him, moaning. He went to her and helped her to sit up, holding her for a moment. Tears streamed down her face.

A small cough caught his attention. Sitting on a rock, Mother Tully watched them like nothing had happened. "If you children are ready, we should leave this place."

He swore. "Give us a moment to recover, Crone." He ignored the frown on her. "I've never hurt that badly in my life. Why didn't you warn us?"

The old woman smoothed the frown from her face. "I did warn you. It is not my fault you did not listen. And now, you are free of your prison, so stop complaining. I have done what I said I would do."

"Enough arguing," Paena said. "We're here now, that's what's important." The girl turned to Mother Tully. "Please, how is the baby?"

Mother Tully smiled and patted her belt pouch. "The baby is fine and safe where I left it."

"How can that be?" he asked. "We were animals. We didn't have any clothing. How did you manage to carry the baby?"

"I transformed our clothing into the fur that covered us. For myself, I changed a bit differently than you did. There is a small creature that carries its young in a kind of pouch around its middle. I transformed myself into that creature to keep the child safe."

"Will you give me back my baby now?" asked Paena.

"I could, or…"

"Or?" he asked.

"Or, I could keep it a while longer so you two can complete your quest. It would be safe with me, and you would not be burdened with the morning sickness or any of the other problems that are part of being pregnant."

"What would become of my baby?"

"The baby would grow normally, just as if it were still in your womb. I can ensure that."

"When this quest is done, you'll give it back to me?"

Mother Tully smiled, showing all her teeth. "Of course, child. I only offer to keep the baby to help you."

"I don't know." Something didn't seem right about this. Kalten couldn't quite put his finger on it.

Paena put her hand on his shoulder. "Kalten, I never wanted to have a child, but now it's happened, I've got to be sure it's safe. If we don't do this, I won't be able to go on much longer. In time I'll be a burden to you and a danger. I won't be as effective because I'll always be worried about the baby. This task is too important for us to take the chance."

He gently turned her to look him in the eyes. "I understand what you are saying. I would always be worried too. But Paena, do you really trust her? Because I still don't."

"I don't care. The baby must be safe. I think we should accept Mother Tully's offer."

Kalten shrugged. "I'll go along with whatever you want to do. The child is yours after all."

She grabbed him and shook him. "No. The child is ours, yours and mine. We may not have meant for it to happen, but that changes nothing. Don't you dare force me to make the decision alone."

"That isn't what I am doing. I just don't trust her."

"Do we have any other choice? If you have any better ideas, I'd like to hear them."

"We could find you somewhere safe to hide until after the baby's born…"

"What would you do while I hide?" she demanded. "Keep searching by yourself? Remember what happened last time? We can't stop looking for the answers the queen needs. Mother Tully is our only choice."

"Fine. I'll go along with it, but I don't have to like it."

"Then we're agreed," Paena said. "Mother Tully, we're agreed that yours is the best way. Please look after the baby for us while we continue to search."

"Excellent. I will do what you ask." She embraced Paena. "Trust me. I will keep the baby safe."

She hugged the old woman. "Thank you. You don't know what this means to me."

"I think I have some idea, child." The old woman clutched Paena a moment longer and untangled herself from the girl. "Now that we have settled that, I must be off."

"Off?" Kalten demanded. "Where are you going?"

"I am going back to my home. That is the best place to keep the child safe while you two adventure."

She made so much sense he could only mumble his response. "Oh. I guess that makes sense."

"But how will we find you?" Paena asked. "You know, when our quest is complete?"

"Don't you worry about that, my dear. I will be watching you. I will know when it's time to meet again. Now, goodbye children. I shall see you again." Mother Tully turned and disappeared between the trees into the forest.

"What now?" he asked.

Paena shrugged. "Now, we find out who's behind this mess." She squared her shoulders. "Well, master scout, find us a way out of this forest. And could you make it one where we don't get captured for a change, please?"

Kalten shook his head. "Follow me."

~ * ~

"It's like we told you, Captain," the guard said. "Looking through the bars, you see people sleeping. When you go in, all you see is straw."

Captain Delus swore. "Get a squad together and find them." When the man hesitated, Delus smacked the guard on the shoulder. "Go man!"

The guard ran off, yelling for his sergeant. Delus grimaced at the sound of panic in the man's voice. He beckoned to his aid. "Corporal."

"Sir?"

"Get a messenger. We must let Duke Samuel know immediately."

"Anyone specific, sir?"

Delus gave him a grim smile. "Pick one of the troublemakers. I'd hate to waste a good man to Duke Samuel's temper. Bring him to my tent. I'll be there writing the missive."

The corporal saluted and ran off.

Captain Delus made his way into the command tent and sat down to write the letter. 'My Lord Duke,' he wrote, and then stopped. What could he possibly say that would appease the man? Nothing probably.

With a sigh of regret, Delus set the vellum aside and pulled out a fresh piece. With a small flourish, he dipped his quill in the inkwell and started writing. 'My dearest Sara, I regret that you will probably not see me again…'

Chapter Twenty-Six

"This is going to take forever." Kalten dodged a protruding root. "I mean, it took us two days to find Lydaroth in the first place, and that was on horseback the entire way. On foot, we'll never get back to town."

Paena looked up at the fading twilight. "How about we continue this complaining around a fire? It's almost dark."

"Normally I would agree with you, but the duke is definitely preparing for war. I am sure of it. We've got to get back to town so we can send word to the queen."

"What are we going to do after that? Simply send a message and wait?" she asked.

"Didn't Roulston suggest we look up a baron if we came this way?" he asked. At the mention of Roulston the mental image of the dead man, hanging from a tree on the edge of town, filled him with sadness.

"I suppose we could do that while we waited for instructions."

"Well, let's pick up the pace then."

She stopped so suddenly, he almost plowed into her. "Okay, fine, mighty scout. You lead for a while. Unlike you, I can't see in the dark."

"No problem. I can easily find my way in the dark. See if I can't." Kalten strode off and tripped over a rock. It took smashing face first into a tree to finally convince him to stop for the night.

While he nursed a bruising eye and scraped forehead, she built a fire and settled their gear. She was cooking their evening meal when she froze, her head cocked to one side.

"What's the matter?"

"Shhh. I thought I heard something moving outside the camp."

Leaves rustled. An owl hooted. Something reached through the bushes behind him and touched his head.

He jumped to his feet. "What *was* that?"

"What was what?" Paena asked.

"Didn't you see it? Something just grabbed me."

"I didn't see anything. Maybe, if we're quiet for a few moments, whatever it is will give its position away." She went still.

A moment later Kalten followed her example. They stood back-to-back and waited. Something, or more precisely some things, moved out in the darkness.

"There's definitely something out there," she said. "It or they seem to be all around us, but… Aiiiieeeee!" A head thrust itself through the bushes.

"It's a horse." He eyed the animal.

A chestnut stallion forced its way through the bushes followed by a slightly smaller palomino mare. Both were saddled and bridled.

"What?" He was stunned.

Two horses showed up just when they needed them most? It was too good to be true.

"Isn't she beautiful?" Paena said, stroking the mare's nose. "And look. There's a note tied to the saddle."

"What does it say?"

"It says: 'Dear Paena and Kalten. I thought these horses might come in handy. Treat them well and good luck. Mother Tully'."

~ * ~

Kalten and Paena arrived at the town at daylight. With horses, the journey back had taken a single additional day. The animals were tireless, and even after a full day of travel, still seemed fresh and ready to go.

He and Paena were a different story. Tired and filthy, they dismounted and joined a small caravan waiting to enter the town. The guards waved them through the front gate without a second look.

Everything appeared much different in the daylight. The inn they patronized the first night was easy enough to find. Kalten still remembered the directions from the previous visit. They left the horses at the livery stable next door to the inn.

Rather than repeat their previous route, he decided to ask for directions. One of the local urchins would do nicely.

"Hey, boy," he called out to a scruffy little waif, "come here for a moment."

The boy backed away. "Why? I didn't do nothin' to you."

Kalten dug into his belt pouch and pulled out a small copper coin. "I only need you to take us to the Trader's Guild house. A copper now and one when you get us there. Deal?"

The boy continued to look suspiciously at Kalten, edging farther away.

"It's not a trick lad, truly." He flipped the coin to the boy.

The boy deftly caught it and looked closely at the coin.

His entire attitude changed with the coin. "Follow me, Master. I'll get you to the Guild house. It's not too far from here. You did say you'd pay me another copper when we get there, didn't you?"

Kalten laughed. "Yes, you young scamp, I did. I will, but not until we're there. No tricks, mind," he said, waving a finger.

"No tricks, Master," the boy said.

He led them down several streets and alleys, always making sure Kalten and Paena were in sight.

In short order he stopped. "In fact, we are here."

"Well done." He handed a second coin to the waif trying to remember his face. "What's your name, lad?"

The boy went immediately on his guard again. "Why do you want to know my name?"

Kalten tried another tact. "My name is Kalten, and the lady's name is Paena. I simply want to know who I should ask for if I've got another errand that needs doing. You seem a trustworthy young man, so I thought maybe you'd be the one the help me out."

The boy's scrawny chest seemed to swell with pride at Kalten's words. "My name's Tom, sir but everyone calls me Scattercat on account of how fast I can run. I'd be happy to help you out again, if you need me. Just ask anyone around here where I'm at. They'll get word to me you're looking."

"Thanks, Tom," Kalten said. He extended his hand to the boy.

The boy shyly shook his hand, and then turned to leave.

"Hold a moment, Tom," Kalten said. He removed a silver coin from his pouch then handed it to the boy. "For future services, my friend. Take it with our thanks."

The boy bowed with a saucy smile then ran off, skipping and jumping. Kalten smiled to himself and turned to Paena. She watched him with the oddest look on her face.

"Just when I think I've figured you out." She turned and entered the Guild house. He could only follow her, wondering what she meant.

The young man from their first visit looked up from his desk when they passed through the door. "Back already? You weren't able to find what you were looking for?"

"Oh, we found him, Randolf," Paena answered. "And we were captured shortly after." She quickly outlined what happened.

"Well, I'm certainly glad to see you here in one piece," Randolf said. "But where is the old woman who came with you the first time?"

"She didn't make it back," Kalten quickly said, catching her eye. "The escape and journey were too much for her."

"That's too bad." Randolf was all business again. "Let's get a message off to Lord Baltar. I'm sure he's anxious to hear about the capture."

"Do you have somewhere quiet where I can write out the details?" Kalten asked. "Paena and I can put everything down, then you can send it off."

"You can write?" he asked with surprise. "Are you sure you don't want to tell me all the details? I can write them down for you and get them sent off in today's courier pouch."

"Thank you, Randolf, but I'd prefer to do it myself," Kalten answered. "Writing the details helps me remember them."

"As you wish. You'll find vellum, quills, and ink in the desk." He got up. "What are your plans after you send the message?"

"Sleep first." Kalten paused for a moment. "Then tomorrow, we'll gather supplies and head out again."

"Where will you go this time? In case I need to send a rescue party. You two seem to have trouble follow you."

"I can't tell you that, I'm afraid."

"What? I'll have you know I'm an appointed representative of the crown."

Kalten held up his hands to ward off further protest. "I can't tell you because I'm not sure where we're going. Out there, that way, I suppose." He pointed nonchalantly toward the west.

"You don't have any plans at all?"

"Not really. But don't worry. When we get... wherever it is we're going, we'll send word."

Randolf's smile seemed a bit strained. "As you wish. Now, if you'll excuse me, I have some errands to run."

"Thank you again, Randolf. When you get back, we'll have the message ready for you to send," Paena said.

He responded with a lazy wave over his shoulder to show he heard her before he closed the door behind him.

Kalten went to the door, opened it then watched him stride off down the street before he closed it and came back to the desk.

"What was that all about?" she asked. "There's nothing wrong with Mother Tully."

"I know that and you know that, but for some reason, I don't want him to know that."

"And the 'no plans at all'? Is that part of your deception too?"

"It is and for the very same bad feeling I have about him."

"Maybe it's because of the difficult time he gave us last time we were here?"

168

Kalten thought for a moment. "Maybe you're right. Still, let's keep Mother Tully and the baby a secret for now and pretend we don't have any idea where to go next. If I'm wrong, we can always bring him up to speed. But if I'm right and there is something..."

"Fair enough. Now, let's get this report written. I could really do with a bath and some sleep."

Chapter Twenty-Seven

Randolf sat at the table and looked around in disgust. A filthy place, this inn, barely good enough for the whores and soldiers who frequented it. He shuddered when one jezebel, long overdue for a bath and caked with layers of grime and old face paint, shuffled past.

She saw him looking and mistook his revulsion for interest. "Like to buy a girl a drink, milord?"

He covered his mouth and waved her away not trusting his stomach to speak. The woman tottered off, muttering angrily.

He was distracted by the arrival of his caller. "Any particular reason you interrupted a good drunk, Randolf?" Pieter threw his leg over the chair and joined him. Despite his teasing, Pieter looked much worse for wear. He hadn't shaved in days, his hair hung in greasy clumps, and the clothes he wore looked like they'd been slept in for several days.

"No names." Randolf checked to see if anyone was watching. "You know the rules."

Pieter snorted. "Just who do you think is following you?" His words were slightly slurred.

"That doesn't matter. If I'm discovered, my life is forfeit."

He leaned back in his chair. "Yes, that would be a shame, wouldn't it?"

Randolf ignored him. "Our employer sent a message for you."

"What is it?"

"You are to follow the traitor and his bitch. Find out where they are going and send back word."

"That's it?"

"Yes. Take a cage of birds to keep him notified."

Pieter leaned closer. "Where might I find them? Last I checked, they had left town."

"Well, they're back and at the Traders' Outpost. Do not lose them this time."

~ * ~

"Did you notice the way Randolf kept looking at us? And he only did it when he thought we weren't watching." Paena spoke for the first time since leaving town. Once again, their time in town had been necessarily brief. They both felt the weight of the queen's mission forcing them on.

"I wondered why you've been so quiet."

"It just strikes me as strange. Almost like... well, I don't know what, but it was creepy." She shuddered.

Kalten grinned. "You shouldn't be surprised he was sneaking peeks at you. You are very pretty." He reached over and wiped an imaginary smudge from her face. "I saw him. I think he's smitten with you."

"Stop teasing me, Kalten. I don't think that's funny." She scrubbed at the spot on her face he had touched.

"Who's teasing? You are pretty. I'd have been surprised if he didn't notice you."

She sniffed and urged her horse to a trot, temporarily leaving him behind. He shifted and gave the stallion a smack on the rump. "Yah." The horse leapt forward, almost unseating him. In half a dozen strides he drew even with Paena.

She glanced over as he caught up and urged her mare faster. Kalten heeled his horse after her.

The trees streamed past while the horses galloped side-by-side, dirt and stones flying off their hooves. Neither animal seemed ready to let the other get ahead. They rounded a corner and came face-to-face with a farmer leading an ox cart. He and Paena reined their horses back hard to come to a bouncing, jarring stop.

Kalten leaned over his saddle, breathing heavily. "That was fun," he said, patting the stallion's shoulder. "And this fellow isn't even winded. I think I'm more tired than he is."

"I'm certainly hotter," she said in agreement.

"Are we friends again, Paena?" he asked after they had ridden the horses around the glaring farmer.

"Perhaps." She frowned at him for a moment, then smiled coyly. "Do you really think I'm pretty?"

He could only laugh. "Of course I don't." He raised his hands to ward off a glare from her. "I think you're beautiful. Now come on, you vain creature. I think that manor house we've been looking for is close by."

"What are we going to do if the baron is already allied with the duke?" she asked.

"I truly hope that isn't the case, but if it is, we're going to have to fight our way out and hope our new mounts are as good as they seem."

"I suppose it is better to start with a more minor, if senior noble."

"We will have a better chance of escape, that's for certain. But I cannot believe Roulston would send us into an enemy's hands."

"We shall see," she said.

The horses shifted and snorted while they talked.

"I think these two want to run a bit more, don't you?" Kalten asked. He nudged the stallion gently with his knees, and it leaped almost instantly into a full gallop, Paena and the mare right beside.

They almost missed the well-maintained lane that led off from the main road. As it was, they had to pull up the horses and turn around after they passed it.

They turned down the lane and rode in. A thick hedge in front of a line of grand old trees grew on both sides of the lane, their massive bows almost touching, forming a living roof over their heads. Both horses began prancing, almost like they could sense the stable and oats they expected to find waiting for them.

Rounding a turn in the road, Kalten saw the manor house. It was built at the top of a hill, solid and forbidding. Made of stone, it had a martial look to it. Not a fortress to his experienced eye, but easily capable of defending itself from invaders. The only windows in the building started well up the wall and were narrow, ideal for archers to do their work from.

As they approached, men patrolling on the roof caught sight of them. A horn sounded out, and men rose from behind the hedges beside them, bows and swords in hand. All were dressed as foresters, clothed in shades of green and brown.

He reined in his horse, keeping his hands well away from his sword. He had no illusions about putting up a fight. The men looked very professional and had them dead to rights. Paena stopped a half step later. The men waited, their weapons ready. No one spoke. He thought it wisest to wait to see what happened next.

From the main building, a man rode toward them, dressed much like the foresters. Only a scarlet badge on his chest and a silver torc around his neck marked him as different.

He halted his horse several paces from Kalten and Paena. He appeared young, possibly Kalten's age, and sat his horse with the ease that came with long practice. He had a strong, handsome face and shoulder length, chestnut colored hair. "What is your business here?"

"We are here on behalf of her majesty, the queen," Kalten said.

"What are your names?"

"My name is Kalten, and my companion is Paena. May we

approach?"

The man ignored Kalten's question. Instead, he wheeled his horse around and called over his shoulder to them. "You will follow me to the house. Do not try to run or you will be struck down in your saddles."

Nothing for it but to follow, Kalten nudged his horse into a slow walk, and Paena followed. Some of the men kept pace along the hedges on foot, weapons still held ready.

The man led them through gates set into a low wall and dismounted at the steps of the manor. Without a word, he went up the steps and into the house. Soldiers trailed them in. It had all happened so fast, Kalten didn't know what to expect next.

He jumped when the great doors boomed shut behind him. Paena crowded close to him, almost tripping him.

"Wait here," the man ordered. "The baron will be down to speak with you shortly." He marched off through a side door, disappearing from sight.

Two pikemen stood at attention on opposite sides of the hall. A massive stairway dominated the middle of the room, and murder holes dotted the gallery walls. He had no doubt archers hid at the ready behind each one. The rest of the room was tastefully, if simply decorated. Richly carved oak paneling covered the walls and a great coat-of-arms with a red boar on a green field hung above the stairs.

"Welcome to my hall."

Paena let out a small gasp. They both looked up to see an elderly man being slowly escorted down the stairway by their guide from the lane. The old man had been tall once, but the years had bent him almost double. A fine crown of white hair circled the sides of an otherwise bald head. His deeply lined face had the weathered look of old leather, and a pair of bright brown eyes sparkled out of sunken sockets. At the foot of the stairs, the old man let go of his escort's arm and hobbled closer to them.

"Please forgive the drama on the road," he said. "There are spies and agents everywhere. I wanted to put on a good show." He smiled. "My name is Baron Estevan, and you are most welcome to my home."

He extended his arm back to the man who had come with him. "And this is my son, Bran. I think you may have already met him outside."

Kalten and Paena bowed to the two men.

"My lords, thank you for meeting with us." Kalten shifted his feet. "I must confess, I was worried about the sort of welcome we'd receive here. The greeting outside just seemed to confirm my fears."

"But, young man. What makes you think your situation is any better now?" The old man's expression was deadly serious. "No one will know if you leave or not. Only that you came in."

Kalten's eyes widened, and the baron let out a great laugh. His son grinned in turn, the dour look erased from his face. "You young people are so gullible. I am only having a joke on you." The baron turned toward a side door. "Please, join me for refreshments. You must be tired and hungry from your ride."

Kalten glanced at Paena. She shrugged and followed the old man through the side doors. He came in after her.

Bran walked beside Kalten. "You must forgive Father," he said. "He has always been a prankster. He thinks it puts people at their ease. Mostly it just frightens the wits out of them, but we let him have his fun."

He smiled, immediately liking the man. "You've obviously had a lot of practice too. You had me totally convinced outside. Then your father really had me worried."

"You must tell him. He'll be pleased his joke was so successful." By this time, they were through the door. Bran waved his arm toward the food-ladened table. "But first, please, take refreshment. There will be time to speak later."

Kalten and Paena joined the baron and his son at the table for the mid-day meal. Although their hosts were clearly curious as to why the two travelers were there, they politely allowed their company to eat their fill. The baron regaled them all with stories of past pranks he pulled on some of his more distinguished guests while they ate.

"Earl Lancshere considered himself to be the greatest horseman in the kingdom. He often bragged to me that he could ride any horse there was, trained or wild. So I bet him one of my prize mares I had an animal he couldn't ride. He, of course, immediately accepted." The baron leaned closer as if to tell a big secret. "Unfortunately for him, he agreed without guaranteeing the animal he had to ride was a horse." The baron had a huge grin on his face.

"What did you have him ride?" Paena asked, fascinated.

"We had caught an old bear wandering around the grounds. I had it penned up in one of the unused stables."

"Did he ride it?" Kalten asked.

"Not at all. He took one look at the bear and realized he'd been fooled. Never said a word. Just tipped his cap to me before he rode out of the yard."

"Then what happened?" she asked.

"Well, miss, a few days later, one of his men delivered a fine young mare to me. The earl has never been back, I'm afraid."

They all shared a laugh for a few moments at the expense of the unfortunate earl before the baron pushed his plate away.

"So, my young friends, while I enjoy sharing my stories with you, I must ask why I have the pleasure of your visit. I am a bit off the beaten path for you to say you were 'in the neighborhood'." He folded his hands in his lap and looked expectantly at them.

Paena carefully wiped her mouth before answering. "Sir, you are absolutely correct. We are here for a purpose."

"You said you were on a mission for the queen. That sounds dreadfully important, especially for a backwater like this. Do you have proof of your mission? And if you do, what is so important that the queen would send you all the way here?" asked Bran. His gaze bored into her.

"We have her warrant, if you'd like to see it," Kalten said.

"It is my experience that warrants can be forged by a skillful hand," the baron said. "I prefer to better understand the mission before I agree to anything."

Kalten leaned toward Bran and the baron. "The queen knows Duke Samuel and other lords of the realm plot against her. Our mission is to travel the land to learn who supports her and who supports the duke."

"Are you saying we are suspected of supporting the duke?" demanded Bran, standing up. His face was flushed.

Baron Estevan placed a hand on his son's arm. "Sit down, Bran. If we were suspected, would the queen only send two people? I did not hear them accuse us of anything of the kind. Now, Kalten, I believe what you are asking is how much we know about the situation and where our sympathies lie, are you not?"

"Very astute, my lord. Yes, you are correct. We do not believe you are plotting against the crown and are hoping you can aid us in our investigations of your neighbors." She smiled fondly over at Kalten. "Unfortunately, Kalten doesn't count intrigue as one of his skills so let me be blunt. Where do you stand in this?"

"Father, don't answer her. We don't really know why they're here. It could be dangerous..."

The old man waved Bran's protestations off impatiently. "Bran, I am tired of hiding in the shadows. It's time to declare whom we are for. If they are against us, they won't be going far."

The old man's casual words chilled Kalten, but he held his peace.

Baron Estevan turned to them. "To answer your question, we are for the queen," he said. "Duke Samuel is a scoundrel and a rogue. We too believe them to be plotting against the crown, and they must be stopped. I will neither condone nor participate in their activities."

"Thank you, my lord. We believe like you do," she said. "And, as said earlier, we are here on behalf of the queen. She suspects that some of her lords are involved in treasonous activities, but doesn't know who they all are."

"Very smart, that girl," said the baron. He turned to his son. "I told you she had a good head on her shoulders?"

Bran let out a small sigh. "Yes father, many times."

"So, what would you have us do? We are not a wealthy county. We have few trained warriors. Really only enough to patrol our own roads against brigands."

"My lord, that I cannot say," said Kalten. "I think the queen first needs to know who she can trust and who is her enemy."

"Well, you can tell her she has the support of me and mine," the old lord declared. "Whatever she asks, we will do our best to fulfill." He stood up, drawing and raising his sword before he spoke his oath.

"Thank you, my lord. Our lady, the queen will be overjoyed to hear of your loyalty," Paena said.

He nodded and took a seat, laying the sword on to the table.

Bran quietly spoke. "If that's settled, how can we help you?"

Kalten thought for a moment before answering. "We don't want to intrude, but would you mind being our hosts for a time while we carry out our investigations?"

Chapter Twenty-Eight

"That was amazing," Kalten said, leaning back in his chair and rubbing his belly. Bits of egg and sausage littered the table in front of him, all that remained of a massive breakfast.

"It should have been. You've been eating since you woke, and it's got to be nearly mid-day," Paena teased. "I'm surprised you haven't burst."

He groaned. "It's not midday. Not by a long shot. The sun's barely up past the trees. Besides, it's not every day I get a chance to eat so much good food."

"I agree with you there. But you're bound to get fat if you keep eating like that." She gave him a sharp poke in the stomach. "Why, I do believe you've got the start of a belly."

"Yow! Stop poking so hard. I do not have a paunch. Look at this lean, mean body." He lifted his tunic to reveal a flat stomach, lined with muscle. "Go ahead. Hit me." At her wicked smile and balled up fist, he quickly held up his hands. "On second thought, maybe not."

"Don't you think we should do something?" she asked.

"What would you have me do? The baron sent messengers to the various lords. Until they come back, there isn't much to do."

"How about some more hand-to-hand training?" She pretended to shadowbox for a moment. "I hear that Bran knows a few moves we don't. How about we ask him? Besides, maybe I can help you get better."

Kalten did his best puppy dog look. "Can't I just let the bruises I've got heal first? Please?"

Paena laughed. "You poor thing. How about you practice your writing and send a message back to Randolf? He should at least know where we are and what progress we've made so he can send Baltar a report."

"Be happy to," Kalten said after a satisfied belch. "But first, I think I'll have a couple more of those sausages." He reached for a covered trencher while he spoke.

She shook her head at him. "While you stuff yourself, I think I'll go and talk to Bran. Maybe he's in the mood for some exercise."

Kalten waved his hand at her before tucking into another plate of sausages. "Have fun."

She left the dining hall still shaking her head. She should have known. The soldiers she'd seen were usually more concerned with where their next meal came from. Why would Kalten be any different?

She walked out into the sunlight, blinking at the brightness. Another beautiful day. She ached to get back on the road just to be doing something. This idleness was intolerable. But the baron had insisted on contacting the local nobility to introduce them in advance. He had asked they stay until replies were received. As guests, they couldn't very well ignore his sensible request.

Across the yard, she saw Bran working with some armsmen in sword drill. From what she could see, he was very good. Maybe even a challenge for her if she took it easy.

He saw her coming and stopped the drill. He threw his sword to one of the men before he greeted her. "Good morning, Paena. You slept well, I trust?"

"Very well, thank you," she answered. She thought he would be arrogant like most nobles seemed to be. It had been a nice surprise to find that he was a regular workingman. "I think breakfast slowed me down a bit. I hoped to work some of it off, if you don't mind."

"Most certainly, lady," he said with surprise. "I knew you carried a sword, but I did not realize you drilled with it."

She laughed. "That's usually the reaction I get. But, if I'm going to carry a sword, I'd better be able to use it. Men don't usually give a woman a second chance."

"Wise words, lady." He collected his sword and signaled for his men to give them some room. He went into a loose guard position. "Whenever you're ready?"

He had barely finished speaking before Paena attacked, driving him relentlessly back into his men. He skipped back to avoid her initial attack. After a moment's hesitation, he gamely fought back. It wasn't long before both were drenched in sweat.

They fought on, laughing and cheering each other on. Paena quickly realized the Bran she had seen earlier had been holding back to fight more closely to his men's level.

It was in the middle of a particularly heated exchange that she heard the voice in her head. *I come.* The shock caused her to momentarily freeze. Bran had to check his swing to avoid decapitating her.

"Paena! What's wrong? You're white as a ghost. Good lord, girl, I almost killed you."

"Warn your men that a dragon's coming," she said. "But tell them to stand down. He's with us, and I don't want anyone getting hurt because they did something foolish."

"Whatever are you talking about? You seriously expect me to believe a dragon is coming here?"

"I told you and your father about my healing last night, didn't I? I'm pretty sure I told you where we were and who healed me," she said.

"Well, yes, but I didn't think you were being serious. I thought you were just joking with my father."

"I was not. And whether you believe it or not, a dragon *is* coming and very soon," she said. "If your soldiers aren't prepared, things could go very badly for us all."

He looked at her for a moment, and then began barking orders at his men. In moments, the area cleared, although the glint of armor could still be seen at windows and rooftop.

"I've done as you asked. Now tell me what's going on. I demand an explanation." He still seemed frightened by what almost happened. "One moment you're giving me the fight of my life, the next I have to stop from killing you with a juvenile overhand slash."

Heat warmed her cheeks. "I'm sorry, Bran, but a dragon spoke to me. I was so surprised I froze. Pretty stupid, I'll admit."

"A dragon spoke to you? You need to explain that further."

"I'll do my best." She tried to find the right words. "I have a, I suppose you would call it, a connection with a dragon. It has something to do with the healing I told you about last night. I don't fully understand it, but it allows me to hear Lydaroth in my mind when he wants to speak with me."

"Lydaroth?"

"The dragon. His name is Lydaroth, and he told me he's coming. It must be something urgent, or he wouldn't be here at all."

"Really? It's still pretty hard to imagine a dragon is coming. I thought the beasts to be myth or at least long gone from these lands."

"He's very real."

"You're sure he's friendly?"

"Yes. Please make sure your men don't attack him. I doubt they'd hurt him much, but he can do a lot of damage himself if he gets angry."

"A dragon. I never thought I would see such a thing." Bran shook his head and strode to the middle of the yard. He cupped his hands around his mouth. "Men. Remain calm and do nothing to provoke the dragon."

A voice could be heard from the roof of the manor. "A dragon? Is he mad?"

"I am not mad although, if you do not follow my orders, I will be very angry!" Bran called out to the manor. "I know the idea of a dragon is hard to take—I don't know that I completely believe it either— but I'm assured it's real and it is allied to Paena and her companion. Therefore, you will do as I command and do nothing unless I tell you too. Is that clear?"

A chorus of "Aye" and "Yes sir" met his question.

"You should be fine," he said. "My men will do nothing unless I signal them otherwise or your dragon friend gets aggressive."

"Thank you." She could see he was nervous despite his brave words. "Trust me. He is an ally. And I have a feeling we're going to need him before long."

A shout went up from the rooftop. "Dragon in the sky!" A man waved and pointed to the north.

She looked to the sky and saw the rapidly growing figure of the dragon approaching. She reached out with her mind to the dragon. *"Lydaroth, is that you?"*

"It is I. Will the humans try to harm me if I approach?"

"No. I have told them about you. You are safe."

"Thank you. I come."

The dragon swooped down, back-flapping his wings to land, raising a cloud of dust in the yard. Paena and Bran were forced to shield their eyes from the flying grit.

Lydaroth was barely on the ground before she had her arms wrapped around his muscular neck. She noticed his normally shining silver scales had taken on an almost coppery, tarnished look, but chose not to mention it. "Lydaroth. I'm so glad to see you."

The dragon shifted uncomfortably. *"I am fine, as you can see. I come with news."*

She stepped back from him and noticed Bran watching at a distance. "Oh, where are my manners? Lydaroth, this is Lord Bran. He is helping Kalten and me. Bran, this is Lydaroth, lord of the Dragon Lands. He is the one responsible for saving my life a few weeks ago."

Bran bowed awkwardly, maintaining his distance. "I am pleased to meet you, Lord Lydaroth. Please be welcome at my home."

"Thank you, my lord," the dragon replied.

Bran looked momentarily surprised but recovered quickly. "So, you saved Lady Paena's life?"

"It was nothing. Please do not take offense, but I cannot dally." The dragon paused for a moment. "The Dark Ones are helping your enemies. We have confirmed this. They have become very bold." The dragon snorted his contempt of the rebels.

Paena's heart sank. "What can we do to stop them?"

"There is nothing you can do." The dragon settled his wings against his back. "They are too powerful. It is up to me to deal with them. I wanted to let you know what was happening so you would not worry."

She shaded her eyes and scanned the sky. "Is there any danger they might attack us?"

He followed her gaze. "That is a possibility. But I will maintain a watch over you. I will listen for your call as well. If you need me, I will come."

"Thank you, Lydaroth. May I tell the queen you and your people will work with her?"

"You may tell her. I believe we must to eliminate this problem. Please send her my pledge to help. And this." The dragon scratched at the tip of his tail, dislodging a scale. He pushed it toward Paena. "I expect your queen will require some proof of my existence. Take this scale. That should satisfy her."

Paena nodded. "I will, Lydaroth. She will be very grateful to hear of your help."

"It is time to bring our two peoples back together as they were in the past." The dragon turned to leave. "Until we meet again, be well." He nodded once to Bran then sprang into the air, his wings pumping hard. Within moments, Lydaroth was airborne and well away from the manor. Only a cloud of dust and debris was left behind to show his passing.

"That was interesting," Bran said, as he drew near Paena. "He's quite an impressive beast."

"He's my friend," she said, annoyed at his choice of words. "And one of the most caring and intelligent beings I've ever met."

"I never said he wasn't, but he clearly isn't the same as you or me. I mean, is he even tame?" he asked.

"Now you are making assumptions. You assume because he is not human, he is an animal. He is a person like you or me."

"If that's true, it makes me question him even more. Does he have the same values we do? Does he consider us his equals? I'm simply concerned that something as powerful as him is being given free access to whatever he wants."

"There are monsters out there that walk on two feet too," Paena argued. "Look at the duke. Would you trust him over Lydaroth? I *know* Lydaroth's heart, and I vouch for him. If that isn't good enough for you…" She left that thought hanging.

Bran held up his hands and took a step back. "Please don't take offense. I meant nothing by what I said. Your good word is enough for me."

"He's already lost his father to this war. I don't want anyone insulting him." Suddenly the young nobleman had lost a little of his appeal in her eyes.

"Very well," said Bran bowing, stiffly formal. "Please accept my apology."

"Certainly," Paena said, her voice flat.

Kalten chose that moment to interrupt.

"Hey Paena," he called from the step of the manor house. "I've got the report ready to send." He ran over to Paena and Bran. "Bran, do you have anyone going into town anytime soon? I'd like to send this right away."

Bran smiled at Kalten. "Of course. I have someone leaving tomorrow morning. Please leave it with me, and I'll make sure it goes with him." Bran turned to Paena. "I'd like to discuss this further. Later, if you don't mind. Kalten. Paena." He nodded to each when he spoke their name and strode off.

"What was that all about?" Kalten asked, scratching his head. "He was sure in a hurry to leave."

She watched Bran enter the manor before she answered. "Lydaroth was here."

"What? When?"

"He left just before you came out. Bran called him an impressive beast, which made me angry. Lydaroth is so much more than a simple animal."

Kalten screwed his face up. "I know that, but why was he here?"

"Hmm? Oh, he came to warn us that the dark dragons were on the move and are helping the enemy."

He put his hands on his hips. "Why didn't you come get me?"

"There wasn't time. Lydaroth only stayed long enough to tell me that and then he left. He didn't want to endanger us."

"So what's the problem with Bran?"

"I just didn't like the way he talked about Lydaroth. We had words, but I don't think anything will come of it."

"Good. We can't afford to make these people angry at us. Now, about Lydaroth…"

~ * ~

Pieter crouched, dipped the quill into the inkpot and wrote on the slip of parchment. 'The traitor has contacted Baron Estevan and works with him. I will continue to follow the traitor.' He lifted the parchment up to his face and gently blew on the ink to dry it.

He had followed Kalten for the past few days, until the man holed up at the baron's manor. The message to Duke Samuel could have been sent that first day, but Pieter had grown cautious in the weeks he tracked the traitor. Kalten simply didn't stay in one place long enough to report on. This time was different. He and his wench were obviously holing up at the baron's for an extended stay.

Satisfied the message was dry, Pieter rolled the slip up into a tiny roll and slid it into a small hollow wooden tube. He held the tube in his teeth while he reached into a willow branch cage and pulled out a pigeon. Pigeon in hand, he tied the message to its leg and tossed the bird into the air. It flapped furiously to catch the air and circled the trees twice before flying off. The duke would know that the baron was allied with the queen soon enough.

Pieter grinned. He wouldn't want to be in the baron's shoes. He made himself comfortable and dozed. For now, he would wait for the traitor to leave. Until then, he might as well catch up on his sleep.

He was just dozing off before a dragon landed in the courtyard of the manor.

Chapter Twenty-Nine

"What a stroke of luck it was finding Baron Estevan," Kalten said to Paena as they rode back from another successful meeting with the baron's allies.

"I agree. Five more lords sworn to support the queen against the duke in the ten days we've been here." Behind them rode the armsman, partially slumped over his mount, bobbing with movement of the horse. "How are you doing back there, Niale?"

The wiry man stretched in his saddle at the mention of his name, stained teeth flashing a smile through a grizzled grey beard. "Just fine, m'lady. Just having a bit of a doze."

"I wish I could," she said, smiling. "But I have enough trouble staying in the saddle when I'm awake."

"It's a soldier's skill, m'lady." His blue gaze danced in amusement above a substantial nose. "You learn to catch a few winks where you can."

Kalten half stood in his stirrups and looked around, hoping to see a familiar landmark in the moonlit night. "How much longer until we get back to the manor?"

Niale squinted up at the full moon. "Dunno, fer sure, young sir. If we ride all night, I'd guess we should get back just before sun up."

"Well, we certainly have enough light to ride by," Kalten said, reining in. "If we're going to keep going, we should give the horses some feed and a quick rest."

"Will do, sir." Niale stopped his horse and dismounted.

Kalten swung from his saddle, arching his back and stretching out his shoulders with a small groan. He pulled a nosebag from his saddlebags and passed it over to Niale.

Kalten went over to Paena who was still mounted. "Coming down from there? Don't you want to give your mare a break?"

"Shhh." She stared up at the sky. "Do you hear that?"

He stopped and listened. "I don't hear anythi…" He was

drowned out by a mighty roar. A jet of flame flashed over his head incinerating a nearby tree momentarily and blinding him.

Kalten jumped up into the saddle behind Paena as she spurred her mare to a full gallop. Niale was already riding into the trees, Kalten's stallion in tow.

He leaned forward, spots still dancing in front of his eyes and yelled into her ear, "Was that a dragon?"

She waved him off. "Yes. Now let me concentrate. I've got to catch up to Niale." Another jet of flame struck a tree just behind them.

A sheet of flame flared in front of Niale. Without missing a beat, the armsman swerved the horses around it and went uphill. Paena and Kalten followed him at breakneck speed, the little mare beginning to breathe heavily from carrying two riders.

The trees thickened, forcing the riders to lean forward onto their horses' necks to avoid being swept off by reaching branches. Niale never slowed while the frequency of the fire jets increased all around them.

They were nearer the cliffs now, and the horses began to show the effects of a long day's ride followed by a wild gallop. And then Niale was gone. Kalten held his breath, afraid Niale had fallen into a gorge.

Paena rode on to Niale's last position. Kalten watched nervously for signs of a gorge. Then they found where he'd gone. A hidden trail into the cliff, perfectly camouflaged by the rock and brush. In the dim light of the moon the trail was almost impossible to see. Ironically, an errant fireball revealed it to Niale.

Paena slowed the mare and let her pick her way into the shelter of the cave.

As they went further in, the darkness was replaced by the soft glow of fluorescent lichen. When the cave widened enough, both riders dismounted to give the exhausted mare a breather. They led her further down a passage until they emerged into a huge dry chamber.

Niale crouched near the middle of the cave, squinting over a pile of shavings, trying to strike a spark from flint and steel.

He spoke without looking at them. "I never expected my misspent youth to ever pay off. This here cave was one of many hidey holes I used to have back then." He struck at the flint a couple more times with sharp, measured strokes. "Couldn't a-guessed I'd be back here though." A fat spark rolled off the flint into the shavings, catching fire in a matter of moments. "Good thing I had a few transgressions back then, else we'd never a known this place was even here." He fed wood into the fire until it burned bright.

He brushed his hands off on his breaches. "Let's get that beast of yours unsaddled and comfortable. She's certainly earned it."

Kalten nodded numbly and uncinched her girth strap while Paena removed her bridle. The mare reached around to nuzzle his hair with velvety lips, then leaned on Paena. "Poor girl," he said, scratching at her shoulder. "You earned your oats tonight."

"I set up a few of these places, just in case," Niale said. "You can't ever say when you might need one." He grinned. Set 'em up with a bit of feed just in case I happened to find myself with a beast or two."

He picked up her feet and checked them for injury. Satisfied she was fine, he let her loose in the cave. She wandered over to a pile of dried grasses where the other two horses were already eating.

"Just what kind of misspent youth did you have?" Paena asked.

"The less you know, the better," Niale said, grinning.

"I wondered where you were going in such a hurry," she said.

"This was the first place I thought of when that dragon flamed. That wasn't one of yours, was it?" Niale asked.

"No, I don't think so," she replied. "Did you get a look at the dragon chasing us?"

His face was deadly serious. "No. I only saw the flame."

"I didn't see anything either. I'm pretty sure it was more than one dragon though," Kalten said. "There was too much flame from too many different places to have been done by only one. When you disappeared, I was afraid you'd fallen over the cliff."

Niale flushed. "Sorry 'bout that. Didn't think I had time to stop and explain myself. I figured that mare of yours could probably see better than you in the dark and would follow, even if you weren't sure."

"Well, you certainly figured right, didn't he, Kalten?"

Niale chuckled. "Glad to help, young lady, glad to help." He peered at the back of the cave for a moment. "If memory serves, there should be some rations in the back. They won't be much, but this here cave is always dry, so they should still be good."

He went to the back of the cave and came back with some wax-sealed packages. "I think there's a bit of jerky in these." He threw a packet to Kalten and one to Paena.

"How did you ever find this place?" she asked, checking her surroundings.

He blushed. "Well, m'lady. Therein lies the story. You see, when I was much younger, I wasn't the fine, upstanding fellow you see before you. I did a few things that weren't, strictly speaking, legal."

"What, like a bit of smuggling?" Kalten asked.

"Could be, could be," the older man said, tapping the side of his nose. "Never did nothin' to hurt anyone, you unnerstand, but there was times I needed to lay low. Found this place when I was runnin' from the authorities. Sort of fell into it, you might say. Once I found it, this here cave became my lyin' low place."

"You old rascal." She leaned over and gave Niale a kiss on the cheek. "Thank you for saving our lives. Your secret is safe with us."

He blushed and knuckled his forehead. "I thank you, miss."

"Is there another way out of here other than through the front?" Kalten asked.

The armsman shook his head. "Sorry, sir. The front is the only way in or out. Used to be a way out the back, but it collapsed some time ago."

"So what do we do now?" she asked.

"We wait, apparently," Kalten replied reclining. "And hope that the dragon or dragons get bored and go away."

"It was going so well too." She sighed and sat in front of the fire to stare moodily at the flames.

"Don't worry, m'lady. We should be safe enough in here. The entrance is too narrow for one o' them beasts." No sooner had Niale finished speaking than they heard the sound of great claws scrabbling at the stone of the cave entrance. The scratching at the stone stopped. It was replaced first by a loud sniffing sound, then by a jet of flame.

The heat from it warming the air of the cave washed over Kalten. "Should we try to call Lydaroth? See if he can bring help?"

"I already tried that when we were running," she said. "Nothing happened. I expect we're simply too far apart."

"I sure hope that changes, and he comes looking for us. Maybe then we can escape."

"Maybe." By her expression, she didn't think help would find them anytime soon. "Or maybe he gets attacked and killed like Golgoroth."

They settled around the fire and stared at the flames. Only the occasional scrape of claw against stone disturbed the crackling of the fire.

~ * ~

Paena was just falling asleep when there was a small explosion in the fire. A fat green spark sprang from the fire into the air and hung spinning above her head.

"Hello Paena. Hello Kalten." The voice of the spark filled the room, catching everyone's attention.

The spark spoke again, glowing brightly, its color changing from green to blue to red and back again in a rhythmic pulse. "Mother Tully sends her blessings to you, her beloved avatars."

"Who are you?" Paena asked. "How do you know Mother

Tully?"

"She sent me." The spark pulsed when it spoke. "I am a creature of her forest. She wanted me to come to you with a message, so here I am." The silvery voice laughed again.

"A message? What message does she send? Why should we care? We've got enough problems."

"Be quiet Kalten," Paena said. "If you've come from Mother Tully, then tell me how the baby is doing."

"Baby?" The voice seemed puzzled. "She did not tell me to say anything of a baby."

"Look, you. We're kind of busy right now," Kalten said.

"Still combative, Kalten? She said you would be." A gay peal of laughter followed the statement. "Still, you're not going anywhere, are you? Not with the dragons waiting outside for you."

"You know about them?" he asked.

"Of course I do, you silly man. That's why Mother Tully sent me. She thought you might need some help."

"What can you do to help?" he asked.

"Me? I can do nothing. Nothing at all." The spark drifted close to his face and orbited his head. "I was sent to tell you how to ask Mother Tully for help. She is the one who will help you."

"We'd love to learn how to ask," Paena said. She gave Kalten a warning look. "What do we need to do?"

The silvery voice giggled. "Kalten, entertain me, first."

"There's no time for that." He swatted at the light without luck.

"Enough Kalten." Paena pushed him toward the back of the cave. "Floating light, or whatever you are, please tell us what to do."

"Very well." The voice sounded disappointed, almost pouty. "If he won't play with me, I'll have to tell you." The spark zoomed over to him. "You're sure you don't want to play?"

Paena ran between him and the light. "He's sure. Now please. Tell us the message?"

The spark dimmed, and its voice continued to sound pouty when it spoke again. "You only need to call out to Mother Tully, either aloud or in your minds. Tell her what you need and ask for her help. If she chooses to help, you will immediately know what to do."

"That's it?" he asked, stepping away from the wall. "And what do you mean, if she chooses?"

"She will help you if there is no other way. She doesn't want you to get lazy after all." The spark seemed to stare at him for a moment. "I've told you how to ask Mother Tully. Now, will you play with me?"

"Maybe another time. Paena, could it really be that easy?"

She shrugged. "Maybe. All we can do is try and see what happens." Paena took his hand. "What do we want to ask for?"

"You're joking, right? We want to get rid of the dragons."

"Yes, of course," she said, flustered. She paused, then spoke in a more commanding voice. "Mother Tully, please hear us now. We are in desperate need of aid from you. Please help us to escape the dragons that wait for us outside the cave."

"Very good, pretty Paena. But you have to tell Mother Tully exactly what you want her to do," the silvery voice said.

"I knew there had to be a catch. That's just like her to play games with us."

"Shut up, Kalten. Your complaining isn't helping. Just let me think for a moment, please." Paena closed her eyes for a moment.

"I seem to remember hearing a tale where the hero stunned a dragon with lightning." Niale, who had been watching the exchange with wide eyes, finally found his voice. "Do you think that might work?"

"It's better than my idea, which is nothing," Kalten said.

"Very well. Let's try it again." She squared her shoulders, faced the spark then spoke again. "Mother Tully. We desperately need your help. Please aid us with light to see by and lightning to drive away or destroy the dragons that have us trapped."

"Excellent, Paena. You've done it," the spark congratulated, glowing brightly.

"Done what? I don't feel any different," Kalten said. "Paena, do you feel any different?"

"You won't feel anything, Kalten," the spark scolded. "You did not ask for aid. Until you ask, you do not get."

"Now that you mention it, I do feel different," Paena said. "I think I know how to make light and call lightning. I can't explain how. It's just at the edge of my mind."

"Grumpy Kalten. Ask Mother Tully for help like Paena did," the spark ordered.

"Why should I? Paena seems to have the power to do it herself."

"Don't ask me how I know this, but I don't think I can do it myself. I need your help." She grabbed his hands. "Please. I really need your help. If we're to get out of here, you must swallow your pride and ask."

He stared at her for a moment. "Fine, I'll ask. But I want it understood, I'm only doing it because of you. No other reason."

"I know it's hard for you, but thank you." She hugged him a hard squeeze then released him.

Kalten nodded to her and spoke. "Mother Tully, Paena needs my help to drive off the dragons. Grant me the same powers she has so we can do this."

"Say please, Grumpy Kalten," the spark said.

He gritted his teeth, jaws clenching and unclenching. "Please." No sooner did he finish speaking than he understood what Paena meant. He could feel power pouring into him like water from a waterfall. Somehow, he knew he could call up both light and lightning. How didn't really matter, it would be there when summoned, and it would be a heck of a show.

"Niale, cover your eyes and the eyes of the horses. Paena and I are going to call light to drive the dragons away from the cave mouth. It will be bright enough to blind you if you don't."

"Aye sir." Niale didn't hesitate to follow Kalten's orders, rushing to the horses. He spoke quietly to them while he covered their eyes with cloths.

"You know what to do?" Kalten waited for Paena's nod. "I don't know how I know this, but I know the light won't blind us. I'll go first, and you follow."

He didn't wait for her agreement, checking to ensure Niale and the horses were blindfolded then called the light.

Immediately, he was surrounded by a brilliant red glow that illuminated the entire cave. A moment later, a green glow pushed back some of the red light. Instead of blending together, the light wavered and danced in crackling strands of red and green brilliance. The air almost appeared to be in flames.

"Wow. You look like me now," the spark said. "So pretty. But I bet you can still get burned by dragon fire. Let me lead the way and make sure the dragons back away from your light and don't cook you when you come out of the cave." The spark, much dimmer in the conjured light, flitted toward the cave entrance.

"Hello dragons. Come out, come out, wherever you are." The spark's voice drifted playfully to them from the cave mouth. A jet of flame answered the spark's calls.

"Nasty dragons," the spark scolded. "That wasn't very nice. Kalten, Paena, you can come closer. The dragons are waiting a little way back from the entrance."

Kalten and Paena slowly made their way out of the cave, preceded by the surrounding light.

"Don't worry, friends," the spark called back. "The dragons seem afraid of your light. They are backing away. It should be safe for you to come out."

Kalten and Paena emerged cautiously from the cave. Once

outside, the light flared up and away, forming a dome above them, half red, half green. Five dragons, thoroughly confused by the light, wheeled above the dome, roaring and breathing blasts of flame, made impotent by distance, down toward the humans.

"Kalten, I don't think this light will last forever. We need to do something to get rid of these dragons soon."

"We need to try the lightning right away."

"Let me try first, then," Paena said. She bowed her head, as if in prayer, then stretched out her arms to the sky and flung her head back. A wind sprang up around them whipping her hair about.

Lightning flashed in the distance as the dragons continued to dive down at the dome of light, flaming at the humans.

A massive surge of lightning struck one of the dragons, blowing it apart. Kalten's hair stood up from the discharge, and spots danced in front of his eyes. He tore his gaze from the dragons. Paena was already starting to slump from fatigue. Her hair danced around her face, crackling with energy.

"Hang on, Paena. I'll try to help you." He too bowed his head before flinging out his arms, just like she had done.

More lightning struck at the dragons. His energy decreased with every strike. Two more dragons were blasted apart, whether by his lightning, Paena's, or some combination, he didn't know.

The flashes of lightning continued, but grew weaker as Kalten and Paena's energy waned. They were leaning on each other now, barely able to stay on their feet. Another bolt struck one of the remaining two dragons, no longer strong enough to destroy, but still enough to kill. The dragon tumbled out of the sky, striking the ground very near them.

The remaining dragon turned tail and fled. The danger over, Kalten and Paena collapsed to the ground, unconscious.

Much later, Kalten opened his eyes long enough to see he was back in the cave, covered by a blanket. His eyes felt grainy, and a coppery taste filled his mouth. "What happened? Did we win?" He could barely mumble the words.

Niale's face entered his line of sight. "Aye, my lad. That we did. When the light show ended, the spark near drove me to distraction until I came out of the cave. You and the young lady were on the ground next to one o' the great beasts. At first, I thought it had killed you. But I could see you were still breathing, so I brought you both back in here to recover.

"The dragons are gone, then?"

"Aye. Gone or dead. Now that you're awake, can I be gettin' you anything?"

"Maybe a drink of water."

The armsman brought over a waterskin and helped Kalten to drink.

"Thank you." He tried to lift himself and failed. "I should give you a hand with Paena and the horses."

"Don't you worry about that. Now, you just be gettin' back to sleep. I'll keep watch until you and the lady are back on your feet."

Kalten would have nodded if he had the strength. Instead, he closed his eyes and went back to sleep.

Chapter Thirty

Duke Samuel impatiently sat his horse in the middle of a clearing flanked by two of his guardsmen. The stallion, sensing the duke's attitude, pawed at the ground and snorted while tossing its head.

The guardsmen held torches aloft to ward off the night as they nervously surveyed the area. Only the dim light of a slivered moon assisted the torchlight.

"Easy boy," Duke Samuel said, reaching down to pat the stallion's neck. "We will only be waiting a short while longer before we turn back."

A gravelly voice floated out of the darkness. "You will not be going anywhere, human."

Immediately the two guardsmen rode forward, between him and the voice. They wildly waved the torches toward the sound, hoping to see who or more precisely what, spoke.

"Show yourself," Duke Samuel ordered. "Come forward and be recognized."

"I do not think that will be necessary." A jet of flame shot out of the darkness and struck the left-most guard and his horse.

Neither the man nor beast had time to utter a sound before they were incinerated. The stench of burning flesh filled the air.

The right guard fought to control his horse and his fear. "My lord, we must flee."

Duke Samuel peered into the darkness. "Hold, man." He nudged his horse a few steps forward. "I say again, show yourself. I am Duke Samuel, and I am a friend to the dark dragons. Why do you show this aggression?"

"You would ask this after sending my people to their deaths?" The voice grew angry as he spoke. "You are bold, human."

Duke Samuel frowned. "What are you talking about? I did no such thing."

A rustling sound came from the trees, and the shadowy form of a dragon marched into the barely lit clearing. "Do you deny asking me for my help to destroy one of your enemies?"

"The traitor? I do not deny it." Duke Samuel settled his gloved hands on the pommel of his saddle. "I would prefer him captured, of course, but I doubt your people can handle an operation that delicate."

The dragon ignored Duke Samuel's intended slight and rambled on. "I sent five of my warriors to destroy your enemies as a favor. Only one returned, and that one will never do battle again. He claimed that the one you would destroy was a wizard of great power who slew four of my warriors before they could strike." The dragon prowled closer. "Why would you send my warriors into such danger without warning?"

"On my honor, I know not what you speak of." Duke Samuel nudged his nervous mount closer to the dragon. "The traitor which you were to kill has no such abilities. He is but a peasant boy."

"You are a liar, Duke. The one my warriors attacked pulled lightning down from the sky."

"Perhaps your warriors attacked the wrong people?"

The dragon roared. "They did not! They tracked and identified your traitor before they attacked him and his party."

Duke Samuel held his hands up in a warding gesture. "My dear Garagoth. What possible reason would I have to kill your warriors? I am the one who helped your people escape their confinement, am I not? I need your support to defeat the bitch queen and her rabble."

"If that were true, then why did you not warn me of the danger?"

"Obviously because I was unaware of it. The boy had no such ability when I knew him, and none of my commanders have reported anything of the like. Except…" He stroked his chin. "I have lost several men who had him in their custody. Perhaps we are both victims of this boy. Would you like the chance to get revenge on him?"

"I am listening."

"There is a baron who is aiding the traitor. If we cannot affect the traitor directly let us work together to punish him through his allies."

"Work together?" The dragon leaned forward. "How?"

"A combination of your warriors and my soldiers in a coordinated attack."

"Keep talking."

Chapter Thirty-One

Still exhausted from the previous night's battle with the dragons, Paena leaned over the mare's neck while she rode. She looked over at Kalten. He maintained a brave front, but he was so pale, his face practically glowed in the morning light.

He met her eyes while she watched and gave her a small smile. "How are you feeling, Paena?"

"Good. I think I could sleep for a week, though." She actually thought it would be more like a month, but didn't want to admit it to him.

"Then you're doing better than me," he replied. "Give me a bed, and I could easily sleep a fortnight."

She smiled to herself. His honesty was so refreshing. "You got me, Kalten. I'm having a hard time staying on my horse. I just didn't want to admit it." She realized they were very close to the baron's manor. The road they travelled was bordered on either side by low stone walls that surrounded fields of pasture and sheep.

They shared a brief smile before Niale interrupted with a discreet cough. "Pardon my interruption, but I can smell smoke. I think it must be from up near the manor."

"Ahead of us?" She tried to see the source. "How close would you say we are from the manor house?"

Kalten strained to see what was in the distance as well. "I would say that we couldn't be more than a short gallop from the entrance. Niale, what say you?"

"I would have to agree with you, my lord. I think we should spur the horses and see what's going on."

"You took the words right out of my mouth." She urged the mare into a gallop and raced past the two men. They followed her at a run.

She and the others thundered down the road until they reached the turnoff to the baron's estate. They slowed the horses to a walk and rode up the lane. Niale and Kalten pulled their bows out and strung them while Paena readied her sword. Whatever the cause of the smoke, it smelled stronger, and she wanted to be ready for it.

Nothing could have prepared her for the sight that met her when they came out of the forest. Smoke and ash filled the air in the clearing that had once been the estate's main yard. The stables and manor house were all burned to the ground, and everywhere she looked, charred and still-smoking bodies littered the yard.

A horse was tied to the remains of a rail near the rubble of the house. A figure lurched out of the yard toward them. Niale let out a surprised yell and readied an arrow.

Somehow, she knew who it was. "Niale, stop! That's Bran." She jumped off the mare and ran toward the staggering man with Kalten close behind her.

Bran all but collapsed in her arms. She slowly lowered him to the ground and grimaced. His hands were a mass of burns. Ash and smoke stained his skin, and what remained of his clothing was black. The soot that marred his cheeks was broken only by the streaks cut by tears running down his face.

He doubled up in a coughing fit, and then looked up into her face. "They're dead. All dead. I tried to find survivors." He held up his damaged hands. "I really tried to find someone left alive." He broke down and held his head, sobbing uncontrollably.

She rocked him and stroked his hair. "You did everything you could, Bran. Don't blame yourself."

"What happened here?" Kalten asked.

Bran's eyes were wild. "Dragons. Dragons and men attacked here. They never had a chance."

"Dragons. Are you sure?" she asked.

"Of course I'm sure!" he shouted. "I saw them flying away from here. Just before the men rode out, they flew away to the north." He grabbed at her arms. "I thought you said they were our allies? Our friends? Why would they do this?"

She gently pried his fingers from her arms. "I don't think they were our friends. There are other dragon factions that are against us. Tell me what they looked like."

"They looked like the one who came the other day," he said, shaking his head. "I don't know what you want me to tell you." His voice had a pleading quality to it.

"Were they bright and gleaming, or were they dull?"

He shook his head again. "I don't know. Dull, I guess, but it could have been the smoke in the air too."

"What about the men? What can you tell me about them?"

He started rocking again, holding his head. "I tried to get them.

I tried to attack, but my horse bolted and threw me into the hedge."

"Lucky for you that happened, or you'd be dead too," Kalten said.

"They had my father's head on a pike. He was just an old man. No threat to anyone. I have to avenge him." Bran broke down in fresh tears, and curled up on the ground.

Kalten took a blanket brought by Niale and covered the stricken man, then helped Paena to her feet. He placed a second blanket under Bran's head.

"You remain here for a while, my friend. We'll take care of things now." Kalten led Paena and Niale away from Bran.

"Did you see his hands? He's been digging through these burning ruins with his bare hands. He's going to need some attention and soon," Kalten said.

"We could ask for healing," she said. At his blank stare she added, "You know. From Mother Tully."

"Oh, yes. From her," he muttered. He sighed. "You're right, of course. Bran needs help badly. We'd never get him to a healer in time to save those hands. But we should let him rest for a little first. He's already suffered a great deal today, and we're still worn out from last night."

"Agreed. And we should warn the baron's neighbors. If it can happen here, they should be prepared for the worst too."

"Good idea, Paena." Kalten waved Niale over. "Niale, are you able to do something for us right now? It's important."

Niale's face was a grim mask, but he nodded without hesitation. "What can I do?"

"We need you to ride over to the two closest neighbors and tell them what's happened. Get help if you can, and have them warn their neighbors as well."

"As you command, my lord," Niale said. He bowed once, mounted his horse then rode out of the yard without a backward look, spurring the animal before he entered the lane.

"There goes a good man," Kalten said. "He keeps his head no matter the situation and does what's right."

"I just hope he doesn't do anything foolish," she said.

"Like what?"

"Like trying to hunt down the men who did this," she replied. "He may just go after them rather than deliver our message."

"No, he'll do his duty. He knows he can't get revenge by himself. And he knows we've got to warn the others who live near here too. He'll do his best to prevent more deaths."

"I hope you're right." She scanned the ruined yard. "We'd better see if there's anyone else left alive here."

They searched the yard for signs of life. Bodies of men were everywhere, most burned beyond recognition. Of the livestock, nothing remained. Every building was burned to the ground.

They only found one body they could identify: the body of the kindly old baron. The invaders had obviously decided to make an example of him. They had stripped the body naked and impaled it on a pole.

While she searched for something to wrap the body in, Kalten removed it from its grisly display. They wrapped the corpse in a charred curtain and carried it over to Bran.

He lay in his blankets staring at them with fevered eyes. "Is that my father?"

"Yes, Bran," she said. "We found him by the steps of the manor."

"This belongs to you now," Kalten said, stepping forward. He pulled the baron's sword from beneath his cloak and offered it to Bran.

He held his hands out for the sword. The palms were a mass of burns and oozing wounds.

"Kalten. Don't be ridiculous. He can't take that with those hands. They must be healed first."

Shock marked Kalten's face. "I'm sorry. I wasn't thinking." He placed the sword beside Bran.

"Let's just focus on what's important right now. We must get his hands healed."

He clenched his jaw. "Do you really think we can heal? Mother Tully never seemed able to do it when we needed her."

"I hope we can, but if you don't want to try?"

"No. I'll do it." He knelt beside Bran and tenderly took the man's hands between his own. Bran grunted in pain when Kalten touched the tortured flesh.

He bowed his head and spoke, both in his mind and aloud. "Mother Tully, we need your help. This man will lose his hands if we don't do something quickly. Please give me the power to heal his wounds so he can fight those who did this terrible thing."

As he prayed, a glow surrounded his hands. It brightened after he finished speaking then disappeared.

He slumped over Bran when he finished the healing. Bran caught him and laid him down in his place. After he scrambled to his feet, he stared first at Kalten, then at his hands, shaking his head in wonder.

"It's a miracle," he said, flexing his fingers. "My hands are healed."

"Yes, I suppose it is," she replied. "Let me have a look." She took each of Bran's hands and inspected them closely. Other than some pinkness, they appeared healthy.

"What about Kalten?" he asked.

"Don't worry about him," she said. "A little time, and he'll be back to normal. Healing you took a lot out of him."

"I'm grateful to you both," Bran said. His voice took on a harder edge as he said, "Now, I must go and hunt the ones who did this."

She grabbed his shoulder. "You won't be hunting anyone right now. You're still weak despite the healing. Your hands may be healed, but look at them. The skin is too soft to last in a fight. You'd rip them to shreds the first time you swung a sword."

"I'll wear gloves."

"Then what? You'll still be outnumbered a hundred to one. They'll cut you down and laugh while you die. And when they're done, they'll have another ornament for their pikes. We need you here. We need you to help us bring the duke and his supporters to justice. Now is not the time to be selfish."

"But look at what they've done," he pleaded with them. "They've killed my father and my men. They've turned everything we had into a charnel house. How can I simply let them ride away from this?"

"They will pay for what they have done. Make no mistake about that. But we must let them think they've gotten away with it for now, if only to stop them from doing it again later," Paena said.

Despite her words, he tried to pull away. "I don't care. I've got to go."

"I won't let you," she said. "If you try to leave, I will stop you. I will tie you up and leave you until you see reason."

He hung his head for a moment. "Fine, we'll do it your way." A fierce expression blazed across his face. "But I will be at the head of the army that avenges this day."

Kalten sat up, shedding the blanket. "What's all the shouting about?"

"Nothing," she replied. "Bran and I were just talking about what to do next." He glared at her for a moment before he stalked off to his horse.

"So, it worked? He's healed?"

She leaned down and helped Kalten to his feet. "Yes, you did it. He's going to be fine."

"I'm glad. I feared I wouldn't be able to help him." He considered Bran who was busy checking his horse's feet. "Did he say who's crest the attackers carried?"

"No, he didn't." She called over to the man, "Bran. Do you remember what livery the attackers carried? Did they have any crest on their shields or any banners?"

He led his horse over to them. "The cowards had their shields covered and wore tunics of plain wool. They were too gutless to announce themselves to their victims."

Kalten swore. "We've got to get word to the queen. She needs to know what treachery is going on here." He jumped up, looking for his horse.

Bran stopped him. "That won't do you any good. I think I know who one of the traitors is."

"Who are you talking about?" Kalten said.

"I'm certain your friend in town is the reason for this attack."

"Friend in town? Who?" he asked.

"Your trader friend, Randolf. I speak of him."

"What're you talking about, Bran?" Paena asked. "Why would you say such a thing?"

"About halfway home, a couple of men jumped out in front of me. I wasn't too worried. I was on horseback and had a sword; they only carried truncheons. What I wasn't ready for was the man behind me. Your man from town. He yelled before he attacked me. That's what saved my life. It gave me enough warning that I managed to dodge his sword. I rode down his men and came straight home fast. I didn't see him again."

"But what makes you think he's responsible for this?" Paena asked with a sweeping gesture.

"Why else would he attack me? Who else knew you were here?" Bran shook his fist at them. "Why else would men and dragons attack this house except for your 'mission' for the queen?"

"Bran, you must believe us when I tell you we never intended to put you or your father in danger." Paena said.

He gave a mirthless laugh. "Oh, I know you meant well. I thought Father and I were too unimportant to draw attention. It looks like we were both wrong." He looked around the ruined estate and sighed. "What would you have me do now?"

"Kalten and I must go to the queen and tell her that the duke is working with dragons. Warn her of the danger she faces. You must gather those lords loyal to her—" The sound of a galloping horse stopped her from speaking.

Niale came flying up the lane, white foam speckling the sides of his horse. He reined up just short of Bran and leaped off his mount.

"They're all dead! Every one of them."

Bran grabbed the man. "What are you talking about? Who's all dead?"

Niale heaved a deep breath. "I went to warn Count Tristan, but it was too late. They're all dead, just like here."

He swore and strode over to his horse. "I've got to warn the others. You didn't mention where you were going next in your dispatch, did you?"

"No," Kalten said. "That news would have been in the next one."

"Well, let's hope they don't know who else you went to see or they'll be dead soon too." Bran swung into his saddle. "Perhaps I'll see you all in the next life." He raised his fist in salute.

Just before Bran rode out of the yard, Kalten called out to him. "Wait. I'll ride with you. That way you'll know where we've been." He turned to Paena. "You and Niale must warn the queen. Bran and I will try to raise her an army."

"How will I contact you?" she asked.

"Lydaroth," he said. "I didn't say anything to you, but I'm hearing his thoughts just like you do. It started a couple days ago. I tried to ignore it, but it won't go away. Anyway, he should be able to find me and speak to me just like he can with you."

Paena clutched at Kalten's head and pulled him down to her level. "You be careful. We've been together too long; I don't want to lose you again."

He grinned. "I'll be fine. Just don't get yourself lost. I have a feeling Bran and I will be too busy to come rescue you." He climbed into his saddle and turned the horse's head toward the lane. "I'll see you soon. Have Lydaroth keep me posted about where you are and what you're doing."

He raised his hand in farewell and rode out of the yard with Bran.

Chapter Thirty-Two

There was no escape. Pieter knew that now.

The duke was insane. Not in the traditional sense where he sat in a corner and dribbled while mumbling. No, this insanity was much worse; the man was insane with power and the desire to take more of it. The fact he had the ability to act on his desires was now beyond dispute.

Pieter had stayed in his small hiding spot, waiting for a response from Duke Samuel. He had seen the dark tide of dragons and soldiers wash over the baron's manor leaving destruction and ruin and death. After watching the massacre and total destruction of the elderly baron from Pieter's perch, it had all become very clear.

He could make a run for it. Hope someone else would take care of the duke. Except, that would mean a life of looking over his shoulder everywhere he went. That was no life at all.

There was nothing for it but to report to the duke.

Pieter chuckled to himself, a sound without mirth. You never knew. Maybe the duke would let him live. He shook his head. Yes, and perhaps pigs would learn to fly too.

~ * ~

After several days of hard riding, Paena and Niale reached the capital. The trip had been anything but uneventful.

First his horse foundered in the middle of nowhere forcing Paena to attempt to heal the beast. She hadn't been sure it would work, but the healing had come. The animal frisked and jumped like a colt for the rest of the day.

Then, highwaymen attacked them. Niale showed his true ability when two were dead before they had a chance to draw their weapons. she had no trouble with two more. They decided to leg it away before they too became casualties.

On the final two days of their trip, rain poured down on them in a continuous torrent, making every step of the way a misery. She sincerely hoped Kalten had better luck.

She and Niale arrived at the city drenched to the skin and shivering. Even the horses were trembling from cold and fatigue. Under the downpour the city took on a grim, hazy appearance. The walls loomed up out of nowhere, monoliths of silent stone.

The guards took one look at her grim face and escorted the travelers directly to the palace without fuss once their names and the passcode were given. She almost wished they said something. The mood she was in, it would have been a welcome relief to scream at someone.

But the guards knew their job and had her and Niale to the palace in short order. They were no sooner inside before staff had them out of their wet clothes and in front of a roaring fire, enjoying a warm drink. She allowed herself to think maybe her luck had finally turned.

They were just getting comfortable when Baltar stormed into the room. "Where in blazes have you been? I've been turning this kingdom upside down trying to find you."

"Nice to see you too," she replied. Niale wisely chose to remain silent.

"Do not give me any of your sarcasm right now, young lady. I am not in the mood for it. I have been worried half to death over you and young Kalten." He looked around the room. "Where is Kalten anyway?"

"Are you quite done acting like an old woman?" she asked. "Niale and I have just ridden through some of the worst weather I've ever seen. What you are hearing is not sarcasm. It is fatigue and anger. I am more than ready to give you my report, but I simply don't have the time or energy to waste on this nonsense."

Baltar stared at her from the doorway, a shocked expression on his face. Then the shock was replaced by a broad grin. He gave a huge laugh and rushed in to give her a rib-cracking bear hug. "I have missed you, my dear. Please forgive an old man his worry."

"I love you too, Baltar. But we really don't have any time to waste. It's worse than you thought. Terrible things have happened that the queen must know about right away."

He sat down, waving Paena back into the padded leather chair across from him. "What have you learned that is of such importance?"

"My lord, Baron Estevan is dead along with many of his neighbors. Killed by treachery, I'm afraid."

"Treachery? From whom? Who would do this terrible thing?"

"One of your own sold him out to the enemy. Your man, Randolf. We are certain he had something to do with the attacks on the baron and all his neighbors. Each lord mentioned in our last report has been wiped out by a coalition of dragons and armsmen."

"Dragons? You must be joking. There has not been a dragon

sighting in decades."

"I sent word about them. Several words, in fact. Did you not receive any of the messages we sent you from Randolf?"

"He sent me regular communications. None of them mentioned dragons, just like none of them mentioned seeing you."

"I'm guessing you know what Randolf's writing looks like by now," she said. "How many of the communications were written by him?"

"All of them were, just like they always are. Why?"

"I ask because Kalten was writing our communications. That explains why you don't know what we were doing and where we were. That is merely the smallest part of Randolf's ill will against the queen."

"You are not joking about the dragons then?" Baltar asked, the merest whisper of hope in his voice.

"I am not. They are back and in force. Kalten and I were attacked by no less than five of the beasts less than a fortnight ago. They are from a rebel faction within the Dragon Lands."

"Rebel dragons? How would you know that?"

"Because we have met and made an alliance with the Dragon Lands itself."

"What? An alliance?" He paced around the room. "Can they be trusted when, by your own words, dragons have attacked and killed several lords of the realm?"

"As I said, there are two factions: the main kingdom of the dragons and a group of rebels who have been banished. They are on the verge of civil war just like we are. It seems their traitors are allied with our own."

He continued to pace. "This is too incredible. Rebel dragons attacking and killing our people. Good dragons allied with Queen Elespeth."

He whirled to face Paena. "If I did not know you so well, I would swear you were delusional. As it is, I will have difficulty convincing Queen Elespeth of this."

"Would it help if I summoned the leader of the Dragon Lands here?"

His eyes almost bulged out of this head. "You can do that?" He collapsed into a chair, shaking his head. "But no... we simply do not have time to send a messenger to this head dragon for proof. We must move now or all is lost."

"No messenger is needed, my lord," Niale said, speaking up for the first time. "The lady here can call out to the dragon with her mind. I've seen it."

"What? How is that possible?"

"I was gravely injured," Paena said. "At death's door, so I'm told. I was badly hurt by rebel soldiers. Kalten and Mother Tully decided to take me to the Dragon Lands for healing. After a long journey, we arrived and were granted an audience with the dragon king." She continued her story, answering his questions whenever he stopped her.

"So, this Mother Tully is a witch woman you met some time before?"

"That's right. We intruded on her forest and had to make a pact with her to leave. She traveled with us until just the past fortnight."

"And Kalten is now traveling with Bran, Baron Estevan's son?" Baltar asked.

"Yes, he is. They wanted to warn the other lords we contacted. We didn't want any more attacks against them."

"Who made those attacks? I know you are saying Randolf is a traitor to me. But who does he work for? The duke?"

"I suspect the duke is behind this, but I don't have absolute proof. We have seen enough of the duke's soldiers to be pretty certain he's up to something," Paena said. "Kalten and Bran continue to search for proof. That, and continue gathering forces for Queen Elespeth."

"I see…," he said, fingers steepled together. "So, you are certain we can trust these dragons?"

"Absolutely certain. Do you want me to call Lydaroth?"

"No. A dragon in the city would cause widespread panic and could alert our enemies. It would be better if we hid the alliance for now."

"That makes sense," she agreed.

"Did you ever mention the alliance in any of Kalten's reports to me?" he asked with a troubled expression. "Since Randolf was clearly intercepting them, I'm worried that information might have gone to Duke Samuel."

"No, we didn't mention the alliance. We felt it prudent to tell you in person."

He breathed a sigh of relief. "Well, that's something then."

"Niale and I have been riding non-stop to get here to tell you."

"Ah yes," Baltar said, turning toward Niale. "And who is this fellow, Paena?"

"Please forgive my rudeness," she said. "Lord Baltar, this is Niale. Niale is, or was, a trusted soldier of Baron Estevan. He has been helping Kalten and me search out allies for the queen."

Niale bowed to Baltar.

"Good to meet you, soldier," he said, standing and shaking Niale's hand. "Your help is most appreciated."

"It has been my honor, my lord," Niale replied. "I just wish I could have been with the baron when the attack came. Perhaps I could have done something."

"Nonsense, man. Unless you have some magic powers I do not know about, you would most likely have been killed along with your fellows."

Baltar turned his attention back to Paena. "Your mission was to gather information that would convince the council of Duke Samuel's duplicity. I'm not sure you have fully done that. What you have done is implicated the duke—not enough for some members of the council—and you have revealed a new threat in the renegade dragons."

He sighed and leaned back in his chair. "Now about this Mother Tully. It might interest you to learn that I already know all about her."

"You do?"

"Yes. A representative from her arrived just two days ago—a young girl travelling alone. She said you would be arriving today and told me a fantastic story I could hardly believe. Now, from what you tell me, I find it to be largely true."

"A representative? Who could that be? Mother Tully lives alone."

"Not anymore, apparently. Like I said, two days ago a little girl arrived claiming to be the emissary for Mother Tully. Ordinarily the palace staff would have turned her away, but she asked for me personally with the message that she knew Kalten and Paena. That got my attention immediately. No one should even know who you are, not to mention that you are traveling together and know me."

"A girl?" She thought for a moment then shook her head. "No, that doesn't make sense. We only met one child in our travels, and that was a little boy, about ten years old."

"That is very odd. But she did correctly predict when you would arrive, and her story nearly matches yours, my dear." He scratched his head for a moment. "She's probably the most mature child I've ever met. She looks very familiar for some reason. You know, she asked to speak to you when you arrived. I thought for sure she made a mistake, because I never expected you two to travel apart."

"We thought it made the most sense to split up, especially since Kalten now seems to hear Lydaroth too. That connection gives us a means to pass messages to each other over a distance."

"Clever thinking." Baltar got up from his chair and moved toward the door. "These attacks change everything. I must inform the queen, immediately. Without full council support being prepared might be our only hope." He stopped at the door. "I may need you to leave the city quite quickly. Will you be ready?"

"We will be ready to go at your order, sir," she replied.

"Excellent. Now, would you like me to send the child in to see you?"

She smiled. "Yes, please. I'm interested to meet this child who claims to know me and Kalten."

"As you wish. She will be here shortly." He left, closing the door behind him.

Niale stood after Baltar left the room. "I think I'll try to catch some sleep while I can. If you'll excuse me?"

"Of course, thank you, Niale." She smiled at the man before he left.

The door had barely closed behind him when a light knock sounded. The door opened before Paena had a chance to respond, and a girl entered.

She had large dark eyes, dark hair, and a dark complexion. To Paena's inexperienced gaze she looked to be about six years old.

"Hello, Paena," the child said with a smile. "It's good to see you."

"Do I know you?" Paena asked, startled.

The child laughed, a silvery little laugh. "Of course you know me, Mother."

"Mother?"

~ * ~

"She called her what?" Kalten shouted out loud, jumping to his feet. Bran glanced at him with a questioning expression, but said nothing.

"Apparently, the child called Paena 'Mother'," Lydaroth replied. *"Please don't shout. I can hear you just fine."*

"Sorry about that. Your news surprised me." Kalten continued to speak to the dragon mentally. *"Could you ask Paena what's going on, please?"*

"Just a moment, Kalten."

He waited while Lydaroth relayed his question. A child calling Paena Mother? And more confusing, she claimed to come from Mother Tully. It didn't make sense. Except it did. Kalten had a growing sense of unease when he thought about the situation.

"Kalten, Paena says the child claims to be yours. Mother Tully did something to accelerate her growth. She seems to know things about the two of you no one else should."

"Face it, Father, I am your daughter," a new voice said in his mind.

He almost leapt out of his skin. *"What do you want?"*

"Father," the voice chided. *"I am your daughter, Kayla. I know Mother has told you about me."*

"Get out of my mind, whoever you are. I am talking to Lydaroth, not you."

"Whatever you say, Father. I heard you talking about me and came. Just call my name whenever you're ready." With that, the voice went silent.

"Lydaroth, are you still there?"

"I am here, Kalten. I told Paena about what just happened. She is as surprised as we are at this. She seems to think this proves the girl's claim even more."

"Could you tell Paena to keep questioning the girl, please? I'm not sure she's telling the truth, but knowing Mother Tully, anything is possible."

"I will tell her." He went silent for a moment. *"Paena wants to know how you and Bran are doing."*

"We've contacted all the lords who have sworn to fight for the queen. They are already gathering their troops and will meet below the city in the next thirty days. Bran and I will continue to search out other loyal lords to bolster the queen's armies. We will also be in the city in thirty days."

"Paena says Lord Baltar wants all soldiers to meet in a large meadow a half day's march north and west of the city. He calls the meadow Ursal's Muster. She seems to think the lords will recognize the name."

"I recognize it, so the lords likely will too. I'll pass that order along."

"Paena says Lord Baltar has already dispatched messengers to the lords you just met with so they will know."

"Thank you Lydaroth. Tell her that will help Bran and me a lot."

"It is done."

"Thank you again, Lydaroth. By the way… how are you doing?"

"I hoped to avoid war between dragons, but my enemies seem determined to bring it to me regardless." The dragon made a mental sigh. *"Since it is inevitable, I can only prepare for the worst, just like you. But I must go now. If you need me, please call. I will answer if I can."* With that, the dragon left Kalten's mind.

He focused back on the campsite.

Bran watched him carefully from the other side of the fire. "Are you back?"

"Yes, I'm here. It seems we are to continue gathering support for the queen."

"We expected that. So why are you looking so out of sorts?"

"Apparently, I have a daughter." At his raised eyebrow, Kalten spoke again. "I knew I was going to have a child. I just wasn't expecting to already have one who can speak to me in my mind. That is going to take some getting used to."

Chapter Thirty-Three

A knock at the door broke Paena from her reverie. "Come in." She turned away from the window at the sound of the door opening.

"Good morning, Paena," Baltar said. He carried a covered silver tray. "The maids told me you had not yet eaten, so I took it upon myself to bring you something."

She gave him a gentle smile. "Thank you, my lord, but I'm not really very hungry."

"That may be so, but you still need to eat. Especially after what I am about to tell you." He set the tray on the small table near the fireplace and pulled two chairs over to it. "Please, come and try some of this food. The cook went all out for you this morning."

Paena reluctantly came over to the table and joined him. The aroma coming from under the tray's cover did smell good. She uncovered a plate filled to overflowing with delicately cooked eggs, cheeses, and smoked meats as well as a sticky pudding drizzled with honey. She ate while he bustled around the room, opening drapes and setting the fire.

"Ah good," he said, finally sitting. "I see you had an appetite after all."

She nodded, surprised to see the plate empty. But it had been very tasty, and she hadn't eaten anything since speaking with the child—her child, she corrected herself—the previous day.

He stared at Paena, as if waiting for her to say something. He cleared his throat before speaking. "Paena, you should know Queen Elespeth is very pleased with what you and Kalten have achieved so far. You have done what no one else has been able to do." He paused and poured himself some water from a pitcher on the tray. "Because of your success, she has requested you go back out to gather more support. Immediately, if possible."

"I can't go out yet. Not until I learn more about Kayla." She leaned toward him. "Did you know she claims to be my daughter? How can that be?"

He took her hand. "I know about the girl, but we need more support if Queen Elespeth is to keep her throne. We cannot afford delays."

Paena pulled her hand away from Baltar and shook her head. "No, I won't go. Not yet anyway. Send Niale, instead. He knows who the lords are and where they live. He can do it."

Baltar grimaced. "I could order you to go."

"But you won't, will you?" She cupped his hand in both her own. "You know I need to do this."

"Paena, I know—" The door opened, interrupting him.

Kayla stepped into the room. Her pretty face was screwed up in a frown that would have appeared comical except for the angry energy she projected. "Paena, you will not stay here." Her voice had completely lost its childish trill.

Paena winced at the tone of Kayla's voice. It sounded so familiar. But where had she heard it before?

"Kayla, not now. This is a conversation for adults only," Baltar said, rising to stand.

"Sit down, Baltar. I have not yet finished." She pointed at Paena. "You wanted to know more about Kayla? Then I shall tell you everything, and you will go and do as you are told."

"But you are Kayla," Paena said.

The smile on Kayla's face was frightening. "Not at the moment. In case you have not guessed it, this is Mother Tully speaking."

Paena sunk back into her seat, jaw hanging open. "What? But, how?"

"Never mind the questions. Just listen. When I left you and Kalten, I took your unborn baby for protection. The only way to ensure her survival was to let it be born. When she was born, I had need for a priestess, so I aged her to what you see now and educated her. I may let her grow and age naturally from now on. It will depend on what I need her to do."

"Priestess? Why would you need a priestess?"

Kayla laughed. "You silly girl. Surely you have figured out who I am by now?"

"I know you are a powerful witch."

"Wrong. That is simply what I have become. Who I am is the goddess of this land. Before I came, this was a wasteland. The people were savages. I tamed the wilderness and brought enlightenment to the people."

The hair on the back of Paena's neck lifted. "So, what

happened?"

"My power has only diminished over the years as my followers disappeared. Before I was Mother Tully the witch woman, I was Tulliandars and I was, as I already said, goddess of this land."

"Wait a minute," Baltar said, his hand stroking his chin. "Mother Tully? Tulliandars?" Shock showed on his face. "You are Tulliandars? I do not believe it. I've heard the name, of course, but only as stories my grandfather would tell around the hearth or when I wouldn't go to bed. "

"You should believe," the child said. "But if it is a demonstration you require?" She gestured at the logs laid out in the fireplace. Sprouts of green appeared on the wood, growing rapidly into a sapling. Stone groaned and mortar powdered under the strain.

"Wait, stop!" he cried, throwing up his hands. "I believe you. Just stop growing that before it tears down the walls."

The child nodded and gestured again. The sapling shrank back into the log, disappearing like nothing had ever happened. "I am glad you chose to see reason without further demonstrations. I can easily provide them if you lose faith again."

Paena sat, close to tears. "Why have you done this? I trusted you."

The child went over to Paena and hugged her. She went rigid in her arms. "You were cold, frightened, and lost. I could not leave you. You would have died." The child released Paena and stepped back. "Even then, I could see you were special. You had an inner spark I knew I could fan into a flame. When Kalten came, I could clearly see that you two were my best chance to regain my power."

Paena flinched as if she'd been struck. "So, we are simply a means to an end? How could you?"

The child slapped Paena on the cheek. Hard. "You ungrateful wretch. Yes, I had been waiting for someone like you, but you have been richly rewarded. I have given you abilities most mortals would kill for."

"I never asked for any of this." Tears filled Paena's eyes.

"No, you did not ask. But, without my help, you and Kalten would have failed long ago. You would be dead and this kingdom lost. Without my help, this child would never have been born."

Paena put her hand to her cheek. "You used us. You never cared about us at all."

"Stop your whining." Kayla/Mother Tully stamped her foot. "You will go back out and gather more support for your queen. You will fight for her, and you will win." The child regarded Baltar, a sly smile on her face. "And you will tell your queen that she will reward me for my help."

"Your help?" he asked. "What do you want?"

"Tell her she will know what I want when it is time. And tell her what I give, I can also take away." The child straightened, sticking her chin out. "Now, both of you. Go."

Paena could only mumble her agreement as she wiped her eyes.

~ * ~

"You have done well, Pieter," Duke Samuel said, clapping a startled Pieter on the shoulder. "Because of your diligence, I have been able to act against my enemies."

He wasn't sure what to say. "Thank you, my lord." He dried his forehead with a sleeve.

The duke went behind the desk in his study to pour himself a goblet of wine. "When I initially heard of your failure to kill the traitor, I was very angry," he said in a conversational tone.

"Yes, my lord." In a daze, Pieter watched the rich red liquid splash into the goblet.

"I had even gone to the trouble of ordering you killed for your failure." Duke Samuel took a sip. "I am pleased my order wasn't carried out."

"As am I, my lord." Pieter stared at his boots. "I only live to serve you, my lord."

"Excellent. Then you will not mind helping me again." It was not a question.

"I am yours to command, my lord."

The duke nodded. "Report to my steward, Marcus. He will get you provisioned."

"Provisioned, my lord?"

"Yes. Your job will be to sow uncertainty amongst the undecided nobility. Tell them whatever you must to get them to follow me or stay neutral. Keep them off balance enough so I can pass unhindered with my armies. You may rejoin me at the place known as Ursal's Muster. It is there we will do war on the queen."

Chapter Thirty-Four

Kalten lay on his blanket, head propped on his saddle for a pillow, and watched the flames of his fire. Around him in the darkness, dozens of campfires burned and hundreds of men prepared for war.

He and Bran had been lucky, so far. Most of the lords they met were eager to give aid when they heard about Baron Estevan's murder. None of them wanted to be on the side of such treachery, regardless of what they thought of Queen Elespeth.

The men around him represented only a tenth of the pledged forces. Mostly peasants, the commanders of the various nobles sent them on with Kalten and Bran while they gathered their armies. The others had to be called in from their farms to bolster their lords' armies.

Somewhere, out in the camp, Bran was hard at work trying to convince the more reluctant lords to join. He was good at it. Diplomacy, he called it. Kalten hadn't even tried. He knew diplomacy wasn't his strong suit. Paena had known it, and Bran agreed with Kalten, and so it went.

There was something wrong too. It wasn't with the gathering of soldiers or the pledging of loyalties from the lords. Kalten hadn't heard from Paena in days. When he called Lydaroth to reach her, the dragon admitted he hadn't heard from her either. She was out there, but her mind was closed to him. It was very strange.

Almost on cue, Kalten felt the presence in his mind that was the precursor to Lydaroth speaking with him. It was akin to someone knocking at the door before coming in.

"Kalten, are you awake?" Although the dragon already knew the answer to his question, he was always unfailingly polite.

"Hello, Lydaroth. Yes, I'm awake," Kalten replied. He had become very proficient communicating with the dragon in the past ten days. He didn't even need to move his lips anymore.

"That is good. I need to speak to you and Paena most urgently, but she still does not respond to my call."

"Perhaps she is upset by something. Can you sense anything?" Kalten asked.

"I cannot. She is healthy, but I do not understand your emotions well enough to know beyond that." The dragon paused until Kalten was afraid he'd left entirely. *"The time is short, and I am disgraced by the news I must bring."*

"What is it?"

"I have proof of the cooperation between the rebel dragons and your rebel lords. A young female dragon was captured during one of our raids. She has confessed nearly all." The dragon, once again, went silent.

"Really? What did she tell you?"

The dragon mentally coughed. *"Please forgive me, but this is very difficult to admit."* He paused again, and then plunged forward. *"The rebels on both sides plan to attack and destroy your queen and her followers. Then, they will combine forces to eliminate me and mine."*

"That is not completely unexpected," Kalten said. *"She gave you the location of the rebel dragons' base, then?"*

"Alas, she did not."

"You are still questioning her? She might still tell you where the slaves are being kept?"

The dragon's words were stilted and sad as he said, *"We will not be questioning her further. Partway through the interrogation she attacked my people. Rather than answer any questions regarding where the rebels were, the female fought her captors. They were forced to kill her to protect themselves."*

"Lydaroth." For a moment, words failed Kalten. *"Lydaroth, you have my sympathy and condolences. I know you never wanted this."*

"No. I never wanted this to pass. But it has, and we must move forward. It is hard to accept. I still have trouble admitting my people's failure to keep the peace. Even those who have been banished."

"Lydaroth, now is not the time to dwell on the short-comings of our two peoples. We must make ready for battle whether we want to fight or not. The rebels on both sides have made sure of that."

"You are right, of course. I will gather my people and prepare to fight." The dragon sighed. *"I had just hoped never to see dragon battle dragon."*

"I understand," Kalten said. *"I wish we had a choice, but since we don't, we must be ready for the worst. Please meet with me at Ursal's Muster, the large grassy plain north and west of the capital city."*

"I will do what you ask. I will see you there in five days."

"Good luck, my friend. I will see you soon." Kalten felt the dragon leave his mind. He was already thinking of how to get in contact

with Paena.

There was no getting around it. Whether he wanted to do it or not, it had to be done. *"Kayla. Kayla, can you hear me?"* He half hoped she wouldn't answer.

"Hello, Father." Kayla's voice echoed in his mind. *"I wondered how long it would be before you accepted me."*

"You can keep wondering, then, because I haven't accepted you yet. I may never. But I need your help."

"Why should I help you when you are being so mean, Father?" Kayla's mental voice sounded sulky.

"Because if you don't, then the queen could lose her throne. Then where would we all be?"

"Very well, Father. What do you want?"

"I want you to contact Paena and pass on some very important information to her."

"Why should I bother?" Kayla sounded almost bored at Kalten's request.

"Now, you listen here…"

"No, Father. You listen. Mother is just approaching your camp. Why don't you just go out to see her yourself?"

"Don't be smart, girl." He was just about to sever the contact before curiosity caught him. *"Just a question for you, before I go. Do you know what is bothering Paena?"*

"I think you should probably ask her that yourself, Father. I will see you very soon. Goodbye for now." With that, Kayla's presence was gone.

There was nothing for it but to go meet Paena. Maybe she could shed some additional light on this whole Kayla business.

He moved toward the southern pickets. If Paena were coming in from the capital, those were the ones she should come in through.

He had only just reached the innermost guard post when he heard Niale's hail from the darkness. Kalten jogged forward, not wanting to wait for them.

A pair of riders emerged from out of the darkness into the light of the guard-post. Niale, in the front, led a second horse and rider. The horses were lathered in foam and dark with sweat. The second rider rode hunched over the saddle, covered head to toe in a black cloak.

Kalten caught the bridle of the second horse just after Niale stopped his mount. "Niale, what happened? Is Paena hurt?"

"Not sure what's wrong with her, sir." Niale wearily dismounted from his horse. "She's been like this since before we left. Don't talk to no one or even really do much of anything."

"Paena. Are you all right?" Kalten asked.

She didn't move a muscle. Kalten reached up to shake her by the leg.

"Paena. Speak to me."

Paena dully lifted her head. Her face was pale, and her eyes were red and puffy.

"Kalten?" She lifted her head a little more and squinted at him. "Kalten is that you?"

"I'm here. It's me."

"Oh Kalten." She half fell, half jumped from her saddle into his arms and buried her face in his shoulder. Muffled sobs wracked her body.

He held her for a moment before taking charge. "You men," he said to two of the guards. "Take these horses and get them taken care of. Niale, bring whatever gear you need and follow me." He pointed to a third man. "You, help him."

Kalten waited for Niale to follow and led the way, carrying Paena. She lay in his arms, face still buried in his shoulder, body shaking.

They got back to Kalten's fire to find Bran had just arrived. "I'm glad you're back. You're just in time for Paena and Niale."

"It's good to see you," the big man said, stepping forward to clasp Niale by the arm. "Can you tell what's wrong with Paena?"

"I really couldn't say, my lord," Niale said, shrugging. "She's been like this since she met with Lord Baltar and the child, Kayla. All I know is Lord Baltar ordered us back here. She hasn't said a word to me the entire time we traveled."

"Niale, you should go and get something hot to eat. No doubt you have orders for us from Baltar. When you're done please come back, and let us know what they are. I'll stay here with Paena. I want to try and find out what's bothering her."

"I'll take him," Bran said. "He can relay any orders while he eats."

"I tell you, my lord, it was unnerving…" Niale's voice faded as he followed Bran.

Kalten gently pried Paena loose from his shoulder. "Paena, it's just you and me, now. What's going on?"

Dark circles rimmed her tear-swollen eyes. "Oh, Kalten. It's that witch. She's been using us since the beginning." She burst into tears again.

"Witch? You mean, Mother Tully?" At Paena's mute nod, he swore. "Now what has she done?"

"She tricked. She took the baby so she would have someone bound to her and to bind us. Remember when we agreed to give her a life to save yours? I'm sure the baby was that life. Everything she's said and done was to get her powers back."

"That makes no sense. She's got plenty of powers that I've seen."

Paena grabbed Kalten's head. "Kalten! Mother Tully isn't a witch. She's a goddess. She was just very weak when we met her. She has been using us to get back what she lost. And she is using our daughter to do it, just like she's using us."

"A goddess?" He laughed.

"Tulliandars. That's what she called herself. She created this land and was worshiped here until all her people either left or died. I didn't believe either until Baltar said he knew of her. Now she's using us to get her strength back. And she has already struck some sort of bargain with Queen Elespeth."

"I knew something was wrong. She actually told you she was using us?"

Paena sniffed and wiped her eyes. "Yes. I wanted to stay in the capital to learn more about Kayla. I told Baltar he had to wait. Then Kayla came in, possessed by Mother Tully. She ordered me to come here and told me we were the means to the return of her power."

"How does she plan to accomplish that?"

"I don't know her entire plan. I do know she has struck a bargain with the queen; if she helps in the coming war she expects to be rewarded."

Kalten swore and shook his fist at the sky. "I knew you were a fake, you crone. Well, I'm done with being led around by you." He unbuckled his sword and threw it to the ground. "You can just do this without me. Do you hear me?"

If he expected an answer, he was doomed to disappointment. Only silence greeted his shouts. Silence punctuated by the sounds of Paena's grief.

~ * ~

"Kalten, where are you going?" Paena asked. Kalten's presence had finally helped her to stop weeping.

"I'm done with being manipulated. I've had enough, and I'm going home."

"To what? There's no one there anymore." That stopped him. "Wasn't that the reason you started this? To find your family?"

He just stood beside his horse, leaning his head against the saddle. "What would you have me do?"

"Let's finish what we started. Let's get the queen her soldiers and then…"

"What?"

"We finish the rebels and find your family." She put her hand on his back. "I know how much you miss them."

"Not as much as you think, obviously."

"What do you mean? That's all you talked about when we met—how you were going to find your family."

"That's true, but until you mentioned them just now, I had actually forgotten they were gone. I've been so busy doing this." He swept his arm out to indicate the camp and soldiers. "I'd managed to forget what was most important to me. I didn't even do that when I was a soldier."

"You're being too hard on yourself. I doubt you ever had the kind of responsibility and pressures we've had since this started."

"Do you really think that matters? Would my mother say 'It's all right that you forgot about us, Kalten. We know you were busy?' My family is counting on me."

"How do you know that? You were dragged away from your home at sword point."

He put his arms around her and held her. "You're right. As usual."

Sounds of the waking camp surrounded them.

"You should know by now that I'm never wrong. Get used to it already."

Kalten hugged Paena tightly for a moment. "I am so glad I was forced to work with you. I never would have gone with you otherwise."

"I was a bitch," she said. "I wouldn't have gone with me either."

"So, what's different?" he said, jumping back and laughing when she threw a punch at him. He warded her off with his hands. "No, no. I surrender. You win."

She stopped attacking him. "That's better. Now, we should think about getting back on the road. We've got a kingdom to save."

"All right, but I want to say one last thing," he said.

"What's that?"

"I won't be used by Mother Tully anymore. "

"I thought we already decided that."

"We had, but part of it is the powers Mother Tully 'grants' us. I won't ask her anymore, no matter what."

"You're sure? We may need those powers in the next few days."

He set his jaw. "I won't be used anymore. No matter what."

Paena shrugged. "I won't argue with you. But we should get started."

He nodded. "I'll get 'em up and ready."

It was well past mid-morning by the time the camp packed up and the men made ready to march out. They took to the road, Bran, Kalten, and Paena in the lead, the troops strung out behind on foot with the provision wagons bringing up the rear.

They marched past abandoned fields and empty towns. The weather held dry, and the roads were good so they made excellent time. There were no people to be seen anywhere.

At about mid-day, the army came around a twist in the road to find thirty mounted knights blocking the way. Arrayed five across and six deep, they waited, visors down and lances ready. The knights wore surcoats of green and teal with a golden sheaf of wheat emblazoned on the chest. Only the leader sat his horse with his visor raised.

Kalten and Bran rode forward to meet with the group. Kalten carried a swatch of white cloth above his head to indicate peaceful parley. The man met them with one of his knights.

"My lord, what is the meaning of this?" Bran asked when they were close enough to speak.

"You may not enter my lands," the man replied. "I am Earl Reitmark, and I wish to remain outside this conflict. You must find another way to the capital."

"Surely, you don't intend to defy the queen's commands, my lord?" Kalten said. "We are out by her orders and must make all haste."

"It is my intention to keep my lands safe, young man," the earl replied. He removed his helmet showing a lean, leathery face, piercing blue eyes and a fringe of thinning brown hair. "I don't believe Her Majesty can do that, so I must stay close to home with my knights to protect my crops and my people."

It was Bran's turn to speak. "My lord Reitmark. Queen Elespeth has commanded us to gather a force to come to her aid. Will you not ride with us?"

"I will not. Have you not been listening? And you will not travel through my lands. My knights and I will battle you if we must."

"You would fight us, rather than let us peacefully move through?" Kalten couldn't believe his ears. "Do you not see that we have you vastly outnumbered?"

The man sneered. "You may have the numbers, boy, but to my eye, they are mostly peasants. I believe my knights can make short work of them."

"If that's the way to want to do it," Kalten said, beginning to turn his horse around.

"Hold," Bran said, grabbing the bridle of Kalten's horse to stop him. "I cannot believe what I am hearing. My father always told me you were a man of honor and courage, not one to hide and avoid the fight."

Reitmark straightened in his saddle, moving his hand to his sword hilt. "Who is this father of yours? And who are you to impugn my honor?"

"My father was Baron Estevan, and I am his son Bran. I would call any man coward who would rather hide on his lands than fight for justice against the murderers of old men." Bran's voice had gotten louder and louder while he spoke until it carried to the knights waiting down the road. They shifted in their saddles, as their mounts danced nervously.

Kalten loosened his sword in its sheath. The next few moments could get very nasty.

"I will challenge each and every man in your party, my lord, if that is what it takes to get past," Bran said. "But we are going through your lands, with or without your permission. I have the murder of my father and all my own retainers to avenge."

The earl's men moved to protect him, but did not attack. Reitmark waved them back. "That is the second time you have used the word murder. But it is not murder to kill cleanly on the field of battle."

"Is that what they told you?" Bran asked, amazement coloring his words. "Then, my lord, you can add lying to the list of crimes perpetrated by these villains." He shook his head and leaned over the pommel of his saddle toward the earl. "My father has not been able to ride into battle for almost a half-score of years. The treacherous attack that killed him and all my men happened at our manor. Men without livery, supported by dragons are responsible. Does that sound like an honorable death?"

Bran shouted now, angered almost beyond reason, "Is it honorable to impale an old man who can barely lift a sword, then behead him and carry away his head for a prize?"

Earl Reitmark wiped his brow and backed his horse away a couple steps. "I had no idea. I only know what I have heard."

Kalten kneed his horse in front of Bran's. "My lord, it is clear you know what's coming, just like it is clear you have been told some of what has already happened. But I say to you, the men who did these things are without honor and cannot be trusted."

The earl appeared uncertain for a moment. "If what you say is true, then I cannot, in good conscience, stop or impede your travel." He studied Kalten for a few moments. "I have decided. My knights and I will escort you through my lands." He gestured to his escort. "Let the men know and get them ready." The man nodded and rode back to the band of knights.

"Thank you, my lord," Kalten said. "Although I'd rather have you and your men coming with us."

"My place is here, lad. My people need protecting." He was interrupted by one of his knights galloping back.

"My lord, the messenger has taken flight. When word was given that you would allow their passage, he killed his escort and made away. I have sent two men after him, but they are riding the heavy horse, and he is on a courier mount. I doubt we can catch him."

Reitmark ran his gauntleted hand through his hair. "Send an alert to all the outposts. Warn them to watch for any kind of surprise attack. And take the men to guard the town. That is most likely where they will go." He waved the man away. "Go. Quickly. I will personally escort these." After the man rode away, he wearily rubbed his eyes.

"My lord, who is this messenger you speak of?" Bran asked.

"A man came to my manor this morning warning of your approach. It is he who told me the story of Baron Estevan's death on the battlefield." The earl sighed. "It is becoming impossible to know friend from foe in these troubled times."

"My lord, we can bring our troops to help guard the town," Kalten said.

"You would do that, even after this foolishness?"

Bran turned his horse back to the levies and called over his shoulder, "Just lead the way, my lord."

"Then we had better get started."

Chapter Thirty-Five

Paena and Kalten rode ahead of the column of troops that loosely marched behind. Four horse-lengths in front of them, Bran and Earl Reitmark rode side-by-side, arguing strategies. Half the knights had ridden ahead to provide advance support for the earl's town.

"Have you heard from Lydaroth?" Kalten asked as he scanned the horizon. After witnessing the slaughter at Baron Estevan's mansion, he had no desire to go in without the aid of the dragons.

Paena reined in her mare next to him. "You already asked me that when we broke camp this morning. I already told you I had last night. Is there a problem?"

"I'm sorry. I always get jittery before a battle." He flashed her a quick smile. "You know what a worrier I am."

She gripped his hand. "I like that you worry. It means you're thinking ahead. The day you stop, I'll definitely start."

"Thank you. I know I'm repeating myself, but I'm very glad you're here."

She smiled fondly. "So am I." Her face took on a look of concentration. "Can you hear that?"

He listened carefully. At first, there were only the sounds of horses and marching men. But with increasing clarity, he heard the sound of large wings flapping through the air.

Both he and Paena searched the skies for signs of dragons. Kalten felt the echoes of Paena's thoughts when she reached out to Lydaroth. He knew at the same moment she did, the approaching dragons were not Lydaroth and his followers.

"To the trees." Kalten turned in his saddle and yelled while kneeing his stallion to the side of the road.

At his orders, men scrambled under the cover of the trees that lined the road. Bran and Earl Reitmark found cover last, waiting until the knights moved off.

Kalten scanned the skies with bated breath, hoping against hope they could evade detection. On the road, they would be easy targets for the rebel dragons.

First one, then three more dragons flew overhead. Every one of the mighty beasts was colored a dark hue that reminded him of nothing else but a dark stain. A collective sigh of relief went up after the last dragon passed.

"Attention men," he shouted. "You saw what just went by. That means the earl's town is about to be attacked." He could see the fear in the eyes of the men closest to him. "You don't need to worry about the dragons, though. Lady Paena has already single-handedly destroyed five of the beasts using her magic. She will protect you from them. While she keeps them off you, your job is to protect the people of the town from the enemy soldiers that are coming. Now, back to the road and march, double-time."

His orders were relayed down the line. Some of the men moved reluctantly, but his command was carried out without exception.

"Why did you tell them I killed five by myself?" Paena asked. "You know very well you had a hand in it."

"I know, but right now, they need something to believe in. They move like men ready to battle. A few moments ago, they looked like they were ready to run away." He watched the men march by. "If I had told them we both were involved, the moment they see I'm not doing anything, they might panic and run."

"But what if I can't do it alone?"

"You can do it," he said. "I know you can. Just like I know I can never ask that crone for her help again." He saw the look on her face. "Don't worry. I'll protect you from soldiers while you take care of the dragons. I won't let anything happen to you."

"I know you won't, but it's still a big risk."

Kalten set his jaw. "I won't ask her help again. Now let's get going before we're left behind." He spurred his horse and galloped back to his place in the column, Paena right behind him. Bran rode back to meet them.

"The earl is readying his knights to ride to the town," he said after they met. "You two should be with them. I'll lead the men in. I want to be with the knights when they get to the town, more than you can know, but judging by what just flew overhead, you are more important than I right now. I will get my chance to exact revenge soon enough, but if you do not take care of the dragons, the knights and levies are useless." He gave them both a hard look. "Now go before I change my mind."

Kalten nodded to Bran and rode up to meet with the knights. Paena nudged her mare to follow Kalten.

As the two met up with the knights, Earl Reitmark gave out a last few words of encouragement. "With the support of our allies, we will win the day and save the town. I know I can count on you all to fight like lions. Good luck."

The knights, to a man, spurred their horses forward, the earl in the lead. Despite having the faster horses, Kalten and Paena could barely keep up.

They galloped up the road behind the knights and came over a rise. An extensive fallow field bordered on one side by a wide stretch of river lay in front of them. A palisaded town occupied the far side of the field.

A large body of men approached the town, and the dragons were already swooping out of the sky, raining fire on the wooden buildings. Smoke billowed from a dozen fires. Atop the palisade, soldiers vainly shot arrows at the flaming beasts. The screams of dying men echoed across the field.

There was no time to lose. "Paena, call the lightning," Kalten said, taking hold of her horse. "I'll take care of you."

"I'm not sure I can do this alone," she said.

"You can do it. I know you can. Pull energy from me if you must. Now destroy those dragons or the town is lost."

She nodded, bowed her head then closed her eyes. He could almost feel the energy begin to build around her.

The sky darkened, and clouds formed above the town. A wind sprang up and within moments, bursts of lightning flashed in the sky. The dragons ignored the impending storm and continued to rain destruction on the buildings.

The earl and his knights lowered their visors and thundered down the hill toward the armed attackers. The attackers changed direction and, as a single unit, turned toward the oncoming riders. The square formed by the attackers never faltered. Despite himself, Kalten had to marvel at their poise and training.

Paena's flung her head back and thrust out her arms. The first blast of lightning struck a dragon while it flew almost directly above the main gate. The charred carcass of the beast spiraled, smoking, to the ground, crashing onto the field. At its death, a faint cheer rose from the walls.

The knights reached the perimeter of the attacking square. With their lances aimed at the shield wall, the first wave of knights smashed into the attackers, driving deep into the formation, scattering men like shorn wheat. A second group harried the edge of the square, allowing the first to make their escape.

The earl's knights rode away from the enemy without casualties although several men clutched at wounds or leaned heavily over in their saddles.

Kalten could see Paena struggle with the effort of summoning lightning. He put a hand on her leg and willed his own energy to aid her. A light-headed euphoria filled him as his own reserves flowed to meet her need.

Lightning lanced from the sky in bright flashes of light and claps of thunder. The remaining dragons were blasted from the sky by a massive, forked bolt. The concussive thunderclap knocked men to their knees, and a guard tower slowly collapsed in on itself in a rising cloud of dust.

Paena moaned and fainted the same moment the guard tower fell. Kalten caught her before she tumbled from her saddle. Instantly, the lightning stopped, and everything went still. The skies cleared.

The knights continued to swarm the attackers, but their numbers dwindled after the enemy reformed its phalanx and repelled their attacks. More than a dozen horses careened around the field with empty saddles.

And through all this, the levies still hadn't arrived to reinforce the knights.

So intent was Kalten watching the battle below, he almost missed the small group of riders who attacked from behind. Only the yell of one of them alerted him to the danger.

He turned to see five riders racing toward him and instinctively kicked his horse in front of Paena to protect her. He yanked out his sword and only barely blocked the first swing. His stallion reared up, striking at the oncoming men, protecting his rider.

Kalten hadn't expected the stallion's defense and, in his weakened state, was thrown to the ground. He gamely jumped to his feet only to almost be knocked back down by a rushing horse.

A man stabbed at him, but Kalten knocked away his thrust at the last moment. He was fending off the hammering blows of the rider above him when he heard the horn. The levies had finally arrived.

He spared a quick glance toward Paena. She was still slumped in the saddle, apparently unconscious. His stallion attacked the enemy riders alone while the mare backed her out of the melee.

That moment of distraction betrayed Kalten. His attacker thrust his sword through Kalten's leather armor into his chest. He screamed and looked down dumbly at the blade where bright red blood already pulsed from the wound.

As he fell to the ground, the levies streamed over the hill. They swarmed toward the attackers on the field.

His killer brutally yanked the sword from his body after Kalten collapsed to the turf. The stallion, with a feral scream, struck the man and his mount to the ground and smashed them into the earth.

The last thing Kalten saw was the stallion crushing his killer's skull beneath its hooves.

Chapter Thirty-Six

There were no more tears to cry. Paena could only stand mutely staring at the shroud that covered Kalten's cold and lifeless body. Bran's men had erected a tent over him where Kalten had fallen. Somehow it just didn't seem real.

Bran ducked into the tent. His face reflected the sorrow she knew she should feel. "Are you going to be all right?"

"I don't know," she answered. She really didn't. Her partner and friend was gone. His loss was almost too much to bear. She wanted to grieve, but the tears refused to come. "I tried to revive him, but the healing was denied. I don't know why."

Bran bowed his head as if in prayer. After a moment, he nodded and straightened. "If you need anything, I'll be just outside."

"Thank you."

She stepped closer to the body. Not body, she corrected herself. Kalten. She gently lifted away the shroud. In the dimness of the tent, his face looked strangely peaceful, if pale. A lock of hair had fallen over his right eye, and there was a smudge of dirt on his cheek. Her hand brushed the hard crust of dried blood over the terrible wound in his chest.

A sob caught in her throat. He'd done what he promised. He had protected her from harm. She had failed him by collapsing when he needed her most. His death was her fault.

She banged her fists against his chest and screamed. Curse him for a hard-headed fool. If he had just used his powers, this wouldn't have happened.

Even while she blamed him, she was ashamed. He had been poorly used by Mother Tully. They both had. He had, ultimately, been the braver one for refusing the old woman's help.

After she thought it, Paena wondered if she had the strength to go on without him. She'd thought she was the strong one. In the end, it had been him.

She tilted her head back and screamed again, a primal sound.

"Mother Tully, why have you done this to us?" She yelled toward the ceiling, "What did we ever do to deserve this? I hate you!" Leaning over Kalten's body, Paena held him and cried.

Through her tears, she could see the light brightening in the tent. "Could you leave us alone, please?" She wasn't ready to face anyone just yet. Light continued to fill the tent.

She turned, ready to scream the intruder out of the tent. Except, her visitor wasn't one of the men.

"So, you hate me now, do you?" Mother Tully asked mildly. The old woman standing in the tent looked much like she had when they last parted. But there was something subtly different about her, a new vibrancy.

"You blame me for this, do you?" The old woman—goddess—Paena reminded herself, drew near Kalten's body. She clicked her tongue when she looked at him. "He always was a stubborn one, was he not? At the beginning, I thought I would have to kill him. Apparently, all I had to do was wait for him to do it to himself."

With a cry of rage, Paena sprang at the old woman, ready to tear her apart. An unseen power slammed her to the ground.

"You are angry," the old woman said. "That I understand. But know you this." She loomed over Paena. "I saved you from the forest. You did not thank me. I gave you powers any mortal would covet, and you scream and rave at me. Now you dare to attack me?" The old woman slapped Paena hard. "I made you. I can destroy you just as easily."

"You made me?" Paena couldn't believe her ears. She climbed to her feet and stood face-to-face with the goddess, their noses practically touching. "You have tricked us, used us and stolen from us." Paena glared at the goddess, hands on her hips. "I will not help you. Go ahead, destroy me. Nothing you can do frightens me anymore."

"It should," the old woman murmured, shaking her head. "It truly should. But I still have use for you, so I shall let you live a little longer."

"Weren't you listening?" Paena screeched. "I've already told you I'm done with being used by you."

"I heard you. But you will do what I say. I still have your daughter, after all."

"What of Kalten?"

"He is dead. What of him?"

"Can you bring him back?"

"Why would I wish to do that?" Mother Tully's eyes flashed at the question. "He refused my gifts and insulted me."

"He's my friend. I need him. I can't finish this without him."

"You will find a way." Mother Tully regarded his body. "I will not bring him back for you. He must pay penance for his mistreatment of me. I will take his body. He was my champion, albeit a poor one, therefore, he belongs to me."

"If I refuse?"

"You will likely die just like he did, and your daughter will be called to take your place."

Paena tried another tack. "She may be the child of my body, but I don't know her. What is that to me?"

Mother Tully smiled. "You do not deceive me, Paena. I know you care for Kayla even though you did not raise her. You would sooner die than put her in danger."

"She is merely another tool to you," she said. "It might be a kindness to put her in where she would be killed."

"There are many ways to die," Mother Tully said, malice filling her voice. "If you disobey, I can promise you her death, when it finally comes, will be one filled with great suffering. Would you be able to live with that knowledge?"

Paena's defiance melted away. "I wouldn't." Her voice was a whisper. "What would you have me do?"

A look of satisfaction crossed Mother Tully's face. "I would have you ride to the queen. Go to her, and fight as her champion. She will need the full benefit of my gifts to win the day against her enemies."

"But…"

"The time for questions is over. The queen needs you now." Mother Tully laid a hand on his body. "I will leave now and take him with me." She faded. "Go with my blessings. I will be watching." With those words she disappeared, along with Kalten's body.

Paena looked around in disbelief. He was really gone, and she hadn't even had a chance to say goodbye. She touched his bloody cuirass that had been abandoned on the floor. "Farewell, my friend. I shall miss you more than you will ever know."

She wiped her eyes and left the tent, blinking at the sudden brightness of the sun.

Kayla moved into Paena's line of sight on a large horse; her feet barely reached the already much shortened stirrups. "Are you ready to go, Mother?"

Paena was confused. "When did you get here? What are you doing here?"

"The goddess brought me while you were weeping over Father." The girl could have been discussing the weather for all the emotion in her voice.

She took a closer look at the girl and her mount. Kalten's horse. It couldn't be. "Kayla, where did you get that horse?"

"Mother Tully gave him to me. She said Father wouldn't need it any longer."

The grief threatened to overwhelm Paena. "How dare you!" She was interrupted by Lydaroth's voice in her mind.

"Paena, I will be arriving shortly. Please let your men know we are coming."

If that were true, she didn't have a moment to lose. Grief for Kalten would have to wait. She ran, calling for Bran and warning everyone she saw.

The final man had just been alerted when the dragons came out of the clouds. Ten dragons in total flew into view in a perfect V-formation. They were a rainbow of colors: silver, green, blue, and red. Lydaroth had turned fully gold now. None bore the dark taint of the rebels, and each one carried a large cage filled with people.

The dragons took turns gently depositing the cages down on the grass near the camp, and then flew to the part of the plain farthest from the baron's town to land and wait.

Lydaroth set his cargo down last. By that point, the men of the camp had released most of the people from the ten cages. Some of the prisoners had to be carried out. Many were old men and women too aged to walk without support.

Lydaroth landed just outside the camp, nearest to Paena.

"Paena, it is good to see you again," he said after she arrived. *"We have brought those people found alive in the rebels' camp. We finally located it yesterday. The rebels had already fled."* His mental voice had a sorrowful tone. *"They took the able-bodied ones with them and left the elderly and infirm behind to die. That is what one of the slaves told me."*

She rushed up to the dragon and wrapped her arms around his neck in a hug. *"Lydaroth, I'm so glad to see you. You look well."*

"I am well, but heartsick at what my kind has done," he said. *"Though I rejoice to see you, I must ask. Where is Kalten? I cannot sense him."*

She released the dragon and stepped away from him, gaze on the ground. *"Kalten is dead."*

With her close proximity, Lydaroth said, "Dead? How did it happen?"

"He died protecting me during the last battle."

"I sorrow for you, Paena. Is there anything I can do?"

She laughed bitterly. "Not unless you can convince Mother

Tully to bring him back."

"I can try to convince her for you," the dragon offered. His voice took on a note of distaste as he said, "I suppose I could… eat her for you if you want."

Her laugh was genuine this time. "That won't be necessary, my friend, but thank you for the offer. Unfortunately, I don't think you could eat her since she is a goddess, not a witch like we thought. Her real name is Tulliandars."

The dragon was silent for several moments. "That makes sense," he finally said. "I always wondered why my father was so eager to maintain the pact he made with her so many years ago. If she were a goddess, he would not have been strong enough to stand against her. None of us would be."

"She used Kalten and me to gain her power back," Paena said. "Everything she did was to get her powers. She never intended to help us at all. And now Kalten is dead." She sighed and shook her head, trying to brighten up. "And you, my good friend. I haven't thanked you for bringing the captives back."

"It was the least I could do," the dragon rumbled, pleased. "I just wish we could have found their camp before they left with all the able-bodied slaves. I shudder to think what might happen to them."

"Lydaroth," she said. "I'm glad to see you and your people here. But this isn't all of them, is it?"

It was the dragon's turn to laugh. "Not at all. I have my people near the meeting place, but out of sight so our enemies do not know about them. And so they do not frighten our allies."

"Very wise, Lydaroth. How many warriors have you brought?"

"At least ten-score. We must win decisively. If too many rebel dragons escape, we will all be fighting for many years to come."

"How many do you think they will have?"

"Three-score, maybe four. But no more than that. Even if all of their females had a hatching every year since their exile, they could have no more."

Suddenly things were looking up. "Then we will have the advantage in the air. That might be very important."

Bran came over. "Correction. It *will* be very important. It is too bad the people you brought were not seasoned warriors, not that I am ungrateful that you freed them. You might as well know… I have just received word from one of our scouts. The enemy troops are almost to the battlefield. Worse, they already outnumber us ten to one."

"Ten to one?" Her brows lifted. "How close did your scout say they were to the mustering grounds?"

"A day's march, maybe less," he replied. "Of course, that was some time ago. Unless they have stopped for some reason, they may already be there."

"Then we've got to get these men to the queen now. Every man counts, especially if the odds are so stacked against us. Lydaroth, with such a huge disadvantage in troops, the queen will need your warriors even more."

"Paena," the dragon's tone sounded unhappy. "Do not count on me or my warriors in the ground fighting with the enemy troops. My apologies, but you expect more than we can give. I thought it would be clear to you. We consider attacking humans to be anathema. We will only join battle if we are struck first and must defend ourselves."

"What?" She couldn't quite believe what she was hearing. "But you threatened us when we first met in the dragon lands."

"That is true," he said with a nod. "You were trespassing on our territory; attacking you in such a situation would be considered self-defense."

"Is there nothing we can say that will convince you to fight on the queen's behalf?"

"I have already agreed to fight on her behalf. We will battle the rebel dragons for you. We will not initiate any aggression against humans, be they friend or foe. You must understand, it was battling humans unprovoked that almost led our race to extinction in the distant past. We have been taught in the generations since to avoid confrontation with humans unless threatened."

"I wish that wasn't the case, Lydaroth. I was counting on your support against the duke's troops," Bran said.

"I am sorry to disappoint you, but we will not go against our natures."

"We," Paena indicated herself and Bran, "are grateful for what you can do. It just means the men we have here are even more important to the queen's cause."

"I do not disagree with you, but be reasonable. The men just finished a hard march followed by a battle. They are not in any condition to go back on the road now." Bran slapped his gloves against his thigh. "Even if we could go now, we would be too late. The rendezvous point is more than a full day's march away."

"I can make it. My mare can run almost non-stop," she said. "It might be close, but with the powers I've been given, I can make some difference in the battle."

The Earl Reitmark joined the group. "May I offer my thanks for your help today, lady," he said, bowing his head toward Paena. "Without you earlier today, those men and their dragons would have massacred us and destroyed the town. For that, and for opening my eyes to the treachery of my peers, I would pledge my support now, if you will have me."

"My lord, we accept both your thanks and your support," she said. "But we still have the problem of how to get to the meeting place."

"We can help you with that," Lydaroth said. "We brought people here with us, and we can take people away as well."

"Brilliant," Bran said with a smile.

"What about me and my men?" the earl asked. "Could you bring both us and our horses?"

Lydaroth pondered for a few heartbeats. "We could definitely bring you, but the horses would be too frightened and too heavy for us to carry."

"Leave the horses, my lord," Bran said. "The queen's forces must have spare mounts. You could ride those."

"A good solution," the earl said, nodding. "I will go and prepare my men. Shall we meet back here?"

"Yes. Bran will work with you," Paena said. "But I must leave now if I am to meet with the queen in time. I will see you at the battlefield."

He stepped forward. "Paena, what would you have me do with Kalten's body?"

She set her jaw. "There is nothing to do. Tulliandars has taken his body away. You will find the tent empty."

"Empty? Then, I will do as you ask and go with the earl," Bran said with a nod.

"Farewell again, Paena," Lydaroth said. "I wish you good speed and safe journey."

She waved farewell and ran to the horse line. The mare waited saddled and bridled, and Kayla sat the stallion nearby waiting. Paena shook her head. She hadn't really paid attention to it before, but the mare always seemed to be ready when needed. She realized she shouldn't be surprised by anything from Tulliandars anymore.

They were on the road in moments, taking their horses out of the camp at a fast trot. They followed the road that would take them past the town and beyond.

Paena edged her mare closer to Kayla. "Kayla, I don't know why you are here, but we need to get to the queen as fast as possible. Even at a full gallop the entire way, we might be too late."

"You must ask the goddess for her help," Kayla said simply. "She will assist us."

Paena considered her words. "We need to ask her for speed so we can get there quicker."

"Yes."

She immediately began praying to Tulliandars for her help, hating the necessity of it. "Tulliandars, grant us the speed to get to the battleground in time." She hoped Kayla was right.

As Paena opened her eyes, the muscles of the mare tensed and got harder. She looked over at Kayla who nodded. "Let's go."

They kneed their horses to a gallop. At first, nothing unusual happened. Then, with a jolt, the world narrowed and twisted, and everything became a blur.

The sensation lasted for a few moments only before the horses were, once again, merely galloping down the road. They reined up the horses and looked around.

The earl's town, easily seen when they left, was gone, and the entire landscape seemed to have changed. They were still on the road, but the land had become hilly, and the forest crouched around them too thick to see into very far. A few ravens perched on a nearby oak. The road had been churned up by the passing of many feet, both equine and human. Paena shrugged and nudged the mare, once again, into a fast trot, with Kayla right behind.

They crested a hill, and Paena gasped in surprise. Below, stretched out across the plain, were two armies.

Queen Elespeth's forces camped next to a river. The queen's pavilion was surrounded by a small city of tents. Her flags and pennants, along with those of her supporters, crackled in the stiff breeze that blew through the valley. Soldiers moved among the tents looking like an army of ants from their vantage point.

On the opposite side of the plain, backed up against a vast tract of trees, the army of the enemy lords filled the area. Their numbers dwarfed those of the queen. The mere idea of battling the massive force sent a shiver down Paena's back. How could they be defeated?

She allowed herself a small smile. They would find a way to win or die trying. There was no other choice.

Chapter Thirty-Seven

The morale in the queen's camp was nearly non-existent. Paena could sense it before the guards half-heartedly challenged them. Few fires burned, tents sagged or lay flat on the ground and soldiers wandered around listlessly. From the stance of the guards, they were ready to run away at the first sign of trouble.

They rode directly to report to Queen Elespeth and Lord Baltar. The command tent, a large, maroon-colored structure, was one of the few tents properly set up. Stern-faced guards in full armor surrounded the tent, their weapons drawn. Only Baltar came out of the command tent to meet with them. Kayla stayed discreetly behind Paena.

He waved off a groom and helped Paena from her horse hugging her as he lifted her down. "Welcome back, my dear. I am so pleased to see you safe and well."

"It's good to see you too, my lord," she replied. "I just wish I brought you better news."

"And what news is that?" he asked. "You have done well to gather the support we already have. Are more on the way?"

"A dozen knights and two-score of foot soldiers should be arriving around nightfall. They are being brought to us by our dragon allies."

At his questioning expression, she explained, "We were a full day's march away from here this morning, my lord. We were lucky to have Lydaroth meet us at Earl Reitmark's town. He agreed to bring the men knowing how urgently the queen needed them. Especially after the treachery of certain other lords."

"She definitely needs them," Baltar agreed, turning his head toward the enemy lines. "One only needs look to the far end of the field to realize how desperate our plight is."

She followed his gaze and nodded. "We have hope more men will come. Kalten did meet many lords who pledged to help. They are to meet us here."

"Yes, and where is young Kalten?" He stiffened a little when his gaze settled on Kayla. He turned to Paena, grabbing her shoulders. "Where's Kalten? And why is that child with you?"

She struggled to keep her emotions under control. "Kalten was…" She paused for a moment. "Kalten died in a battle earlier today defending me." Tears threatened to fall, but she savagely fought them back. "Tulliandars sent Kayla in his place to help me."

Baltar held her in a fierce embrace. "Paena, I am so sorry. Kalten was a fine man."

Paena let the older man hold her for a few moments before she gently pushed him away. "Yes sir, he was. He was a good friend, and now he's gone." She was amazed at how calm she sounded.

He stared at her for a moment. "Yes, of course." He was suddenly all business. "How long before you expect the other men to arrive?"

"I don't know, my lord. Kalten told me the men were on the march almost immediately after he met with their lords."

He sighed. "I hope they come soon, then. Men have already begun to desert because of the odds against us."

"Stay strong, my lord. I will be able to provide some help too. Not to mention that Lydaroth is bringing ten-score dragons to our aid."

"Ten-score?" Baltar whistled. "That is good news indeed. I must tell Queen Elespeth and her strategists at once. It may change the plans they are making."

Kayla stepped forward. "Then she must also be told about the number of dragons that support the enemy, my lord. They have fewer, but will still bring some into the battle. Lydaroth estimates that they may have four-score themselves, and the enemy dragons have proven to be without mercy. I'm not sure he fully understands how ferociously they will fight."

"You must also tell her Lydaroth and his followers will not engage the enemy soldiers unless attacked first. He will battle the rebel dragons and no more unless provoked," Paena said.

"Is there no changing his mind on this?" Baltar asked. "Ten-score of dragons would even things up considerably."

"He will not budge," she said, shaking her head. "I tried to convince him, but it is all but law for his people to not attack humans. I wish it were otherwise."

"As do I. Very well. I will tell her, the good and the bad," Baltar promised. "Now, you two should get some rest. There is a tent beside Queen Elespeth's pavilion set aside for you to share."

"Thank you, my lord," Paena said. "We will retire there as you suggest."

"Good. I may have some questions for you both later." At her nod, he strode off leaving them alone.

She shrugged. What had she expected? He had responsibilities. She turned to Kayla. "Let's get the horses stabled and then retire. I have a feeling we're going to need it."

"You are starting to sound like Father you know, Mother."

"What did you say?" she asked the girl.

"I said you're starting to sound like Father." Kayla smiled. "You know Father would still be here if he had listened to the Goddess."

She raised her hand to slap Kayla. "What would you know about it?" She took a deep breath and lowered her hand. "Do not mention Kalten again. Do you understand?"

"As you wish, Mother."

"Kayla."

"Yes?"

"Do not call me Mother. To you I am simply Paena." Paena's voice was tinged with ice.

"As you wish... Paena." The girl kept her voice carefully neutral.

"Better. Now let's settle the horses and get some sleep."

~ * ~

Paena half sat up and leaned on her elbows. She could have sworn she heard someone rummaging around in the tent. A sliver of light came through the tent flap. It vaguely showed a silhouette inside the tent that looked like a person standing at attention.

She glanced at Kayla and was surprised to see the girl sitting cross-legged on her cot, watching.

"The goddess left you a gift, Paena," Kayla said. The girl pointed toward the silhouette, her arm barely visible in the gloom.

"What is it?" Paena slipped out of her bed and crept toward the silhouette. She shivered, partially from the cool air in the tent and partially from anticipation. Reaching out, she touched it and felt cold, hard metal beneath her fingertips.

She flung open the tent flap to let the light in for a better look. The figure she had mistaken for an intruder was a shining set of armor hung on a stand: a supple chain mail coat, helm, greaves, gauntlets, and a surcoat with the embroidered pattern of a tree. Leaning against the armor was a shield with the same emblem embossed on the front.

Real armor just like the knights wore. She had never dared to dream of such finery; women didn't become knights. Apparently champions of certain goddesses did.

She tried on the armor, laughing with delight. She twisted and flexed, marveling at how little it impeded her movement.

"The goddess thought you might like it."

Paena stopped trying out the armor for a moment, and her eyes narrowed with suspicion. "Why is she giving me this now? What does she want?"

The girl shrugged. "You ride into battle tomorrow as her warrior. She wanted you to look the part."

Paena let that soak in for a few moments before she continued donning the armor. Kayla joined her to help fasten and adjust the straps.

They stepped out of the tent just as Bran drew near. The sun showed slightly past halfway across the sky.

"Whoa, you are bright," he said, shielding his eyes. "You almost blinded me."

"Bran, you made it," she said, delighted. She ran over to him and gave him a big hug.

"Oooofff!" he said with a wince. "My goodness. My ribs are bruised. You are as hard as a rock."

"Stop teasing, Bran," Paena scolded. "What do you think?"

"Brilliant is the only word that comes to mind," he said. He studied her critically. "Nice armor. Where did you get it?"

She shrugged. "It turned up in our tent. Tulliandars gave it to me."

"Tulliandars?" He peered more closely at her armor. "It is very well made. Your goddess is generous. I would guess it could take a direct sword thrust or even an arrow from a crossbow."

"Really?" She was impressed. She had a pretty good idea what armor of that quality could cost. It was much more than she had ever been able to afford. Then she thought about Kalten and frowned. If he had been given such armor, he would still be alive.

"You almost made me forget," Bran said. "I just reported in, and Lord Baltar asked me to get you."

"Thank you, Bran," Paena said. "Did everything go well?"

"We were dropped off a short way from the camp. Lydaroth was not ready to be seen yet."

"I know he'll do what's best when the time comes," she said. "But I guess I had better get over to the command tent. See you soon." She gave Bran a wave before she left.

It was only a few steps to the command tent. The guards ushered her and Kayla in when they arrived. Stuffy warmth assailed them as they stepped from the brightness of the afternoon sun into the gloom of the tent. Braziers were spread around and burned with little smoke, providing just enough light to see.

Clustered around a table in the center of the tent stood Baltar, Queen Elespeth, and several men Paena didn't recognize. They all looked up when she and Kayla entered into the tent.

"Paena." Baltar straightened up from the table. "Did you get any sleep?" He didn't wait for her answers. "Good, good."

A grizzled older bear of a man with a scar across one cheek spoke. "Where are these other men you promised us?" He scowled at them. "How about these so-called dragons? So far you have been big on promises and small on delivery."

"Rufus. That is enough." The queen rose from her chair. "This lady and her companions have delivered more than all the agents you ever sent out."

The man bowed to the queen. "Pardon me for saying so, Your Highness, but it seems to me they have also brought us closer to war than we have ever been too."

"What is happening was inevitable, General, and you know it," Baltar said. "Duke Samuel and his ilk have been plotting and planning for years. We all knew it was only a matter of time."

"Have you seen the size of the army facing us?" Rufus said.

"We are aware of what we are up against," Baltar said. "Paena did what she could to bring us support. Her partner, Kalten, gave his life for us. I know her to be honorable and trustworthy. If she says the dragons will come to our aid against the rebel dragons, I believe them."

"But will it be enough?"

"Did you tell them of the limitations to the dragons' aid?" Paena asked Baltar.

"I have told the queen but no others," he replied. "It is your news to share."

"Very well," she said with a nod. "I have unexpected and unwelcome news regarding the help the dragons will provide. The dragon lord, Lydaroth, told me only hours ago that he and his warriors will not engage any humans within the duke's forces unless they are attacked first."

"What?" Rufus roared. "Then what good are they to us? I say again, have you seen how many we face in the duke's army? Without the dragons we will be slaughtered."

"They will do their part to protect us from the rebel dragons," she said.

"Do not forget that Queen Elespeth has the support of the goddess," Kayla said, speaking up for the first time. She had been standing behind Paena.

"The goddess? You mean this so-called Tulliandars, don't you? More hocus pocus, if you ask me." Rufus shook his head. "First dragons, and now this? I am almost afraid to look outside the tent for fear that our soldiers are mere smoke."

"Your Majesty, perhaps a demonstration is in order?" Kayla grew dark and solemn, her eyes gleaming in the light. "Mother. If you would be so kind?"

Paena obeyed the compulsion and immediately called light at Kayla's request.

Radiance flooded the tent. Unlike the last time Paena invoked this power, only pure white light shone from her body. Now, even her armor glowed with a vibrant luminosity that surrounded her like a nimbus.

"Satisfied?" Kayla's voice had a smug quality about it. "Or does she need to call lightning down on you before you are convinced?"

The general visibly trembled while he spoke, but somehow managed to keep his voice steady. "That will not be necessary. I am convinced. But what can you do?"

"Paena has already destroyed nine dragons in the past number of days," Kayla said. "The goddess has given you her warrior for this conflict. Paena's aid should turn the tide of battle in your favor."

Paena hastened to say, "I will not fail you, Your Majesty. I can win this battle for you." She wasn't exactly sure she believed her own words, but she knew they needed to be said.

"We do not have much choice," the queen said. "Our options are severely limited. We either win here or we die."

Baltar massaged the small of his back. "Will the dragons be ready tomorrow?"

"Just a moment, I'll reach out to him and check," Paena said, going silent, listening for his reply. "Lydaroth tells me they will be ready whenever we call. His people are keeping a close watch for the enemy dragons."

"Good," Baltar said. "With your permission, Your Majesty, let us adjourn this meeting until tomorrow. Morning will arrive soon enough. We all have much to do. Let us prepare as best we can so we can be ready for whatever greets us on the morrow."

Queen Elespeth nodded, and the meeting broke up.

Paena and Kayla returned to their tent.

"Paena, I will be joining you on the battlefield tomorrow," Kayla announced once they entered the tent.

"What? There's no way a child like you can go into battle."

"Paena... Mother." Kayla took Paena's hand. "I must come with you. I can boost your powers with my own vitality. We cannot have you fall on the battlefield tomorrow because you have used up all your energy. If you do, we will lose, and none of us can afford that. I will ensure your energy levels remain high."

Paena tried to resist, but the earnest expression in Kayla's eyes could not be ignored. "I don't like it, but you'll come whether I want you there or not, won't you?"

Her grin was impish. "Yes, I will."

"There's more, isn't there?"

"There are some things we can do tonight to weaken the enemy. I must warn you, it will take considerable energy. Perhaps you should rest until then."

"I'm sick of resting," Paena said. "I need to get out and get some fresh air. See exactly what we are against."

"Very well, Mother," Kayla said. "I will wait here for you. Please be back before full night falls."

~ * ~

"Come with me," Kayla said shortly after Paena's return. She exited the tent and led her mother to the edge of the camp closest to the enemy. They looked across the field at the encamped enemy.

"I want you to think about the forest that sits behind and to the sides of the enemy," Kayla said. "Now, think about the trees surrounding the enemy and the animals of the forest attacking the enemy soldiers." She waited and watched Paena for a few moments. "Now I want you to pray to the goddess and ask her to give you the power to make it happen."

Paena closed her eyes and prayed. The prayer was answered with an immediate rush of power, which allowed her to feel the collective mind of the forest.

At first, the forest resisted, but then Kayla's mind linked to hers, and a surge of energy flowed through them. The forest's resistance disappeared.

A strong wind blew into their faces and, through the link with the forest, Paena felt the trees begin to move. For a time, they just maintained the link. The trees surrounded the enemy's army and then the animals attacked from the shadows.

Shrieks and screams from the enemy's camp echoed through the darkness.

"That will not stop the enemy, only slow them down a little," Kayla said. "We must be increasingly diligent now. The enemy must know more is going on than they expected. We should be ready for an attack any time now."

~ * ~

Duke Samuel had just began eating his evening meal when he heard the first shouts of alarm. Within moments, the camp came alive with calls to arms, cries of fear, and screams of pain.

In one motion, he flipped the table away and leapt to his feet. He snatched his sword and jogged out of the tent. Outside, it was chaos with men dashing around in mindless panic.

Duke Samuel stopped a soldier as he was sprinting past. "What is going on? Are we under attack?"

The man's eyes were wide with fear. Samuel thought the man might be deranged.

He tried to pull away, looking wildly from side-to-side. Foam speckled his cheek. "Monsters! The very trees attack us." With unnatural strength he jerked out of the duke's grasp and scampered off screaming.

The growls and snarls of predators seared the night air accompanied by another less identifiable but equally terrifying sound. A creaking, rustling roar sounded in the background. Duke Samuel turned to see the colossal form of an ancient oak tree looming over him. Gnarled and twisted, the massive oak advanced with snapping, disjointed lurches and had two flailing soldiers clutched in its branches.

He backed away from the thing and barely avoided stepping directly into one of the campfires. With a gloved hand, he snatched a burning log. As he straightened, he threw the wood toward the groaning tree.

The burning brand struck the tree and caught in its branches, flames sputtering feebly for a few breaths, before setting the dried bark ablaze. Moments later, the tree was a raging pyre for the ill-fated men trapped in its branches.

The blazing tree lit up the camp, revealing more moving trees on all sides, many clutching men in their branches. Burning leaves from the oak fell among those trees, igniting them and their unfortunate captives.

The duke grabbed a guard who remained close by during the danger. "Find my captains and have them get the men under control. They must get the men and supplies away from this fire or we are lost. Report back to me when you have delivered that message."

The man straightened, saluted then trotted off.

The attack couldn't be a coincidence. It had to be the work of the queen. Her use of foul magic was further proof she had no right to the throne.

That was fine. Duke Samuel had his own resources. Clearly, it was time to deploy them.

Chapter Thirty-Eight

Paena was dozing in her tent when a feeling of wrongness struck her. She jumped to her feet and buckled her on sword belt. No armor this time; whatever was wrong, she would need speed and stealth.

When she looked outside the tent, nothing seemed amiss. It was very late and dark. Watch fires burned around the camp, and men lay sleeping in bedrolls. Out in the darkness one of the soldiers was doing a very good impression of a saw and snoring loudly. Sentries patrolled the camp. Although it felt peaceful, she couldn't shake the feeling something bad was happening.

Slipping out of the tent, she began a patrol of her own. The sense of danger grew stronger the closer she got to Queen Elespeth's tent. Whatever was going on, it appeared to be directed at the queen.

The front of the queen's tent seemed fine. She saluted the two guards when she strode past, and they returned the gesture.

Paena almost tripped over the body of the guard behind the tent. If not for a moment where the moon shone from behind a cloud, she never would have seen it in the darkness. A large cut in the tent canvas was directly behind the guard's body.

There was no time to lose. She leapt through the hole in the canvas with a yell. An assassin dressed all in black leaned over the queen's sleeping form about to plunge a dagger into her. The shadowy figure froze after Paena yelled. That brief moment saved the queen's life.

Paena pulled the dagger from her belt and threw it at the assassin. Her aim was good, and the dagger buried itself in the intruder's throat. He dropped to the ground with a gurgle, clutching at the protruding knife.

As the man fell, Queen Elespeth woke and screamed. Two more attackers garbed in black charged into her chamber from the outer room, swords ready.

Paena drew her sword, and the blade burst into flame before it cleared the scabbard. She didn't have time to wonder at the flames. The radiance from the blade showed two men with dead black eyes and intricately scarred faces. They wore black trousers tucked into black boots along with black shirts belted at the waist.

The nearer man faltered at the sight of her sword, and Paena thrust it at his head. He dropped his own blade, screaming and pawing at his face. She finished him off with a lunge through the heart ignoring the sound and smell of sizzling flesh.

The second intruder was cut down from behind by one of the guards who rushed in at the sound of the queen's screams. It was all over in moments.

Another guard ran for reinforcements while Paena stared down at her sword in astonishment. As her anger cooled, the flames flickered and went out.

With the deaths of the assassins, she realized the sense of wrongness had disappeared. She hoped it didn't come back.

The camp stayed on high alert for the remainder of the night. Paena personally guarded Queen Elespeth and was exhausted by the time morning came. When the sun came up, Baltar and several of the queen's personal guard relieved her.

Kayla led Paena back to their tent and brought food. While she ate, Kayla stood behind her and restored her energy much like the healing Paena had done in the past. There wasn't much time to relax. A page came to warn them that the enemy had begun to form ranks. She finished eating.

Baltar came to the tent shortly after the page left. "The duke is waiting in the middle of the field carrying a parley flag. Queen Elespeth wants you to accompany her when she goes out to meet him."

Paena frowned. "Is that a good idea? Won't that put her at unnecessary risk?"

"Our queen is willing to explore any option that might save lives," Baltar replied, shaking his head with obvious dismay. "If that means talking to a traitorous subject, she wants to do it, no matter what we say to her."

"Then I had best get my armor on." Paena slowly got to her feet, still chewing. She hurried to don her armor with Kayla helping her to dress.

Paena reached out with her mind while she dressed. *"Lydaroth, are you there?"*

"I am here, Paena," the dragon's voice replied. *"We are waiting for your word."*

She had a mental picture of Lydaroth and his followers hiding in a forest. *"Are there any signs of the rebel dragons?"*

"No, but they may be circling high above. I believe we should

remain hidden until they begin their attack."

"I agree. You will be most effective if the enemy doesn't know about you. Can you be here quickly?"

"We can be there very fast."

"I'm glad to hear that. I will be accompanying the queen to a parley with Duke Samuel. I may need you if the duke tries something."

"I will watch you closely for signs of treachery. Do not worry."

"Thank you Lydaroth. See you soon."

"Good luck, Paena."

Paena came back to herself to see Kayla watching her.

"How's Lydaroth?" Kayla asked. "Is he ready?"

"Lydaroth... how did you know?"

"You had that look. Will he be ready in time?"

"He's ready." She gave a nervous laugh. "I'm just not sure I am."

"Don't worry, I'll be right there with you," Kayla said.

"I still don't like the idea of you on a battlefield. You're just a little girl."

"I'm sorry, Mother," Kayla began, "but the goddess has commanded me to accompany you."

"But you're just a girl."

Kayla folded her arms across her chest. "Don't argue, Mother. It won't make any difference in the end."

Paena could only shake her head with a sigh. Kayla had never really been her daughter. It became more obvious every time they talked.

The horses waited outside the tent, fully saddled and ready to go. Paena carefully checked her horse's gear. The old tack had been replaced with a new harness that matched her armor. The sign of the tree was worked in silver on the bridle and saddle, and chainmail now protected the chest of the mare. Tulliandars had definitely been at work here. Kayla's stallion was similarly clad but without the silverwork.

Mother and daughter rode out to where the queen and her knights waited. Queen Elespeth looked very much the warrior. She wore a shaped breastplate over a gown of light chainmail. Snow-white gauntlets covered her hands, and a small steel circlet was set on her brow. Her mare was harnessed in white leather, and a white skirt embroidered with the royal coat-of-arms covered the horse to its ankles. Ribbons were braided into the mane.

"Your Highness," Paena said with a half-bow after she stopped beside Queen Elespeth. "I understand you wish to speak with Duke Samuel."

The queen turned her head only enough to look in Paena's direction. "Yes, Paena. I have hopes we can come to an accord without bloodshed. I would have you at my side when I speak to him." Her voice was rich and husky.

"As Your Majesty wishes." Paena shifted in her saddle and scrutinized the field.

"Then let us go and meet with our rebel duke." The queen clucked her tongue at her mare and started forward. Paena and the knights moved in escort of their queen.

They rode about a quarter of the way onto the field and stopped. The queen turned to her knights. "My noble knights, would that I could take you with me, but the terms of the parley forbid it. I am allowed only a single companion. I must ask you all to wait here for me."

A grizzled older knight nudged his horse forward. "My queen, take me instead of this girl, I beg you." He nodded to Paena. "No offense to the lady, but would my steel not better serve you?"

Paena decided to be gracious. "Noble knight, I take no offense at your words, but you should know I have been gifted with special abilities by the Goddess Tulliandars. I believe I can be of service to our queen in ways the duke cannot know." She held a gauntleted hand up and allowed a trickle of electricity to flow between her outstretched fingers.

The elder knight paled but stayed silent for a moment. "I... I see. Perhaps you are right, lady."

The queen spoke again. "The duke is on the move. I ask you men to keep me in your prayers and watch for treachery." She urged her mare back into motion. This time only the queen and Paena moved forward, horses walking shoulder to shoulder.

Across the grass the duke and a lone escort advance on their mounts to the center of the field. Both parties rode until they were a scant stone's throw apart.

"Duke Samuel. You requested this parley," the queen said. I trust you have come in good faith to bring a peaceful end to this confrontation?"

The duke sat his horse straight-backed, but appeared haggard and weary. His eyes were bloodshot and rimmed with heavy dark circles. Still, the look he directed toward the queen was one of distaste. "I have come to offer you terms for your surrender."

"Terms?" Queen Elespeth almost laughed. "You would expect me to give up to you without a fight?"

Duke Samuel gestured to his army. "As you can see, I have you grossly outnumbered. You claim to have the welfare of your subjects at the forefront of your mind." He smiled then, almost a sneer. "I would expect you to concede to me to avoid pointless deaths."

"All I see is a traitor trying to take what is not his," she retorted. "You crave power no matter the cost."

"Perhaps," Duke Samuel said, sounding bored. "But I would make a better ruler than some slip of a girl who hides behind her army."

The queen stiffened. "I see I have wasted my time talking to you. I hoped you might have come to your senses. I see now I was wrong." She turned her horse.

"Ah, but you haven't wasted my time, girl." The duke raised a gauntleted fist, and a horn rang out from his camp. He wheeled his horse and galloped back toward his army.

"Your Majesty, it is a trap," Paena called before she herded the queen's mare along. From overhead came the sound of giant wings.

Paena spared a glance over her shoulder to see a blue dragon flying toward them. The beast seemed to have a dark stain across its entire hide. One of the rebels then.

As the two women charged toward the queen's lines, Paena tried to call for help from Tulliandars, but nothing came. She bit off a curse and looked again at the rapidly approaching dragon.

The creature was almost within flaming range and visibly inhaled while it flew. It was only a matter of moments before it would exhale a killing ball of fire at her and Queen Elespeth.

Paena reached out with her mind to call the one being she knew listened. *"Lydaroth. Help!"*

Before the rebel dragon could breathe fire, a massive golden streak dove out of the clouds. Lydaroth had come to defend her. The gold dragon slammed into the rebel dragon, tearing at it with steel-sharp talons. The rebel dragon tried to escape the Dragon Lord's wrath but had been caught completely unaware. The battle was fierce but short, with the rebel dragon crashing to the field, torn and bleeding in a dozen places. The creature tried to stand, but collapsed before a single step could be taken.

Lydaroth roared once when he circled the field. He disappeared back up into the clouds.

It was all over before Paena and the queen were even back to the knights. The small party found safety back behind the lines of friendly troops.

~ * ~

Sergeants lined up their troops while captains rode back and forth across the battle line exhorting their men to readiness. The queen's army waited, a mismatched set of soldiers. Old men stood shoulder to shoulder with boys barely old enough to grow a beard. Some wore patchworks of leather armor, and others were covered in chain mail. All wore the same expression of hopeless determination. Across the field, the enemy soldiers prepared for battle, a black churning mass of men. Both armies faced each other in silence. Time seemed to stand still.

Everywhere Paena looked she saw Kalten's face. How could he have been so stubborn? He had protected her before and now when she needed his help most, he was gone. It was almost too much to bear.

Across the field, horns blared, and the enemy surged forward. The order quickly passed down the line, and the queen's forces surged to meet their foes.

Paena and Kayla waited back with the knights and watched while the foot soldiers marched toward the enemy. Four rows deep, the first two rows of soldiers were made up of pikemen. The men behind carried short swords and shields.

As they neared the center of the field, Paena felt the same sense of wrongness she had the night before. She looked to the skies and saw death descending.

Chapter Thirty-Nine

"Dragons." Kayla pointed to the sky above the enemy.

Five darkly gleaming dragons, two blues and three greens, swooped in, jetting a swath of flame that ended at the first row of soldiers. A dozen men were instantly incinerated, and many others fell rolling to the ground.

Paena called out. *"Lydaroth, we need you now!"*

"We are coming," the dragon replied.

She anxiously watched the sky for signs of Lydaroth while the dark dragons came around for a second attack. The ranks of foot soldiers were already in disarray as terrified men tried to get away from the flaming terror.

The rebel dragons were just beginning their second attack when Lydaroth led a score of brightly colored dragons down from the clouds, smashing into the attackers. The darker dragons were hurled to the ground where they lay unmoving in broken heaps.

The allied dragons remained in the air above the battlefield wheeling and diving in the air, keeping watch for the rebels. The sergeants managed to get their men back into ranks and resumed their steady march toward the enemy troops, avoiding the smoldering bodies of their comrades.

"Lydaroth, I know you and your warriors will not attack the duke's forces. But they might not be aware of it. Perhaps stay above the battlefield to give us moral support," Paena said.

"That we can do," he said. *"That will also give us a good position to prevent further attacks by the rebel dragons."*

Queen Elespeth's vastly outnumbered troops drew closer to the enemy. They locked their shields and lowered their pikes for attack.

The enemy waited until the last minute before spreading apart. From within their ranks a dozen dragons rose up from covered pits, necks waving sinuously, hissing at their enemy. The first opened its mouth and belched out a sheet of flame at the closest soldiers. Another dozen men disappeared in the fire.

Lydaroth and his warriors tried swooping down to attack the rebels, but they couldn't get close enough. Enemy archers raked them with arrows. One of his warriors, wings torn and flapping from dozens of arrows, crashed into the enemy ranks, crushing dozens.

At the first attack from the ground-based dragons, the queen's troops retreated, trying to stay out of the range of the scorching flame. At the same time, the enemy advanced.

Around them, the knights were lowering helms and preparing for attack. Paena followed suit, praying for protection from the dragon's flame. The knights rode out, Paena near the front, Kayla at her side.

As they closed in on the enemy, they spurred their horses to a full gallop. Paena and Kayla, with their stronger mounts, surged to the head of the column. Paena's sword blazed with fire.

As they neared the enemy force once again, the troops separated to allow a dragon to climb up out of a covered pit to come forward. The enormous blue-black monster spread its jaws and jetted a stream of fire as thick as a tree trunk at her.

The fire splashed against an invisible shield. She felt the lash of the heat, but was unaffected by it. Her mare bolted forward, unimpeded. Paena raised her blazing sword and struck at the dragon, shearing off a large part of its snout.

The creature roared, thrashing and bellowing, crushing several of the enemy soldiers near it, as dark blood poured from its wound. She closed in and hacked at the creature while Kayla's stallion slashed at it with his hooves. The knights fought the duke's foot soldiers to keep them away from Paena and Kayla while they battled the dragon.

Kayla continued to harass the dragon with hoof strikes from her stallion, and Paena rode the mare in close, just behind its head. She drove her sword between the creature's neck and jaw and wheeled the mare around. The dying creature swung its head into them, knocking Paena and her mare to the ground. The mare struggled to its feet, breathing heavily, and Paena tried to swing into the saddle.

Her right arm refused to respond. Kayla saw her plight and grabbed her under her left arm and tried to pull her up onto the stallion. A knight Paena didn't know helped Kayla get Paena into the saddle. Kayla scrambled over to the mare's saddle and with the knights protecting them, once mounted they galloped back to their own battle lines.

Kayla helped her from the stallion. "Paena, can you tell me what's wrong?"

"I think my arm's broken."

A yell of fear from the men around them distracted Kayla. At least a score of the dark dragons led by a massive gold-hued dragon swooped down from the clouds and attacked Lydaroth and his dragons.

He was singled out by the rebels and had no less than five dragons, including the gold one, attacking him. On the field, both sides backed away from each other to watch the aerial battle.

Paena spoke through gritted teeth. "Kayla, you must do something to help Lydaroth." She reached out to Lydaroth with her mind, but got no answer.

"I am, Mother. I'm healing you."

As Kayla said it, Paena realized her arm no longer hurt.

She closed her eyes and prayed. Lightning wouldn't work this time. It would kill Lydaroth just as quickly as it would his attackers.

She picked up a head-sized rock, looked up at the battling dragons, and threw it. Her arm blurred as she launched the heavy stone. It flew straight as an arrow at one of the five dragons surrounding Lydaroth and hit it squarely in the belly.

A ball of flame spurted out of its mouth, and the dragon doubled up around itself, plunging to the ground. It smashed into the earth between the opposing armies.

The surprise of the attack distracted one of the remaining dragons. Lydaroth slashed at its belly with his talons, disemboweling the creature. It fell shrieking to the ground, landing near its dead companion. It vainly struggled to get to its feet before it collapsed one last time.

Paena tossed another stone at the attacking dragons but missed. One of the attackers broke off and came directly at her, flaming while it dove. She picked up another, larger rock and threw it straight down the dragon's gullet, knocking it back.

The dragon swung its head around and tried to jet flame again. A startled look crossed its face just before its belly expanded and exploded. Bits of flesh and scale rained down across the field. At that moment, the rest of Lydaroth's followers came out of the clouds to attack the remaining rebel dragons.

As the dragons fought, the duke's forces marched forward, spearmen at the fore. A volley of arrows arched into the queen's lines.

The queen's forces, momentarily stopped as they watched the dragons battle, began to move again as they realized they were under attack. They slammed into the duke's army near the middle of the field. The screams of men battling and dying filled the air.

Lydaroth and the enemy gold dragon continued to battle. The gold rebel was larger than Lydaroth but slightly slower. The combatants warily circled each other before coming together with a crash. They became a blur of slashing talons and teeth, thrashing each other with tails and wings.

Lydaroth managed to grab the gold dragon by a wing with his jaws. He bit hard, and the wing bone shattered. The gold dragon screamed and grappled at Lydaroth, trying to keep from falling. Its claws scrabbled at Lydaroth's scales. For the briefest of moments, time seemed to stand still, and then the gold dragon fell, a flaming streak. It hurtled to the ground among the enemy troops, crushing many. It did not get up.

Lydaroth's roar was a mix of pain, victory, and despair. He soared once above the battlefield before he flew back into the clouds.

With the change in fortunes above them, the enemy soldiers retreated back to their lines. When they left the field, the queen's troops also withdrew. Above them, the dragons battled, with the enemy dragons being knocked out of the sky one after the other by Lydaroth's superior forces. In short order, the remaining rebel dragons were in full retreat, chased by the allied dragons.

~ * ~

"At best, we managed a draw," a general said. Queen Elespeth and her commanders, including Kayla and Paena, were once again meeting in the command tent. The man turned to Paena. "I thought you said the dragons would attack the duke in self-defense. They were attacked, so why do they still refuse to attack humans?"

"I can answer that, sir," Kayla said. "I spoke with Lydaroth a short time ago, and he explained it further. Dragonkind was almost driven to extinction by humans they attacked in the distant past. To save themselves, they made a pact with humanity. It is still very much in effect for them. They cannot go against what has been agreed unless they are attacked themselves."

"But wasn't one of their number killed by the duke's soldiers?"

"Only because that dragon threatened his troops. At least, that's what Lydaroth believes."

"Bah. I should have known better than to hope for their help," the general said with a frown. "Untrustworthy beasts—"

"But they have helped us, Rufus," Queen Elespeth said, interrupting him. "Or have you forgotten how they destroyed and drove off those dragons that supported our enemy? Without that aid, our army would be no more."

Rufus ran his hands through his thinning hair and grimaced. "Of course, you are right, Your Majesty." His laugh was bitter. "Still, it would just be nice to have an advantage in this battle."

"We do have an advantage," Bran said, stepping forward. "Paena has abilities and strengths that will tip the balance in our favor."

Rufus sneered. "I saw the young woman throwing rocks. Rocks! No offense, but the duke's forces have arrows and spears to throw our way. I cannot see us winning this with some rocks."

"I used rocks because lightning would have killed both our friends and our enemies," Paena said. "There are other things I can do."

"Would you mind telling us what those other things might be or is it a secret?" he asked. "Just so we mere mortals can be ready." His words were punctuated by a loud crash from outside the tent.

A sentry rushed into the tent. "My lords, we are under attack."

Paena stepped out of the tent in time to see a massive boulder hit the ground and bounce through the tents scattering men and equipment. She reached out with her mind. *"Lydaroth, what is happening?"*

The dragon's reply was confused. *"I do not know. I have only seen two large rocks hurled from the enemy camp. Could they also have someone like you?"*

"It's unlikely. It could be that they're using a machine to throw the stones. Could you take a look?"

"I am already above their camp," the dragon replied. *"I do see something. It looks like a wooden arm. Wait a moment. The arm is lowering. Yes. They are placing a rock in a cradle on the end. Watch out!"*

The dragon's warning gave her time to spot the rock flying toward them. She tried calling for aid from Tulliandars, but no answer came. She turned to Kayla. "Tulliandars is refusing help to stop the stone."

"If the goddess refuses to give you aid, it is because you are able to do something on your own," Kayla said. "Think the problem through, and you will find the answer."

Paena swore under her breath and started shouting at people to get them to move out of the rock's path. Despite her warning, several people were crushed by the bouncing stone.

"That's convenient," she said. All around them, men were running and shouting. "Keep me from getting hit while I talk to Lydaroth."

"Yes Mother." Kayla guided her to a quieter spot beside one of the tents.

"Lydaroth, we need your help."

"I cannot. They have archers ready for me if I try to burn the device. I would never make it." The dragon sounded angry, frustrated.

"That's okay, my friend, but I was thinking of a different kind of help."

"What do you suggest?"

"Let's use their own weapon against them. Take some of your stronger people and gather large stones. Fly over the enemy camp and drop the stones on the machine. The soldiers around the machines should flee when they see you coming."

"It will be done." With that, his voice was gone.

Paena refocused on her daughter. "Kayla, I've got to get back to General Rufus. We've got to ready the troops."

Kayla gave her a questioning look, but carved a path for her mother through the rushing people. Paena shouted over the din, calling for the general. They finally found him near the front of the camp, shouting out orders.

"Go away!" The man was clearly agitated. "I really do not have time for you two right now."

"You need to get your soldiers formed up right away. I believe this attack is a diversion."

"Surely you jest? Of course it is a diversion. But we are getting wiped out right now."

"Not for much longer. Lydaroth and his people are about to destroy the machine. When they do, the enemy will surely attack."

"Destroy the machine? How?" he asked. "Never mind. I will do as you say." Without a backward glance, he began gathering his commanders, issuing orders.

"We'd better get to the horses," she said, nodding at Kayla. "When they attack, we should be ready."

"The goddess wishes you to stay out of the battle for a time."

"What are you talking about?" Paena asked. She tried to move the girl out of the way. "We've got to get in there, or the queen's soldiers will be destroyed."

But the girl would not be moved. "You have heard her command. You are not to question her will. You are only to obey it."

Still, Paena tried to get around the girl. "I won't let innocent men be slaughtered."

Kayla shook her head sadly and grabbed her arm. Paena froze in place. "I'm sorry, Mother, but you will obey the goddess." Kayla held her there until the battle was underway.

They arrived at the battlefield just after the queen's soldiers marched forward. General Rufus rushed over to meet with them.

"Thank the gods you are here," he said. "But where are your mounts?"

"We have been ordered by the goddess to stay out of the battle," Paena said in a monotone. "We are to stand back and watch."

"What? But we need you out there."

"There's nothing we can do," she said. She watched the ranks of soldiers move out onto the field.

With a grunt of disgust, the general turned his back to them and strode away, once again calling out orders to his commanders.

The enemy met the queen's soldiers in the middle of the field, and the battle began once again. Horse archers rode behind the combatants, loosing arrows into the opposing forces. Men died and were ground underfoot. With a dreadful inevitability, the queen's soldiers were pushed back, their numbers dwindling by the step.

Paena fidgeted while the battle lines drew closer. "We need to do something soon. Our men can't afford to keep fighting much longer. There's simply too many of them. Why won't Tulliandars let me do something?"

"Earth," Kayla finally said. "It is time, Mother. The goddess wishes for you to destroy the enemy now. Open the ground beneath those men, just like the goddess did to save you and Father. I will help you."

"I can do that?"

"Of course, you can. I would not have suggested it otherwise. Now stop asking questions and listen to me. I will boost your power."

"What of the remaining men?" Paena asked.

"They are of no consequence. Now ask for Her help."

"No consequence? They are the queen's people. We can't simply treat them as unimportant!"

"If you do nothing, they will die anyway, Mother. Also, many others. Now, stop stalling and doing as I say," Kayla commanded.

Realizing the truth of the girl's words, Paena reluctantly closed her eyes and prayed to Tulliandars. In moments, the familiar surge of power filled Paena. She visualized the opening of the ground and released the power.

She heard a low rumbling, and the ground shook. She checked the advancing army. The enemy troops had stopped moving and were looking around wildly.

As the shaking intensified, cries of alarm rose from the enemy. The ground caved in below the enemy troops along the entire attacking line. Loyal men who were fighting the enemy fell in screaming too. In a single moment, the duke's army was gone along with many of Queen Elespeth's troops. Where the battlefield had been a short time before was now a massive sinkhole. All that remained of the enemy's army were a few knights and the rebel lords themselves.

Paena trudged out onto the battlefield, a feeling of self-loathing filling her. So many dead. Could she have done anything differently to save those men? She saw a dead young soldier, buried up to his shoulders, and could only see Kalten's lifeless face. Would things have been different if he were still with her?

The grief she had been holding back overwhelmed her, and she fell to her knees in the mud, bawling for her friend and all the other dead.

~ * ~

"Going somewhere?" Pieter cradled his left arm, blood still flowing from a nasty slash near his elbow.

Duke Samuel ignored Pieter's question and finished cinching the saddle.

He stepped closer. "My lord?"

The duke turned, a sour grin on his face. "It would appear we are undone. I believe a tactical retreat might be in order."

"You would leave your men and allies behind?"

"Of course. They are of no use to me now." The duke turned and gathered up the reins of his horse.

"Where will you go?"

Duke Samuel seemed to consider this for a moment. "I have other alliances I can call upon. I believe I will go to one of them to build a new army.

Pieter took a step forward. "Let me get a horse. I will come with you."

"No, I don't believe you will. Your wound will only slow me down." He swung into his saddle.

Pieter looked down for a moment. "I thought you might feel that way." He pulled a knife from a hidden sheath at his left wrist and threw it in a single, fluid motion.

The blade flipped end over end burying itself into the duke's neck with a meaty *thunk*. He touched the knife. Blood bubbled from the wound, and Duke Samuel tried to speak. Blood flowed from his mouth as he slowly toppled from the saddle, a surprised expression on his face.

Pieter grabbed the uneasy horse and scrambled into the saddle. He laughed and bowed at the body of his former lord. "Thank you for the horse and provisions, my lord. I will make good use of them."

Still holding his injured arm, Pieter turned the horse and trotted away from the battlefield.

Chapter Forty

General Rufus recovered quickly from the sudden change of events. He ordered his knights to gather the remaining enemy and bring them to heel.

The spirit of the rebel lords was broken by the destruction of their army and even more by the discovery of Duke Samuel's body. Before nightfall, the remnants of the opposing army were either under guard or dead. Queen Elespeth had her victory.

The queen made her judgment against the traitors quickly. The insurgents were either executed or banished for the remainder of their lives. To return meant death. Their lands were forfeit and seized by the crown.

The body of Duke Samuel was prominently placed at the main gate of the city in a crow-cage.

The unhappy job of escorting the traitors fell to Paena and a dozen knights. They rode around the wagon that carted the surviving lords to their banishment.

At the edge of the kingdom, the men were cast out of the wagon they had been forced to ride in. Those who refused to leave were chased down the rocky track with whips and prods. In the end, they all left, weaponless, with nothing but the clothes on their backs in a pitiful parade.

The knights stayed behind to ensure the traitors didn't try to sneak back into the kingdom. Paena traveled the dusty roads back to the capital, making better time on the return journey.

On the main avenue leading to the palace, a new building was being built. It was constructed of massive blocks of marble fronted by tall, fluted pillars.

She was met at the palace by both Baltar and Kayla.

"Welcome back, my dear," Baltar said with a smile. "I never got a chance to tell you how proud I am of you. Queen Elespeth is very pleased with your performance."

"I don't deserve your praise, Baltar," Paena said. "I killed as many of the queen's men as the enemy did."

"What is wrong with you?" Baltar asked. "We won the day. The enemy is defeated."

"Mother feels guilt over the deaths of the queen's soldiers," Kayla said.

"I would be worried if those deaths didn't bother her," Baltar said. "Still, if you hadn't intervened as you did many more would have died and we most likely would have lost the war."

"Perhaps that's true. But if I'd done something else fewer may have died."

"Maybe. Maybe not," Baltar replied. "Only the gods, or goddess in this case, know with any certainty. Without your help we would have been doomed. Take some comfort in that, at least."

"Thank you, sir," Paena said. "I was glad to help. I know Kalten felt that way too."

Kayla stepped from behind Baltar. "The goddess is also pleased with you."

Paena bowed. "Thank you." Somehow that praise made her more uneasy than Baltar's words.

"Any problems taking the traitors to the border?"

She frowned. "No, sir. But it did seem to be too lenient a punishment for what the men have done."

"Trust me, the queen was ready to execute the lot of them, but several of her allied lords convinced her to show mercy. They felt if she was too heavy-handed, there could be problems with others in the future." Baltar leaned closer to her, speaking in hushed tones. "I tell you this because you deserve to know. But please do not bring it up to Her Majesty. It is still a very touchy subject and weighs heavily on her mind." He brightened after he straightened. "Now, if you two would come with me?"

Paena nodded and followed him into the palace. Instead of the council chamber, Baltar led them directly to the throne room. Two guards stood at attention outside the massive doors.

"Baltar, why did you bring us here?" she asked.

The older man simply winked at her and asked one of the guards to announce them. The guard slipped through one of the doors, closing it behind him. She gave Kayla a questioning glance. The girl avoided Paena's gaze and moved off to the side.

The doors swung open, and Baltar quickly entered the throne room. He cleared his throat and looked meaningfully at Kayla and Paena with a smile. "Introducing the warrior Paena." He moved aside, clapping his hands.

The gallery surrounding the throne room was filled with applauding people, the lords and ladies of the kingdom, dressed in every color, bright as songbirds. On her throne, Queen Elespeth sat resplendent in a gown of shimmering white, the crown of state sitting on her brow. Smiling, she rose up and beckoned for Paena to come forward.

She gulped and stepped into the room. She stopped to look at the cheering throng.

"Go on, Mother," Kayla urged.

Paena nodded and, head held high, marched down the carpeted aisle to the queen. At the base of the throne, she fell to one knee and bowed her head.

"Please rise, my champion," the queen said.

Champion? Paena looked up in surprise.

Queen Elespeth continued to speak in loud ringing tones, scanning the entire room. "You should all know that I am most pleased with this warrior. If it were not for her, our cause could have been lost. Without her bravery, a usurper might now sit on this very throne."

The queen gazed out at the gallery, once again and held up her hands for silence. "The goddess, Tulliandars, has blessed us indeed with the timely gift of this warrior. We, in return for this gift, are building a temple so, as it once was in this land, our people and Tulliandars will exist together." She turned her attention to Paena. "But what can we do for you, to show our thanks?"

"Your Majesty?"

"Please, Lady Paena, rise." The queen stepped down from the throne and took Paena's hand.

She got up, her legs shaking.

"Now, Paena, what reward could I grant you?"

Paena cleared her throat. "Your Majesty, there is nothing I want but a place in your guard."

"Done," the queen said in surprise. "But that is hardly a just reward for what you have done for this kingdom and me. Is there nothing else you desire?"

"Perhaps…" Paena had to stop and clear her throat again. "Perhaps you would honor my friend Kalten? He died defending me just before the last battle."

"Of course. I shall have a statue erected in the plaza in his honor."

The voice of Kayla rang out from near the door drawing the attention of the entire room. "That will not be necessary." She stepped forward. "Your Majesty, if I may?"

At Queen Elespeth's permission, Kayla spoke again. "Your Majesty, I am afraid that the goddess will not allow such an honor for Kalten. His disobedience to her led to his death."

Paena turned an anguished face toward Kayla. "Surely Tulliandars would not deny Kalten such an honor? Hasn't he suffered enough?"

Kayla straightened taller. "What the goddess does is not your concern." She turned toward the queen. "Also, Paena may not be your champion. She may only serve the goddess."

"I see," the queen said. She remained in thought for a moment. "What does it mean for Paena to be her paladin, exactly?"

"A warrior dedicated to the goddess, my lady," Kayla answered.

"Could such a warrior be a knight?"

Kayla appeared momentarily confused. "I suppose that could be the case. But Paena has no such a title."

Queen Elespeth flashed a smile of triumph. "She does now." She beckoned Baltar to step closer. "Lord Baltar, please get me the Sword of State."

He bowed and hurried out of the chamber, returning moments later carrying a large, ornate sword. He bowed to his queen holding it out to her.

"Kneel, Paena," the queen ordered. She waited until Paena had knelt before continuing, "Since I am unable to have you in my direct service, let me grant you this honor instead."

She descended from the dais and stood over Paena. Grasping the sword with both hands, the queen tapped her shoulders, first left, and then right. "By my right of birth and the authority of this kingdom, I name you Lady Paena, knight protector of the realm." She leaned down and kissed the top of Paena's head.

Queen Elespeth raised Paena up and turned her to face the gallery. "I give you Lady Paena. She is to be accorded all honor and respect. You are to provide her with lodging and food when on quest and as our friend, she is to be given all aid when asked for. This is my command." The queen stepped back up to the dais and seated herself on the throne. She spoke more quietly, her words only for Paena's ears. "An estate shall be set aside for your use when you are not on quest. Is this acceptable to you?" Queen Elespeth sat, looking stern, but Paena thought she could see a faint twinkle in her eyes.

Things had happened so fast. But she had no problem answering the question. "Yes, Your Majesty."

"Excellent. Then I declare this audience over." The queen stood and swept out of the room through a door behind the throne.

At that moment, Paena was alone before the throne, stunned by events. Baltar came to her aid and led her from the hall before well-wishers mobbed her.

As she left the throne room, Kayla joined them. "Mother. The goddess has an assignment for you…"

Chapter Forty-One

Paena, with a frown on her face, looked down from the crest of a hill across a sea of trees. The "assignment" Tulliandars had given her was to guard the borders of the kingdom.

"Too many men of the kingdom perished in the war to properly defend it," Kayla said.

Paena had not even had the chance to sit at the banquet before leaving.

That so many had died had been her fault. Actually, that wasn't true, she reminded herself. The fault had been Tulliandars. If only she had found a different solution.

"It isn't fair," she spat. Instead of celebrating the victory and mourning Kalten, she was banished to the edges of the kingdom. Her 'reward' was no different than the traitors' punishment.

"*Stop sulking, Mother.*" Kayla interjected. "*You agreed to follow the goddess, and what you are doing is important. It will not be forever.*"

"*Get out of my mind, girl.*" Paena replied. "*I don't need your lectures just now, nor do I crave your company.*"

Kayla's mental voice remained, mercifully, silent. Paena looked over the trees and brooded. She hoped Kalten was in a better place.

She finally tired of the view and climbed back into the saddle. At least she had the mare for company. She patted the horse's neck and lightly tapped her heels to its flank. Back on patrol.

Kalten had never gotten the chance to find his lost family. Maybe that was something she could do to honor his memory.

She urged the mare to a gallop and careened recklessly through the trees. Maybe then she could lay his memory to rest.

Epilogue

The goddess, Tulliandars stood in a clearing behind her cabin, looking intently at the body laid out on a stone slab. Not a sound could be heard.

She circled the body, clucking her tongue and tapping her chin.

"What am I going to do with you? You fought me at every turn and refused to use my gifts despite my commands. And for that you died.

"Is death enough of a punishment? You bound yourself to me to save your child. I have gifted you with powers to be my warrior, yet you have resisted. I need you in that capacity, and I think you need more of a lesson before you are ready to accept my gifts. But what lesson will that be?"

She poked the grey flesh of the corpse with an index finger while she pondered the question. Where her finger touched, the flesh took on a pink hue.

She snapped her fingers. "I have it. I know what is to be done with you." She closed her eyes in concentration for a few moments before she turned away and went back to the cabin.

As the sound of birds started again, only the stone slab remained. Of the body, there was no sign.

About the Author

Michell (Mike) Plested is an author, editor, blogger, closet superhero (not to mention sock herder and cat wrangler), podcaster, and publisher living in Calgary, Alberta, Canada.

He began his writer's journey by reading every Fantasy and Science Fiction novel he could find on his long bus rides to and from school. That grew into the dream that one day his own stories would be similarly enjoyed.

The Goddess Renewed is infused with his love of the genre, creating a beautiful, deadly world that could easily spell your doom should you decide to visit it.

Mike loves to hear from his readers. You can find and connect with him at the links below.

Website/Blog: www.michellplested.com
Facebook: https://www.facebook.com/michell.plested

~ * ~

Thank you for taking the time to read *The Goddess Renewed*. If you enjoyed the story, please tell your friends, read another by Mike, and leave a review. Reviews support authors and ensure they continue to bring readers books to love and enjoy.

And now for a look inside *Jack Kane and the Statue of Liberty*, a humorous steampunk with heroic leads, goofy villains, and adventure galore mixed with cool gadgets.

EXPLODING SHIPS.
A DIABOLICAL MASTERMIND.
JAKE AND BETSY HAVE NEVER HAD SO MUCH FUN.

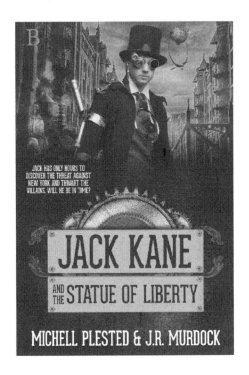

TURN THE PAGE
FOR A LOOK INSIDE!

Chapter One

Felonious Fenduke Filcher the Fourth stood on the upper patio with a brass spyglass held up to his right eye. The object of his attention was a heavily laden cargo ship entering New York Harbor a good half-mile away.

A warm breeze blew across the house, ruffling his hair.

Some might have once called Felonious handsome if it weren't for the maniacal look in his eyes. His thirty short years of driven, single-minded existence had changed that. He now had a gaunt, haunted expression the fairer sex described as cadaverous.

It didn't matter to him. He had more important things to do than woo love.

"Excuse me, sir," his butler said with a subtle clearing of throat.

"What is it? I said I was not to be disturbed!" Felonious allowed a hint of anger to seep into his voice. "I told you to call me 'my lord' not 'sir'!"

"I know, my lord. But you have a call on the wireless." The man shuffled his feet on the worn stone of the veranda taking the admonishment in stride. "It's the baron, my lord."

The baron. What was that windbag doing calling, especially now? "Bring the wireless out here to me. At once," Felonious said.

"Yes, my lord." The man snapped his fingers, and two hulking brutes wrestled the wireless into place. It was a massive thing, all brass and wood. An ornate microphone decorated a wooden top and a huge speaker faced out behind it.

Felonious tugged on a lever. "Baron? How nice of you to call."

"No time for idle chit-chat, Felonious," a voice with a distinct British accent crackled through the speaker. "Has the item arrived?"

"I was watching the vessel sail into the harbor, my lord," Felonious said. "It shouldn't be long now."

As if on cue, the night sky was lit with bright light. Moments later the concussive boom of an explosion echoed across the water.

Felonious pulled out his pocket watch. "Ah, right on time, my lord. The ship has been blown up according to schedule."

"Excellent work, Felonious!" The voice of the baron actually sounded pleased. "Congratulations. I will have to speak with my colleagues in the House of Lords to get your recommendation moving through the proper channels. After the sinking has been confirmed, of course."

Felonious forced his irritation into hiding. "Of course, Baron. I wouldn't have it any other way."

The butler stepped into Felonious's field of vision and spoke quietly. "Do you need anything, my lord?"

"Did your man call you, 'my lord', Felonious? You are not getting airs or presenting yourself above your station, are you? You know how the Peers of the Realm feel about that sort of thing."

"Never, my lord," Felonious said with a grimace. "You know how these servants can be, holding their beloved master in awe. I will chastise them again after we have completed talking with each other."

"Well done, old boy. Now as to the reason for this call. I have taken the liberty of sending one of my best men to you on the Zeppelin. He should arrive this afternoon. I was certain you would be successful, but I sent along some extra help just the same. One can never be too sure."

"Quite," Felonious said. "Well, it was unnecessary, but thank you. As you no doubt heard, the ship has been sunk."

"Oh yes," the voice crackled. "It was the explosion that sounded across the world, to coin a phrase. I will be quite delighted to hear about it on the news later. But I must dash."

"Before you go, my lord, answer me this. How will I know your man when he arrives?"

"Ah. Excellent question," the baron said. "He is quite a well-dressed fellow. Carries an interesting walking stick. Has a silver skull on it. He goes by the *nom de guerre* of 'Mister Y'."

"Thank you, my lord," Felonious said, his mind whirling with plans for the agent.

"Well, ta ta for now."

The voice went silent, and Felonious shut off the wireless with a push on the lever. Only after the machine had gone dark and silent did he allow himself a grin, the baron's reprimand about title already forgotten.

"Bennington! Fetch me some of the 1828 Napoleon brandy." Felonious tipped the coffee dregs out of his stained and cracked cup and held it up for the butler. "Fill it up. I feel the urge to celebrate."

The butler was at his arm almost immediately, an expensive

crystal decanter of dark liquid in his hands. "I thought you might, sir." He wrinkled his nose. "Would you like me to strain the brandy through my socks before I pour it into your, ahem, mug, sir?" The wryness of the tall man's statement barely registered.

"No, that won't be necessary, Bennington. Just fill it up and keep it full. There's a good chap. And as I said before, call me, 'my lord'."

"But the baron—"

"Is not here." Felonious raised an eyebrow at the man. "Do I make myself clear?"

"Crystal, my lord," Bennington said, emphasizing the final two words.

"Excellent! Then you may pour."

Bennington grimaced and tipped the pristine decanter over the grimy cup, filling it with the dark, expensive liquid.

Felonious tipped the cup back and took a big swig. With a belch, he held the mug out for Bennington to refill. "Top 'er up, old top."

"As you wish, my lord." Bennington did as directed and refilled it.

"That will be all, Bennington," Felonious said with a wave of his hand.

He picked up the spyglass and lifted it to his eye, sloshing some of the brandy on his tunic. It took him a few seconds before he had the spyglass sighted in. When he finally got the image, he sighed happily. Boats surrounded a burning patch of harbor. Fire department patrol boats sprayed torrents of water on the fire, which spread from the destroyed cargo hauler.

Heads bobbed in the water. It didn't bother him in the least to see the floundering sailors. They were either French or American. It wasn't terribly likely any Englishmen were out there, and if they were... He shrugged. If they were, they were traitors to good Queen Victoria and the empire and deserved what they got.

He watched for a few moments more, chuckling to himself and guzzling the brandy. Things were going extremely well. At this rate, his tarnished family name would regain its previous luster, and he would be back in the ranks of gentlemen.

Felonious adjusted his gaze to the street in front of his estate and grimaced. The first thing he would do is get a house in a better part of town. No more living near the stockyards and the slaughterhouses.

He laughed under his breath. It would also mean his "estate" would not consist of the rotting remains of machines and old coaches. It would also likely mean a new title for himself. No longer "King of Junk" but something more suitable for a gentleman patriot of the empire. Then perhaps that fop of a baron would serve him as his family served Felonious' in the not-so-distant past.

The junkyard served him well. It provided a good income and an even better place to hide his life's work—the overthrow of the American government. And it gave him all the resources he could ever need to experiment and build his machines.

Deep within the confines of the yard lay his workshop, his lab. There his ideas and inventions were created. There the planning and execution of the agenda took place.

He swirled the remnants of the brandy in the mug before gulping it down. He was about to call Bennington for something stronger when he saw the truck chugging and wheezing its way up the street. It would not be long before Felonious could get a firsthand account of the glorious explosion and sinking of the ship bringing that monstrous symbol of American and French defiance.

"There will be no Statue of Liberty," Felonious muttered. "Not now that I've destroyed it."

He peered down at the struggling steam truck. "Might as well make myself comfortable. Those clowns will be a while before they get here to report."

~ * ~

Felonious was sitting behind his massive desk when his minions trudged in. The men, both modeled after the great apes with massively muscled frames and sloping foreheads, were a mess. Their clothes were soaked and torn, and the minion on the right lacked part of an ear.

Felonious pulled the cigar out of his mouth and stared at them. "What in heaven's name happened to you two?"

Minion number one, who had his entire ear, stared at the floor and shuffled his feet. "Well, Boss. It's like this…"

"Yes?"

"Well…the thing is…" The big man couldn't seem to get the words out. He looked at his companion. "You tell him Lenny. Youse is better wit words than me."

Minion two, Lenny, who was missing part of his ear, seemed stunned to be put on the hot seat. "Well, Boss. Um…" He stumbled over the words, dragging them on.

Felonious banged his fist on the desk making both gorillas jump. "Will you two stop dancing around and tell me what's going on? I saw you blow up the ship. So why are you looking so guilty? Hmm? Tell me what's going on right now."

"Well, Boss, the thing is, we did blow up a boat like you said. We put the floating bombs into the harbor like you ordered. Thing is… Well, the wrong boat hit the bomb." Lenny cringed as he spoke the final words as if he expected to be struck.

Felonious glared from one minion to the other, his cigar dangling in his hand. "So, the wrong ship hit it. You managed to sink the cursed French vessel that carried the statue, didn't you?"

"The *Isere*?" Minion one mumbled.

"What?"

"The French ship carrying the statue is the *Isere*," Lenny supplied helpfully.

"I don't give a damn what the ship is called. Did you or did you not sink the blasted French ship?"

"That's what we've been trying to tell you, sir," Lenny said.

Felonious rubbed his fingertips against his throbbing temples, momentarily closing his eyes. He leaned back in his chair and tried another tactic when he opened them. His voice was calm when he spoke again. "Yes, gentlemen. That is what I hope you will tell me. Did you blow up the French ship?"

"The *Isere*?" Lenny asked, staring everywhere but at Felonious.

He ground his teeth together. "If one of you don't tell me in the next minute what I want to know, I shall have you both killed. Is that understood?"

"Yes, sir," both henchmen said in unison.

Felonious looked at them. They looked back.

"So?"

"Not as such, sir," Minion one said, his voice barely audible.

"I'm sorry," Felonious said. "I didn't quite catch that."

Lenny sighed. The breeze almost knocked Felonious over. "No, sir. We didn't sink it because the other ship hit the explosives and blew up. There was nothing left to blow up the French ship with. I tried to move the bomb, but all I managed was to get caught up in the blast myself."

Felonious turned his back to the men and stared out the window. "You mean to tell me I give you two one thing to do—blow up the dirty French dogs and their abomination of a statue—and you can't even get that right?"

He paced. "I thought I had the right men for the job when I hired you two. Now I find out I was wrong." Felonious spun about the room, speaking to himself—the only person he trusted. "I was so certain you two were the right men. But if I was wrong, what am I going to do? I can't have you two going around telling the world I was wrong. What would people think?"

"Boss, youse wasn't wrong," Minion one said. "We are the right guys for the job. It wasn't our fault the wrong ship hit the bomb. The current grabbed it and carried it into the other ship's path."

Felonious continued talking, ignoring that the goon had spoken at all. "What should I do with these two? Perhaps I should simply kill them. Isn't that what happens to people who fail?"

"Boss, give us another chance," Lenny pleaded. "We can do it, I promise. We need the chance to go and try again. No one will ever know about the screw up."

Felonious stopped pacing and stared out the window. "Perhaps I should be lenient. These men aren't bad people." He laughed, happy at his own joke. "Well, they are bad people, but they are not bad at what they do. Perhaps if they were to leave right now and try again and get it right, mind you, maybe, just maybe, I can let them live. I believe there is another explosive device in my workroom. It is clearly marked as 'Explosive'. All any clever minion who wanted to get on his employer's good side would need to do is put the explosives in a nondescript case, take said case and plant it on or near the French ship so it can be blown up. If they are as smart as their employer wants them to be, they will have the case in place by 10:00 a.m. so the explosion will happen during the big celebration. Maybe I should give them another chance, after all."

He clapped his hands together and spoke as he turned to face the henchmen. "That is exactly what I'll do…" He feigned surprise. "Well, what do you know? They're gone. Perhaps they left to try again?" He grinned. "Felonious, you clever scoundrel you. You certainly know how to motivate your staff, don't you?"

~ * ~

The early morning hours suited Jack fine. There were far fewer people out for one thing, but those who were awake at this hour were always doing something productive to get ready to start the day: packing or unpacking crates or loading or unloading lorries to be pushed back along the rails to the piers. These men would work until the sun rose and another shift would take over. Just like Jack, New York City never truly slept.

The aroma of a distant bakery caught his nose. "If we're lucky, Franklin, we'll get ourselves a treat before heading home. How's that sound, boy?"

Franklin gave an approving whimper as Jack scratched him behind the ears.

"You get one for being such a good boy. For me, I think I'll treat myself to a pastry for getting the double wall done on my project. So many failures, and all it took was to build a double thick wall to resolve the pressure containment issue. Not only does it solve my problem, but this will also make my work go far more efficiently at the yard once it's up and running."

The yard was in fact a junkyard that lay a few blocks back on the corner of Hudson and Jay Streets. Franklin had been found scavenging in a pile of trash on Franklin Street during Jack's early morning walk the previous morning, and he took pity on the poor creature. He'd told himself, "Jack, you can't leave this poor fellow here to root through the trash."

Normally Jack would get to Beach Street and take a right at the New York Central and Hudson River Railroad Freight Depot and make his way over to Broadway before heading back to the yard, but something made him hesitate. It wasn't something he could easily explain, but the feeling caused him a moment's pause. Perhaps it was a shift of the breeze or a change in pitch of the harbor bells, but Jack Kane stopped on the corner of Hudson and Beach and turned toward the piers.

There were no screams, not at first anyway, but only a bright flash of light that turned the early morning darkness into daytime for an instant. A concussive blast quickly followed the flash and knocked Jack end over teakettle. Poor Franklin rolled along with him.

Thankful for the early morning hour being free of heavier traffic, Jack shot to his feet. As he started to run along Beach to get to the pier, Franklin gave a whimper and refused to follow. Jack nearly fell thinking his partner would follow him anywhere.

"What is it, boy? Come on. We've got to get to the pier and see if anyone needs assistance. It's all right. Come along now."

Franklin refused to budge no matter how hard Jack tugged on the leash. He had to get to the piers to see what happened. Nothing ever exploded in this area on accident, and he knew of nothing that was planned to explode at such an early hour. It didn't matter that few residents actually lived in this part of the city. Things didn't go boom before the sun came up. They just didn't.

"All right. You win. You'll have to wait for that snack until I get back. You be a good boy. I won't be long."

Jack tied Franklin to the fireplug on the street corner then paused. If something had exploded on or near the pier that was a bad thing indeed, and deserved more caution than he was about to give it. He needed to move higher to get a good appraisal of the situation before hurrying in. Unfortunately, people weren't happy about a person scampering across the rooftops unannounced. It was for occasions like this Jack Kane had created his very own alter ego.

From within his long coat he pulled the two halves of a metal mask he'd fashioned from bits of scrap metal and various parts. Most of the mask's composition was of blackened steel with rivets keeping it all together. Two large, but different-sized, gears made the eyes. A brass skeleton key created a fine nose. The mouth was a simple rectangular slit covered with a mesh screen to hide the voice modulator.

It was more than a mask, but closer to a full helmet, once expanded. Tiny hooks on its top allowed him to replace his hat and ensure he wouldn't lose it once he took to the rooftops. As an almost badge of honor he pinned a hand-sized gear on his chest. This he'd painted with gold paint.

With his alter ego in place, he was ready to go. As he ascended the ladder, he thought of what to call himself. Stories of his escapades had been in print in the *Wilkes' Spirit* a few times talking about minor things he'd done to help people in the area. The paper usually put a good spin on his handiwork, but he hoped they'd be more helpful in giving him a name. Jack was never good with naming things.

"Metal Head? No, no. Gearheart? No no. I need a better name than that. What can I call myself?"

After ascending the fire escape to the top of the building, Jack realized a minor error in calculation. He'd climbed up a building on the wrong side of Hudson. He needed to be on the opposite side of the street in order to get himself to the piers via the rooftops. He'd already wasted enough time scaling one building. He didn't want to waste more climbing down and then up another.

A bundle of telegraph wires drooped between two poles heading in the direction of the harbor. It was what Jack needed. Within one of the many pockets in his coat he removed what could best be described as a giant's fishing hook with a non-barbed hook on one end and a loop on the other.

He put his hand through the loop and leapt off the building, holding the hook out to catch the wire. His falling speed allowed him to gain momentum. The hook caught the wire as Jack planned, and he slid along it and continued to gain speed as he crossed the street toward the smaller building on the other side. The zinging of the hook running across the wire caught the attention of the people below him.

The one thing he hadn't planned on when he started his race was his dismount. Oh sure, he could let go of the hook at the right moment, but now he heard people yelling as they saw him. He had to do this right. It had to be impressive. People knew his alter ego in this part of town. They expected more than a zip across the street.

As Jack approached the other side and was on his upward turn, he kicked his legs into the air. Unfortunately, this caused the hook to tilt and lose contact with the telegraph wire. The next thing Jack realized was he was no longer traveling up at the proper speed to get to the top of the building; he was going higher. And faster!

Once he left the telegraph wire he sailed up and over the roof's edge, the hook trailing out behind him. His momentum propelled him high, and the hook caught onto a circular chimney and circled him around not once, but three times before it wound off the top of the chimney and sent him flying across Beach. His arc carried him up where he managed to land on his feet atop the building.

Cheers rose up from the street. Jack Kane turned and waved to the workers below. He could just see them in the gas lamplight clapping and pointing. Even Franklin gave an approving bark from the street. This wasn't the time to stand around though. Jack sprinted along the edge of the roof. The space between the buildings on the ends of one block and the next heading toward the piers was significantly less, and he made short work of the distance. A few hops, a couple ladders, and he had the perfect vantage point atop the main receiving building.

The rooftop gave him a great view of not only the piers, but of the entire Upper Bay. Small ferries and tug boats made their way out to a sinking ship. Jack could make out the American flag on its fantail. Alongside the vessel was a second ship that appeared mostly undamaged save for some black scorch marks on its side. This one flew a different red, white, and blue flag—that of the French.

Usually up on the comings and goings of the harbor, he hadn't known a French vessel was due to arrive this morning, or even what it might contain. He'd have to look into that, but first, he had to see if there was anything he could do to help out before the ship slipped under water.

The gears that made the eyes of his mask were more than decorative. They also served to hold items such as the spyglass Jack tugged from his pocket. The spyglass fit snugly over the right eyehole. With movements of his brow he was able to tighten the focus and take in the scene. It took a few seconds, but he focused on the action below.

The French ship had made its way further along and away from the sinking American ship. The scorching on the French ship's side appeared to be the only visible damage, and three of the ship's crew were at the rail accessing the damage.

The American vessel, on the other hand, had all but disappeared. Many of its crew were being dragged up onto a small ferry, but that wasn't what grabbed Jack's attention. What appeared to be a second ship, far smaller than the American, was also sinking. Much of it had been blown apart, but it was most certainly another ship.

That's when something paddling away from the scene caught his eye: a man swimming from the sinking vessels. He didn't appear to be heading for safety; his frantic movements suggest he was trying to flee the scene.

Jack knew, he knew deep down, this person must've been piloting the smaller ship and detonated an explosive device to sink the American ship. Thankfully, the French ship hadn't sunk. The French and American's were on great terms and having one of their ships destroyed could ruin that relationship. Jack had to catch this man and quickly.

~ * ~

Bennington Bartholomew Bentley the XVIth was a butler through and through. His family had a long and distinguished history of butlering to the rich and powerful throughout history. That Bennington worked for Felonious was not as much an indication of failure, as a need by his society to change the order of the world.

"That foolish boy is going to muff the whole thing up," he said.

He sat at a modest reading desk in his sparsely furnished bedroom staring into a small screen that was cleverly designed to fold into the back of the desk itself. On the screen, Felonious could be seen prancing about, dancing with a lady's nightshift.

"I'm going to have to do something to ensure the plan is carried out." Bennington tapped a tiny button on the side of the flat panel and the image of Felonious went blank. It was replaced with a woman. One who would be instantly recognizable to most of the world should they see it.

"Yes?" Her voice was majestic, cultured, and extremely British.

Bennington bowed his head. "I apologize for the late hour, Majesty, but I needed to speak with you."

"Bennington?" The woman smiled. "I always have time for you. Please, tell me what troubles you."

"As you know, Majesty, my charge is young and foolish. I fear he will do something to jeopardize the mission."

"You are speaking of Four-F? Bennington, I would not have sent you to the Americas if I did not think you were the man for the job. I have complete faith in you."

"Thank you, Majesty." He straightened in his chair. "Majesty, if I may ask a boon?"

"Name it, and if it is in my power, it is yours," Queen Victoria said.

Bennington's stomach churned. "Do we have any, ahem, men in the field here?"

She looked away from the screen and spoke to an unseen person then turned back a second later. "We do indeed. I will have my secretary send you the contact information." Queen Victoria frowned and waggled a finger at him. "But Bennington, these agents are very well placed for some of my future plans. Do not expose them lightly."

His smile seemed a bit forced. "I will use them with utmost discretion, Your Majesty."

"See that you do," she said.

The screen went dark, and Bennington sat, thinking about whether helping Felonious succeed warranted risking his queen's wrath.

Chapter Two

It took Jack far longer than he would have liked to get down. With his spyglass still in place he was able to keep track of the person's progress. That was a plus. But he needed to go to the pier. The man swam *away* from the rescue ships. He had to have done something wrong, and Jack Kane was the man to catch him.

Five stories below on the street were several lorries covered over and ready to push out onto the pier to load whatever ship might be coming in that day, and just as many empty lorries waiting to unload ships. There was no way to tell what was in the covered lorries, and Jack dared not jump onto one.

Most nights he hit the street prepared for such a situation, but he'd been so excited about completing his doubled-walled invention he only grabbed his coat—holding his mask, badge, and a few other implements—but left his satchel behind. Perhaps there was something on the rooftops he could use.

Jack scanned about him. There wasn't much on the roof of the receiving building: a broken crate, several articles of unidentifiable clothing, a housing for what might have been a pigeon coop in a previous life, a zeppelin-docking ring with a tether...

That was it! He wasted no time in getting the suspiciously thin zeppelin tether cable and tossed it over the side of the building. From within his pocket he fetched the hook and a small attachment from another pocket. The attachment for the hook had four flywheels and inside steel alloy gear strong enough to support his weight. The device, when attached to a rope or cable, would slow his descent. He built this gizmo for angled drops, not for going straight down, but he had to make do and hope for the best.

Jack did one more check on the person swimming for the pier. No ships steered toward the man, and he made no motion to signal them. A guilty act if Jack had ever seen one.

He attached the gizmo on the inside of the hook and clipped it onto the zeppelin tether. A pull to ensure the tether was secure, though he had little doubt it would be loose, and Jack lowered himself over the side of the building. He took a deep breath. Then a second. Finally a third, and he began to descend.

The 'ping' noise from the gizmo concerned him for only a second. It spun then locked up leaving him hanging about ten feet from the rooftop. He hefted himself up with both arms and dropped, trying to unfreeze the gears. He tried putting his feet against the side of the building and yanking. That didn't free anything up either. He braced his feet inside the fifth floor window frame where he stopped and jumped. This drop freed the gears with a loud pop.

Immediately Jack's heart leapt into his throat. The gizmo, as best as he could tell, had failed, and he was falling far too rapidly toward the ground. When he slapped the toes of his boots together, small spikes popped out the bottom of the boots. He'd built his boots more for climbing over slippery trash, but now he used them to slow his descent. They helped a bit, but what helped more was a second pop from the gizmo, and Jack came to another stop that almost popped his arm out of its socket.

He had no desire to see how far he was from the ground. Turning around to try and spot the swimmer, Jack was confronted with a lorry blocking his view. Planting his feet in to the wall he tried to peer over the top of it, but it was too tall. It was best to unhook the gizmo and drop the rest of the way to the ground. He gritted his teeth and let his legs dangle as far as he could stretch. Once his feet hit the ground, he'd roll up into a ball and hopefully prevent himself from suffering any permanent damage.

With his left hand, he unlatched the gizmo from the tether. And let go.

He was going to count the number of heartbeats that passed before he hit the ground, but there weren't any. Instead his feet touched almost instantly. This startled him and, with his legs loose and relaxed, he fell on to his rump.

"Well then. No damage done."

Getting up and slipping around the lorries in front of him, he then sprinted up pier twenty-seven to where he'd last seen the swimming man. No ship was moored at the pier. It was possible the sinking ship would have been tied there had it not been blown to pieces. He needed to know not only what was on the ship, but why it'd been targeted. Things like that didn't happen. The person in the water most likely didn't work alone either. Interrogation was in order once he got the man out of the bay.

A few workers, likely those whose job it was to secure the incoming ships, milled about on the pier watching the activity beyond.

Those on pier twenty-eight were busy mooring up the French ship that had been pushed into place by the tugs. Jack couldn't make out the name of the vessel, but that wasn't his main concern.

He stowed the spyglass attachment and now, with his vision clear, he could make out the reddish glow of the lantern on the water. Eerie. It hadn't been so spooky from atop the building. Down here the reflections danced and swayed with each ripple on the water's surface.

No one gave him any notice as he made his way along the dimly lit pier. Though the mask had minor blind spots, it allowed him to focus on where he wanted to go. The first version of the mask, or helmet, had no padding and beat him about the head and neck when he ran. This model, he liked to think of it as version 3.0 as it was really the third iteration of the design, had not only padding, but ventilation and a tiny, inside fan to allow his head to breathe. Version 2.0 caused him to sweat too much.

At the end of the pier, he caught sight of the man, still swimming toward the pier. There was no one else around and no ladder descended. Jack raised the sleeve of his jacket. Strapped to his wrist was another device he built to help with his job at the junkyard. Made from scrap parts, it was a winch with a cable almost as strong as that of the zeppelin tether, but thin as thread. His own special design. The spool of thread could be launched or thrown—which was what he'd do. But how was he going to pull the man in?

The hook. Jack attached the hook to the thread, removed the gizmo, and threw the hook to the swimming man. The man was tired, out of breath. That would make him easier to capture.

The hook caught the swimmer behind the right ear and bounced into his clothing then held fast. He shrieked and floundered. Jack winced. Ouch. Like a fisherman with a prize fish on the line, he yanked. The reel on its mechanism had a handgrip that would wind the thread in.

He squeezed and pulled. Squeezed and pulled. The man dragged through the water easily enough, but once he had him to the pier, Jack had to lift the man's entire significant weight. The tide had only begun to come in, and the water was low. Jack braced himself and, inch by inch, lifted the man up and onto the pier.

Once on deck, the big fellow, around six foot two and two-hundred-twenty pounds, lay like a dead fish, barely breathing.

Jack, in stark contrast, puffed and panted and feared he might pass out. He couldn't do that, though. He had his suspect who needed to be questioned.

~ * ~

Lenny and his pal Squiggy practically flew from Felonious' office.

The two gorillas hadn't waited for their boss to finish his monologue before they hit the door running.

"What do ya think that was all about," Squiggy said.

"I dunno, Squiggy," Lenny replied. "I just know that when the boss starts talking like that, it's time to leave." Lenny's damaged ear was beginning to bleed again as it flapped in the breeze from their running. "Geez, this ear is a pain." He pulled a pink polka-dotted kerchief from the breast pocket of his suit and tied it around his head like a bandanna. "That's better. Now maybe I can think about what we need to do."

"What was the boss jabbering about?" Squiggy asked, his words coming out in short gasps.

Lenny abruptly stopped and waited for his colleague to do the same. "Yeah, what was he saying?" He tapped the side of his head as he thought, wincing when he hit his injured ear. "Something about an explosive, I think."

"You're right, Lenny," Squiggy said, his expression brightening. "He did say those words." The expression didn't last long. "What do you suppose he meant by that?"

Lenny wrapped a beefy arm around Squiggy's shoulders. "You know, Squiggy. That's what I like about you. You don't let little things slow you down too much."

"Thanks, Lenny," Squiggy said. "Uh, Lenny? What do you mean by that exactly?"

"Oh nothing," Lenny said. "Now about that explosive the boss mentioned. I think he was talking about us taking another shot at blowing up that Frenchy ship. Maybe we can get back on his good side?"

"Gee. Do you think that would work?"

"I sure hope so, 'cause I hate being on the boss' bad side," Lenny said. "He's crazy. There's no knowing what he might do to us if we really made him mad."

"You got that right, Lenny." Squiggy frowned. "Where do you suppose we would find some explosives at this time of night?"

Lenny tapped his head. "Leave it to me, Squiggy. I do believe the boss mentioned something about his workroom in all that babbling. Surely we'll find something in there."

"That's some good thinking." Squiggy held the front door of the manor open for his friend.

"Thanks, buddy. Let's hurry before the boss changes his mind and has us put on ice." The big man led his companion out into the darkness that was the front yard of the junkyard. Off to the left a hound bayed. "Aw geez. The dogs are out. We'd better make a run for it if we don't want them jumping all over us and slobbering on our clothes."

The two men broke into a trot and crossed the dark courtyard into the junkyard proper. They zigzagged their way through mounds of metal and rusted machines. The tiny bit of moon lit their way just enough they avoided any accidents. The baying of the hounds grew closer with every passing second.

"We ain't gonna make it, Lenny," a panting Squiggy said. "Them dogs must be just about nipping on our heels."

"Don't worry, Squiggy. We'll make it," Lenny said, indicating a light a few yards away. "There's the boss' workshop now."

The barking of the dogs sounded only inches away, spurring both men to a final burst of speed. They rushed through the door and slammed it closed behind them looking at each other with relief. The door shuddered as several bodies smashed against it. The sound of scratching and whining traveled through the thick wood.

"See, Squiggy. I told ya we'd make it," Lenny said. "Now, spread out and get looking for the explosives."

"You got it, Lenny." Squiggy ran around the room picking up and throwing items over his shoulder in wild abandon.

"Squiggy!" Lenny waited for the man to stop his rampage. When he didn't Lenny called out again. "Squiggy, what are you doing?"

Squiggy stopped and turned to face Lenny. "I'm looking for explosives like you told me too."

Lenny walked up to the man and put a meaty hand on his shoulder. "Do you even know what you're looking for?"

Squiggy scratched his head. "Stuff that goes boom?"

"Squiggy, you saw the explosives we put out in the water, didn't you?" Lenny corrected himself quickly. "Before we put them in the water?"

"Oh yeah," Squiggy said with a look of comprehension.

"That's what we're looking for. And for the record, I don't think the boss wants us to trash his workroom, okay?"

Squiggy's expression fell. "Oh, yeah. I didn't think of that."

"Good. Now you know. So just look for a crate or box with the word 'explosives' on it."

"Will do." Squiggy rummaged more carefully through the workroom. After five minutes he turned back. "Um, Lenny?"

"Yes, Squiggy?"

"How do you spell explosives?"

"Oh for crying out loud. It starts with an 'e'."

"Oh." He went silent for another minute. "Lenny?"

"Yes, Squiggy."

"What does an 'e' look like?"

Lenny checked his partner to see if he was joking. "Don't you know how to read?"

Squiggy blushed. "I was kicked out of school when I was in the first grade. Teach said I was too dumb and was holding back the other kids."

"No kidding?" Lenny felt a sense of sadness for his friend. "Come over here, Squiggy. I'll write the word you want to look for, okay?"

Squiggy's smile was a warm glow. "That would be great, Lenny. Thanks."

Lenny pulled a piece of paper out of his suit pocket followed by a pen. He started to write the word 'explosive' when the communication console in the workroom buzzed. He flipped a switch, and a screen with the glaring Felonious rose from the console.

"Change of plans, boys," Felonious said. "I want you to hold off on the explosives for a bit longer and come over to my main workroom to help me with something. If you have the explosives, bring them along. I can use them, otherwise, just come to give me a hand."

"Sure thing, boss," Lenny said. He toggled the switch to lower the screen and end the call. "Looks like the boss wants us in his workroom."

Lines formed on Squiggy's forehead. "But isn't this his workroom? I don't understand."

"This is one of his workrooms. You know the boss has labs and work places all over the estate."

"Yeah, I guess so," Squiggy answered. "So what are we gonna do?"

"We do as the boss says and go to his main workroom." Lenny spied something out of the corner of his eye. "Hey, what do ya know? There is the crate of explosives too."

He walked over to the box and picked it up. It was heavy and took most of his effort to carry it. "Hey, why doncha give me a hand here?"

"We're taking this too?" Squiggy said nervously. "What about those dogs out there?"

"Oh, don't worry about them," Lenny said. "The main workroom is attached to this one by underground tunnels. We don't have to go back outside at all."

"I wonder why the boss wouldn't have the workrooms attached to the house," Squiggy asked.

"You know, I think they are," Lenny said.

"Then why did we go outside where the dogs could get us?"

"I honestly don't know. Now shuddup and grab the box."

Lenny led his befuddled comrade to the tunnel door, and they made their way to the main workroom. Felonious was already there working hard on a beautiful gleaming carriage. The vehicle shined in a malignant black and was a vision of pipes and chrome. The wheels were made of the finest rubber and a single seat was at the front for the driver. The steam-powered carriage was the picture of grace and power.

When Felonious saw them he spoke. "Ah, gentlemen. How good of you to come. And with the explosives too, I see. Excellent."

"What can we do to help you out, boss?" Squiggy asked.

"Well, it occurred to me that the French ship might be quite impossible to approach, what with the ceremony and dignitaries who will be attending it. Only those people who look like they belong will be allowed close enough to attend."

"Okay, boss. But how does that include us?"

Felonious's nose twitched. "I'm getting to that, lackey. Do not interrupt me."

"Sorry, Boss."

Satisfied that Squiggy wouldn't speak again, Felonious continued, "This carriage will guarantee you won't be stopped when you go to the dock."

"I can see how the fancy steam carriage might do that. Even if Squiggy and me are doing the driving. But how will that help us to blow up the ship?" Lenny asked.

"It won't," Felonious said. "I have other plans for the carriage. I simply need you to get it close to the French ship for now. I could blow it up during the press conference, but it would kill most of the reporters." He paced. "While I don't have any particular love for reporters, they are necessary to my plan. I need someone to spread the word of my victory, after all."

"Oh, I get it, boss," Squiggy said. He smiled for almost a minute before confusion showed on his face once again. "Um, Boss?"

"Yes, minion?"

"Boss, I lied. I don't get it at all."

Felonious sighed. "I don't expect you to understand, but I will try to explain anyway. I want you two at the dock to scope out the situation. See who is there and how security is set-up. Get people used to seeing you too. I want to be sure they accept you as normal people when everything happens. That will make it all much easier."

"Whatever you say, boss," Lenny said.

"Exactly. Whatever I say," Felonious replied.

He pulled a stylish gentleman's case from under a workbench and handed it to Lenny. Then Felonious opened the box marked explosives and grabbed several sticks of dynamite. He handed them to Squiggy. "Here, fill the case with these and hook this detonation device to them."

Lenny held the case open while Squiggy filled it with the explosives and connected the detonator.

Felonious remained silent until Lenny snapped the case closed. "Place it near the French vessel, close enough the ship will sink from the blast. Do you understand?"

"Yes, boss," Squiggy said, nodding his head vigorously.

Felonious waited.

"So, what do you want us to do now, boss?" Squiggy asked.

Felonious counted to ten before he answered his large minion. "I want you to take the carriage to the dock and blend in with the crowd. Place the case which you filled with explosives near the ship."

"Yes, boss, but you said the press conference is at 10:00 a.m.," Lenny said.

"And?"

"It's not even 6:00 a.m. yet, Boss. Wouldn't it look suspicious if we were at the dock this early?"

Felonious stared at Lenny for several seconds, tapping his bottom lip, before he answered. "You raise a very good point, minion. It is too early to go." He paced again, talking aloud for his own benefit. "What should I have my faithful minions do for the next few hours?"

"You could let us have forty winks," Squiggy said in a pleading tone. "We've been up all night, and I'm beat."

"Hmm? Beat you say? What a novel idea," Felonious said.

"Squiggy just meant he's tired, Boss," Lenny said quickly. "We both are. I could use some shut-eye."

"Well, why didn't you say so," Felonious said with a wicked smile. "I have just the thing for that."

He wandered over to a steel cabinet and removed a key from the breast pocket of his lab coat. With great care, he unfastened the lock on the cabinet and opened the steel door, which made no sound as it moved.

Both henchmen leaned forward to catch a glimpse of the contents of the cabinet. Inside, gleaming like a new penny, was a brass colored ray gun. A globe of dazzling light shone from the back of the weapon, and polished brass and wood decorated the entire surface. Felonious gently withdrew the gun from its padded stand and cradled it like a newborn baby.

"What is it, Boss?" Lenny asked, awe coloring his voice.

"I call it my rejuvenation ray," Felonious said.

"What does it do?" Squiggy's voice cracked as he spoke.

Felonious patted the barrel. "One shot from this, and you will be filled with new energy to get things done. You won't feel tired at all."

"Gee, boss, look at the time," Squiggy said, holding up a bare, watchless wrist. "Me and Lenny here got to run out and do an errand for the boss."

"Minion, you don't have a watch, and I am the boss. I don't recall giving you anything to do for me."

"Um…"

"Relax, minion. It won't harm you at all. I've tested it thoroughly on rats and they hardly ever explode." Felonious eyed the two men. "Ha, ha," he said with little mirth. "That was a joke, gentlemen, in case you missed it."

"Oh! Ha ha," Lenny said, his face twisted in fear.

"Oh for heaven's sake," Felonious said. Facing Squiggy, he said, "You, minion, go get me one of those hamster cages from over there." He indicated a shelf covered with animal cages.

Squiggy walked over to the wall and fetched a cage containing one sluggish, fat hamster. The small animal was plodding along on a wire wheel.

"Place the cage on that table," Felonious ordered.

Squiggy put the cage on the indicated table and stepped back. With the two henchmen watching, Felonious lifted the weapon and aimed it at the cage. He pulled the trigger, and an ominous hum sounded. The glowing ball of energy in the weapon brightened, and a wavy beam of violet light flowed through the air and struck the cage. The sluggish hamster froze for a moment.

Then all hell broke loose.

The hamster went from motionless to full speed in mere seconds. The creaky wire wheel was suddenly moving so fast it was almost invisible. The axle started glowing a cherry red in seconds. The glow stretched from the axle to the rest of the wheel. The hamster let out a startled squeak and burst into flame. As fast as it started, the whole thing ended with a well-cooked hamster stuck to the slowing, melted wire wheel.

"If it's all the same to you, Boss, I think Lenny and I will go out and grab a cuppa joe," Lenny said, backing away from Felonious, case and explosives clutched tightly in his arms.

"Yeah, what Lenny said." Squiggy followed his comrade.

But Felonious ignored them. He was busy examining the gun. "That shouldn't have happened. I wonder if it would do the same thing to a bigger animal?"

~ * ~

Jack glanced at his chronometer. How long had he been lying on the dock? The sun had gone from creeping up on the horizon to nearly up. And if he'd been there for any length of time, why had no one come to their aid? The man beside him made no noise save for quiet breathing.

Jack rolled onto his right shoulder then wished he hadn't. It hurt terribly. He was lucky he hadn't pulled it out of its socket pulling the man up to the pier and after the abrupt stop during his descent from the top of the building. Jack tried moving the left, but he hadn't unattached the hook from the big man. Using his left arm, Jack righted himself into a sitting position.

The hook, after bouncing off the man's head, had caught on his belt. A lucky catch. Jack had to turn the man to the side, again using his left arm and release the hook from the big man's belt. This he did with his right arm which hurt to move. Once the hook was removed, Jack stowed it back in his jacket and finished reeling in the line. Each squeeze of his hand brought new pain to his shoulder and arm.

The man next to him stirred slightly. Jack was glad for that. Looking along the pier he could see no one had noticed them yet. That was both good and bad. Good in the fact Jack would have a few moments with the fellow to interrogate him as to why he sunk the ship, bad in the fact that both of them were in possible need of medical attention.

Jack appraised the wound on the top of the man's head. It oozed blood slowly, but it oozed nonetheless. He dug into a pocket of his jacket and produced a small bundle of cloth. It wasn't intended to be a bandage, but in this situation, it would have to do. He pressed it to the man's head. Now if only he had something he could use to secure it.

From within another pocket Jack got out a tiny nail gun. He looked at the man's head for only a second before putting the gun back. From another pocket he retrieved a length of twine. He made a mental note that for future adventures he'd need to make sure to have some sort of medical supply kit, no matter how small.

With the twine he secured the bundle of cloth to the top of the man's head. As long as he didn't move around too much it would stay in place just fine.

But Jack couldn't sit here and wait all morning for this man, whoever he was, to come to. Others might show up, and Jack would lose the element of surprise. Surely the man wasn't expecting to be captured so quickly.

He nudged him. "Sir. Sir! Are you all right?" The voice modulator gave Jack's voice an intentional mechanical quality.

The big man mumbled something incoherent.

"I said, 'are you all right?'"

The man rubbed at his ears. "What hit me?"

"That's not important right now. I was able to pull you out of the water. Are you all right to talk?"

He reached up to the top of his head and touched the bundle there. "What's this?"

"You got a cut on top of your head. Can you answer a few questions for me?"

"I guess."

He tried to sit up. Jack put a gentle hand on the man's shoulder. "Just lay there. There's a good fellow. It's quite a nasty bump and cut you've got there. I'll make sure you get the proper medical attention you need. Now, I must ask you a few questions."

"Who the devil are you? What is that you're wearing? Some kind of…iron mask?"

A name? The Iron Mask? The Man in the Iron Mask? Iron Masked Man? No. None of those would do at all. "I have no name you can call me. Yet. I must ask you some questions though. I need to know what you think you were doing."

"I was swimming for the pier. The ship, it was sinking." The man pointed out to the bay.

"Sinking indeed. How did that happen?" Jack wished he had something on which to take notes. Something else to remember to bring on his next outing.

Waving his hands in the air the man asked, "Didn't you see the explosion? It nearly blinded me."

"I did see the explosion. Why did you sink that ship?"

"Me? Why did *I* sink that ship?" He sputtered. "Say, who are you? Is this some kind of a joke?"

Again the man tried to sit up, but Jack prevented him.

"I assure you I am most serious. I saw you swimming away from the crime. Everyone else swam for the rescue boats. Everyone except you, that is."

"You think I tried to sink my own ship? Are you insane?"

"I am not. Why didn't you swim toward the rescue boats?" Jack motioned with his head to the boats around the wreckage of the sunken ship.

"Because I was blown off the ship from the blast. I see this smaller ship come riding up alongside of us, and I went off to tell them to veer away. They were going to hit us. I waved my lantern. I blew my horn, but the vessel kept coming at us. Then it blew up."

Jack lifted a brow. "So you didn't try to blow up the ship?"

"Look, buddy, it was *my* ship. Why would I blow up my own ship and ruin my livelihood? Now I'm going to have to pay to get that shipment off the bottom of the bay. The insurance is never going to believe this one."

"So you did it for the insurance money?"

"No! Look, I told you what happened." The man sat up and the bundle of cloth fell into his lap. "I'm not going to sit here and let some patsy in a mask ask me questions when I'm the one who needs to find out who sunk my ship and why. So why don't you and your...mask, take a hike, and I'll get to the bottom of this."

"Hold on. You've got a nasty cut on your head. You should stay sitting. Sir, sir! Where are you going? I'm not done asking you questions. Sir?"

Once the man got to his feet, he started to leave. Jack reached out to stop him, almost catching his sleeve. There were so many questions and no answers. He didn't know the name of the ship or its captain. He didn't know what cargo had been on board. He didn't even know where it hailed from. Nothing. And this man was obviously not going to give him anything.

"Now you hold it right there."

Jack cringed and tried to stay hidden behind the big man. He knew that voice.

"How many times have I told you that if we need *your* help we'll call you?"

Officer O'Malley told Jack, well, not Jack but his persona that still needed a name, not to interfere. In fact there had even been the threat of physical violence on more than one occasion. Officer O'Malley had the physical presence to do damage to nearly anyone he came in contact with. It was amazing there was enough material to make O'Malley's uniform. Jack didn't want to think of how many cows it took to make the belt to encircle the officer's midsection.

"Sir," O'Malley said to the other big man leaving. "I hope this man didn't bother you."

"Just you tell him when he accuses a captain of sinking his own ship, he could end up swallowing a few of those teeth even if they are hidden behind some kind of mask."

All the moisture left Jack's mouth, and he found it difficult to swallow. As he tried to respond, his voice came out in a squeak. He licked his lips and found his voice. "How was I to know?"

The captain gave one final glare at Jack and stomped off. O'Malley's brow creased, and he appeared like he wanted to leave. Instead he walked up close to Jack.

"I can't tell what you're thinking behind that mask you're wearing. I'm pretty good at telling what people got going on by the look on their face. I'm sure you mean well, son, but listen to me and listen real good now. Don't be interfering in a crime scene. The police are in this city for a reason. We don't need no vigilantes running around wearing masks and causing more trouble than help. Have I made myself clear or do we need to go down to the station to have us a little talk again?"

Jack was suddenly very glad for two things. One, that Officer O'Malley couldn't see the look of fear on his face, and two, the fan and vents keeping the sweat from running down his neck. "Can I at least stay around and keep an eye on things? I did see the explosion. There's more than one ship involved."

"And how would you be knowing that?"

"I was on top of the Central Receiving building immediately after it happened. I saw the second smaller ship sinking, and that man confirmed what I saw."

"I think that's all we need out of you. Why don't you go home, hang up your mask, and call it a day? Please keep off the building tops. I don't want to have to scrape your body off the ground one of these days. Run along now, and for your own safety, stop playing hero."

Jack didn't let O'Malley's words get to him. There was something a-foot here, and it centered around the sunk ship. He needed to know not only the name of the ship, but what it was carrying. Vital clues needed to be dug up, and if he had to do that on his own, so be it.

Out Now!

What's next on your reading list?

Champagne Book Group promises to bring to readers fiction at its finest.

Discover your next
fine read!
http://www.champagnebooks.com/

~~~

We are delighted to invite you to receive exclusive rewards. Join our Facebook group for VIP savings, bonus content, early access to new ideas we've cooked up, learn about special events for our readers, and sneak peeks at our fabulous titles.

https://www.facebook.com/groups/ChampagneBookClub/
Join now.

34853922R00160